12/20/07

Wolf Woman Bay

And Nine More of the Finest Crime and Mystery Novellas of the Year

EDITED BY
Ed Gorman
AND **Martin H. Greenberg**

CARROLL & GRAF PUBLISHERS
NEW YORK

WOLF WOMAN BAY:
And Nine More of the Finest Crime and Mystery Novellas of the Year

Carroll & Graf Publishers
An Imprint of Avalon Publishing Group, Inc.
11 Cambridge Center
Cambridge, MA 02142

AVALON
publishing group incorporated

Carroll & Graf books are available at special discounts for bulk
purchases in the United States by corporations, institutions, and other
organizations. For more information, please contact the Special Markets
Department at the Perseus Books Group, 2300 Chestnut Street, Suite
200, Philadelphia, PA 19103, or call (800) 255-1514, or e-mail
special.markets@perseusbooks.com.

Cataloging-in-Publication Data is available from the Library of Congress.

ISBN-10: 0-7867-1980-X
ISBN-13: 978-0-7867-1980-8

9 8 7 6 5 4 3 2 1

Interior design by Maria E. Torres

Printed in the United States of America

Contents

Permissions   *iv*

Honor Code
Joyce Carol Oates   *1*

Junior Partner in Crime
Carole Nelson Douglas   *51*

Grieving Las Vegas
Jeremiah Healy   *81*

The Resurrection Man
Sharyn McCrumb   *123*

The Temptation of King David
Brendan DuBois   *209*

Gustav Amlingmeyer, Holmes of the Range
Steve Hockensmith   *245*

Wolf Woman Bay
Doug Allyn   *299*

Merely Hate
Ed McBain   *375*

Diamond Dog
Dick Lochte   *477*

Arizona Heat
Clark Howard   *515*

Permissions

~~~~~~~~~~

Honor Code

Joyce Carol Oates

~~~~~~~~~~

Joyce Carol Oates has authored nearly three dozen novels, nearly thirty short story collections, compilations, books of plays, collections of her non-fiction writings, books of poetry, and books for young adults and children. A Distinguished Professor of Humanities at Princeton University, where she has taught since 1978, Oates has been recognized and honored with numerous awards including several Pushcart Prizes, The National Book Award, the O. Henry Award, the Rosenthal Award (National Institute of Arts and Letters), the *Boston Book Review's* Fisk Fiction Prize, the Bram Stoker Award, and three nominations for the Pulitzer Prize, as well as other honors. Her latest releases are *High Lonesome Stories,* a collection, and *Black Girl/While Girl.*

1.

Seems like forever I was in love with my cousin Sonny Brandt, who was incarcerated in the Chautauqua County

Youth Facility outside Chautauqua Falls, New York from the age of sixteen to the age of twenty-one on a charge of manslaughter. You could say that my life as a girl was before-Sonny and after-Sonny. Before-*manslaughter* and after-*manslaughter.*

That word! One day it came into our lives.

Like *incarceration.* Another word that, once it comes into your life, the life of your family, is permanent.

No one says "incarcerate" except people who have to do with the prison system. "Manslaughter" is a word you hear more frequently, though most people, I think, don't know what it means.

"Manslaughter."

Those years I whispered this word aloud. Murmured this word a precious obscenity. I loved the vibration in my jaws my teeth clenched tight. "Man-slaughter." I felt the thrill of what Sonny had done, or what people claimed Sonny had done, reverberating in those syllables not to be spoken aloud in the presence of any of the relatives.

"Manslaughter" was more powerful than even "murder" for there was "man" and there was "slaughter" and the two jammed together were like music: the opening chord of an electric guitar, so deafening you feel it deep in the groin.

What Sonny did to a man who'd hurt my mother happened, in December 1981, when I was eleven. A few years later my mother's older sister Agnes arranged for me to attend a private girls' school in Amherst, New York where one day in music class our teacher happened to mention the title of a composition, for piano—"Slaughter on Tenth Avenue"—and in that instant my jaw must have dropped, for a girl pointed at me, and laughed.

"Mickey is so weird, isn't she!"

"Mickey is so funny."

"Mickey is funny-weird."

At the Amherst Academy for Girls I'd learned to laugh with my tormentors who were also my friends. Somehow I was special to them, like a handicapped dancer or athlete, you had to laugh at me yet with a look of tender exasperation. When I couldn't come up with a witty rejoinder, I made a face like a TV comedian. Any laughter generated by Mickey Stecke was going to be intentional.

"Hurry! No time to dawdle! This is an emergency."

It was Hurricane Charlie in September 1980 that broke up our household in Herkimer, New York and caused us to flee like wartime refugees. So Momma would say. That terrible time when within twenty-four hours every river, creek, and ditch in Herkimer County overflowed its banks and Bob Gleason's little shingleboard house on Half Moon Creek where we'd been living got flooded out: "Near-about swept away an all of us drowned."

Momma's voice quavered when she spoke of Hurricane Charlie and all she'd had to leave behind, but in fact she'd made her decision to leave Herkimer and Bob Gleason before the storm hit. Must've made up her mind watching TV weather news. This confused time in our lives when we'd been living with a man who was my brother Lyle's father, who was spending time away from the house after he and Momma had quarreled, and every time the phone rang it was Bob Gleason wanting to speak with Momma, and Momma was anxious about Bob Gleason returning, so one night she ran into Lyle's and my room excited saying there were "hurricane warnings" on TV for Herkimer County, we'd have to "evacuate" to save our lives. Already Momma was dragging a suitcase down from the attic. "You two! Help me with these damn bags." Momma had a way of keeping fear out of her voice by sounding as if she was scolding or teasing. It became a game to see how quickly we could pack Momma's old Chevy Impala in the driveway. Momma had just the one suitcase that was large, bulky, sand-colored, with not only buckles to snap shut but cord belts to fasten. She had cardboard boxes, bags from the grocery store, armloads of loose clothes carried to the car on hangers and dumped into the back. Already it was raining, hard.

Our destination was my aunt Georgia's house in Ransomville, three hundred miles to the west in the foothills of the Chautauqua Mountains, we'd last visited two summers ago.

I asked Momma if Aunt Georgia knew we were coming. Momma said sharply of course she knew. "Who you think I been on the phone with, all hours of the night? *Him?*"

Momma spoke contemptuously. I was to know who *him* was without her needing to explain.

When a man was over with, in Momma's life, immediately he became *him*. Whatever name he'd had, she'd once uttered in a soft-sliding voice, would not be spoken ever again.

"Pray to God, He will spare us."

It was a frantic drive on mostly country roads littered with fallen tree limbs. From time to time we encountered other vehicles, moving slowly, headlights shimmering in the rain. Ditches were overflowing with mud-water and at every narrow bridge Momma had to slow our car to a crawl, whispering to herself. Where it was light enough we could see the terrifying sight of water rushing just a few inches below the bridge yet each time we were spared, the bridge wasn't washed away and all of us drowned. To drown out the noise of the wind, Momma played Johnny Cash tapes, loud. Johnny Cash was Momma's favorite singer, like her own daddy, she claimed, lost to her since she was twelve years old. In the backseat in a bed of wet, rumpled clothes Lyle fell asleep whimpering but I kept Momma company every mile of the way. Every hour of that night. I was Aimée then, not Mickey. I wasn't sorry to leave the shingle-board house on Half Moon Creek that was run-down and smelled of kerosene because Lyle's daddy was not my daddy and in Bob Gleason's eyes I could see no warmth for me, only for Lyle. Where my own daddy was, I had no idea. If my own daddy was alive, I had no idea. I had learned not to ask Momma who would say in disdain, "Him? Gone." From Momma I knew that a man could not be trusted except for a certain period of time and when that time was ending you had to act quickly before it was too late.

Through the night, the rain continued. In the morning there was no sunrise only a gradual lightening so you could begin to see the shapes of things along the road: mostly trees. Then I saw a shivery ray of light above the sawtooth mountains we were headed for, the sun flattened out sideways like a broken egg yolk, a smear of red-orange. "Momma, look!" And awhile later Momma drove across the suspension bridge above the Chautauqua River at

Ransomville and when at midpoint on the bridge we passed the sign CHAUTAUQUA COUNTY she began crying suddenly.

"No one can hurt us now."

These words that came to be confused in my memory with Johnny Cash's manly voice. *No one can hurt us now,* the words to a song of surpassing beauty and hope that was interrupted by applause and whistles from a vast anonymous audience. *No one can hurt us now* soothing as a lullaby, you drift into sleep believing it must be true.

My aunt Georgia Brandt lived in a ramshackle farmhouse at the edge of Ransomville. Of the original, one hundred acres, only two or three remained in the family. Georgia was not a farm woman but a cafeteria worker at the local hospital. She was a soft-fleshed fattish woman, in her mid forties, ten years older than my mother, a widow who'd lost her trucker husband in a disastrous accident on the New York Thruway when her oldest child was in high school and her youngest, Sonny, was five months old. Aunt Georgia had a way of hugging so vehemently it took the breath out of you. Her kisses were like swipes with a coarse damp sponge. She smelled of baking-powder biscuits and cigarette smoke. To keep from crying when she was in an emotional state Aunt Georgia blurted out clumsy remarks meant to amuse, that had the sting of insults. First thing she said to Momma when we came into her house after our all-night drive was: "Jesus, Dev'a! Don't you and those kids look like something the cat dragged out of the rain!"

If Sonny happened to overhear one of his mother's awkward attempts at humor he was apt to call out, "Don't listen to Ma's bullshit, she's drunk."

Aunt Georgia was a hive of fretful energy, humming and singing to herself like a radio left on in an empty room. She watched late-night TV, smoking while she knitted, did needlepoint, sewed quilts—"crazy quilts" were her specialty. Some of these she sold through a women's crafts co-op at a local mall, others she gave away. After her husband's fiery death she'd converted to evangelical Christianity and sang in a nasal, wavering voice in the choir of the Ransomville Church of the Apostles. She was brimming with prayer like a cup filled to the top, threatening to spill. Even Sonny, at mealtimes, bowed his lips over his plate, clasped his restless hands and mumbled *Bless us O Lord and these thy gifts which we are about in receive through Christ-our-Lord AMEN*. My aunt Georgia was the second-oldest of the McClaren girls who'd grown up in Ransomville and had always been the heaviest. Devra was the youngest, prettiest, and thinnest—"Look at you," Georgia protested, "one of those 'an-rex-icks' you see on TV." In an upscale suburb of Cleveland, Ohio lived the oldest McClaren sister, my aunt Agnes, who was famous among the relatives for being "rich" and "stingy"— "snooty"—"cold-hearted." Agnes was the sole McClaren in any generation to have gone to college, acquiring a master's degree from the State University at Buffalo in something called developmental psychology; she'd married a well-to-do businessman whom few in the family had ever met. Agnes disapproved of her sisters' lives for being "messy"—"out of control"—and never returned to the

Chautauqua Valley to visit. Nor did she encourage visits to
Cleveland though she'd taken an interest, Momma
reported, in me: "Aggie thinks you might take after her,
you like books better than people."

I did not like books better than people. I was nothing
like my aunt Agnes.

I hated Momma's brash way of talking, that my cousin
Sonny Brandt might overhear.

First glimpse I had of Sonny that morning, he came outside in the rain to help us unload the car, insisted on carrying most of the things himself—"Y'all get inside, I can
handle it." Sonny was just fifteen but looked and behaved
years older. Next, Sonny gave up his room for Lyle and me:
"It's nice'n cozy, see. Right over the furnace." The Brandts'
house was so large, uninsulated, most of the second floor
had to be shut up from November to April; the furnace was
coal-burning, in a dank, earthen-floored cellar, and gave
off wan gusts of heat through vents clogged with dust.
Sonny was always doing some kindness like that, helping
you with something you hadn't realized you needed help
with. He was a tall lanky lean boy with burnt-looking skin
and pale ghost-blue eyes, said to resemble his dead
father's. His eyebrows ran together over the bridge of his
nose. Already at fifteen he'd begun to wear out his forehead with frowning: one of those old-young people, could
be male or female Momma said, who take on too much
worry early in life because others who are older don't take
on enough.

Like his mother, Sonny was always busy. You could hear
him humming and singing to himself, anywhere in the
house. He slept now in a drafty room under the eaves, at

the top of the stairs, and his footsteps on the stairs were thunderous. He had a way of flying down the stairs taking steps three or four at a time, slapping the wall with his left hand to keep his balance. He could run upstairs, too, in almost the same way. It was a sight to behold like an acrobat on TV but Aunt Georgia wasn't amused, calling to him he was going to break his damn neck or worse yet the damn stairs. Sonny laughed, "Hey Ma: chill out."

Sonny was in tenth grade at Ransomville High but frequently out of school working part-time or pickup jobs (grocery bagger, snow removal, farm hand) or helping around the house where things were forever breaking down. The previous summer, Sonny had painted the front of the house and most of what you could see of the sides from the road but the color Georgia had selected was an impractical cream-ivory that looked thin as whitewash and required a second coat. Disgusted, Sonny said he'd have been better off working for a painting contractor, at least he'd have been paid.

Momma teased Sonny for being a "natural-born Good Samaritan" and Sonny said, scowling, "Screw 'Good Samaritan.' Asshole, you mean."

Lyle and I were crazy for our cousin like puppies yearning for attention, any kind of attention, even teasing, swift hard tickles beneath the arms, attacks from behind. Sonny never hurt us, at least not intentionally. He was likely to be clumsy, not cruel. Georgia complained of him growing out of clothes as fast as she could buy them. Already he was just under six feet tall, built like a whippet with shoulders and arms hard-muscled from outdoor work. His hair was a damp-wheat color and sprang straight from the crown of his head. He had to shave every other day, otherwise his jaws were covered in dark stubble. His skin looked perpetually sunburnt and he wore ratty old clothes yet girls called him on the phone at all hours, provoking Georgia to answer the ringing phone, speak sharply, slam down the receiver. Sonny seemed indifferent to the calls, we never heard him call any of the girls back, still Georgia complained, "All that boy has got to do is get some damn girl pregnant. Wind up married, a daddy at sixteen."

Sonny tried to laugh these remarks off. A flush rose into his face, he hated to be teased about girls, or sex. Anything to do with sex. He'd tell Georgia chill out, and slam out of the house.

As soon as we moved in, Sonny changed my name: "Mickey" and not "Aimée" he'd been trying to pronounce "Aim-ée" as Momma wanted it.

" 'Mickey' kicks ass, see? Instead, of getting her ass kicked, like 'Aimée.' "

It was the most obvious logic! The way Sonny explained it, like adding up a column of numbers.

Sonny called Lyle "Big Boy." (Which was a sweet kind of teasing, since Lyle was small for his age at six.) Sometimes, Sonny called my brother "Lyle-y" if the mood between them was more serious.

Sonny had a formal way of addressing adults, you couldn't judge was respectful or mocking. He could provoke my aunt Georgia by referring to her as "ma'am" in the politest voice. In town, adults were "ma'am"—"sir"—"mister"—"missus." (Behind their backs, Sonny might have other, funnier names for them.) But he took care to call Momma "Aunt Devra" both to her face and to others. To Lyle and me he'd say, "Your momma," in a serious voice. The way his eyes shrank from Momma, even when she was trying to joke with him, which was often, you could see he didn't know how to speak to her. Much of the time, he didn't speak. Though he did favors for Momma, constantly. Climbing up onto the roof to repair a drip in Momma's bedroom, changing a flat tire on Momma's car, taking a day off from school to drive Momma to Chautauqua Falls seventy miles away. (Sonny had a driver's permit which allowed him to drive any vehicle so long as a licensed driver was with him. What Momma was doing in Chautauqua Falls wasn't for us to know. She would claim she "had business" which might mean she was interviewing for a job, looking for a new place to live, or contacting a friend. So much of Momma's life was secret, her own children wouldn't know what she'd been planning until she sprang the surprise on us like something on daytime TV.) When Momma tried to thank Sonny for some kindness of his he'd squirm with embarrassment and scowl, mumbling *Okay, Aunt Devra* or *Well, hell* and make his escape, fast. Momma hid her exasperation beneath praise, telling Georgia her son was the shyest boy—"For somebody growing up to look like Sonny is going to look."

Georgia said defiantly, "I hope to God he stays that way."

A few months in Ransomville, we'd begun to forget Herkimer. The shingleboard house on Half Moon Creek we'd almost come to believe, as Momma said, had been flooded and swept away by Hurricane Charlie. The glowering man who wasn't my daddy and had no wish to pretend he was. (If Lyle missed his daddy he didn't say so. His big brother now was Sonny he adored.) Now I was Mickey and not Aimée, I behaved with more confidence. I became brash, reckless. I infuriated my aunt and my mother by careening around the house at high speed, taking the stairs from the second floor two and three at a time, slapping my hand against the wall for balance. (Unlike Sonny, I sometimes missed a step and fell, hard. Skidding down the remainder of the stairs to lie in a crumpled heap at the bottom. The pain made me whimper but embarrassment was worse, if anyone happened to have noticed.) Another roughhouse game if you could call it a game was running and sliding along the hall on my aunt's "throw rugs"; Lyle imitated me, in a shrieking version of bumper cars. When Momma was home she scolded and slapped at me—"Aimée! You're too old for such behavior"—but more and more, Momma wasn't home.

Aunt Georgia's was the kind of household where a single bathroom had to suffice for everyone and the hot water heater was quickly depleted. The kind of household where a shower, a bath, was an occasion. I hid in wait to catch a glimpse of Sonny hurrying into the bathroom barefoot, bare-chested, and in beltless trousers, pajama bottoms, or white jockey shorts dingy from many launderings, quick to shut the door behind him and latch it. Slyly I would draw near to hear him whistling inside as he ran water from the rusty old faucets, flushed the toilet, showered. I drew Lyle into teasing Sonny with me, rapping on the bathroom door when Sonny was inside, managing to jiggle the latch-lock open and reaching inside to switch off the light, to provoke our cousin into shouting, "Put that light back on! God *damn!*" More daring, we crept into the steamy bathroom when Sonny was showering, pushed aside the shower curtain so that I could spray Sonny with shaving cream from his aerosol can, all the while shrieking with laughter like a cat being killed. Nothing was more hilarious than Sonny flailing at us, streaming water, trying to grab the shaving-cream can out of my hand. Once or twice I caught a glimpse of Sonny's penis swinging loose, limp and seeming not much longer than his longest finger, innocent-looking as a red rubber toy between his narrow hips. In his rage, Sonny wouldn't trouble to wrap a towel around his waist. The sight of my cousin's penis did not upset or alarm me. If I'd been asked I might have said *Anything that is Sonny's, anything to do with Sonny, could never cause me harm.*

Furious and flushed with indignation, Sonny lunged from the dripping shower stall to shove Lyle and me out of the bathroom with his wet hands, and shut the door behind us, hard.

"Damn brats!"

Of course, Sonny would exact his revenge. If not immediately, in time. Somewhere, somehow. We would not know when. We trembled in anticipation, not knowing when.

It would be years before I glimpsed another penis on another young male. And more years before I saw an erect penis. In my naiveté taking for granted that adult men looked like my boy cousin surprised naked in the shower. In my naiveté taking for granted that, like my protective boy cousin, no man would truly wish to harm me.

That environment my aunt Agnes would say, after Sonny

was arrested. *Those people, that way of life* my aunt would speak in disgust as if any sensible person would agree with her. And I would want to protest *It wasn't like that!* I would want to say *I loved, them, we were happy there, you don't understand.*

"If I could trust you, Dev'a. My mind would be more at peace."

It was difficult to interpret my aunt Georgia's tone of voice when she spoke like this to Momma. She didn't seem to be scolding or sarcastic. She didn't sound reproachful. She laughed, and she sighed. (Fattish people sighed a lot, I knew. Like they were made of rubber pumped up like a balloon and when they felt sad, air leaked out more notice-ably than it did with thinner people.) The way Momma murmured in reply as if she was too much in a hurry to be angry, "Georgia, you can trust me! I'm an adult woman," I understood my aunt and Momma had had this conversa-tion before and that, on her way out of the house, Momma would pause to kiss Georgia's cheek, squeeze her hand, and say in her taunting-teasing way, "And you can mind your own business, Georgia. Any time you want us out, we're out."

This hurt my aunt, I knew. (It hurt me, overhearing. Momma was so careless in her words slashing like blades.) So Georgia would say no she didn't mean that, didn't want that, Momma had to know she didn't want that.

Through the winter and into January 1981, Momma sold perfume in a department store at the mall. Then, Momma was "hostess" in a restaurant owned by a new friend of hers. Then, Momma was "receptionist" at Herlihy's Realtors whose glaring yellow and black signs were everywhere in Chautauqua County, and Mr. Herlihy (who drove a showy bronze-blond Porsche) was Momma's new friend.

It seemed that every few days, a new friend called Momma. Male voices asking to speak with "Devra Stecke" but Momma wasn't usually home. Some of the men left names and telephone numbers, others did not. Some of the men my aunt Georgia knew, or claimed to know, others she did not. This was an "old pattern" repeating itself, Georgia said. Complaining to anyone who would listen how her younger sister who'd already had such turmoil in her personal life, was "growing apart" from her—"growing estranged"—"secretive"—and this was a signal of trouble to come. Sonny rolled his mother by saying, in the way you'd explain something to a slow-witted child, "Ma, the fact is: Aunt Devra has got her own life. Aunt Devra ain't *you*."

The plan had been that Momma, Lyle, and I would live with my aunt Georgia only for as long as Momma needed to get a job in Ransomville, find a decent place for us to live, but months passed, and Momma was too busy to think about moving, and Georgia assured her there was no hurry about moving out, there was plenty of room in the house. My aunt's daughters were grown, married, separated, or divorced, and dropped by the house with their noisy children at all times, especially when they wanted favors from their mother, but Georgia liked the feel of a family living together day to day. "Like, when you wake up in the morning, you know who you'll be making breakfast for. Who you can rely upon."

It began to be that Momma "worked late" several nights

a week at Herlihy Realtors. Or maybe, after the office closed, Momma had other engagements. (Swimming laps at the Y? Taking a course in computers at the community college? Meeting with friends at the County Line Café?) If Momma wasn't back home by seven P.M. we could expect a hurried call telling us not to wait supper for her, and not to keep food warm in the oven for her. Maybe Momma would be home by midnight, maybe later. (Once, our school bus headed for town passed Momma's car on the road, headed home at 7:45 A.M. I shrank from the window trying not to notice and wondered if my little brother at the front of the bus was trying not to notice, too.) In winter months when we came home from school, ran up the snowy driveway to the old farmhouse so weirdly, thinly painted looking in twilight like a ghost-house, sometimes only our aunt Georgia would be home to call out, "Hi, kids!" Georgia would be changed from her cafeteria uniform into sweatpants and pullover sweater, in stocking feet padding about the kitchen preparing supper (Georgia's specialties were hot-spice chili with ground chuck, spaghetti and meatballs, tuna-cheese-rice casserole with a glaze of potato chip crumbs); or having lost track of the time, sitting in her recliner in the living room watching late-afternoon TV soaps, smoking Marlboros and rapidly sewing, without needing to watch her fingers, one of her crazy quilts—"Look at this! How it came to be so big, I don't know. Damn thing has a mind of its own."

Georgia tried to teach me quilting, but I hadn't enough patience to sit still. Since I'd become Mickey, not Aimée, seemed like tiny red ants were crawling over me, couldn't stay in one place for more than a few minutes. Momma said it would be good for me to learn some practical skill, but why'd I want to learn quilting, when Momma hadn't the slightest interest in it herself?

Georgia Brandt's quilts were famous locally. She'd made quilts for every relative of hers, neighbors, friends, friends-of-friends. For people she scarcely knew but admired. Georgia's most spectacular quilts sold for two hundred dollars at the women's co-op. She was modest about her skills ("I'm like the momma cat that's had so many kittens, she's lost count.") and scowled like Sonny if you tried to compliment her. It was difficult to describe one of Georgia's quilts for if your first impression was that the quilt was beautiful, the closer you looked the more doubtful you became. For there was no way to see the quilt in its entirety, only just in parts, square by square. And the squares did not match, did not form a "pattern." Or anyway not a "pattern" you could see. Not only did Georgia use mismatched colors and prints but every kind of fabric: cotton, wool, satin, silk, taffeta, velvet, lace. Some quilts glittered with sequins or seed pearls scattered like constellations in the sky. Georgia said she could see a quilt in her mind's eye taking form as she sewed it better than she could see a quilt when it was spread out on the floor. A "crazy" quilt grew by some mysterious logic, moving through Georgia's fingers, grew and grew until finally it stopped growing.

People asked my aunt how she knew when a quilt was finished and Georgia said, "Hell, I don't ever know. I just stop."

May 1981 my cousin Sonny turned sixteen: bought a car, quit high school, got a job with a tree-service crew.

Aunt Georgia had begged him not to quit school, but Sonny wouldn't listen. He'd had enough of sitting at desks, playing like he was a young kid when he wasn't, in his heart. The tree-service job paid almost twice what he'd been making working part-time and he was proud to hand over half of his earnings to Georgia.

Georgia wept, but took the money. Sonny would do what he wanted to do, like her deceased husband. "Now I got to pray you don't kill yourself, too." We picked up the way Georgia's voice dipped on *you.*

Sonny, the youngest member of the tree-service crew, soon became the daredevil. The one to volunteer to climb one hundred feet wielding a chainsaw when others held back. The one to work in dangerous conditions. The one to be depended upon to finish a job even in pelting rain, without complaining. He liked the grudging admiration of the other men some of whom became his friends and some of whom hated his guts for being the good-looking brash kid who clambered into trees listening to rock music on his Walkman and was still fearless as most of them had been fearless at one time, if no longer. "Hey Brandt: you up for this?" It was a thrill to hear the foreman yelling at him, singling him out for attention. Sure, Sonny wore safety gloves, goggles, work boots with reinforced toes. Sure, Sonny insisted to Georgia and to Momma, he never took chances and didn't let the damn foreman "exploit" him. Yet somehow his hands became covered in nicks, scratches, scars. His face looked perpetually sunburnt. His backbone ached, his muscles ached, his pale-blue eyes were often threaded with blood and his head rang with the deafening whine of saws that, on the job, penetrated his so-called ear-protectors. Away from a work site, Sonny still twitched with vibrations running through his lean body like electric charges. One evening he came home limping, and Georgia made him take off his shoe and sock to reveal a big toenail the hue of a rotted plum, swollen with blood from beneath. Momma cried, "Oh, sweetie! We're going to take you to a doctor."

Sonny waved her off with a scowl. Like hell he was going to a doctor for something so trivial.

His first month with the tree service, Sonny came home staggering with exhaustion, fell into a waking doze in the shower, and crawled into bed without eating supper. By degrees he became accustomed to the work and claimed to like it. The mood of the crew wavered. Some days, things were fine. Some days, tempers were short. The other guys were Sonny's buddies, or anyway a few of them were. The foreman was a "good guy, basically" unless he was a "bastard"—"not to be trusted." Sonny was the young brash kid wearing the Walkman, a boy with a quick smile and a readiness to take on difficult tasks, unless Sonny was taking on the moods of his buddies, who were sometimes sullen, irritable, quick to take offense. When the foreman yelled, "Brandt? You up for this?" Sonny might mouth *Up yours* to amuse whoever was watching, though usually he did as he was instructed. In theory, at sixteen Sonny was too young to go out drinking with the men after work but if they invited him, cajoled and teased him, how'd he say no?

Drinking, the men were apt to get into fights. With men they met in bars, or with one another. Sonny was an accidental witness to an incident that might have turned fatal:

One of his buddies slammed another man (who'd allegedly insulted him) against a brick wall so hard his head made a cracking sound before his legs buckled beneath him and he fell, unconscious. (No one called an ambulance. No one called police. Eventually, the fallen man was roused to a kind of consciousness and taken home by his friends.) On the job, Sonny tried to keep out of the way of the meanest men, who'd been working for the tree service too many years, yet once, in the heat of midsummer, one of these men took exception to a remark of Sonny's, or a way in which, hoping to deflect sarcasm with a grin, Sonny responded, and before he could raise his arms to protect himself he was being hit, pummeled, knocked off his feet. His assailant cursed him, kicked him with steel-toed boots, and had to be pulled away from him by others who seemed to think that the incident was amusing. Sonny was shocked, thought of quitting, but how'd he quit, where'd he work and make as much money as he made with the crew, so he reported back next morning limping, favoring his right leg that was badly bruised from being kicked, a nasty cut beneath his left eye, face still swollen but Sonny shrugged it off saying, as he'd said to his mother and his aunt Devra, "No big deal, okay?"

We began to notice, Sonny was getting mean. He was short-tempered with his mother, even with his aunt Devra. The kinds of silly jokes Lyle and I had played with him only a few months before just seemed to annoy Sonny now. One evening Lyle crept up on Sonny sprawled on the sofa, drinking a beer and eliciting through TV stations with the remote control, and Sonny told him, "Piss off." His voice was flat and tired. He wasn't smiling. His jaws were bristling with dark stubble and his T-shirt was stained with sweat. Whatever was on TV, he stared without seeming to see. Compulsively he poked and prodded a tooth in his lower jaw, that seemed to be loose.

Poor Lyle! My brother crept away wounded. He would never approach Sonny again in such a way.

I knew better than to tease Sonny in such a mood for he didn't seem to like me much any longer, either. *I hate you! I don't love you. Fall out of some damn tree and break your damn neck, see if I give a damn.*

These brash-Mickey words I whispered aloud, barefoot on the stairs a few yards away. Where I could watch my boy cousin through the doorway, slumped on the sofa poking at a tooth in his lower jaw.

In the fall, Momma had her hair trimmed in a feathery cut that floated around her face and made her eyes, warm liquidy brown, look enlarged. She was living her secret life that left her moody and distracted vehemently shaking her head when the phone rang and it was for her and whoever wanted to speak with her left no name and number only just the terse message *She'll know who it is, tell her call back.*

She was still working at Herlihy Realtors. Unless she'd quit the job at Herlihy Realtors. Maybe she'd been fired by Mr. Herlihy? Or she'd quit and Mr. Herlihy had talked her into returning but then after an exchange she'd been fired, or she'd quit for a second, final time? Maybe there'd been a scene of Momma and her employer Mr. Herlihy in the office after hours when everyone else had departed, when the front lights of HERLIHY REALTORS had been switched

off, and Momma was upset, Momma swiped at her eyes
that were beginning to streak with mascara, Momma
turned to walk away but Mr. Herlihy grabbed her shoulder,
spun her back to face him and struck her with the flat of
his hand in her pretty crimson mouth that had opened in
protest.

And maybe there'd been a confused scene of Momma
desperately pushing through the rear exit of Herlihy Realtors, blood streaming from a two-inch gash in her lower
lip, Momma running and stumbling in high-heeled shoes
to get to her car before the man pursuing her, panting and
excited, could catch up with her.

Maybe this man had pleaded *Devra! Jesus I'm so sorry!
You know I didn't mean it.*

Or maybe this man had said, furiously, snatching again
at Momma's shoulder *Don't you walk away from me, bitch!
Don't you ever turn your back on me.*

It was 9:50 P.M., a weekday night in December 1981. Aunt
Georgia picked up the ringing phone, already pissed at
whoever was calling at this hour of the evening (knowing
the call wouldn't be for her but for her sister Devra who'd
been hiding away in her room for the past several days
refusing to talk to anyone even Georgia, even through the
door, or her son Sonny who'd been out late every night that
week). A voice was notifying her that it was the Chautauqua County sheriff's office for Mrs. Georgia Brandt
informing her that her sixteen-year-old son, Sean, Jr., resident of 2881 Summit Hill Road, was in custody at headquarters on a charge of aggravated assault. It seemed that
Sonny had confronted Mr. Herlihy of Herlihy Realtors in

the parking lot behind his office earlier that evening, they'd begun arguing and Sonny had struck Herlihy with a tire iron, beating him unconscious. Georgia was being asked to come to headquarters as soon as possible.

Aunt Georgia was stunned as if she'd been struck by a tire iron herself. She'd had to ask the caller to repeat what he'd said. She would tell us afterward how her knees had gone weak as water, she'd broken into a cold sweat in that instant groping for somewhere to sit before she fainted. She would say afterward, over the years, how that call was the second terrible call to come to her on that very phone: "Like lightning striking twice, the same place. Like God was playing a joke on me He hadn't already struck such a blow, and didn't owe me another."

Sonny would say *Well, hell.*

Sonny would swipe his hand across his twitchy face, he'd have to agree *Some kind of joke, like. How things turn out.*

Cupping a hand to his ear, his left ear where the hearing had been impaired following a beating (fellow inmates at the detention center? guards?) he refused to speak of, refused to allow Georgia to report saying *You want them to kill me, next time? Chill out, Ma.*

Each time we saw him, he was less Sonny and more somebody else we didn't know. In the orange jumpsuit printed in black CHAU CO DETENTION on the back, drooping from his shoulders and the trouser legs so long he'd had to roll up the cuffs. The guards called him kid. There was a feeling, we'd wished to think, that people liked him, Sonny wasn't any natural-born-killer type, not a

mean bone in that boy's body my aunt Georgia pleaded to
anyone who'd listen. If only Mr. Herlihy hadn't died.

I only just hate that man worse, God forgive me.

Georgia made us come with her to church. Not Momma
(you couldn't get Momma to step inside that holy-roller
Church of the Apostles, Momma proclaimed) but Lyle and
me. *Pray for your cousin Sonny, may Jesus spare us all.*

Visits to see Sonny at the detention center, and afterward at the "youth facility," were discouraged for Lyle and
me. I wanted to be taken with my aunt, but maybe not,
maybe I was just as happy to be left behind. Each time I'd
seen Sonny he was less Sonny and more somebody else
and a few times, he'd refused to come out to the visitors'
area. No reason given, the guard told us with an indifferent
shrug. Inmates got their moods.

I wrote to Sonny, saying how I missed him. How we all
missed him. We missed him *so!* But Sonny never
answered, not once.

Aunt Georgia said Sonny meant to answer, but was
busy. You wouldn't believe how they keep them busy at
that damn place.

Momma said maybe Sonny didn't "write so good." Maybe
Sonny hadn't paid much attention at school when writing
was taught, maybe that was it. So he wouldn't want to
show how like a little kid he'd write, that other people
might laugh at.

Laugh at Sonny! I was shocked at such a thought. I
could not believe that Momma would say such a thing.

Still, I loved Sonny. My heart was broken like some
cheap plastic thing, that cracks when you just drop it on
the floor.

2.

"Aimée."

Mrs. Peale's voice was low and urgent. My heart kicked in my chest. I saw a look in the woman's eyes warning *Take care! You are a very reckless girl.* Later, more calmly I would realize that Mrs. Peale could not have been thinking such a thought for Mrs. Peale could not have known why the dean of students had asked her to pass along the pink slip to me, discreetly folded in two and pressed into my hand at the end of music class.

My trembling hand. My guilty hand. My tomboy-with-bitten-fingernails hand.

It was a rainy afternoon in October 1986. I was sixteen, a junior at the Amherst Academy for Girls. I had been a student here, a boarder, since September 1984. Yet I did not feel "at home" here. I did not feel comfortable here. I had made a decision the previous day and this summons from the dean of students was in response to that decision I could not now revoke though possibly it was a mistake though I did not regret having made it, even if it would turn out to be a mistake. All day I'd dreaded this summons from the dean. In my fantasies of exposure and embarrassment I'd imagined that my name would be sounded over the school's loudspeaker system in one of those jarring announcements made from time to time during the school day but in fact the summons, now that it had arrived, was handwritten, terse:

Aimée Stecke
Come promtly to my office end of 5th period.
M. V. Chawdrey, Dean of Students

This was funny! *Promtly.*

My first instinct was to crumple the note in my hand and shove it into a pocket of my blazer before anyone saw it, but a bolder instinct caused me to laugh, and saunter toward the door with other girls as if nothing was wrong. I showed the note to Brooke Glover whom I always wanted to make laugh, or smile, or take notice of me in some distinctive way, but my bravado fell flat when Brooke, who'd wanted to leave the room with other friends, only frowned at the dean's note with a look of baffled impatience, like one forced to contemplate an obscure cartoon. That Dean Chawdrey had misspelled *promptly* made no impression on Brooke for whom spelling was a casual matter. She'd misunderstood my motive in showing her the note, made a gesture of sympathy with her mouth, murmured, "Poor you," and turned away.

Now I did crumple the incriminating note and shove it into my pocket. My face pounded with blood. A terrible buzzing had begun in my head like the sound of flies cocooned inside a wall in winter.

I left Mrs. Peale's classroom hurriedly, looking at no one. *Well, hell.*

To get you out of that environment. Away from those people, that way of life. My aunt Agnes had come for me, to save me. Her expression had been frowning and fastidious as if she smelled something nasty but was too well-mannered to acknowledge it. Aunt Agnes refused to discuss Sonny with Georgia, though Sonny was her nephew. She refused to hear what Momma had to say about the situation. Yes it was tragic, it was very sad, but Agnes had come to Ran-

somville to rescue me. She would arrange for me to attend
a girls' boarding school in a Buffalo suburb, a "prestigious"
private school she knew of since her college roommate had
graduated from the Amherst Academy and was now an
alumni officer. She would arrange for me to transfer from
Ransomville High School as quickly as possible. At the
time, I was fourteen. I was ready to leave Ransomville.
Momma had accused her oldest sister *You want to steal my
daughter! You never had a baby of your own* but Agnes
refused to be drawn into a quarrel nor would I quarrel with
my mother who'd been drinking and who when she drank
said wild hurtful stupid things you did not wish to hear let
alone dignify by replying *Momma you're drunk, leave me
alone. Haven't you hurt us all enough now leave us alone.*

At this time Sonny was gone from Ransomville. There
was shame and hurt in his wake. There was no happiness
in the old farmhouse on Summit Hill Road. No happiness
without Sonny in that house he'd started to paint a lumi-
nous cream-ivory that glowed at dusk. Sonny was "incarcerated" in the ugly barracks of the Chautauqua County
Youth facility north of Chautauqua Falls and he would not
be discharged from that facility until his twenty-first
birthday at which time he would be released on probationary terms. I had not seen Sonny in some time. I still
wrote to Sonny, mostly I sent him cards meant to cheer
him up, but I had not seen Sonny in some time and from
my aunt Georgia the news I heard of Sonny was not good.
*Like he doesn't know me sometimes. Doesn't want me to
touch him. Like my son is gone and somebody I don't know
has taken his place.*

When Sonny was first arrested after Mr. Herlihy was

hospitalized in critical condition, the charge was aggravated assault. He'd told police that he had only been
defending himself, that Herlihy had rushed at him,
attacked him. He had never denied that he'd struck Herlihy with the tire iron. But when Herlihy died after eleven
days on life support without regaining consciousness the
charge was raised to second-degree murder and Chautauqua County prosecutors moved to try Sonny as an
adult facing a possible sentence of life imprisonment.

At this time, we'd had to leave my aunt's house. Momma
had had to move us to live in a run-down furnished apartment in town for she and Georgia could not speak to each
other in the old way any longer, all that was finished.
Always there was the shadow of what Sonny had done for
Momma's sake, that Georgia could not hear. There was no
way to undo it, Momma acknowledged. Her voice quavered
when she uttered Sonny's name. Her eyes were swollen
and reddened from weeping. When Georgia screamed at
her in loathing, Momma could not defend herself. She
spoke with police. She spoke with the prosecutors and
with the judge hearing Sonny's case. She pleaded on
Sonny's behalf. She blamed herself for what he'd done.
(She had not asked him to intervene with Mr. Herlihy,
Momma insisted. Though she had allowed him to see her
bruised face, her cut lip. She'd told him how frightened she
was of Herlihy, the threats he'd made.) Momma testified
that her nephew had acted out of emotion, to protect her;
he'd had no personal motive for approaching Herlihy. He
had never seen, never spoken with Herlihy before that
evening. Sonny was a boy who'd grown up too fast,
Momma said. He'd quit school to work, and help support

his family. He'd taken on the responsibilities of an adult man and so he'd acted to protect a member of his family, as an adult man would do. Others testified on Sonny's behalf as well. Authorities were persuaded to believe that the killing was a "tragic accident" and Sonny was allowed to plead guilty to voluntary manslaughter as a minor, not as an adult, which meant incarceration in a youth facility and not in a nightmare maximum-security prison like Attica.

Lucky bastard it was said of Sonny in some quarters. His tree-service buddies seemed to feel he'd gotten off lightly: less than five years for breaking a man's head with a tire iron when not so long ago in Chautauqua County, as in any county in New York State, the kid might've been sentenced to die in the electric chair.

At the Amherst Academy where I was one of a half-dozen scholarship students out of approximately three hundred girls, I would speak only guardedly of my family back in Ransomville. Now my mother had married, a man I scarcely knew. Now my aunt Georgia had sold the farm-house and was living with one of her married daughters. In this place where talk was obsessively of boys I would not confess *I'm in love with my cousin who is five years older than me. My cousin who killed a man when he was sixteen.* Never would I break suddenly into tears to the astonish-ment of my friends *I am so lonely here where I want to be happy, where I am meant to be happy because my life has been saved.*

Three days of rain and the grounds of the Amherst Academy for Girls were sodden and treacherous underfoot as quicksand. Where there were paths across lawns and not paved walks hay had been strewn for us to tramp on. Soon most of the lovely-smelling hay became sodden too, and oozed mud of a hue and texture like diarrhea and this terrible muck we were scolded for tracking into buildings, classrooms. We were made to kick off our boots just inside the doors and in our stocking feet we skidded about on the polished floors like deranged children, squealing with laughter.

I was Mickey, skidding about. My laughter was shrill and breathless even when a husky girl athlete, a star on the field hockey team, collided with me hard enough to knock me down.

"Mickey, hey! Didn't see you there."

I had friends at the Amherst Academy, I could count on the fingers of both hands. Sometimes, in that hazy penumbra between sleep and wakefulness, in my bed in the residence hall, I named these friends as if defying Momma. *See! I can live away from you. I can live different from you.* Some of the girls at the Academy did not board in the residence hall but lived in the vicinity, in large, beautiful homes to which I was sometimes invited for dinner and to sleep over. And at Thanksgiving, even for a few days at Christmas. After my first year at the Academy, my grades were high enough for me to receive a tuition scholarship so now my aunt Agnes paid just my room, board, expenses. It was strange to me, that my aunt seemed to care for me. That my aunt came from Cleveland to Amherst to visit with me. That my aunt was eager to meet my roommates, my friends. That my aunt did not ask about Momma, or Lyle. My aunt did not ask about

Georgia, or Sonny. Not a word about Sonny! *You are the one I take pride in, Aimée. The only one.*

Aunt Agnes was a slender quivery woman in her early fifties. She did not much resemble her younger sisters in her appearance or in her manner of speaking. Her face was thin, heated, vivacious. Her teeth were small, like a child's teeth, and looked crowded in her mouth that was always smiling, or about to smile. Where Momma would have been awkward and defensive meeting my teachers, having to say quickly that she "never was very good" at school, my aunt smiled and shook hands and was perfectly at ease.

At the Academy, it may have been assumed by girls who didn't know me that Agnes was my mother.

Even those girls to whom I'd introduced my aunt seemed to hear me wrong and would speak afterward of "your mother": "Your mother looks just like you, Mickey"— "Your mother is really nice."

My mother is a beautiful woman, nothing like me. My mother is a slut.

My first few months at the Academy, I'd been homesick and angry and took the stairs to the dining hall two or three at a time slapping my hand against the wall for balance not giving a damn if I slipped, fell and broke my neck. I'd glowered, glared. I was so shy I'd have liked to shrivel into a ball like an inchworm in the hot sun yet there I was waving my fist of a hand, eager to be called upon.

I was Mickey not Aimée. Screw Aimée!

I tried out for the track team but ran too fast, couldn't hold back and so became winded, panting through my month. Staggering with sharp pains in my side. I helped other girls with their papers though such help was forbidden by the honor code we'd solemnly vowed to uphold. I said outrageous things, scandalizing my roommate Anne-Marie Krimble confiding in her that I didn't have a father like everyone else: "I was conceived in a test tube."

Anne-Marie's mouth dropped softly. She stared at me in disbelief. "Mickey, you were not."

"*In vitro* it's called. My mother's 'egg' was siphoned from her and mixed with sperm from a 'donor male,' shaken in a test tube the way you shake a cocktail."

"Mickey, that did not happen! That is gross."

Anne-Marie had taken a step back from me, uncertainly. I was laughing in the way my cousin Sonny Brandt used to laugh, once he'd gotten us to believe something far-fetched. "*In vivo,* that's you: born in an actual body. But not me."

Tales quickly spread of Mickey Stecke who said the most outrageous things. But mostly funny, to make her friends laugh.

"These are very serious charges, Aimée."

Aimée. In the dean's flat, nasal voice, the pretentious name sounded like an accusation.

Dean Chawdrey was peering at me over the tops of her rimless bifocal glasses. In her hand she held the neatly typed letter I'd sent to her the previous day. I was sitting in a chair facing her across the span of her desk, in my damp rumpled raincoat. I heard myself murmur almost inaudibly, "Yes, ma'am."

"You saw, you say, 'someone cheating' last week at midterms. Who is this 'someone,' Aimée? You will have to tell me."

M.V. Chawdrey was a frowning woman in her early fifties, as solidly fleshy as my aunt Georgia but her skin wasn't warmly rosy like my aunt's skin but had a look of something drained, that would be cold to the touch. Her mouth was small, bite-sized. Her eyes were distrustful. It was rare that an adult allowed dislike to show so transparently in her face.

"Aimée? Their names."

I sat miserable and mute. I could see the faces of the girls, some of whom were my friends, or would have believed themselves my friends as I would have liked to think of them as my friends. I could see even the expressions on their faces, but I could not name them.

Of course, I'd known beforehand that I could not. Yet I'd had to report them. It was the phenomenon of cheating I'd had to report, that was so upsetting.

At the Amherst Academy much was made of the tradition of the honor code. Every student signed a pledge to uphold this "sacred trust"—"priceless legacy." The honor code was a distinction, we were repeatedly told, that set the Amherst Academy apart from most private schools and all public schools. On the final page of each exam and paper you were required to say *I hereby confirm that this work submitted under my name is wholly and uniquely my own.* You signed and dated this. But the honor code was more than only just not cheating, you were pledged also to report others' cheating, and that was the dilemma.

Punishments for cheating ranged from probation, suspension from school, outright expulsion. Punishments for failing to report cheating were identical.

*Who would know, who could prove. You have only to say
nothing.*

I knew this, of course. But I was angry and disgusted,
too. If I did not want to cheat, I would be at a disadvantage
when so many others were cheating. My heart beat in
childish indignation *It isn't fair!* It wasn't just incidental
cheating, a girl glancing over at another girl's exam paper,
two girls whispering together at the back of a room. Not
just the usual help girls gave one another, proofreading
papers, pointing out obvious mistakes. This was system-
atic cheating, blatant cheating. Especially in science
classes taught by an affable distracted man named Werth
where notes and even pages ripped from textbooks were
smuggled into the exam room, and grades were uniformly
A's and B's. In English and history it had become com-
monplace for students to plagiarize by photocopying material from the periodicals library at the University of Buffalo
that was within walking distance of the Amherst Academy.
Our teachers seemed not to know, unless they'd given up
caring. It was easier to give high grades. It was easier to
avoid confrontations. "Well, Mickey: I know I can trust
you," Mrs. Peale had said once, mysteriously. The
emphasis on *you* had felt like a nudge in the ribs, painful
though meant to be affectionate.

My first few months at the Academy, eager to be liked,
I'd helped girls with homework and papers but I'd never
actually written any part of any paper. I'd wanted to think
of what I did as a kind of teaching. *This isn't cheating. This
is helping.* Uneasily I remembered how at freshman orientation questions had been put to the Dean of Students
about the honor code, those questions Dean Chawdrey

had answered year following year with her so-serious expression *Yes it is as much a violation of the honor code to fail to report cheating as to cheat. Yes!* A ripple of dismay had passed through the gathering of first-year students and their parents, crowded into pine pews in the school chapel. Aunt Agnes had accompanied me and now she murmured in my ear *Remember what that woman is saying, Aimée. She is absolutely right.*

I felt a stab of guilt, thinking of my aunt. Agnes had such hopes for me, her "favorite" niece! She wanted to be proud of me. She wanted to think that her effort on my behalf was not in vain. I seemed to know that what I was doing would hurt Agues, as it would hurt me.

For nights I'd lain awake in a misery of indecision wondering what to do. In Ransomville, nothing like this could ever have happened. In Ransomville public schools there was no honor code and in fact there hadn't been much cheating, that I had known of. Few students continued on to college, high grades were not an issue. Here, I'd come to think, in any anxiety, that our teachers had to know of the widespread cheating and were amused, that girls like me, who never cheated, were too cowardly to come forward.

The irony was, I wasn't so moral—so "good"—that I couldn't cheat like the others. And more cleverly than the others. But something in me resisted the impulse to follow the others who were crass and careless in their cheating. *I am not one of you. I am superior to you.* Finally, I'd written to the dean of students a brief letter of only a few sentences and I'd mailed the letter in a stamped envelope. Even as I wrote the letter I understood that I was making a mistake and yet I'd had no choice.

I thought of my cousin Sonny whom I loved. Whom I had not now seen in years. My boy cousin who'd been beaten in the youth facility yet refused to report the beatings out of what code of honor or fear of reprisal, I didn't know. I thought of Sonny who'd killed a man out of another sort of honor, to protect my mother. Sonny had not needed to think, he'd only acted. He had traded his life for Momma's, by that action. But he'd had no choice.

Dean Chawdrey persisted, "*Who* was cheating, Aimée? You've done the right thing to report it but now you must tell me who the girl is."

The girl! I wanted to laugh in the dean's face, that she should imagine only one cheater at midterms.

I mumbled, ". . . can't."

"What do you mean, 'can't'? Or 'won't'?"

I sat silent clasping my hands in my lap. Mickey Stecke had bitten fingernails, cuticles ridged with blood. One of my roommates had tried to manicure my nails, painted them passion-flower purple, as a kind of joke, I'd supposed. Remnants of the nail polish could still be detected if you looked closely enough.

"What was your motive, then, Aimée, for writing to me? To report that 'someone was cheating' at midterms but to be purposefully vague about who? I've looked into your schedule. Perhaps I can assume that the alleged 'cheating' occurred during Mr. Worth's biology midterm, last Friday morning? Is this so?"

Yes. It was so. By my sick, guilty look, Dean Chawdrey understood my meaning.

"I hope, Aimée, that there is merit to this? I hope that

you are not making a false report, Aimée, to revenge yourself upon a friend?"

I was shocked. I shook my head. "No . . ."

"Or is there more than one girl? More than one of your
'friends' involved?"

I opened my mouth to speak, but could not. The buzzing
in my head had become frantic. I wondered if a blood
vessel in my brain might burst. I was frightened recalling
how my aunt Georgia had described finding an elderly relative seated in a chair in his home, in front of his TV, dead
of a cerebral hemorrhage, blood "leaking" out of one ear.

"Aimée, will you look at me, please! It is very rude, your
way of behaving. By this time, you must certainly know
better."

Through the buzzing in my head I heard the dean chide
me for my "mysterious subterfuge." Wondering at my
"motive" in writing to her. If I refused to be more forth-
coming, how was the Academy's honor code upheld? "I
wonder if, in your mutinous way, you are not making a
mockery of our tradition. This, perhaps, was your inten-
tion all along."

At this, I tried to protest. My voice was shocked,
hushed. In classes, as Mickey Stecke, I was a girl whose
shyness erupted into bursts of speech and animation. I
was smart, and I was funny. My teachers liked me, I
think. I was brash and witty and willing to be laughed at,
but not rebellious or hostile; no one would have called me
"mutinous"; I did not challenge the authority of my
teachers for I required them desperately, I adored my
teachers who were all I had to "grade" me, to define me to
myself and my aunt Agnes. Dean Chawdrey should have

been one of these adult figures, yet somehow she was
not, she saw through my flimsy pose as my cousin Sonny
had once laughed at me in a Halloween costume flung
together out of Aunt Georgia's castoff fabrics *What in
hell're you s'posed to be, kid?*

Dean Chawdrey had dropped my letter onto her desk
with a look of distaste. It lay between us now, as evidence.

"I've looked into your record, 'Aimée Stecke.' You are a
trustee scholar, your full tuition is paid by the Academy.
Your grades are quite good. Your teachers' reports are, on
the whole, favorable. If there is one recurring assessment,
it is 'immature for her age.' Are you aware of this, Aimée?"

I shook my head, no. But I knew that it was so.

"Tell me, Aimée. Since coming to our school, have you
encountered any previous instances of 'cheating'?"

I shook my head, yes. "But I . . ."

" 'But'?"

". . . didn't think it was so important. I mean, so many
girls were cheating, not such serious cheating as lately, so
I'd thought . . ."

" 'So *many*'? 'So *many girls*'? What are you saying,
Aimée?"

An angry flush lifted into the dean's fleshy face. I tried
to explain but my voice trailed off miserably. So stared-at,
by an adult who clearly disliked me, I seemed to have lost
my powers of even fumbling speech. Thoughts came dis-
jointed to me as to one tramping across a field, of mud
half-conscious that her boots are sinking ever more deeply
into the mud, being actively sucked into the mud, not mud
but quicksand and it's too late to turn back.

"But why then, Aimée, did you decide just the other day

to come forward? If it has been so long, so many instances of 'cheating,' and you'd been indifferent?"

"Because . . ." I swallowed hard, not knowing where; this was leading, ". . . I'd signed the pledge. To uphold the . . ."

"To uphold the honor code, Aimée. Yes. Otherwise you would not have been permitted to remain at the Academy. But the honor code is a contract binding you to report cheating at all times, and obviously you have not done that." Dean Chawdrey's small prim mouth was creasing into a smile.

I was sitting very still as if paralyzed. I was listening to the buzzing in my head. Remembering how, in the late winter of our first year of living with my aunt Georgia, Lyle and I had heard a low, almost inaudible buzzing in the plasterboard wall in our room. Above the furnace vent where, if you pressed your ear against it, you could hear what sounded like voices at a distance. My brother had thought it might be tiny people inside. I'd thought it had something to do with telephone wires. It was a warm dreamy sound. It was mixed in with our warm cozy room above the furnace, that Sonny had given up for us. Then one day Aunt Georgia told us with a look of amused disgust that the sound in the wall was only flies—"Damn flies nest in there, hatch their damn eggs then start coming out with the first warm weather." And so it had happened one day a large black fly appeared on a window pane, then another fly appeared on the ceiling, and another, and another until one balmy March morning the wall above the furnace vent was covered in a glittering net of flies so groggy they were slow to escape death from the red plastic swatter wielded in my aunt's deft hand. "You were one of them, Aimée. Weren't you."

This wasn't a question but a statement. There was no way to defend myself except to shake my head, no. Dean Chawdrey said in the way of a lawyer summing up a case, "How would you know, otherwise? And until now, for some quaint reason, you haven't come forward as you'd pledged you would do. What you've alleged, because it's improvable, is dangerously akin to slander. Mr. Werth will have to be informed. His integrity has been impugned, too."

I said, faltering, "But, Dean Chawdrey—"

"The only person who has reported cheating at midterms is you, Aimée." Dean Chawdrey paused, to let that sink in. "Naturally, we have to wonder at your involvement. Do you claim that, since coming to the Amherst Academy, you have never participated in 'cheating'?—in any infraction of the honor code?"

It was as if Dean Chawdrey was shining a flashlight into my heart. I had no defense. I heard myself stammer a confession.

". . . sometimes, a few times, freshman year, I helped other girls with their term papers. I guess I helped my roommates earlier this fall, with . . . But I never . . ."

" 'Never'—what?"

I lowered my head in shame, trying not to cry. I could not comprehend what had gone wrong yet I felt the justice of it. Honor was a venomous snake that if you were reckless enough to lift by its tail, was naturally going to whip around and bite you.

The rest of the visit passed in a blur. Dean Chawdrey did all the talking. You could see that the woman was skilled in what she was doing, other girls had sat in the chair in which I was sitting and had been severely talked-to, many times in the past. Behind the rimless bifocals, Dean Chaw-drey's eyes like watery jelly may have glittered in triumph. Her flat, nasal voice may have trembled with barely restrained exhilaration but it was restrained, and would remain restrained. I heard myself informed that I would be placed on "academic probation" for the remainder of the term. I would be summoned to appear before the discipli-nary committee. More immediately, Dean Chawdrey would notify the headmistress of the Academy about my allega-tions and the confession I'd "voluntarily made" to her, and the headmistress would want to speak with me and with a parent or legal guardian before I could be "reinstated" as a student. The buzzing was subsiding in my head, I knew the visit was ending. The terrible danger was past now that the worst that could happen had happened. I saw Dean Chawdrey's mouth moving but heard nothing more of her words. Behind the woman's large head and oblong-shaped leaden window glared with the sullen rain-light of October. It was no secret that the dean of students wore a wig that fitted her head like a helmet: the color of a wren's wet feathers, shinily synthetic, bizarrely "bouffant." Her right hand lay flat on my letter, that incriminating piece of evi-dence, as if to prevent me from snatching it away if I tried. I gathered my things, and stood. I must have moved abruptly, Dean Chawdrey drew back, I tried to smile. I had seen Momma smiling in a trance of oblivion not knowing where she was, what had been done to her or for her sake. I seemed to be explaining something to Dean Chawdrey but she did not understand: "It was a test, wasn't it— 'promtly.' To see if I would say something. The misspelling. 'Promptly.' " Dean Chawdrey was staring at me in alarm, with no idea what I meant. I turned and ran from the room. In the outer office, the dean's secretary spoke sharply to me. Under my breath I murmured *Get the hell away*. In my stocking feet (I'd had to kick off my muddy boots in the vestibule of the administration building, all this while I'd been facing the dean like a child in dingy white woollen socks) I ran down a flight of stairs, located my fallen boots covered in mud and bits of hay and kicked my feet back into them. I ran outside into the rain, across a patch of hay-strewn muddy lawn that sucked at my feet with a lewd energy. Somehow, it had become dusk. The edges of things were dissolving like wet tissue. A harsh wind blowing east from Lake Erie tasted of snow to come that night but for the moment it continued to rain as it had rained for days. *Raveling-out* was my word for this time of day, after classes, before supper. Neither day nor night. I thought of my aunt Georgia in the days before her son had been taken from her humming to herself as she'd unraveled knitting, castoff sweaters, afghans, energetically winding a ball of used yarn around her hand. My aunt would use the yarn again, nothing in her household was discarded or lost. I would pack my things while the other girls were in the dining hall. What I wished to take with me of my things, my clothes, a few books to read on the bus, not textbooks but paperbacks, and my notebooks, my journal to which I trusted the myriad small secrets of my life in full knowledge that such secrets were of no more worth than the paper, the very ballpoint ink, that contained them. In a flash of inspiration I saw that I would leave a message of farewell on the pillow of my neatly made bed for my roommates and I would leave the residence hall by a rear door and no one would see me. I would never see them again, I thought. Aloud I said, preparing the words I would write: "I will never see any of you again."

No time to dawdle! This is an emergency.

I had money for a bus ticket, even a train ticket. I had money to escape.

This was money scrupulously saved from the allowances my aunt Agnes sent me to cover "expenses" at the Amherst Academy. And money from Momma, five-, ten-, twenty-dollar bills enclosed as if impulsively in jokey greeting cards. *Lyle & I say hello & love & we miss you. Your MOMMA.* I'd hardened my heart against my mother but I'd kept the money she sent me, secreted away in a bureau drawer for just such an emergency.

It was my cousin Sonny I wanted to see. Somehow, I'd become desperate to see him. Not my aunt Agnes who loved me, not my mother who claimed to love me. Only Sonny whom I hadn't seen in almost five years and who never replied to my letters and cards. I'd been told that in September, when he'd turned twenty-one, Sonny had been released into a probationary work program and was living in a halfway house in Chautauqua Falls. Momma had sent me the address and telephone number of Seneca House, as the place was called, saying she hadn't had time to see Sonny yet but she meant to take the trip, soon. Sonny's work was something outdoor like tree service, highway construction—"That boy was always so good with his hands."

Momma was the kind of woman who could say such a thing in utter unconsciousness of what it might mean to

another person. And if you'd indicate how you felt, Momma
would stare in perplexity and hurt. *Why, Aimée. You don't
get that sarcastic mouth from your mother.*

The Greyhound bus that passed through Chautauqua
Falls didn't leave until the next morning so I hid away,
wrapped in my raincoat; with the hood lowered over my
face, in a corner of the bus station. This night unlike any
other night of my life until then passed in a delirium of
partial sleep like a film in which all color has faded and
sound has been reduced to mysterious distortions like
waves in water. In the morning it was revealed that a gritty
snow had fallen through the night, glittery-white like scattered mica that melted in sunshine as the bus lumbered
into the hilly countryside north and east of Buffalo.
Repeatedly I checked the address I had for Sonny: 337
Seneca. I hadn't yet written to Sonny at this address, discouraged by his long silence. It was sad to think that it was
probably so, as my mother had said, Sonny's writing skills
were crude and childlike and he'd have been embarrassed
to write to me. I had the telephone number for the halfway
house but hadn't had the courage to call.

My fear was that Sonny wouldn't want to see me. There
was a rift between Momma and the Brandts, I didn't fully
understand but knew that I had to share Momma's guilt
for what she'd caused to happen in Sonny's life.

I stored my suitcase and duffel bag in a locker in the
Chautauqua Falls bus station. I located Seneca Street and
walked a mile or so to the halfway-house address through
an inner-city neighborhood of pawn shops, bail-bond services, cheap hotels, taverns and pizzerias and X-rated video
stores. In the raw cold sunlight everything seemed height-

ened, exposed. I felt the eyes of strangers on me, and walked quickly, looking straight ahead. Seneca House turned out to be a three-story clapboard house painted a startling mustard yellow. Next door was Chautauqua County Family Welfare Services and across the street a Goodwill outlet and a storefront church, New Assembly of God. I rang the doorbell at Seneca House and after several minutes a heavyset Hispanic woman in her thirties answered the door. I said that I was a cousin of Sonny Brandt and hoped that I could see him and the woman asked if I meant Sean Brandt and I said yes, he was my cousin. The woman told me that Sean was working, and wouldn't be back until six. "There's rules about visitors upstairs. You can't go upstairs." She must have assumed I was lying, I wasn't a relative of Sonny's but a girlfriend. My face pounded with blood.

"How'old'r you?"

"Eighteen."

"You got ID?"

The woman was slyly teasing, not exactly hostile. I wondered if there was a law about minors visiting residents of Seneca House without adult supervision. In my rumpled raincoat, looking exhausted and dazed from my journey, speaking in a faltering voice, I must have looked not even sixteen. I saw, just off the squalid lobby in which we were standing, a visitors' room, or lounge, with a few vinyl chairs and formica-topped tables, wanting badly to ask if I could wait for Sonny there, for it wasn't yet four P.M. The woman repeated again, with a cruel smile, "There's no visitors upstairs, see. That's for your protection."

I went away, and walked aimlessly. Outside a Sunoco

station, I used a pay phone to call the latest telephone number I had for my mother in Ransomville, but no one answered and when a recording clicked on, a man's voice, I hung up quickly. My latest stepfather! I could not remember his name.

I knew that I should call my aunt Agnes. I knew that, by now, the Amherst Academy would have contacted her. And she would be upset, and anxious for me. And she would know how mistaken she'd been, to put her faith in me. Her "favorite niece" who'd betrayed her trust.

"Fact is, I'm Devra's daughter. That can't change." The weirdest thing: I had a strong impulse to speak with my brother. Lyle was eleven now, a sixth-grader at Ransomville Middle School, almost a stranger to me. We had Sonny in common, we'd loved our cousin Sonny in the old farmhouse on Summit Hill Road. Lyle would remember, maybe things I couldn't remember. I called the school, to ask if "Lyle Stecke" was a student there (though I knew that he was a student there) and after some confusion I was told yes, and I said that I was a relative of Lyle's but I did not have a message for him. By this time the receptionist to whom I was speaking had begun to be suspicious so I hung up, quickly.

I walked slowly back to the mustard-yellow clapboard house with the handpainted sign SENECA HOUSE. It was nearing six P.M. I was very hungry, I hadn't wanted to spend money on food and had had the vague hope that Sonny and I might have dinner together. I thought that I would wait for my cousin on the street, to avoid the Hispanic woman who suspected me of being Sonny's girlfriend. At 6:20 P.M., a battered-looking bus marked

Chautauqua County Youth Services pulled up to the curb in a miasma of exhaust and ten, twelve, fifteen men disembarked. All were young, some appeared to be hardly more than boys. All were wearing work clothes, work boots, grimy-looking caps. Nearly all were smoking. A fattish disheveled young man with sand-colored skin and a scruffy goatee, several young black and Hispanic men, a muscled, slow-moving young Caucasian with a burnt-looking skin in filth-stiffened work clothes, a baseball cap pulled down low on his forehead . . . The men passed by me talking and laughing loudly, a few of them glancing in my direction, but taking no special notice of me, as I stared at them unable to see Sonny among them, confused and uncertain. Waiting for Sonny, I'd become increasingly anxious. For soon it would be dark and I was in a city I didn't know and would have to find a place for the night unless I called Momma and in desperation told her where I was, and why. I had no choice but to follow the men into the residence. I saw that the young man in the filthy work clothes and baseball cap was Sonny, moving tiredly among the others, staring at the cracked linoleum floor. His jaws were unshaven. His hands were very dirty. I called to him, "Sonny? Hey, it's Mickey."

He hadn't heard. One of the young black men, eyeing me with a smile, poked at Sonny to alert him to me. When he turned, the sight of him was a shock. His face had thickened, coarsened. The burnt-looking skin was a patchwork of blemishes and acne scars. I could recognize the pale blue eyes, but the eyes were hardened in suspicion. I'd expected that Sonny might smile at me, even laugh at the sight of me, in surprise; I'd expected that he would come

to me, to hug me. But this man held back, squinting.
There was something wrong about his gaze. I saw to my
horror that his left eye seemed to have veered off to the
side as if something had caught its attention while his
right eye stared straight at me. His lips drew back from his
teeth that were discolored and crooked. "Dev'a? Are you—
Dev'a?"

Devra! Sonny was mistaking me for Momma. I told him
no, I was Mickey. His cousin Mickey, didn't he remember
me?

I tried to laugh. This had to be funny. This had to be a
joke. This had to be Sonny's old sense of humor. But he
wasn't smiling; he continued to stare at me with his one
good eye. The lines in his forehead had sharpened to
creases. His nose was broad at the bridge as if it had been
broken and flattened. However old you might guess this
man to be, you would not have guessed twenty-one. "Did
you come to see me? Nobody comes to see me." Sonny
spoke slowly, as if he had to choose his words with care,
and yet his words were slightly slurred, like speech heard
underwater. He'd been injured, I thought. His brain had
been injured in a beating. But I came forward, to take
hold of one of Sonny's hands, so much larger than my
own. Sonny loomed above me, six feet tall but somewhat
slump-shouldered, his head pitched slightly forward in the
perpetual effort of trying to hear what was being said to
him. "I'm Devra's daughter, Sonny. Remember, 'Aimée'? I
was just a little girl when we came to live with you and
Aunt Georgia. You changed my name to 'Mickey.' 'Mickey
kicks ass,' you said. You—"

Sonny jerked his hand from mine, as if my fingers had

burnt him. He might have heard something of what I'd said, but wasn't sure how to interpret it. From what I could see of his hair, beneath the grimy cap, it had been shaved close, military-style, at the sides and back. His skin looked stitched-together, of mismatched fabrics like one of Georgia's crazy quilts. His face shriveled suddenly in the effort not to cry. "You lied to me, Aunt Dev'a. That wasn't the man, the man that I hurt, it was somebody else, wasn't it! Some other man you'd been married to. You lied to me, I was told you lied to me, Aunt Dev'a, why'd you lie to me? I hurt the wrong man, you lied to me." Sonny spoke in the aggrieved voice of a child, pushing at me, not hard, but enough to force me to step backward. I was astonished at what he'd said. Though I'd heard something like this from my aunt Georgia, who'd had more than a suspicion that the man who'd actually hurt my mother had been Bob Gleason, not Herlihy. I couldn't make sense of this, I couldn't allow myself to think of it now. I was trying to smile, to laugh, in the old way, as if Sonny's confusion was only teasing and in another moment, he'd wink and nudge at me and we'd laugh together. I said, "Do you still like pizza, Sonny? We can have pizza for dinner. I have money." Sonny said, " 'Piz-za,' " enunciating the word in two distinct syllables. His face shriveled and he clenched his fists as if he was considering breaking my face. A middle-aged black man who wore a laminated ID badge appeared beside us, laying a restraining hand on Sonny's arm. "Hold on there, Sean. Take it slow, man." I told this man who I was, I'd come to see my cousin, and the man explained to Sonny who listened doubtfully, staring at me. "I'm Mickey. You remember, your cousin Mickey. That's me." I spoke eagerly, hopefully. The filmy look in Sonny's good eye seemed suddenly to clear. " 'Mickey.' That's you. Well, hell." Sonny's lips parted in a slow smile that seemed about to reverse itself at any moment. I said, "I'll get the pizza. I'll bring it back here. I'll get us some Cokes, we can eat right there." I meant the lounge area, where there was a table we could use. On the wall beyond, a mosaic of crudely fashioned bright yellow sunflowers in shards of tile that looked handmade.

I hurried outside. The fresh air was a shock after the stale smoky air of Seneca House. Up the block was Dino's Pizza. I went inside and ordered a large pizza as if it was the most natural thing in the world for me to do. Years ago, in the old farmhouse on Summit Hill Road, Sonny had brought home pizzas for us on evenings Georgia hadn't wanted to cook, our favorite was cheese with pepperoni and Italian sausage, tomatoes, no onions or olives. Lyle and I would drink soda pop, Georgia and Sonny and Momma, if she was home, beer. I wondered if beer was allowed in Seneca House and I thought probably not, I hoped not. I hoped that Sonny would be waiting for me in the lounge, that he hadn't for-gotten me and gone upstairs where I couldn't follow. The guy behind the counter was about twenty, olive-skinned, dark-eyed, hair straggling to his shoulders. Half his face creased in a smile. "You don't look like anyone from here."

"What?"

"You don't look like anyone from here but maybe I know you?" I'd been pretending to be looking through my wallet, to see how much money I had. I laughed, feeling blood rush into my face. But it was a pleasant sensation, like the feel of hot sun on bare skin, before it begins to burn.

~~~~~~~~~

Junior Partner
in Crime

Carole Nelson Douglas

~~~~~~~~~

Former newspaper reporter Carol Nelson Douglas is an award-winning author who has written mainstream novels, historical romance, fantasy, science fiction, and mystery. The first book in Douglas's Irene Adler series, *Good Night, Mr. Holmes,* was honored as a *New York Times* Notable Book of the Year. It also won an American Mystery Award for Best Novel of Romantic Suspense, and a *Romantic Times* Best Historical Romantic Mystery Award. Also known for her feline sleuth Midnight Louie cat-titled mysteries set in Las Vegas, Douglas's current release is *Cat in a Quicksilver Caper.* Douglas also writes wonderful short stories and has edited several anthologies, including *Marilyn: Shades of Blonde.*

Once upon a time in 1973, a stray cat called "Midnight Louey" lived at or about a motel in ritzy Palo Alto, California, one of the nation's wealthiest suburbs. Cats abandoned at motels, no matter how upscale, become feral. They go untreated if injured, often starve, and live short, brutish lives.

Midnight Louey, however, frequented the motel koi pond for lunch, and weighed a strapping eighteen pounds. This hairy lothario hung out by the Coke machine in the evenings to pick up lonely ladies who would take him into their rooms and out of the northern California chill for the night.

When the motel management decided to send this feline gigolo to the local pound to preserve their expensive decorative fish collection, a visiting Minnesota woman couldn't stand to see his superb survival instincts rewarded with certain death. So she shipped him two thousand miles back to her St. Paul home.

That's where Carole Nelson, a metropolitan daily newspaper reporter, saw the thirty-dollar ad in the classifieds offering Midnight Louey, who was "equally at home on your best couch as in your neighbor's garbage can," to the right home for a dollar bill. Intrigued by the fiscal contradiction, she wrote a feature article about Midnight Louey. By 1985, Carole had left Minnesota and journalism for full-time fiction writing in Texas, but she revived the black cat as the part-time narrator of a romantic suspense quartet of novels. And nineteen years after Carole met Louey, Midnight Louie, P.I. debuted as cover boy and star of his own mystery series in 1992's Catnap.

Obviously, the "real and original" Louey would be a very senior citizen of the cat world by now. We don't think about that. We know he's still out there somewhere, copping koi and seducing dames.

But Louey's inimitable beat goes on. During the first Midnight Louie Adopt-a-Cat book signing/cat adoption tour sponsored by Forge Books in 1996, Carole Nelson Douglas met Midnight Louie, Jr., in the Lubbock, Texas, shelter. Oh, he wasn't called that then, and he was an entirely different kettle of fish from the real and original, but he was as good at picking up dames as his namesake, and he eventually came home with her to join the Douglas household.

How he got to the shelter is the real mystery.

—CAROLE NELSON DOUGLAS

ACT I: Legend

It's hard living up to a legend.

Especially a legend that's mostly a figment of some author's imagination, as most legends are, if you ask me.

The trouble is, nobody does. Ask me, that is.

I am just a cat.

I am not a hard-boiled, hairy-chested Las Vegas P.I. who's had serial tangles with murderers, like my old man, Midnight Louie, Sr. I do not write books, interrogate neighborhood dogs, visit casinos, or chase Persian showgirls.

There is only one way I take after my old man: I do like a little nip now and then.

I mean, what can the average dude do to ease the pressure? How would you like to be the son of Superman? All the kids would want to know if you'd hopscotched over any tall buildings lately.

I get asked if I've nailed any big-league baddies. How is a house-bound soul supposed to do that? I think about these matters often these days as I lounge about one of my many condos, polishing my handsome spats to the sheen of black patent leather.

Yeah, I am strictly a hot-house cat these days. I loll by the water fountain, nibble from fine crystal, unwind on the king-size bed, and enjoy naps on the custom-built screen porch over the kitchen sink.

Unlike my supposed sire, I am politically correct to the tips of the whiskers on my chinny-chin-chin: I do not wander the mean streets, I had the required surgery (nut cut) early in life, I almost had a claw draw, too, but my post-street blood numbers were a little iffy and prevented it, plus I am such a little gentleman at nail-trimming time that I retain the "four on the floor" that Senior boasts of.

Nevertheless, I am a peace-loving type, even though the platinum-blonde who was here first didn't warm up to me at first. But Summer, the silver Persian, has come around. The other cats, Smoke, the mother-daughter act of Victoria and Secret, and our token dog, Xanadu, have always been friendly. I don't much like that upstart roof rat, Amber-leigh, that the humans plucked off a neighbor's eaves last fall, but I suppose in time I'll soften my stance.

I basically like being the good guy.

So my main role in life now is acting as a body double for my old man, being he's so camera shy: Miss Carole poses with me in photographs, and my mug has been on posters and dust jackets. Everybody says what a hand-some fellow I am. And I am. Miss Carole boasts of my short-cropped black-velvet head and limbs and the flowing long fur on my body and tail.

I do get a perverse little kick out of thinking that Mid-night Louie, Sr., the Sam Spade of pet detectives, is being repped by a dude who was once seriously mistaken for a girl.

Of course that wee misapprehension saved my life, so I try not to take it too personally.

My life has had its ups and downs.

The downs explain why I was to be found in the Lubbock city shelter at the tender age of one year, give or take a couple months, with my tail broken in two places, my tummy shaved, my midnight coat as dull as ditch water, and the name "Jasmine" written on a tag attached to my cage. Jeez, might as well have had my nose tattooed with the name "Rosie," although my nose, like the rest of me, is a solid, no-nonsense black.

Every guy and gal in a joint like a shelter, whether accurately labeled or not as to gender, has a story. Like the fancy Himalayan huddled on the highest perch with a deep gash on his aristocratic nose. Lubbock isn't a big town, and the shelter director managed to find his owner. "Oh," she says, "as long as you've got him, you might as well keep him." So here he sits with the usual lowlifes, scared to death.

Our holding cell is pretty nice for a shelter. We have a big open room, with perches and condos scattered between our nighttime cages. You could call it a colony. We are free to move around, stretch our legs and our territorial instincts. That's why Mr. Himalayan is so nervous. He's not used to establishing territory in a common holding cell.

Frankly, it was no piece of catnip for me, either, being I'm small for my age, and downright skinny. Not to mention that "girl" part.

I had a home once. They meant well, or at least they liked kittens in a kind of careless way. But they didn't keep us inside because they never thought about all the dangers waiting outside, even if they got me "fixed."

So I ended up footloose and fancy free, and I even had One Big Case before I was shoveled into stir and then worked my way out of the Big House. Here is how it all went down:

ACT II: The Sting

It was a day like any day. My owners went to work and let me out for the duration.

Frankly, I never did like these day-long outings. I am just a little guy and there are a lot of big, tough cats and dogs in the neighborhood that my owners never see.

After cavorting for an hour or so, I was ready to find a safe place to hunker down.

It is April in Lubbock. The sidewalks are already hot, and I had to amble through a few neighboring yards in search of water. Nobody was watering their lawns because my neighborhood didn't exactly have lawns so much as dirt patches with weeds.

While I might stumble over a birdbath in the shade, which had a little gruel in the bottom mixed with water and, er, bird droppings, my best bet was breaking into the plastic bags at the curbs and finding those big plastic water bottles with a few drops left in the bottom. Sometimes I had to work their caps off, but if I put a lot of effort into it, I could almost wet my whistler enough to make it worth the effort.

So there I am, curled up like a dead roach around this empty plastic bottle that is bigger than I am, kicking and chewing and working that screwtop loose, when I feel a hot breath of wind singeing the nape of my neck.

This is no ordinary high plains breeze. As I turn around to look, I see the huge face and fangs of a drooling English bulldog.

Only mad English bulldogs go out in the noonday sun in Lubbock, so I scoot upright, kick the bottle into the bulldog's stupid toothy kisser, and take off across the hot pavement.

With a yowl and a bay and scrabble of nails long enough for Nosferatu (I have watched a lot of late-night cable television and have a vivid imagination), the dog is on my tail.

I dash through yards, forced to bypass familiar hiding places, knowing nothing will fool this infuriated hound. Before I know it I am in foreign territory where there is not a safe house to be seen.

I finally claw my way up a mesquite tree behind a dilapidated shack. Now mesquite trees are not very high, or wide, or handsome. It is a good thing I am a lightweight, I think, as I sway to and fro on a top branch in the hot sun. My coat is black and thick, and I soak up every sizzling ray. Luckily, even a white-coated bulldog can't take the Texas heat. After an hour of howling and bow-legged leaping, it goes swaggering off like it has actually accomplished something.

I skitter down the tree trunk and head for the nearest shade by a wooden house, which is deserted.

Well, the bulldog has accomplished something nasty, after all, I realize as I survey my situation. I am far from home and I am lost. And there are not even plastic bags at the curb in this neighborhood. There are not even curbs! In fact, there are not even other houses, be they ever so humble.

You have no doubt heard of remarkable journeys made by lost pets across half the country to return to their homes. Forget it. That is all Disney propaganda.

It's not easy to sniff your way back to your old neighborhood when you've run willy-nilly away from it without having time to mark any territory along the way.

Besides, I don't see any pressing reason to find my way back. The food was pretty mediocre, the kids teased me without any parental objections, and I was fending for myself outside all day, anyway.

So I wait until evening shadows fall, then start hoofing my way back to town. That darn bulldog has chased me halfway to the Great Salt Desert.

My pads are pretty tender, but I know I need to find civilization to find garbage. The more civilization, the more garbage. I believe this is the motto of some political protest groups, but I am too hungry, footsore, and thirsty to be a political animal at the moment. *Vive le garbage!* It is all Chef Surprise to me.

To make a long story short, I pad it back to more occupied territory and get seriously into a career of garbage inspector. Frankly, I have not been brought up to hunt wild game, although there is some wild game out here that has been brought up to hunt me. Besides coyotes, there are domesticated dogs and feral cats.

For the next few days, I manage to scout up enough rank food and liquid to survive, but not well. I hole up and sleep by day, hunt the polyvinyl chloride herds at the curbs by night.

I am not doing well. My sides are concave and I have fleas. I am doing so poorly that when I run into some homeless people, they set aside their bottles of Mission Bell muscatel to give me pinches off their soggy Quarter Pounders. This is like getting a sawdust sandwich drenched in radiator fluid, but I gobble it down. Any port wine in a storm.

Then one day I am looking for a place to go to ground and I sniff a little something gourmet on the breeze. A window is open in the Land of Air Conditioners!

I run around to the back of a neatly painted bungalow to discover that there is a window with a screen and inside the screen is a raised sash and inside the room is a hot meal. With meat.

I bound up to the sill and hook my front shivs in the screen. I am so weak I can barely balance there.

I hear a creaking sound, and then this old lady comes wheeling toward me in a moving chair. Her hair is white and fluffy like popcorn.

"Kitty," she says, like she knows me.

Well, "Kitty," is my middle name. Me and a million like me.

"Poor Kitty," she purrs at me, and I know she can be trusted.

In a minute, *she* is clawing at the screen, too, except that she is making a much better job of it. Maybe it is those cuticle scissors she wields like a single wicked claw. Clever, these humans.

Before I know it, a few fresh pieces of roast beef are sitting on the sill, waiting for my delectation.

I delectate rapidly, and get more. And more. More is not enough.

Then there is another creak, of a door to the room. The old lady quickly shuts the inner glass window and her chair spins around.

I blink, watching a shadow advancing to the window.

Down. Fast. Trust no one.

I huddle at the cool, damp stone foundation beneath the window, burping. A voice, muted, wrangles above. I cringe at its grinding tone. I have heard that sound many times in my journey. The raging of an angry human.

It is not shouting at me, I realize, but the old lady who fed me.

Who would shout at a kind old lady? I stick by the window, not willing to give up the drive-through at Chez Grandma. When darkness comes, I have to go out scouting for water, and finally score a dead sprinkler still sitting in a small pond of liquid.

I return to the window. I want to know the old lady is all right. Hopping up to the sill, I see the room is quiet and dark.

I meow softly.

Something stirs. Something creaks. The old lady is at the glass, struggling to lift it. "Kitty," she whispers. I see her eyes in the moonlight as if they were behind maroon-tinted lenses. They are sad and confused. I know the feeling.

"I saved you something, Kitty. Now, shush. Oh, I'm so tired. Here, I have to push open this bit of screen I've worked loose. Maynard and Lucille would be so mad. Here. Pork patty."

Bits of meat are pushed through, and I gobble the first bit. It tastes stale. Or something. I take the rest up in my teeth and jump down.

I must have overeaten earlier. My stomach rebels. I'll save it until later, bury it somewhere. Under the house where there's a crack in the stone.

Easily sated, even queasy, I slink off to a nearby out-building, and shelter behind some piled stones. There may be snakes, spiders, and scorpions, but I have to hide somewhere.

I sleep, and in that sleep my stomach undergoes earth-quakes. I wake and spit up, not a hairball, but liquid I can't afford to lose. I know I am in trouble if getting food makes me sick. I am not just hungry, but starving.

Yet I must eat something, so I stumble back to my cache. *Eureka.* A dead mouse has fallen into my fangs. It lies there in the moonlight. *Fresh, Dead. Mine!*

Then I look. The meat I hid is gone. The mouse's belly is high and round . . . an acrid pile of vomit lies near it.

I draw back, all hunger turned to dread.

The meat is bad. The meat is fatal. The old Lady!

I lope back to the window.

The room is dark with night. There is no sound, no motion. I sit vigil until the skies blush blue with dawn.

I see the old lady in her bed, tossing and moaning in her sleep. A furrow grows in the short fur on my forehead. I don't like what I'm thinking.

Later, I hear the other people enter the room. A rangy, raw-boned woman is crooning at my benefactor, pushing a tray of food onto the bed.

The minute she leaves I yowl plaintively at the window. The old lady's eyes light up as they focus on me through the round spectacles that sit crookedly on her nose.

She pushes out of the bed into the wheeled chair, takes a dish from the tray and comes wheeling toward me.

In a minute the inside window is pushed open a few inches, and sausage meat decorates the windowsill.

I yowl and pace back and forth until her fingers push through the screen and manage to pat my sides.

"So skinny," she cries. "Here, Kitty. Eat all this. I have more."

The sausage has the same musty taste as the pork. I nibble delicately, then take as much as I can into my mouth and jump down to the ground.

In a moment I am on the sill again, begging, pacing, yowling. I get more, taste a touch, then grab the rest and disappear beneath the window view.

I am not eating this bounty, of course, much as I could use some easy protein. It is tainted, and not accidentally. Luckily, the old lady is so kindhearted that she eventually gives me the whole mess.

The only bad part is that I have to take a few morsels into my mouth to make her think I'm gobbling it all up, and my stomach is already burning.

Once it's all gone, she shuts the window, eyes the door to her room uneasily, and rolls back to the bed. A few minutes later, the big-boned woman is back for the tray, and clucks with pleasure at the short work I have made of the breakfast sausage. The old lady has only eaten toast, but I'm betting that it is not spiced and suitable for poisoning.

I bury the sausage deeper than diarrhea.

Then I walk around to the front of the house. We are in a row of houses at least, though they are modest. I hear a TV blaring in the front room.

"She eat?" a man's voice asks.

"Some toast and all the sausage," the woman answers triumphantly and softly, but I have big ears I can manipulate to pull in whispers as well as mice scrabblings.

"Meat seems to work with her."

"And it's easy to fix, too. Just like handling a stray dog in the neighborhood."

"I'm sure glad we heard about your widowed aunt needing some live-in care," he says. "I'm ready for retirement."

"It won't be long now," Lucille comments, popping the top on a soda can dewed with water.

I salivate from my watching post in the parlor window.

"Sure is hot and dry in this damn place," Lucille adds. "Maybe I can hurry it up."

"Don't want to overdo it," Maynard says. "We can wait a little while."

But I can't. What's a homeless, inconsequential, mute dude to do? I have not yet even heard of He Who Is Soon To Be My Old Man. I do not know a private eye from a privy. I am just a youngster and in trouble myself. But I can't let someone who wants to help me go undefended.

I've got some time. It's clear I can cadge the old lady out of her meat indefinitely, although I doubt I can safely tooth that lethal stuff much longer without succumbing myself.

I settle under an oleander bush to rest up and think. A couple hours later I hear the stomp of big, soft-soled shoes. Someone is coming up the cracked sidewalk to the house!

That's what I need! A human helper. I peer out and like what I see: a big girl, tall and solid, with a long red braid down the back of her shirt and a broad, friendly, freckled face. She looks cheerful, strong, and confident. She is carrying a big leather satchel like it is cotton candy.

Best of all, she is wearing a U.S. government uniform. I could use a little official help.

I waylay her before she gets too close to the door, throw myself down on my side in her path and cry piteously. Believe me, the piteous cries are not faked at this point.

She stops on a dime, which is good because the next thing she would have stopped on would have been my concave guts. "Why, Kitty! What a sweetie!" My empty tummy is being tickled. It is all I can do to avoid the dry heaves, but I must appear to be a happy, healthy cat.

She unbends and clomps up to the door, pauses at the big metal bin nailed up next to it, then knocks.

"Yeah?" Lucille doesn't look or sound happy.

"Sorry to bother you," my savior says. "I was just wondering if Mrs. Sargent had gotten a new cat."

"That?" Lucille eyes me like I am a case of the clap. "Some darned stray. Mrs. Sargent don't need no cat. She needs a miracle."

"I'm sorry to hear that," the mail carrier says, sounding it. "I used to enjoy chatting with her on my rounds. She'd always wheel up to the screen door just before I got here, and we'd talk."

"What about?" Lucille sounds suspiciously suspicious.

The mail carrier blinks. "The weather, her health, my aching feet. I'd think a cat would be just the kind of company Mrs. S would need in her situation."

"She's lucky to have me and Maynard, and between us, she won't be in her situation for long, so you'll have to mark that mail RETURN TO SENDER. Last thing she needs is a damn stray cat. If I have anything to say about it, that animal will be gone before my aunt will."

"I'm so sorry to intrude." The mail carrier has stuffed a

fistful of catalogs and flyers in the box and backed away. "You must be very sad right now."

Lucille looks about as sad as a striking rattlesnake.

"Tell Mrs. S that Erin the mail girl called, and I wish her the very best of everything."

Lucille mumbles something ungracious under her breath, and my strapping cohort walks away.

For lunch we have hamburger, and I con the whole patty out of Mrs. S in four minutes flat. I bury it next to the breakfast sausage near the foundation, musing that the property will be vermin-free for a very long time.

Dinner is meatballs. All mine. But I've had to tongue too much and can barely jump up onto the parlor sill after dinner.

Maynard and Lucille are watching *Touched by an Angel,* of all things.

"Meat go down?" Maynard wants to know. He is a beer belly with a five o'clock shadow and that's about it.

"Every last crumb. But it's not working fast enough. She seems to be doing better, oddly enough. I don't get it."

"Maybe we need a concentrated form. Something liquid."

I quail. There is no way I can keep Mrs. Sargent from drinking something.

Lucille gets up, goes into the kitchen and returns with a bottle of Ozarka spring water.

"Maybe a hypodermic. We could always say one of those nutso product tamperers had done it."

"Gad," says Marnard. "That crap tastes like fairy juice. Tropical fruit flavor. That ought to cover up anything. We'll bring her to the parlor tomorrow morning, and make a damn toast out of it."

I more fall than jump to the ground. I am very hungry, very thirsty, very weak. And very desperate.

There is more sausage for breakfast, and more sausage buried by the foundation, and more sausage in my system than there should be.

I save my strength by snoozing in the oleander shade. Oleander leaves are poisonous to animals, you know, but I could not open my mouth to eat even a filet mignon at this point.

Mrs. Sargent is in the parlor. She had wheeled herself to the front door and asked that it be opened. She doesn't know that this is a last request. Maynard and Lucille shrug.

"I'm glad you're feeling better, Aunt Betty," Lucille coos in that meat-offering voice. I've heard people trying to trap me and they sound just like that, all honey and hypocrisy.

"How about a nice tall cool glass of spring water?"

I am on the front stoop peering through the screen. They have left the latch off. I paw it open, slip through. Better.

"I'm feeling poorly lately," Mrs. Sargent says, eyeing the Ozarka askance. "That stuff is all bubbly. It might upset my stomach."

"It might soothe your stomach," Lucille urges, lifting the bottle.

Well, I am nearly dying of thirst.

I launch myself into the air, right at the Ozarka bottle.

We land like paired ice-skaters, the bottle in my arms as we go spinning across the hardwood floor together. I am kicking, I am unscrewing the cap faster than I have ever before. It is a world record. In a minute a sizzling flood of adulterated spring water is washing over the floor and over me.

"Get that cat!" Lucille screeches. "Kill that cat!"

"No!" the old lady yells. "Don't touch it. It's my friend."

My ears prick up as I leap to avoid the arc of Maynard's kicking work boot.

Other boots, coming up the walk.

"Shut the door," Lucille screeches, rushing for the heavy oaken slab that stands ajar.

I rush to beat her to it.

It's swinging shut like a steel safe door, momentum behind it.

Before me I see Erin's open, puzzled face nearing the mesh of the screen.

Mrs. S is screaming, "Don't hurt it! Don't hurt it!"

If that door closes, everything will remain hidden behind it. Everything bad that can happen, one way or the other, will happen.

That door must not close.

I dash through with no inches to spare. It is a good thing I am so skinny. My forelegs push open the screen door, inviting, drawing Erin in. Her face is alarmed, confused, and grim. She is not going to go away.

I grit my teeth. I stop on the threshold, close my eyes, and leave my tail trailing behind me like a doorstop.

Then all goes black and bright white. I hear howls of pain. I rocket into the front yard, pursued by agony.

Erin has pushed the ajar door open and is filling the front room. "Mrs. S? They said you were too weak to see company."

"Weak! A little, but that's from the food they give me.

Mush like you've never seen before. Oh, the poor kitty, where is the poor kitty?"

"They said you couldn't see anybody," Erin goes on, talking as if Maynard and Lucille weren't there. "I missed our talks."

"They said you had a different route, and never came anymore—"

So there it was: they said, she said.

I am out of there, but I knew that Maynard and Lucille soon would be too.

ACT III: The Great Escape

So what do I get after saving the day and the old lady and ingesting enough acid rain to be the Great Lakes? The Big Boys on the street are waiting for me when I finally stop panting in a vacant lot.

Death, taxes, and tomcats are unavoidable. Unfortunately, two of those negative outcomes were right in front of me, snarling and hissing and mincing sideways with their backs up and their tails and ears down. (And I don't mean the IRS.)

Luckily, the excruciating pain in my tail means that I was having a Very Bad Hair Day. It is standing up all over my body as if I'd stuck my tongue in an electrical outlet, which I know better than to do.

So I let myself really feel that pain-pulsating tail of mine, broken in two places the exact thickness of a hardwood front door. I yowl out my agony and run right through their ranks like a bolt of cold lightning . . . you know, that weird gray flash people sometimes see running along the baseboards?

I am an electrical phenomenon, all right. Wish someone had captured this Kodak Moment for posterity, not that I will ever have any.

I don't have the Big Boys' advantage of numbers (about nine), or the edge of body weight, 'cause every last and least one of 'em is twice my heft. But I do have speed and a tail that feels like the long, burning line of a firecracker fuse. I blast past them like the lead car in the Indy 500 and head right for sanctuary.

Some would call it prison, but at this point I need something between me and the cruel, cold world, not to mention about a gross of cold, cruel claws.

I dart right into the open cage and throw all my weight on the food holder.

Clang.

I don't bother eating the glop, although I feel hungry when I'm not hurting. I turn in a flash of pain and triumph and have the satisfaction of seeing the pursuing phalanx mashing their kissers into the metal mesh, ears and whiskers crumpled against steel wire. They all look like a bunch of Scottish Folds, that breed of cat with crimped ears. The tartan plaids impressed on their faces by the wire patterns go right along with the Caledonian theme. Scotland's burning, boys, and if my tail had to go for broke in the course of a humanitarian act, your pusses are gonna look like chopped haggis on a birthday cake with a rash of candles for a couple of days.

They scream and caterwaul and claw at me through the grid, but I am safe until the feral catch-and-cut crew come to retrieve me, and then I will be out like Flynn because I've already had my politically correct procedure.

So I squat on the unpleasant metal grid floor, which turns my tender pads into waffle-patterns, and watch the Big Boys raise their blood pressure to no avail. I would wrap my tail around my throbbing toes but it doesn't move so good. It finally dawns on me that I have sacrificed my pride and joy, my panache, my posterior plume, for all eternity. The cause was good, true, but the effect will be a lifetime maiming.

I would offer my tail a parting snuffle or two, but I dare not show weakness in front of these bully boys, even if they are out of reach at the moment.

I have gravely underestimated the risks of turning myself in voluntarily. When the collection van pulls up as expected a couple hours later, the gang scatters like rats facing a Bengal tiger. I am left to stand alone, like the cheese in the old song. I am "It" in a game of tag, and all the players have vanished except the parents, who come to break up the game for the night.

A woman approaches my prison on soft cat feet to bend down and peer at me. These catch-and-cut types are usually women. My old man would call them "dames," but I am more enlightened.

"Got one! Oh, what a pretty cat," she says.

This sounds promising. The other woman bends down. I wait for them to unlatch the cage to move me so I can dash out and find another shelter before the Big Boys are smart enough to come back.

My world shakes, then spins. I am not to be removed, with an opportunity for fleeing, but will be transported in the trap.

Somebody has figured out that we street types are tricky.

But I am trickier than any "somebody" out there. Outwitted murderers, didn't I?

I stand and totter over to the cage side, rubbing against the grid, as close as I can get to Woman Number One.

"Merrrowwww," I say.

"This is a friendly one," she purrs right back. "We may be able to foster her and find her a home."

Her.

Thus it begins, the greatest masquerade of my crime-fighting career.

"Look," says Woman Number Two. "She can hardly hold her tail up. Something must have happened to it."

Duh.

"Oh, not the cage door closing, I hope," whimpers Woman Number One.

I mew piteously, small and wee. Nothing like a big lump of guilt to get humans on the right track.

"We'd better have the vet look at the tail before surgery."

Yeah, you'd better! The vet had better look *under* the tail, because I sure as heck do not want an unnecessary hysterectomy!

"Linda, I think we can place this one. She must be in awful pain, but she's still so sweet and friendly. I don't think she's feral at all."

Sweet and friendly does not cut it on the street, but among the Cage Set, it's the best pedigree there is. Even if you have to undergo a temporary sex change.

I purr so loud I sound like a snoring frog.

"Poor little thing!"

By now *my* eyes are watering. Well, my tail is a poor little thing, all right.

Soon I am ensconced, cage and all, in a van that smells like collies and cat-marking behavior.

Every jolt on the journey makes my tail quake, and I make the silent scream many times, which is the downside of the silent meow, but I grit my teeth. I do not want to scare anyone on the other end.

Frankly, the pain and the hunger and poison and the stress catch up with me, and I am pretty much out of it by the time I arrive wherever I arrive.

I recall much sympathetic cooing, and ginger inspections of my maimed posterior appendage. I am lifted and my weight is found wanting. I am turned upside down and my stomach is shaved.

This is when the cluckings become shock, and I am quickly turned right side up.

Voices say that I am "friendly" and a "candidate." I am moved into another cage, and then another van, and then another cage.

I wake up in a room with a window wall on the bleak high plains emptiness of beyond-suburban Lubbock. A bare-naked tree, all trunk and limbs, awaits in a fenced area like a denuded traffic cop.

The room is crawling with my kind. All kinds of my kind, with but one thing in common: We belong to no one, and that could get us killed.

But we have one other thing in common, I know it in my bones. We have been chosen to live, at least long enough to get a chance at conning some human into a home.

Let us not kid ourselves. This is not a resort hotel. In a way it is as rough as the empty lot where the Big Boys rule.

A male attendant comes into the room, dispensing dry food. Finally, my cage is approached.

"So this is the new kitty."

The door opens. I am carefully lifted out.

"Bad tail," the young man says, squinting at the card affixed to my cage. "Name of . . . Jasmine. One- or two-year-old female. Yellow eyes. Long tail. Trapped. How'd you get yourself caught in a big ole trap, Jasmine? Must have been awfully hungry. You weigh as much as a six-month-old kitten in my hand. Here. You sit on this cat condo and make friends with the others."

I am left, high, dry, and handsome (if my tail were in any normal condition) for all the other cat eyes in the room to stare at. They are not mean, those eyes, but they are wary and hungry and hurt, probably like my eyes. Which are *green!* Or so my mama done told me, and I tend to believe her.

And my tail is not particularly *long,* but it is broken and hurts like hell.

And my name is not Jasmine, because I am not a girl, but I can see why with all the animals they have coming and going they made the mistake.

I am light on my feet, and jump down to try some food nuggets in a bowl.

Hisses, humped backs, and the delicate prod of nail-tips.

I sigh. This may not be the Big Boys' lot, but I still will have to fight for every crumb.

Despite the initiation rituals, which leave me with minute scabs on my neck and shoulders, this place offers a certain routine. There are sunny times out scrabbling up the bare tree limbs.

There are the rare times a browser meanders through our quarters, eyeing each of us, murmuring at some, passing through, all too seldom picking . . . one.

We watch with found envious eyes as the lucky pickee is groomed, then handed over, never to be seen again. We hope the escapee heads toward the heaven of laps and Fancy Feast and a secure old age.

We know, of course, only that one is gone, and it is not us.

How long can they keep us? Others crowd to join us, many times more than the few who leave. A grain of sand sifts through the narrow neck of the hourglass, and a thousand new grains pour into the wide gaping maw at the top.

So many are called homeless. So few are chosen.

My tail mends, though it is still tender, and I am still underweight. I bask in the sun on the bate-limbed tree. I take my nicks of the colony's claws. I wait. I am looked at. And left.

Then one day there is a buzz of activity. Several shelter people enter our colony cage at once. They need, they say, a black cat.

Eight of us perk up ears, widen eyes, purr.

Someone laid-back.

Three flip over on their sides and purr. I am not normally a side-flipper, and I will not start now.

Good for media.

Four lift paws, blink.

I am too weary still to perform. I can only recline elegantly, my twisted tail hidden between my legs.

"Here," someone says. "Jasmine is so calm. She should do well under the hot lights."

I am picked, picked up, put into a small carrier that is dark and close and taken to a van. This time my tail doesn't hurt as much as we jolt to a strange place.

I sit for a long time in the carrier, ignoring the water, food, and cardboard box of litter.

I am finally extracted into the glare of fourteen suns and settled on someone's lap.

Someone's lap.

This is my Big Chance.

My moment in the sun.

A few precious seconds to impress, please, survive.

I knead my nails into the lap. I purr. I blink in the bright lights. I remain very, very calm.

I hear voices discussing an adoption event. For the first time I hear the name "Midnight Louie." I hear my "name" Jasmine and statistics given. I hear that I have a "good personality" and am available.

Then the lights vanish. The cage returns. The humans gather around me and talk above my head as usual. They think it went very well. The noon news show resumes. The attractive anchor lady says, "And now the latest on a shocking case of elder abuse. Mrs. Sargent is safe in a foster home after her niece and the niece's live-in boyfriend were arrested on charges of abuse and attempted murder. An alert mail carrier noticed that—"

An alert mail carrier indeed! What about an "alert male carrier" of a once-proud tail?

But I am happy to hear the outcome, and the journey in the van soon returns me to the shelter common room. It is all over. And after two days, no one calls my name. I have been on TV and I have not been adopted. I know that Mrs. Sargent and Erin have been too busy to watch TV, but still, I had hopes. . . .

Needless to say, I am a little depressed.

Then another flutter of activity. An eminent visitor. Again I hear the name Midnight Louie. I begin to curse it, for it is not mine.

A woman enters the common room. She is being shown around, a VIP. Many thoughts flash through my mind. Midnight Louie is one big wheel to be mentioned on television. This woman is associated with Midnight Louie. It would be a smart move to associate with this woman.

But so many cats occupy the space, high and low and in-between. All are sweet and deserving and variously attractive. What can I do?

I sit on the concrete door by the woman and meow. My dry, dusty life on the Lubbock streets has left my voice scratchy and faint. I doubt she will hear me.

But she looks down, "Oh, this is a little one."

She bends down and picks me up.

Hosanna to Bastet! I purr. I rub my face on her shoulder. I am light (thanks to long-time hunger) and laid-back (thanks to weakness).

She cradles me like a baby, tummy up.

"The tummy is growing out from a shaving. She must be spayed."

The attendant agrees that it looks like that.

I agree, too. I am politically correct, whatever gender I am taken for. I am quiet and friendly. I deserve a home.

I am put back down on the concrete floor and the

woman leaves. The sun no longer shines on the naked tree outside and the high plains are empty, and evening comes.

The attendants arrive in a flutter. Many are chosen, lifted into carriers, carted away. I am one.

I end up in the bottom, floor-level cage in a Tic-Tac-Toe board of piled cages in a fluorescent-lit store somewhere in Lubbock. Kittens cavort above me, easily accessible. I am old, a year or two, and inhabit the lowest level where people have to squat on their knees to see me.

But suddenly I am released. The woman who knows Midnight Louie has asked me out on a date! I sprawl on her lap and purr. I knead my sharp claws into the fiber of pure silk. I sit on the table that is piled with books and rolling pens and a white foam cup that recently held water. I always tend toward water, like a cactus. I stick my nose in the cup, lift it up and everybody laughs.

"Robocat," the woman names me as I pose with the cup on my nose and head.

Later, she is on the phone discussing me. I am a year-old female, she says, small and portable. I've been on TV and am ideal for media appearances. I have a wonderful purrsonality, but my tail is a mess. I will never be able to loft it higher than a croquet hoop. But it won't show much; she didn't even notice it at first.

I am being discussed! The shelter director has brought a collapsible travel cage so I can fly away with the Midnight Louie woman tomorrow.

I am out of the cages and free to be me. (Even if it is Jasmine, the female impersonator.)

And then I am returned to the cage, the cages are loaded into the van, and we return to the shelter.

Nothing whatsoever else happens. I bask briefly in the tree. I accept and give my sharp-pointed badges of courage to my peers. A lot of cats come, a few cats go. And I wonder how long Jasmine of the Crooked Tail can be kept without disappearing into That Room From Which No Cats Return.

Days go by. Then a flurry. Maxie, a big black short-hair, is suddenly brushed and spiffed up. The lucky devil. Someone has adopted him.

My tail droops even lower than usual. Time must be running out.

Flutter. Visitors in the colony. Attendants, a man and woman.

Maxie is presented.

"This is the wrong cat," the Midnight Louie woman declares. "This is not Jasmine."

I am dredged up from the concrete floor. I am suddenly being combed.

"Oh," she says, "I was afraid for a moment—" She looks regretfully at Maxie, freshly brushed. "We really can't take two—"

While she worries, I purr. I rub my face on her shoulder.

Money is exchanged. I am worth something! I am put into the soft portable carrier I never left in before. We drive away, and I am released into a room with a bed and a window and a bathroom. I have my own little bathroom in a cardboard box, and my carrier is left open, and there is food and water in bowls, but I am too excited to use any of it.

The man and woman vanish, speaking of dinner.

When they return, I have examined the room from stem to stern and they are surprised that I am so calm. They go to bed.

Bed. A room. Night. I am home.

I jump up on the bed. I jump up on the man and woman, only I cannot jump up on both at once, so I alternate every fourteen purrs. I meow. I alternate. I purr. I meow. All night.

I have a home! I've got a home!

I am hoarse by morning and the people have not slept much, but they are pleased with me for some reason. They have never seen such a happy cat, they say. I am so smart. I am so pretty. I am such a sweet, pretty girl.

Oh, well. I have a home. I would pretend to be Lassie to have a home.

To make a long story short, I am the new unofficial Midnight Louie body double. I drive home five hours to Fort Worth, and when I get there I eat, drink, and make merry. I gain weight. I go to the vet, who says that my liver numbers are bad and I must have eaten something toxic, but after a month they are on the money.

My coat goes from dull to glossy. My tail recovers full range of motion, even to the tip. Although I will never be able to hold it straight up like a pennant, my filling-out coat covers all signs of my heroic breaks.

But one thing bugs me. They keep calling me "Midnight Louise" and "she."

Otherwise, everything is perfect.

So I have to figure out what to do about it and finally decide that the shortest route is the best.

When they are playing with me one day I roll over and leave nothing to the imagination.

"Louise!" they exclaim, as if I had done something wrong. Get with it! Different strokes for different folks.

"I can't believe it," he says.

"He . . . she was such a small little cat, and it's hard to tell a neutered male from a female in crowded shelters," the woman says. "Remember Goldie, the stray we took to a no-kill shelter and left spaying money for so she'd get a home faster? Then they called and said she was a neutered he?"

"But there is no other Midnight Louie than Midnight Louie," he says. "What can we call . . . him?"

There is a silence. "Midnight Louie. *Junior.*"

And that is that.

So I am out of the detecting business and female imper-sonator racket, and into the luxuriating indoor house-cat class. Permanently.

~~~~~~

Grieving Las Vegas

Jeremiah Healy

~~~~~~

Jeremiah Healy is the creator of two Boston-set series: John Francis Cuddy, a private-investigator run, and, writing as Terry Devane and Mairead O'Clare, a legal-thriller series. Healy has written eighteen novels and over sixty short stories, including *Rescue, Invasion of Privacy, Spiral* (Cuddy novels), *Uncommon Justice, Juror Number Eleven,* and *A Stain Upon the Robe* (O'Clare books). Fifteen of his works have won or been nominated for the Shamus Award. *A Stain Upon the Robe* was optioned for feature film in 2003. *Off Season and Other Stories* is his collection of short stories. His books have been translated into French, Japanese, Italian, Spanish, and German.

Ed Krause lay on his back, staring up at the night sky, his sports jacket surprisingly comfortable as a pillow beneath his head. The desert air in mid-May was still warm, considering how long the sun'd been down. And the stars so bright—Jesus, you could almost understand why they called it the Milky Way, account of out here, away from any city lights, more white star showed than black background.

At least until Ed turned his head to the east, toward Las Vegas, which glittered on the horizon, like a cut jewel somebody kept turning under a lamp.

Jewel?

Ed coughed, not quite a laugh. Better you stuck with carrying diamonds and jade. But no, this new deal had sounded too good to pass up, especially the final destination and the cash you'd have for enjoying it. From that first day, at Felix . . .

. . . Wasserman's house. In San Francisco, on one of those crazy fucking hill streets near Fisherman's Wharf that had to be terraced and handrailed before even an ex-paratrooper like Ed Krause could climb up it.

Felix Wasserman was an importer, which is how Ed had met him in the first place, seven—no, more like eight— years ago. Just after Ed had mustered out of the Army and was nosing around for something to do with his life. A buddy from the airborne put him onto being a courier, which at first sounded like the most boring duty Ed could imagine, worse even than KP in the Mess Hall or standing Guard Mount outside some Godforsaken barracks in the pits of a Southern fort.

Until the buddy also told him how much money could be made for carrying the right kind of stuff. And being able to stop somebody from taking it away from you.

After climbing thirty-five fucking steps, Ed found himself

outside Wasserman's house. Or townhouse, maybe, since it shared both its side walls with other structures, what Ed thought was maybe earthquake protection, since he'd seen signs down on more normal streets for stores that were temporarily closed for "seismic retrofitting." Wasserman had his front garden looking like a Caribbean jungle, and Ed had to duck under flowers in every shade of red that grew tall as trees before he could ring the guy's bell.

His doorbell, that is, seeing as how Ed Krause was what he liked to call in San Fran a "confirmed heterosexual."

Wasserman himself answered, turned out in a silk shirt that looked as though his flower trees out front had been spun into cloth for it. Pleated slacks and soft leather loafers that probably cost—in one of the tonier "shoppes" off Union Square—as much as Ed's first car.

"Felix, how you doing?"

"Marvelously, Edward," said Wasserman, elegantly waving him inside. "Simply marvelously."

Give him this: The guy didn't seem to age much. In fact, Wasserman didn't look to Ed any older than he had that day when Ed—working for a legitimate, bonded courier service then—first laid eyes on him. It was after maybe the third or fourth above-board job he'd carried for the gay blade that Wasserman had felt him out—conversation-ally—on maybe carrying something else for his "import" business. At a commission of ten percent against the value of the parcel involved.

Now Ed just followed the guy up the stairs to a second-floor room with the kind of three-sided window that let you look out over the red-flower trees across to the facing houses and up or down the slope of the hill at other

people's front gardens. Only, while there were two easy
chairs and a table in the window area, Wasserman never
had Ed sit there during business.

Too conspicuous.

Another elegant wave of the hand, this time toward the
wet bar set back against one wall. "Drink?"

"Jim and Coke, you got them."

"Edward," Wasserman seeming almost hurt in both
voice and expression, "knowing you were coming to see
me, of course I stocked Mr. Beam and your mixer."

Ed took his usual seat on one couch while his host first
made the simple bourbon and cola cocktail, then fussed
over some kind of glass-sided machine with arching tubes
that always looked to Ed like a life-support system for wine
bottles. Coming away holding a normal glass with brown
liquid in it and another like a kid's clear balloon with some
kind of red—is this guy predictable or what, color-wise?—
Wasserman handed Ed his drink before settling into the
opposing couch, a stuffed accordion envelope on the redwood—see?—coffee table between them.

"Edward, to our continued, and mutual, good fortune."

Clinking with the guy, Ed took a slug of his drink, just
what the doctor ordered for that forced march up the
screwy, terraced street. Wasserman rolled his wine around
in the balloon glass about twelve times before sniffing it,
then barely wetting his lips with the actual grape juice. Ed
wondered sometimes if the wine was that good, or if the
dapper gay guy just didn't want to get too smashed too
quick.

"So, Felix," gesturing toward the big envelope, "what've
we got this time?"

Wasserman smiled, and for the first time, Ed wondered if maybe the guy had gone for a face-lift, account of his ears came forward a little. But after putting down the wine glass, Felix used an index finger to just nudge the package an inch toward his guest. "Open it and see."

Ed took a second slug of the Jim and Coke, then set his glass down, too. Sliding the elastic off the bottom of the envelope and lifting the flap, he saw stacks of hundred-dollar bills, probably fifty to the pack.

Ed resisted the urge to whistle through his bottom teeth. "Total?"

"One-quarter million."

Since they both knew Ed would have to count it out in Wasserman's presence over a second drink, the courier just put the big envelope back on the table, three packs of cash sliding casually over the open flap and onto the redwood.

Ed said, "For?"

A sigh and a frown, as Wasserman delicately retrieved his glass by its stem and settled back into his couch. "I expect you're aware—if only in a general way—of the rather distressing state of the economy."

"I remember hearing something about it, yeah."

A small smile, not enough to make the ears hunch. "Ah, Edward, both dry and droll. My compliments." Wasserman's lips went back to neutral. "My rather well-heeled clientele hasn't been consuming quite as conspicuously these last few seasons, feeling that fine jewels, no matter the rarity nor brilliance, can't quite replace cash as hedges against the uncertain miasma within which we find ourselves floundering."

Ed just sipped his drink this time, kind of getting off on the way Wasserman made up sentences more elaborate than his garden out front.

"However, the landlord still expects his rent for my shop, and the bank its mortgage payments for my home. And so I've shifted my sights a bit, importwise."

"Meaning?"

Wasserman took an almost normal person's belt of his wine. "Heroin."

Ed would have bet cocaine. "Let me guess. I take the package of money from here to there, and pick up the powder."

"Precisely. Which, of course, would do me no good, since fine Cabernet," swirling the wine in his glass now, "constitutes my only source of substance abuse. Fortunately, though, I have a business contact in the Lake Tahoe area who will gladly buy said powder from you, as my representative, at . . . twice the price."

Ed did the math. "You're saying my cut of this will be ten percent of five hundred thousand?"

"Precisely so. From Tahoe you'll transport the remainder of the cash involved to Las Vegas."

Christ, even a bonus. Growing up in Cleveland, Ed'd always had an itch to sample the glitzy life, but in all his time in San Fran, he'd never been to Vegas. He'd heard everything there—thanks to the casino action—was bigger and better: spectacular tits and ass on the showgirls, classy singers and magicians, even lion tamers. Not like the trendy shit that passed for culture in the "City by the Bay."

In fact, Ed had also seen—three times, at cineplex

prices—that Nick Cage movie, *Leaving Las Vegas.* Got the guy an Oscar, and he fucking well deserved it. I mean, who'd ever believe that anybody'd want to check out of the genuine "City That Never Sleeps"?

Felix allowed himself another couple drops of his wine. "When you reach Las Vegas itself, a friend of mine will—shall we say, hand-wash—the actual bills for his own fee of a mere five percent, after which you shall bring the balance back here to me."

Ed thought about it. A little complicated for his taste, given the number of stops and exchanges. But fifty thousand for what would be maybe three, four days tops of driving? And he didn't give a shit whether his share was laundered or not, since Ed would be passing it in far smaller amounts than Wasserman probably had to pay his creditors.

"Felix, with all this running around, I'm gonna need a cover story, and an advance against expenses."

Now a pursing of the lips. "How much?"

"That'll depend on where I'm picking up the powder to begin with."

Another sigh, but more—what the fuck was the word? Oh, yeah: wistful. "Edward, I actually envy you that, even though the Cabernet varietal, in my humble opinion, doesn't really thrive there. You'll make your first exchange in Healdsburg. Or just outside it."

Ed had noticed the town's name on maps, maybe two hours up U.S. 101 from the Golden Gate, in one of the many parts of the state called "wine country."

He said, "Three thousand, then, upfront, given the cover story I'm thinking about."

"Which is?"

"Bringing a chick along, camouflage for flitting around all these vacation spots like a butterfly."

"A woman." The deepest frown of all from Felix Wasserman. "That I don't envy you, Edward."

"Let me get this straight," said Brandi Willette, trying to size up whether this guy who never plunged for more than three well-drinks at a sitting—but did tip her twenty percent every time he settled a tab—was on the level. "You want to take me—all expenses paid—with you on this whirlwind trip over the next four days?"

A nod from his side of the pub's bar, the guy wearing an honest-to-God, old-fashioned sports jacket. "Maybe even longer, we like it in Vegas enough."

Brandi had been there only once, on the cheap with a girlfriend, splitting every bill down the middle. The girlfriend turned out to be a drag, but Brandi loved the gambling, believing firmly that if she could just sense her luck changing, she'd make a fortune, even from the slot machines. The kind of money that'd let her get out from behind a smelly, tacky bar, listening to offers from guys like this . . . "It's 'Eddie,' right?"

"No. Just 'Ed,' like you're 'Brandi' with an 'I'."

She shook her head, then had to blow one of the permed blond curls out of her face. "Okay, Ed. We go together, same room, same bed, but if I don't feel like doing the nasty, we just share the sheets, not stain them?"

"That's the deal."

Brandi gave it a beat. Then, "So, how come you're asking me?"

The guy seemed to squirm a little on his pub stool, which sort of surprised her, since Ed had struck Brandi as the ultra-macho type. Probably six-one, one-ninety, with a military haircut and big, strong-looking hands. Her pre-dick-tion: A fuck buddy who'd come up skimpy on the fore-play but be a pile-driver during the car chase.

"Well?" she said, wondering if maybe the guy was a little slow in the head.

"It's part of a business transaction."

"What kind of 'transaction'?"

"Just some documents. I exchange what this person gives me for what that person gives me, then I do the same thing a couple more times."

"What, these 'persons' don't trust Federal Express?"

"They trust me more."

"And why is that?" asked Brandi.

"It's confidential."

"Confidential." The curl spilled down over her eye again, and Brandi blew it back away. "You're a spy?"

"No."

"Private eye?"

"No."

Given the guy's limited active vocabulary, Brandi didn't waste her breath on "lawyer," but she did cock her head in a way that she knew guys dug, kind of a "persuade me" angle, like Sarah Jessica Parker did on *Sex and the City*. "So, we're gonna be sleeping together, in the same room, and you can't even share why you're picking me?"

"All right." More squirming. "It's because we don't know each other very well."

Huh, that was sure the truth. On the other hand, Brandi

figured she could always just fuck the guy senseless, then while he snored away, search through his stuff, find out what was really going on.

And Vegas would put Brandi one step closer to making her fortune. To attending catered dinner parties at swank homes instead of nuking some frozen muck in the microwave before spending the night surfing the cable channels.

"Okay, Honey," said Brandi, "I want to see your driver's license, and then I'm gonna call three of my girlfriends—who you don't know at all—to tell them I'm going on this grand tour."

Ed seemed to mull that over. "All right."

"And one other thing."

"What?"

Brandi leaned across the pub's bar, used her forearms to push her breasts a smidge higher against her tank-top, give him a little more reason to be nice to her. "You ever eaten at Masa's?"

As the slipstream from a passing trailer-truck tried to knock the little Mustang convertible onto the shoulder of U.S. 101, Ed Krause heard Brandi say from the passenger's seat, "I think it's another two exits from here."

He glanced over at the chick, her pouty face buried in a road map from the rent-a-car company, and began to question his own judgment. Not that Brandi with a fucking "I" wasn't the right type. Just to the "maybe not" side of slutty, with only one nose-stud and six earrings as body piercings, a small tattoo on the left shoulder that looked professional, not homemade. Decent boobs and legs, too, but overall not so smart or good-looking he thought she'd turn down his offer of a free trip.

Or his offer to help her through the night.

But "eating" at Masa's on Bush Street the night before turned out to be at the bar, since they didn't have reservations. Actually, Ed kind of counted his blessings on that one, because the very chi-chi, black-and-chrome restaurant didn't exactly price out as reasonable. He had to admit, though, he'd tried stuff off the "tastings" menu that the bartender suggested, and it was the best fucking food he'd ever eaten. Ed even had wine, served in Felix-like balloons, and Ed could tell that Brandi was impressed by the way he rolled the grape juice around the inside of his glass before sniffing and sipping it.

Not, however, impressed enough to take him to her place or vice-versa to his, for a little "tour preview." No, Brandi begged off, saying she needed to pack something more than the tote bag she'd carried from the pub to the restaurant—"It's Nine West, Honey, and only forty-nine-ninety-nine, but the real reason I bought it is how the last three numbers on the price tag all lined up the same, like it was gonna bring me luck?"

Thinking, Vegas at the end will make all this shit worth my while, Ed just picked her up the next morning outside Macy's on Geary Street, thinking too that once he got her hammered on a wine tour and fucked her senseless back in their room, he could always go through the chick's stuff, get a last name and address off her driver's license.

In case you ever want to . . . visit her later.

And Brandi was good enough at navigating, Ed could keep his eyes on the rear and side mirrors, make sure nobody stayed with them as he first did fifty-five for a while, then sixty, then a little over before dropping back down to fifty-five. It was a beautiful day, and frankly the slower speed with the top down was a lot more enjoyable than just putting the pedal to the metal.

There were a bunch of exits for Healdsburg, but give the chick credit: She picked the right one for the Inn on the Plaza. As they were shown to their rooms by a pert brunette younger than Brandi, Ed could tell his cover story was watching him to see if he was watching their guide. But all he did was listen to the brunette tell the story of the "bed-and-breakfast," how it had so many skylights because it used to be a "surgery," which Ed took to be where doctors operated before there were hospitals, much less electricity to let them see what they were cutting.

The room was pretty spectacular, even by Ed's images of the Las Vegas glitz to come. For now he could see high ceilings and a king-sized brass bed, a big tiled bathroom and Jacuzzi for two. If all went according to plan.

Just as Ed was about to tip the brunette and get her out of there, he heard Brandi behind him gush, "Oh, God, he's so cute!"

Which is when Ed noticed the chick grabbing a teddy bear off one of the many throw pillows at the head of the bed and hugging it between her boobs.

Right on cue, the brunette said, "They're even for sale, at our desk downstairs." As Brandi squealed with delight, Ed Krause hoped that the tab for their dinner the night before wouldn't be an omen for the stuffed animal and everything else on the trip to Vegas, even if Felix Wasserman was fronting expenses.

* * *

"I still," said Brandi Willette, around a hiccup she thought she stifled pretty well, "don't understand why we couldn't stop at that last winery?"

Driving them, top down, along the nice country lane, Ed—not "Eddie"—seemed to put a little edge on his voice. "Same reason we didn't stop at the other two—of seven, I'm counting right—you wanted to hit: I couldn't see the car from the tasting room."

Brandi swallowed a second hiccup. "Five wineries in one afternoon isn't really enough, I don't think." Then she got an idea. "Is that the same reason you brought your brief-case from the car to the room and then back again?"

"Yes," the edge still there.

The idea turned into a brainstorm. "And how come we have to put the roof and windows up at every stop," she gestured at the beautiful day around them like she'd seen a stage actress do once, "even though there's not a cloud in the sky?"

"That's right." Ed pointed toward the glove compartment. "A little yellow button inside pops the trunk, and I don't want somebody giving it a shot."

"Couldn't—" Brandi tried to stifle yet another hiccup, but it was just not to be denied, "—Oh, excuse me, Honey. Couldn't 'somebody' take a knife to the roof, or break one of the windows, or jimmy open one of the doors, and then pop the trunk?"

"They could," Ed's voice getting a little nicer, so when he slid his right hand over and onto her left thigh, Brandi didn't brush it away like she had on the drive up from the city. "But they're not likely to try it when I can see the car, and anyway that'd give me time to get out there and stop them."

Brandi didn't ask Ed how he would stop them, because

she'd kind of accidentally stumbled into him at the fourth winery—or maybe the fifth?—and felt something really hard over his right hip.

A gun.

Which, to tell the truth, excited Brandi more than scared her. She figured when he pitched the trip to her back in the pub that something was maybe a little dangerous about the guy, with his overall aura and "confidential transaction."

And besides, Brandi thought—closing her eyes and letting her head just loll against the back-rest, living the moment with the breeze in her hair and the sun on her face and the birds singing around her—what girl doesn't like something . . . hard now and then?

"I still don't see why I can't come in with you?"

Ed Krause just looked at her, sitting in the passenger's seat of the Mustang. He'd left the top down for fresh air, but put Brandi in the shade of a big tree in the circular driveway of a large stucco house with orange roof tiles. Let her kind of doze off some of the incredible amount of wine she'd put away, maybe—please, Christ?—even lose the hiccups doing it.

Of course, despite all the "I still don't understand this" and "I still don't see that" bullshit from her, there was no reason to make the chick mad, just as she was letting his nondriving hand, and then his lips, start to soften her up for later, in that brass bed.

Or better, the Jacuzzi.

"Like I told you," he said to Brandi, nice as he could. "This is the business part."

She nodded. Sort of. "The confidential part."

Con-fuh-denture-pah. Ed shook it off with, "Yeah. Just sit tight, enjoy the afternoon, and I'll be back in a few minutes."

Brandi seemed to buy it, slumping deeper into the seat with a sappy grin on her face, so he kissed her once and quickly, slipping his tongue in just enough to know she wouldn't fight more of the same back in their room. Then Ed opened the trunk, took out the briefcase Felix Wasserman had given him to hold the money, and went up to the front entrance, painted the same orange as the roof tiles.

The door swung inward before he could knock or ring, an Asian guy standing there, but more like an owner than a servant. Ed shouldn't have been surprised, since he knew Wasserman dealt with a lot of Chinese guys on the imports, only Ed also thought his gay blade could have prepared him for this by providing more than just a first name.

"Edward?"

"Yeah, though 'Ed' is fine. You're Tommy?"

"The same. Please, come in, though I take it your friend is more comfortable outside?"

"Let's just say I'm more comfortable that way."

A wise smile. "I see."

The guy led Ed into a first-floor living room done up all-Spanish with heavy, dark woods, bullfighting capes and swords, and funny lamps. The guy took one patterned chair and motioned Ed toward its mate.

The courier looked around before sitting down, feeling on his right hip the heft of the Smith & Wesson Combat Masterpiece with its four-inch, extra-heavy barrel—for pistol-whipping, in case he had to discourage some jerk who didn't require actual shooting. "No security?"

Another wise smile. "None evident, shall we say?"

Ed nodded, kind of liking the guy's—what, subtlety maybe? "Any reason not to get down to business?"

"As you wish, especially since I don't wish to keep you from your friend." Tommy clapped his hands twice, and two more Asian guys appeared from around a corner. One carried a briefcase the same make and model as the one Ed had, the other a submachine gun so exotic that even the ex-paratrooper didn't recognize it.

Letting his stomach settle a minute, Ed took his time saying, "And if you clapped just once?"

"Then, regrettably, you'd be dead, and your friend soon thereafter."

Ed trusted himself only to nod this time. They exchanged briefcases—both unlocked, as usual—Ed looking into the one he was given. "Felix told me I didn't have to test the stuff."

"If you did," said Tommy, "he wouldn't be doing business with my family in the first place."

"Good enough." Ed glanced at the guy with the exotic piece. "Okay for me to leave?"

"Of course," said Tommy, standing, "Enjoy your visit to our valleys."

"My friend already has," Ed rising and feeling he could turn his back on these guys as he walked to the door.

"Oh, God," said Brandi Willette, nursing the worst hangover she could remember and afraid to look over the side of the car, because the road just fell away down the steep, piney slope. "I think my ears are popping again."

"The change in altitude," said Ed from behind the wheel.

"And that bottle from the last winery you brought back to the room probably isn't helping any."

"Please," Brandi holding her left hand out in a "stop" sign while her right palm went from the teddy bear in her lap to cover her closed eyes. "Don't remind me about last night, all right?"

"Oh, I don't know. I think we both liked what happened next."

Well, you can't disagree with the guy on that one, at least the parts of it you remember.

Which were: Coming back to the room around five-thirty, after hitting the last row of wineries with names like Clos du Bois, Chauteau Souverain, and Sausal. Feeling free as could be from all the great stuff she'd tasted, and, although Brandi was still hiccuping, ready for anything. Including letting Ed slip her clothes off, the guy more gentle than she could have hoped. After a quick shower together, him touching her just about everywhere, them getting into the Jacuzzi—the guy must have had it filling up while he was stripping her in the bedroom and soaping her in the stall. And then getting a real good look at that snake he had down there, the head on it big as a cobra's. And Brandi telling him to get in first, sit down, before lowering herself onto his soldier-at-attention. She stayed balanced by resting her palms on his shoulders, her nipples just skimming the surface of the sudsy water as she rocked up and down and back and forth—him laughing, because she still had the hiccups—until she came so violently and thoroughly it was like one long shudder that wasn't a hiccup at all. In fact, took them away.

And then him lifting her up, not even bothering to dry

themselves off, and onto the soft mattress of the brass bed—her new teddy bear watching—for another, and another, and. . . .

"Hey," from the driver's side, "you're gonna puke, hold on till I can pull over."

"Yeah, yeah," said Brandi, hoping she'd have better luck controlling her gag reflex than she did with the hiccups.

"Okay," said Ed Krause, nudging the chick on her bicep with his fist, "we're here."

He watched Brandi's head try to find its full and upright position in the passenger's seat. After three hours of complaining about everything under the sun, she'd finally fallen asleep—or passed out—a good ten miles from Tahoe City, and therefore she'd missed some of the best fucking scenery Ed had ever driven through. Snow-capped, purple mountains, sprawling vistas down to pine-green valleys. The whole nine yards of America the Beautiful.

And now Lake Tahoe itself.

Brandi said, "I'm cold."

"Like I tried to tell you before, it's the altitude. Walk slow, too, or you'll start to feel sick." Stick in the knife? Sure. "Again."

The chick raised her hand like she had before, reminding him of a school crossing guard, but she managed to get her side door open.

After checking into the Sunnyside Lodge, Ed got them and their luggage to the suite, which had a little balcony off the living room and overlooking the waterfront, more mountains with snowy peaks kind of encircling the lake from high above. Brandi shuffled into the bedroom and flopped face down on the comforter, not even bothering to kick off her shoes. Ed heard snoring before he could secure his briefcase with the heroin behind the couch in the living room, pissed that the key fucking Tommy gave him for the handle lock didn't fucking work, so all Ed could do was click the catch shut.

Leaving the chick to sleep it off, he went back downstairs and did a walkaround, first outside, then in. Big old lodge, dark-log construction, security doors you'd need a computerized room key to open. A moose's head was mounted on a wooden plaque over one fireplace, a bear's over another, a buffalo's over a third.

Ed liked the place. Rugged, with the taxidermy adding just a hint about the history of killing the lodge had seen.

But no pool, and when he asked at the lobby desk, the nice college-looking girl told him it was way too cold to swim in even the lake, because it never got warmer than sixty-eight degrees, "like, ever."

When Ed got back to the room, Brandi was still snoring. But checking how he'd wedged his briefcase behind the bureau, it had turned a few degrees. Ed tilted the briefcase back to its original angle, then stomped his foot a couple of times, harder on the third one.

Brandi's voice trickled out of the bedroom. "What the hell are you doing out there?"

The briefcase never budged. "Testing the floorboards. Be sure they can take us rocking that mattress."

A different tone of voice with, "Wouldn't we be better off doing your testing . . . in here?"

And that's when Ed Krause knew in his bones that Brandi Willette—given how shitty she must still be feeling—had snuck a peek into his unlockable briefcase, just as he'd gone through her "lucky" totebag the night before at the Inn on the Plaza in Healdsburg.

"Honey," said Brandi Willette, in the best seductive/hurt tone she knew, "I still don't understand why I can't come in there with you."

"Keep your voice down."

She watched Ed shut the driver's side door, even almost slam it, in the yard he'd pulled into, a big Swiss-chalet style house on the lakeside in front of them.

Ed turned back to her. "It's like the last time."

"Confidential?"

He glanced into the next yard. "I said, keep your voice down. And stay put."

"All right, all right," Brandi flicking her hand like she couldn't give a damn.

Only she did. After seeing all that "snow" in his briefcase back at the lodge, Brandi could care less about the real thing on the mountaintops and melting in the shaded clumps still on the ground under trees that must block the sun. As they drove, many of the houses—like the one next door to the chalet—looked like something out of that ancient *Bonanza* TV show with Michael Landon that Brandi caught on the cable sometimes, a program she figured he must have done even before that old show *Little House on the Prairie,* account of how much younger he looked as a son/cowboy instead of a father/farmer.

But the snow in the briefcase? Heroin or cocaine, had to be. Which meant big-time bucks, and maybe an opportunity for her luck really to change, even just riding with Ed.

Or figuring out a way to hijack him. After all, the three friends Brandi called from the pub in the city would go to the police only if *she* didn't make it back.

Brandi watched Ed move slowly through the yard and toward the chalet. There'd been a wooden privacy fence between it and the road that wound around the lake. On each side of the fence's gate were these totem poles, like Brandi remembered from a Discovery Channel thing on Eskimos—or whatever they were called when they lived more in the deep woods and not so much on icebergs.

And, sure enough, there were three guys doing land-scaping in the next yard who could have been Eskimos themselves. Short, blocky guys, with square, copper-colored faces. The oldest of them seemed to be bossing the other two, one gathering up broken limbs and throwing them onto a brushpile, the other sweeping the driveway of huge pine cones from even huger trees looming overhead. Probably getting the neighbor's place ready for the season.

Brandi noticed Ed giving the three Eskimos the eye as he reached the stoop of the chalet. Then the guy knocked and disappeared inside.

Brandi couldn't believe how cold it could be in mid-May nor how her breathing still wasn't back to normal from banging Ed and then just walking downstairs in the lodge and over to the Mustang. In fact, about the only other thing Brandi did notice was how, about five minutes after Ed entered the chalet, the oldest Eskimo in the next yard came strolling toward her side of the car, smiling and taking a piece of paper—no, an envelope?—out of a bulging pocket in his jacket.

And right then, Brandi Willette, even without knowing

what was going to happen next, could feel her luck changing, and visions of what that would mean in Vegas— and beyond—began slam-dancing in her head.

Natalya, a fat-to-bursting fortysomething who looked like no drug pusher Ed Krause had ever encountered, settled the two of them into over-stuffed chairs that suited her like Felix's red flowers back in San Fran' suited him, only different.

She said. "Tell me, do you prefer 'Edward,' 'Ed' . . . ?"

"Just 'Ed,' thanks."

Natalya smiled. Not a bad face, you suck a hundred pounds off the rest of her, let the cheekbones show. She seemed to arrange their seating so he could enjoy the dynamite view of the lake through a wall of windows. Ed was pretty sure the chalet had been designed to be appreciated from the water, not the road.

But the view turned out to be less "enjoyable" and more distracting, as some fucking moron in a scuba wetsuit went water-skiing past, and Ed automatically glanced at all the interior doorways he could see.

The fat lady turned her head toward the skier, then turned back, smiling some more. "There's a rather famous school that teaches that between here and your lodge, though I've always felt it a bit too frosty and . . . strenuous to be diverting." As soon as he'd entered the room, Ed had seen the sample case on the tiled floor next to the chair Natalya had picked for herself. He'd rather it be at least the same size as his briefcase, but then the two-fifty in hundreds had barely fit in its twin on the way to Healdsburg, and this would be twice as much, maybe some of it in smaller denominations to boot.

Natalya said, "May I offer you refreshment?"

"No, thanks. I gotta be going soon."

"As you wish," the fat lady sighing, as though if he'd said "yes," maybe she could break some kind of weight-watching rule of her own by joining him. "I will be needing to test your product."

A switch from Tommy in wine country. "And I'll be needing to count yours."

"Let us begin, then."

"Before we do," said Ed, leaning forward conversationally but also to free up his right hand to move more fluidly for the revolver under his sports jacket and over his right hip, "any security I should know about, so nobody accidentally gets hurt?"

"Security?" A laugh, the woman's chins and throat wobbling. "No, Tahoe City is a very safe place, Ed."

"Not even those guys next door?"

"'Those guys?'"

"Mexicans maybe, doing yard work."

"Oh," a bigger laugh, shoulders and breasts into it now. "Hardly. And they're Mayans, Ed. They drift up here from the Yucatan to do simple labor—like opening up the houses after the winter's beaten down the foliage? My neighbor's a retired professor of archaeology, and the one who first got them to do landscaping for a lot of us along the lake. In fact, that figurine on the table and the stone statue near the fireplace are both gifts from him." Natalya paused. "I'd have said it was too frigid up here for them, frankly," the fat broad stating something Ed had been thinking from the moment he saw them, "but my neighbor tells me our gorgeous topography reminds them in some ways of their native land."

Ed thought that still didn't ring right: Most people he knew who ever traveled far from home went from colder weather to warmer, not the other way around.

On the other hand, what do you know about Mexicans, period, much less "Mayans" in particular?

Then Natalya opened her hands like a priest doing a blessing. "Shall we?"

Ed brought his briefcase over to her, and he took her sample case back to his chair, accidentally scraping the bottom of the case against the tiles, the thing was that heavy.

"This is supposed to be the best restaurant in town."

Brandi Willette heard Ed's comment, but she waited till the waitress at Wolfdale's—who looked like one of the retro-hippies back in the city—took their drink orders and left them before glancing around the old room with exposed ceiling beams and a drop-dead-gorgeous view of the lake, kind of facing down its long side from the middle of its short one. "It better be the best, all the time you spent back there."

Ed just shrugged and read the menu.

Brandi didn't want to push how long it took him inside the chalet, but she did notice he was carrying a different bag coming back to the convertible. The guy wants to keep things "confidential," that's fine. But it didn't take a genius to figure that if what Ed brought in there was drugs, what he brought out was money. Lots of it. And, given the size of the case, lots more than he used in Healdsburg to buy the shit with.

Then Brandi thought about the oldest Eskimo, and what he'd given her while she was waiting for Ed, what was now nestled in her lucky totebag. Plus what that gave her to think about from her side. For her kick, even her fortune, which was a nice fucking change of pace.

The dinner at Wolfdale's turned out to be maybe the best food Brandi had ever eaten in her life—medallions of veal, asparagus, some kind of tricked-out potatoes. And a merlot that made even a lot of the great wines she'd tasted the day before seem weak. A perfect experience.

Just like the catered dinner parties you'll be going to soon.

But, just as they were finishing dessert, Ed said, "How about we take a drive, see the lake by night?"

Remembering the mountains closer to the wine country they'd already gone up and down with her hangover that morning, Brandi said, "I'd rather see our bed by night."

"We can do that, too. Afterwards."

Well, what could a girl say to that? A guy who'd rather drive than get laid, there was just no precedent for dealing with such a situation.

"Ohmigod, ohmigod," said Brandi Willette in a tone that made Ed Krause think of the word *shriek*.

"What's the matter?" him taking the Mustang through its paces on the ribbon of road—lit only by the moon— switchbacking up one of the mountains on the southwest end of the lake.

"What's the matter?" came out as more what Ed would call a "squeal." The chick pointed over the passenger's side of the car without looking down. "There's no fucking guardrail here!"

"Highway Department probably thinks it wouldn't help.

Either you'd go through it and down, or bounce off it and into a head-on with somebody coming the other way."

"Don't even say that."

Another couple of miles—Brandi now groaning, even shaking—and Ed saw his lights pick up the "SCENIC VISTA" sign that fat Natalya had told him about back at her chalet, after she recommended Wolfdale's for dinner. "Let's give you a break."

He pulled into the otherwise deserted parking area, which seemed, even at night, like just a man-made platform jutting out from the side—nearly the top—of the mountain. They'd passed a few other viewing points—not to mention the entire Nevada town of South Lake Tahoe, but when Brandi had said, "Why don't we stop here for a while, try our luck?" Ed had glanced around at the penny-ante casinos with Harrah's, Trump's and a bunch of other evocative names on them, chintzy motels sprinkled among them, and replied, "Nah, I want to wait for the real thing. In Vegas."

As Ed now came to a stop in one of the vista's parking spaces, Brandi finally opened her eyes. "It's dark out. What're we gonna be able to see?"

He opened his door, came around to hers. "A fat broad told me a story about a guy, said nobody should miss it."

Ed could tell the only reason the chick'd leave the car would be to feel her feet on solid ground again, and that was fine. She got out of the Mustang, leaving her lucky fucking totebag on the floor between her feet, and Ed took her hand, guiding her over to the edge of the vista's platform.

"I don't want to go any closer."

"You have to, to appreciate the story I'm gonna tell you."

"Honey, please. I'll do you every which way but loose back in the room—"

"—the suite—"

"—whatever, but please don't. . . ."

"Hey, there it is."

Ed had his hands on the sides of her shoulders now, marching her in front of him, teach her a lesson about going through his briefcase. She was arching over, pushing her butt into his groin, the grinding sensation of their little "dance" making him hard.

"Honey, please. . . ."

"See? Right there, through the tree branches?" Brandi's butt was writhing, like a wet cat trying to get free of the drying towel. "The moon's lighting it up like noontime."

"It's a . . . all I see is this island—ohmigod, way down there?"

"This fat broad told me that back in the old days—eighteen-hundreds we're talking—there was a caretaker for the house that's on the mainland, back under the trees."

"I don't—"

"Seems this caretaker stayed all winter," said Ed, "but he liked the island more, and his booze the best. Fact is, he'd row all the way from here to where we're staying in Tahoe City—miles and miles through the cold, though the lake doesn't freeze over like you might expect—to hit a saloon, then he'd row all the way back."

"Honey, let's go, huh?"

"But this caretaker, he fell in love with that island, so he built his own tomb on it. For when he died, to be buried there."

"Why are you—"

"Only thing is, the poor old coot was rowing back from town one night with too much of a load on, and he went over into the water. They found his boat, but not him. Not ever. And so he's at the bottom of the lake someplace, and his tomb's just falling apart, empty, down there on that pretty little island."

"Honey, this is too weird for—"

Ed dropped his hands from her shoulders to her biceps, and then lifted her off the ground—swinging her legs straight out—and sat her down, hard, on the ledge overlooking the drop-off.

Brandi lifted her face to the sky and screamed like a baby.

Ed said, "I invited you along on this trip—a complete freebie—and I didn't move on you 'til you let me know you were ready for it."

"Yes, yes," the tears streaming down her cheeks from eyes clenched shut.

"And I don't expect you to help me at all in what I'm doing, just be half the cover story of the nice couple on a vacation."

"Anything, Honey, I will."

"But if I ever . . ." Ed thrust his pelvis forward, into her butt, like Brandi was giving him a lap-dance and he was pounding her doggy-style. She screamed till her voice broke, then began just sobbing and gasping for breath. "Ever . . ." he banged her harder, nearly over the edge but for him holding her upper arms, Brandi now just choking on her own breaths, ". . . think you're double-crossing me, you're gonna join that fucking caretaker down there, deep at the bottom of the fucking lake. Or worse."

"Don't . . . Please, don't . . ."

Ed pulled Brandi with an "I" back off the ledge, almost having to carry her toward the car. He would have done her on the rear seat, too, finish the lesson, but he could smell what she'd already done to herself, and so Ed Krause wanted her back in their suite and cleaned up first.

Standing under the showerhead, the water so hot she almost couldn't bear it, Brandi Willette thought, Girl, nobody does that to you and gets away with it. Nobody.

Fuck Ed, the goddamned homicidal maniac, hanging you over the fucking edge of that fucking cliff. Literally fuck him as soon as you dry off, keep Dickhead happy and his fucking mind off killing you, but really fuck him good tomorrow, just like the Eskimo's note said, just before telling you to tear it up.

Fuck Ed with the other thing that gardener gave you, too.

And, for the first time in hours, Brandi actually smiled, even if only to herself. Feeling the luck changing, guiding her toward the fortune she'd always felt she deserved.

About two hundred miles into the drive that next afternoon, the scenery now pretty much scrub desert on the eastern side of the California mountains, Ed Krause noticed that Brandi wasn't all that interested in small talk anymore.

Hey, count your blessings, he thought, glancing again to the rearview mirror, not such good viewing with the convertible's top up, but necessary against the withering heat outside: At least today the chick's not complaining every two minutes.

No, their time at the moonlit vista over Lake Tahoe seemed to have had the right effect on little Brandi. Or so Ed would have thought, from the way she romped him in bed after her shower back at the lodge. Good thing he'd taken the trouble, though, while she was still in the bathroom, to go through her stuff a second—shit!

Checking the rearview, like always, Ed saw the same vehicle again. Making three times in the same day, even after stopping the Mustang for lunch and once more for gas.

A dark Chevy Suburban, or some other fucking station-wagon-on-steroids, coming around the last turn behind their Mustang along one of the narrow state roads in Nevada that linked together like a poorly designed necklace from Reno to Las Vegas. Between the sun's glare and the Suburban's tinted windshield, though, Ed couldn't make out the driver, much less how many others were in the thing.

"What's the matter?" said Brandi.

Ed thought about how to play it, both with the Suburban and her. "Don't turn around, but we've got somebody tailing us."

Predictably, the stupid bitch started to turn her head, so he reached over and squeezed her thigh like he wanted to break the bones underneath.

"Owwww! That hurt!"

"It was supposed to. I told you, don't turn around. Right now, they've got no reason to think I've spotted them, and I don't want to give them one."

"You didn't have to hurt me for that."

Ed just shook his head, not trusting his voice right then.

"So," said Brandi, "what are we going to do?"

Different tone now, kind of "We're still a team, right?"

He glanced again in his rearview, the Suburban dropping back a little. "Try to lose them."

Ed nailed the accelerator, Brandi making a moaning noise, kind of like when they'd started again in bed back at the lodge the night before. But the Mustang at least didn't give him any trouble, the V-8 he'd insisted on at the rent-a-car agency coming into its own.

Maybe five minutes later, Brandi said, "Aren't you, like, worried about the police or anything?"

"Lesser of two evils," said Ed, noticing nobody behind them now. Problem was, based on his study of the map that morning before heading out from Tahoe City, there were only so many roads you could take to get to Vegas, so the tail could probably find him, and he didn't have the firepower onboard to stage an effective ambush.

At least not until he found a perfect spot, and after dark.

Brandi piped up now with, "Are they gone?"

Ed tried to remember whether he'd ever said "they" in talking about the tail, decided he had. "For now."

"So," the tone growing a little more impatient, "what are we gonna do?"

"Stay ahead of them. At least for a while."

"How long a while?"

"Until sunset."

"Uh-unh, no way, Honey."

"What the fuck do you mean, no way?"

"I gotta pee."

"So, do it in your clothes, like you did last night."

"That's not funny."

Jesus Christ. "Okay. Around this next bend, then."

"No. I want a real bathroom, not . . ." Brandi with a fucking "I" waving her hand ". . . some spot behind a bush in the desert where a snake could get me."

"The desert, or your clothes. You decide how you want to feel, the next hundred miles to Vegas."

"God, I hate you, you know that?"

Checking the rearview again, Ed was beginning to get that impression, yeah.

Brandi Willette, who'd looked forward so much to enjoying this trip to Vegas, now found she'd run out of tissues.

God, she thought, shaking herself dry as best she could before pulling up her panties. I can't wait for this to be over.

Straightening from behind the bush, she looked over to the convertible. Dickhead was slouched in the driver's seat, head back, eyes closed, still wearing that ugly sports jacket to "hide" his gun.

Well, girl, look on the bright side: He doesn't suspect a thing, and that'll make it all the sweeter, once it happens.

"No," said Brandi, out loud but softly as she picked her way back to the car. "When it happens."

Having slowed to fifty-five about twenty minutes before—just after he put the top down to enjoy the clear, crisp night air of the desert—Ed Krause kept one eye on the rearview and the other on the highway in front of him, figuring he didn't have to worry about Brandi trying anything until they came to a stop.

She said, "Is it dark enough yet?"

Right on cue. "Dark enough for what?"

Brandi blew out a breath in the passenger seat next to

him, like he noticed she did a lot of times—even during sex—to get the hair out of her face.

Why wouldn't you just get a different 'do, the hair thing bothered you so much?

Brandi said, "Dark . . . enough . . . for whatever you're planning?"

Another thing Ed didn't like about the little bitch: the way she kept hitting her words hard—even just parts of words, like he was some kind of idiot who couldn't get her points otherwise.

Shaking his head, Ed checked the odometer. Thirty miles from Vegas, give or take, its lights just blushing on the horizon. "Yeah, it's dark enough for that."

The Suburban had appeared and disappeared a couple times over the prior two hours, not taking advantage of at least three desolate spots where it could have roared up from behind, tried to force him off the road. Which made Ed pretty sure they were waiting for him to make the first move.

Or, like Brandi, the first "stop."

"Okay," Ed abruptly pulling off the road and onto the sandy shoulder. "Here."

"Honey?"

Ed turned to her. Brandi was leveling a nickel-finish semiautomatic at him in her right hand, a Raven .25 caliber he'd seen only once before.

Brandi Willette had thought long and hard about how to phrase it to him—even rehearsed some, with the teddy bear as Ed—but decided in the end that less was more. And so she was kind of disappointed that Dickhead didn't look shocked when she said just the one word, and he saw what Brandi had in her hand.

But that was okay. The asshole thought he was so smart, and so macho, and now Ed finds himself trapped and beaten by a girl, one whose luck had finally changed.

"Just what the fuck do you think you're doing?" he said.

Funny, Dickhead didn't sound scared, either, like Brandi also expected. "I'm taking the money. Honey."

Now it seemed like Ed almost laughed, even though she'd worked on that line, too. Make it kind of poignant, even.

"Brandi, Brandi, after all we've meant to each other?"

Okay, now she really didn't get it. "You're going to open the trunk and take out the case with all the money. Then you're going to leave it with me and just drive off."

Brandi saw Dickhead's eyes go to the rearview mirror again, and she thought she caught just a flash of headlights behind them along with the sudden silence of an engine turning off, though Brandi didn't dare look away from Ed, what with that big gun over his right hip.

No problem, though. Her luck was both changing and holding, just like it would in Vegas, when she hit the slots and the tables, or even the—

Dickhead said, "Your friends are here."

That stopped Brandi. "My . . . friends?"

"When we got back to the room at the lodge, after our little talk about the Tahoe caretaker? While you were in the shower, I went through your totebag there and found that gun. I'd done the same thing at the Inn back in Healdsburg, and it wasn't there then. So, I figure the only time you were out of my sight long enough to come up with a piece was when I was inside the chalet, and those Mayans were working in the yard next door."

Mayans? "I thought they were Eskimos?"

Now Ed did laugh, hard. "No, you stupid fucking bitch. The fat broad in the chalet—Natalya—told me they were her neighbor's crew, but I'm guessing they were hers instead, and one of them passed you that gun."

Oh, yeah? "Well, smart guy, that wasn't all he passed me."

"Some kind of instructions, too, right? Like, wait till the courier stops, at night, near Vegas?"

Brandi was beginning to think she hadn't torn up the note in the envelope, though she clearly remembered doing it. Then Brandi let her luck speak for her. "You're the one who's stupid, Honey, you know that? The Eskimo or whatever told me you'd never think to look for the little thingy he put under your bumper."

No laughing now. Just a squint, the eyes going left-right-left.

Good. Finally, Brandi gets her man. The way it hurts him. Your luck has changed for sure, girl.

Dickhead said, "A homing device, probably based on GPS."

Brandi got the first part, at least. "So they could keep track of us, they lost sight of the car."

"Christ, you dense little shit. Don't you understand the deal yet?"

"The deal is that I get ten percent of all the money in the trunk, because I'm making it easier for them to take it from you."

"No, Brandi." A tired breath. "The deal is that as soon as

they see me get out of this vehicle, they're going to charge up here, kill both of us, and take a hundred percent of the money."

"No, that's not what the note said." Brandi kind of used the gun for emphasis. "What it said was, if you don't get out of this car now, I'm supposed to shoot you."

Ed's chin dipped toward his chest. "Good trick, seeing as how I unloaded your little purse piece there."

As Brandi Willette couldn't help looking down at her gun, she felt Dickhead's hand strike like a rattlesnake at her throat, clamping on so tight and yanking her toward him so hard, she barely could register the silver thing—like a Pez dispenser?—in the fingers of his other—

"Christ!" Ed Krause yelled, as Brandi's head exploded next to his, the round carrying enough punch to spiderweb the windshield after it came out her right temple, leaving an exit wound like a rotten peach, blood and brains spattered over the dashboard and that fucking teddy bear. Ed ducked as a second round shattered the driver's portion of the windshield, a sound like somebody whistling through water trailing after the impact.

Ed shoved Brandi's rag-doll corpse against the passenger door, then yanked the floorshift back to DRIVE and took off. A second later, he thought the Mustang might be in the clear based on acceleration alone when he first heard and then felt the blowout of his right rear tire, the convertible wanting to pivot on that wheel rim, send him off the pavement.

Ed wrestled with the steering, finally getting it under some control, and whipped right, over to the shoulder and beyond it, he pictured the three Mayans from the yard next-door to Natalya's chalet, and he hoped he'd put the Mustang's engine block between him and any likely fields of fire from their vehicle. Ed also hoped they didn't have much weaponry beyond the sniper rifle but knew he was probably wrong on that score, the way they'd handled everything else.

And, after their killing Brandi, there was no bargaining with them, no chance of "Take the money and let me live, or I'll nail at least one of you right here." Nobody leaves a body *and* a witness behind.

Ed grabbed the little Raven .25 from the floor mat, slapped the magazine back into the butt of its handle, and slid the semiautomatic into the left-side pocket of his sports jacket. Then he slipped out the driver's door, waiting for the Mayans to make their move. They took long enough before starting the Suburban's engine, he was pretty sure one of them did the same thing he'd done: dropped out of their vehicle and into the desert, to flank him while the others rolled slowly toward him. Just like Ed learned in Small Unit Tactics, back in the airborne. And just like the big land yacht was doing now.

Down on his hands and knees, Ed scuttled like a crab across the desert floor, away from the Mustang. And the money, but it was his only chance: Outflank the flanker, and come around behind all of them.

Ed went into the desert fifty or sixty meters at a diagonal to the road, angling slightly toward the direction he'd driven from. Figuring that was far enough, given the superiority of numbers and firepower the Mayans would think they had over him, Ed assumed the prone position to wait.

Listening to the desert sounds. Trying to pick up anything that didn't move like a snake. Or a lizard, even a tarantula.

Or whatever the fuck else there'd be in this kind of desert.

And he did hear some slithering sounds, then a scratching sound, like maybe a mouse's foot would make on wood, then a little squeak that Ed figured was curtains for that particular rodent.

But now, footfalls. Halfway between him and the road, moving parallel to it. Jogging, the guy moving with confidence toward the Mustang.

Ed rose to a sprinter's start, waiting for the Suburban to draw even with him. Then he used the noise of the receding vehicle to cover his own.

The running Mayan stayed on a line with the big vehicle's rear doors. Smart: That way, its headlights wouldn't silhouette him for a shooter still at the Mustang.

Bad luck, though, too: That relative positioning did pinpoint the guy—a pistol of some kind held muzzle up—just right for the angle Ed had from behind.

Closing fast on an interception course, Ed was all over the Mayan—Christ, no more than five-four, max?—before the little guy could have heard him. Ed used the extra-heavy barrel of the Combat Masterpiece to pistol-whip the Mayan across the back of his head, pitching him forward onto the sand with a "whump" sound from his body but nothing from his mouth.

Then Ed planted his left foot on the Mayan's spine, and—with his free hand—hooked under the little guy's chin and snapped his neck.

Scooping up the Mayan's pistol—another semiautomatic,

maybe a nine-millimeter but not enough light on it to be sure—Ed put it in his jacket's right side-pocket, kind of balancing off Brandi's Raven .25 in the other. Then be started to run, trying to match the pace of the Mayan he'd just killed.

Thinking: one down, two to go.

The Suburban was now enough ahead of him, he could see it clearly approaching his Mustang. When the driver nailed the gas and kicked in his high-beams, the third Mayan began shooting two-handed from the rear seat, Ed closing his eyes against the blaze from the muzzles, so as not to ruin his night vision. He heard both magazines empty into and around the convertible as they passed— some richochets, some thumps, depending on what the rounds hit. Then, hanging a U-ey, the Suburban came back hard. Ed was already prone again, eyes turned away from the headlights, but his ears picked up the sound of the third Mayan emptying another two magazines into the Mustang from the opposite direction.

Christ, a good thing you left the car. And picked off their flanker, who'd otherwise be standing over you right now, capping three rounds through your skull.

Ed turned again toward the Suburban. It hung another U-ey, this time moving back toward the Mustang real slow and weaving a little, let its high beams maybe pick up a dead or wounded courier against the convertible or some-where near it.

Fuck this.

Ed got into another crouch, then sprang forward, letting Brandi's .25 fill his left hand, since he couldn't waste time fiddling with the maybe-on, maybe-off safety from the first

Mayan's semi. He matched that dead guy's pace again as best he could, let the two Mayans exiting the Suburban— one at the driver's side, of course, the other at the passenger rear door—think their pal was joining up. Until they were clear of the vehicle and fixated on the Mustang, each just forward of the Suburban's front grille, using its high beams to blind anybody left alive to shoot back at them.

After drawing a deep breath and releasing it slowly, Ed emptied both of his weapons into those two Mayans, being careful not to hit their vehicle.

His new transportation, after all.

Ed's targets spazzed out like puppets as his slugs hit them, Ed himself now pulling from his jacket pocket the first guy's semi, to close and finish the fuckers. Then he caught the flash of another muzzle from the rear-passenger's window of the Suburban and simultaneously the impact of two, three rounds spinning him around and down, hard.

Shit: A fourth fucking Mayan?

Hoping the semi did have its safety off, Ed squeezed the trigger, putting five shots into the rear door. Hearing a scream, he decided to save the remaining slugs, in case the guy was playing possum. But Ed started feeling dizzy, too, knew he was losing too much blood to wait any longer. Levering up on his elbows—Christ, like somebody's hit you in the chest with a haltering rain, tough even to breathe shallow—Ed staggered toward the Suburban, keeping the semi as level as he could. Getting there seemed to take an hour, but when he inhaled as much air as his lungs would hold, he yanked open that rear door, and saw the top half of fat Natalya ooze more than flop onto the pavement, another semiautomatic clattering on the asphalt like it was the tile floor in her chalet. Fucking bitch didn't trust her Mayans after all.

Then Ed walked around to the front of the Suburban, let its high-beams spotlight his shirt under the sports jacket. He said, "Shit," and, a moment later, the same once more. After that, he didn't see much else to say.

So Ed inched out of the jacket as best he could, found a soft, level spot on the desert floor, and rolled the jacket into sort of a pillow, rest a little easier.

Ed Krause opened his eyes, realized he didn't know how long he'd been out, still just lying there on the desert floor. He was starting to feel cold, which he didn't remember from before. And while some of the stars above him seemed to have changed position, there was no sign yet of dawn to the east.

Just the glorious, heavenly effect from the lights of Vegas.

Ed shifted his head on the sports-jacket pillow as best he could, to be able to stare at those lights, the promise of real money and seeing a place he'd always wanted to visit. Last two times he'd coughed, though, blood came up, so right now he wouldn't bet on even seeing morning.

You're gonna bleed out in this fucking desert, you might as well stay focused on the prize, huh? Shows . . . lions . . . showgirls . . . magic acts . . . tigers . . . casinos.

The Vegas lights started to go funny against Ed's eyes, so he closed them.

Help the imagination, you know?

Slick cars like Maseratis, Ferraris, Rolls-fucking-Royces.

Cruising the Strip, just like they did in the movies he'd seen. All the filet mignon and trimmings you could eat, all the Jim and Coke you could drink. Call-girls that'd make Brandi with an "I" look like fucking Spam.

Action of all kinds, nonstop. The genuine "City That Never Sleeps."

Only you're never gonna see it now.

Vegas, Las Vegas. Grieving . . .

The Resurrection Man

Sharyn McCrumb

Sharyn McCrumb is the author of *Ghost Riders, The Songcatcher, The Ballad of Frankie Silver, The Rosewood Casket, She Walks These Hills, The Hangman's Beautiful Daughter,* and *If Ever I Return, Pretty Peggy-O,* which have been named Notable Books for the Year by *The New York Times* and *The Los Angeles Times.* Her novels have been translated into German, Dutch, Japanese, and Italian, and she has lectured on her work at Oxford University, the University of Bonn-Germany, and at the Smithsonian Institution; taught a writers' workshop for WICE in Paris, France, and served as writer-in-residence at King College in Tennessee. In 2003, McCrumb was honored by the East Tennessee Historical Society with the Wilma Dykeman Award for Regional Historical Literature, as well as having been honored for Outstanding Contribution to Appalachian Literature by the Appalachian Writer's Association; the Sherwood Anderson Short Story Award; Appalachian Writer of the Year Award from Shepherd College; the

Flora McDonald Award; Morehead State University's Chaffin
Award; and the Plattner Award from Berea College. Her work has
also twice received the AWA's Best Appalachian Novel Award. Her
latest novel is *St. Dale*.

Haloed in lamplight the young man stands swaying on the
threshold for an instant, perhaps three heartbeats, before
the scalpel falls from his fingers, and he pitches forward
into the dark hallway, stumbling toward the balcony
railing where the stairwell curves around the rotunda.
From where he stands outside the second floor classroom,
it is thirty feet or more to the marble floor below.

The old man in the hall is not surprised. He has seen too
many pale young men make just such a dash from that room,
from its stench of sweet decay, hardly leavened by the tobacco
spit that coats the wooden floor. They chew to mask the odor—
this boy is new, and does not yet know that trick. The tobacco
will make him as sick as the other at first. It is all one.

He makes no move to take hold of the sufferer. They are
alone in the building, but even so, these days such a thing
would not be proper. The young man might take offense,
and there is his own white linen suit to be thought of. He
is not working tonight. He only came to see why there was
a light in the upstairs window. More to the point, he has
long ago lost the desire to touch human flesh. He stays in
the shadows and watches the young man lunge for cold air
in the cavernous space beneath the dome.

But the smell of the dissecting room is not escaped so
easily, and the old man knows what will happen if the student does not get fresh air soon. Somebody will have to
clean up the hall floor. It won't be the old man. He is too

grand for that, but it will be one of the other employees, some acquaintance of his, and it is easy enough to spare a cleaner more work and the young man more embarrassment. Easy enough to offer the fire bucket as an alternative.

A gallon bucket of sand has been set outside the dissection room in case a careless student overturns an oil lamp, and in one fluid motion he hoists it, setting it in front of the iron railing, directly in the path of the young man, who has only to bend over and exhale to make use of it, which he does, for a long time. He coughs and retches until he can manage only gasps and dry heaves. By the time he is finished he is on his knees, hunched over the bucket clutching it with both hands. The retching turns to sobbing and then to soft cursing.

A few feet away the old man waits, courteously and without much interest in the purging process. If the student should feel too ill to return to his work, he will call someone to tend to him. He will not offer his shoulder unless the tottering young man insists. He does not care to touch people: The living are not his concern. Most of the students know him, and would shrink from him, but this one is new. He may not know whom he has encountered in the dark hallway. For all the boy's momentary terror and revulsion, he will be all right. He will return to his task, if not tonight then tomorrow. It is the night before his first dissection class, after all, and many a queasy novice has conquered his nerves and gone on to make a fine doctor.

The young man wipes his face with a linen handkerchief, still gulping air as if the motion *in* will prevent the motion *out*. "I'm all right," he says, aware of the silent presence a few feet away.

"Shouldn't come alone," the old man says. "They make you work together for a reason. 'Cause you joke. You prop up one another's nerve. Distractions beguile the mind, makes it easier, if you don't think too much."

The young man looks up then, recognizing the florid speech and the lilt of a Gullah accent beneath the surface. Pressing the handkerchief to his mouth, he takes an involuntary step backward. He does know who this is. He had been expecting to see a sweeper, perhaps, or one of the professors working here after hours, but this apparition, suddenly recognized, legendary and ancient even in his father's student days, fills him with more terror than the shrouded forms in the room he has just quit.

He is standing in the hall, beside a bucket filled with his own vomit, and his only companion is this ancient black man, still straight and strong-looking in a white linen suit, his grizzled hair shines about his head in the lamplight like a halo, and the student knows that he looks a fool in front of this old man who has touched more dead people than live ones. He peers at the wrinkled face to see if there is some trace of scorn in the impassive countenance.

"I was here because I was afraid," he says, glancing back at the lamp-lit room of shrouded tables. He does not owe this man an explanation, and if asked, he might have replied with a curt dismissal, but there is only silence, and he needs to feel life in the dark hall. "I thought I might make a fool of myself in class tomorrow—" He glances toward the bucket, and the old man nods. "—And so I came along tonight to try to prepare myself. To see my—well, to see it. Get it over with. Put a cloth over its eyes." He dabbed at his mouth with the soiled handkerchief. "You understand that feeling, I guess."

"I can't remember," said the old man. He has always worked alone. He pulls a bottle out of the pocket of his black coat, pulls out the cork, and passes it to the young man. It is half full of grain alcohol, clear as water.

The young man takes a long pull on the bottle and wipes his mouth with the back of his hand. The two of them look at each other and smile. Not all of the students would drink from the same bottle as a black man. Not in this new century. Maybe once, but not now. The prim New Englanders would not, for his race is alien to them, and while they preach equality, they shrink from proximity. The crackers would not, because they must always be careful to enforce their precarious rank on the social ladder, even more so since Reconstruction. But this boy is planter class, and he has no need for such gestures. He has traded sweat and spit with Negroes since infancy, and he has no self-consciousness, no need for social barriers. It is the way of his world. They understand each other.

"You don't remember?" The young man smiles in disbelief as he hands back the bottle. "But how could you not recall the first time you touched the dead?"

Because it has been nigh on sixty years, the old man thinks. He points to the bucket. "Do you remember the first time you ever did that?"

His life is divided into *before the train* and *after the train.* Not after the war. Things for him did not so much change after the war as this new century's white folks might suppose. The landmark of his life was that train ride down from Charleston. He remembers some of his earliest life, or perhaps he has imagined parts of it for so long that they have taken on a reality in his mind. He remembers a rag quilt that used to lay atop his corn shuck mattress. It had been pieced together from scraps of cloth—some of the pieces were red and shiny, probably scavenged from silk dresses worn by the ladies up at the house. His memories are a patchwork as well: a glimpse of dark eyes mirroring firelight; the hollowed shell of a box turtle . . . someone, an old man, is making music with it, and people are dancing . . . he is very young, sitting on a dirt floor, watching legs and calico skirts flash past him, brushing him sometimes, as the dancers stamped and spun, the music growing louder and faster . . .

There was a creek, too . . . He is older by then . . . Squatting on a wet rock a little way out into the water, waiting for the frog . . . waiting . . . So still that the white birds come down into the field for the seeds as if he were not there . . . Then crashing through the cattails comes Dog, reeking of creek water and cow dung, licking his face, thrashing the water with his muddy tail . . . frogs scared into kingdom come. What was that dog's name? It is just sounds now, that name, and he isn't sure he remembers them right, but once they meant something inside his head, those sounds . . . He has never heard them since.

Older still . . . Now he has seen the fields for what they are: not a place to play. Sun up to sun down . . . Water in a bucket, dispensed from a gourd hollowed out to make a dipper . . . the drinking gourd. He sits in the circle of folks in the dark field, where a young man with angry eyes is pointing up at the sky. The *drinking gourd* is a pattern of stars. They are important. They lead you somewhere, as the Wise Men followed stars . . . But he never set off to follow those stars, and he does not know what became of the angry young man who did. It is long ago, and he resolved to have nothing to do with drinking gourds—neither stars nor rice fields.

He listened to the old people's stories, of how the trickster rabbit smiled and smiled his way out of danger, and how the fox never saw the trap for the smile, and he reckoned he could do that. He could smile like honey on a johnny cake. Serenity was his shield. You never looked sullen, or angry, or afraid. Sometimes bad things happened to you anyway, but at least, if they did, you did not give your tormentor the gift of your pain as well. So he smiled in the South Carolina sunshine and waited for a door to open somewhere in the world, and presently it did.

The sprawling white house sat on a cobblestone street near the harbor in Charleston. It had a shady porch that ran the length of the house, and a green front door with a polished brass door knocker in the shape of a lion's head, but that door did not open to the likes of him. He used the back door, the one that led to the kitchen part of the house.

The old woman there was kind. To hear anyone say otherwise would have astonished her. She kept slaves as another woman might have kept cats—with indulgent interest in their habits, and great patience with their shortcomings. Their lives were her theatre. She was a spinster woman, living alone in the family house, and she made little enough work for the cook, the maid, and the yard man, but she must have them, for the standards of Charleston's quality folk must be maintained.

The old woman had a cook called Rachel. A young girl with skin the color of honey, and still so young that the corn pone and gravy had not yet thickened her body. She was not as pretty as some, but he could tell by her clothes and the way she carried herself that she was a cherished personage in some fine house. He had met her at church, where he always took care to be the cleanest man there with the shiniest shoes. If his clothes were shabby, they were as clean and presentable as he could make them, and he was handsome, which went a long ways toward making up for any deficiency in station. By then he was a young man, grown tall, with a bronze cast to his skin, not as dark as most, and that was as good as a smile, he reckoned, for he did not look so alien to the white faces who did the picking and choosing. He was a townsman, put to work on the docks for one of the ship's chandlers at the harbor. He liked being close to the sea and his labors had made him strong and lean, but the work was hard and it led nowhere. The house folk in the fine homes fared the best. You could tell them just by looking, with their cast-off finery and their noses in the air, knowing their station—higher than most folks.

The fetching little cook noticed him—he took care that this should be so, but he was patient in his courting of her, for he had more on his mind than a tumble on a corn shuck mattress. For many weeks he was as gentlemanly as a prince in a fairy story, taking no more liberties than pressing her hand in farewell as they left the church service. Finally when the look in her eyes told him that she thought he'd hung the moon, he talked marriage. He could not live without her, he said. He wanted no more of freedom than the right to grow old at her side.

Presently the determined Rachel ushered him into the presence of her mistress, the old woman who kept her servants as pets, and he set out to charm her with all the assurance of golden youth, condescending to old age. The gambit would not work forever, but this time it did, and he received the mistress's blessing to wed the pretty young cook. The mistress would buy him, she said, and he could join the household, as butler and coachman—or whatever could be done by an assiduous young man with strength and wit.

The joining took place in a proper white frame church, presided over by a stately clergyman as dignified and elegant as any white minister in Charleston. No broom jumping for the likes of them. And the mistress herself even came to the wedding, sat there in the pew with two of her lady friends and wept happy tears into a lace handkerchief.

Then the newlyweds went back to their room behind the kitchen that would be their home for the next dozen years. Being a town servant was easy, not like dock work. The spinster lady didn't really need a coachman and butler, not more than a few hours a week, so she let him hire out to the inn to work as a porter there, and she even let him keep half of what he earned there. He could have saved up the coins, should have perhaps. One of the cooks there at the inn had been salting away his pay to purchase his freedom, but he didn't see much point in that. As it was, he and Rachel lived in a fine house, ate the same good food as the old lady, and never had to worry about food or clothes or medicine. The free folks might give themselves airs, but they lived in shacks and worked harder than anybody, and he couldn't see the sense of that. Maybe someday they'd think about a change, but no use to deprive himself of fine clothes and a drink or two against that day, for after all, the old missus might free them in her will, and then all those years of scrimping would have been for naught.

All this was *before the train ride* . . .

Dr. George Newton—1852

Just as Lewis Ford and I were setting out from the college on Telfair Street, one of the local students, young Mr. Thomas, happened along in his buggy and insisted upon driving us over the river to the depot at Hamburg so that we could catch the train to Charleston. When Thomas heard our destination, he began to wax poetic about the beauties of that elegant city, but I cut short his rhapsody. "We are only going on business, Dr. Ford and I," I told him. "We shall acquire a servant for the college and come straight back tomorrow."

The young man left us off the depot, wishing us godspeed, but I could see by his expression that he was puzzled, and that only his good manners prevented his questioning us further. *Going to Charleston for a slave?* he was thinking. *Whatever for? Why not just walk down to sale at the Lower Market on Broad Street here in Augusta?*

Well, we could hardly do that, but I was not at liberty to explain the nature of our journey to a disinterested party. We told people that we had gone to secure a porter to perform custodial services for the medical college, and so we were, but we wanted no one with any ties to the local community. Charleston was just about far enough away, we decided.

For all that the railroad has been here twenty years, Lewis claims he will never become accustomed to jolting along at more than thirty miles per hour, but he allows that it does make light of a journey that would have taken more than a day by carriage. I brought a book along, though Lewis professes astonishment that I am able to read at such a speed. He contented himself with watching the pine trees give way to cow pastures and cotton fields and back again.

After an hour he spoke up. "I suppose this expense is necessary, Newton."

"Yes, I think so," I said, still gazing out the window. "We have all discussed it, and agreed that it must be done."

"Yes, I suppose it must. Clegg charges too much for his services and he really is a most unsatisfactory person. He has taken to drink you know."

"Can you wonder at it?"

"No. I only hope he manages to chase away the horrors with it. Still, we cannot do business with him any longer, and we have to teach the fellows somehow."

"Exactly. We have no choice."

He cleared his throat. "Charleston. I quite understand the need for acquiring a man with no ties to Augusta, but Charleston is a singular place. They have had their troubles there, you know."

I nodded. Thirty years ago the French Caribbean slave Denmark Vesey led an uprising in Charleston, for which they hanged him. All had been quiet there since, but Dr. Ford is one of nature's worriers. "You may interview the men before the auction if it will ease your mind. You will be one-seventh owner," I reminded him. We had all agreed on that point: All faculty members to own a share in the servant, to be bought out should said faculty member leave the employ of the college.

He nodded. "I shall leave the choosing to you, though, Newton, since you are the dean."

"Very well," I said. Dr. Ford had been my predecessor— the first dean of the medical college—but after all it was he who had engaged the services of the unsatisfactory Clegg, so I thought it best to rely upon my judgment this time.

"Seven hundred dollars, then," said Ford. "One hundred from each man. That sum should be sufficient, don't you think?"

"For a porter, certainly," I said. "But since this fellow will also be replacing Clegg, thus saving us the money we were paying out to him, the price will be a bargain."

"It will be if the new man has diligence and ingenuity. And if he can master the task, of which we are by no means certain," said Ford.

"He will have to. Only a slave can perform the task with impunity."

We said little else for the duration of the journey, but I was hoping for a good dinner in Charleston. After my undergraduate days at the University of Pennsylvania, I went abroad to study medicine in Paris. There I acquired a taste for the fine food and wines that Charleston offers in abundance. It is the French influence—all those refugees from the French Caribbean improved the cuisine immeasurably.

When we had disembarked and made our way to the inn to wash off the dust of the journey, there were yet a few hours of daylight before dinner, and after I noted down the costs of our train fares and lodging for the college expense record, I decided that it would be prudent to visit the market in preparation for the next day's sale. Slaves who are to be auctioned are housed overnight in quarters near the market, and one may go and view them, so as to be better prepared to bid when the time came.

It was a warm afternoon, and I was mindful of the mix of city smells and sea air as I made my way toward the old market. I presented myself at the building quartering those who were to be sold the next day, and a scowling young man ushered me inside. No doubt the keeping of this establishment made for unpleasant work, for some of its inhabitants were loudly lamenting their fate, while others called out for water or a clean slop bucket, and above it all were the wails of various infants and snatches of song from those who had ceased to struggle against their lot.

It was a human zoo with but one species exhibited, but there was variation enough among them, save for their present unhappiness. I wanted to tell them that this was the worst of it—at least I hoped it was.

I made my way into the dimly lit barracks, determined to do my duty despite the discomfort I felt. *Slave* . . . We never use that word. *My servant,* we say, or *my cook,* or *the folks down on my farm . . . my people . . . Why, he's part of the family,* we say . . . We call the elderly family retainers by the courtesy title of Uncle or Aunt . . . Later, when we have come to know and trust them and to presume that they are happy in our care, it is all too easy to forget by what means they are obtained. From such a place as this.

In truth, though, it hardly matters that I am venturing into slave quarters, for I am not much at ease anywhere in the company of my fellow creatures. Even at the orphan asylum supported by my uncle, my palms sweat and I shrink into my clothes whenever I must visit there, feeling the children's eyes upon me with every step I take. I find myself supposing that every whisper is a mockery of me, and that all eyes upon me are judging me and finding me wanting. It is a childish fear, I suppose, and I would view it as such in anyone other than myself, but logic will not lay the specter of ridicule that dogs my steps, and so I tread carefully, hearing sniggers and seeing scorn whether there be any or not.

Perhaps that is why I never married, and why, after obtaining my medical degree, I chose the role of college administrator to that of practicing physician—I hope to slip through life unnoticed. But I hope I do my duty, despite my personal predilections, and that evening my duty was to enter this fetid human stable and to find a suitable man for the college. I steeled myself to the sullen stares of the captives and to the cries of their frightened children. The foul smell did not oppress me, for the laboratories of the college are much the same, and the odor permeates the halls and even my very office. No, it was the eyes I minded. The cold gaze of those who fear had turned to rage. I forced myself to walk slowly, and to look into the face of each one, nodding coolly, so that they would not know how I shrank from them.

"Good evening, sir." The voice was deep and calm, as if its owner were an acquaintance, encountering me upon some boulevard and offering a greeting in passing.

I turned, expecting to see a watchman, but instead I met with a coffee-colored face, gently smiling: an aquiline nose, pointed beard, and sharp brown eyes that took in everything and gave out nothing. The man looked only a few years younger than myself—perhaps thirty-five—and he wore the elegant clothes of a dandy, so that he stood out from the rest like a peacock among crows.

The smile was so guileless and open that I abandoned my resolve of solemnity and smiled back. "How do you do?" I said. "Dreadful place, this. Are you here upon the same errand as I?" Charleston has a goodly number of half castes, a tropical mixture of Martinique slaves and their French masters. They even have schools here to educate them, which I think a good thing, although it is illegal to do so in Georgia. There are a good many freedmen in every city who have prospered and have taken it in turn to own slaves themselves, and I supposed that this light-colored gentleman must be such a free man in need of a workman.

There was a moment's hesitation and then the smile shone forth again. "Almost the same," he said. "Are you here in search of a servant? I am in need of a new situation."

In momentary confusion I stared at his polished shoes, and the white shirt that shone in the dimness. "Are you—"

He nodded, and spoke more softly as he explained his position. For most of his adult life he had been the principal manservant of a spinster lady in Charleston, and he had also been permitted in his free time to hire out to a hotel in the city, hence his mannered speech and the clothes of a dandy.

"But—you are to be sold?"

He nodded. "The mistress is ailing, don't you know. Doesn't need as much help as before, and needs cash money more. The bank was after her. So I had to go. Made me no never mind. I'll fetch a lot. I just hope for a good place, that's all. I'm no field hand."

I nodded, noting how carefully he pronounced his words, and how severely clean and well-groomed his person. Here was a man whose life's course would be decided in seconds tomorrow, and he had done all he could to see that it went well.

"And the mistress, you know, she cried and carried on to see me go. And she swore that she would never part with my wife."

I nodded. It is regrettable that such things happen. Money is the tyrant that rules us all. I said, "I am the dean of a medical college in Augusta. In Georgia. Do you know where that is?"

"A good ways off, sir."

"Half a day's journey south by train. Over the Savannah River and into the state of Georgia."

"A college. That sounds like a fine situation indeed, sir. What kind of place is it?"

"We teach young men to be doctors and surgeons."

"No, sir," He smiled again. "The *place.* The position you've come here wanting to fill."

"Oh, that." I hesitated. "Well—Porter, I suppose you'd say. General factotum about the college. And *something else,* for which, if the man were able to do it, we should *pay.*" I did not elaborate, but I thought he could read expressions much better than I, for he looked thoughtful for a few moments, and then he nodded.

"You'd pay . . . Enough for train fare?"

"If the work is satisfactory. Perhaps enough, if carefully saved, to make a larger purchase than that. But the extra duty . . . it is not pleasant work."

He smiled. "If it was pleasant, you wouldn't pay."

And so it was done. It was not the sordid business of buying a life, I told myself, but more of a bargain struck between two men of the world. True, he would have to leave his wife behind in Charleston, but at least we were saving him from worse possible fates. From cane fields farther south, or from someone who might mistreat him. He could do worse, I told myself. And at least I saved him from one ordeal—that of standing upon the block not knowing what would become of him. I thought the man bright enough and sufficiently ambitious for the requirements of our institution. It may seem odd that I consulted him beforehand as if he had a choice in his fate, but for our purposes we needed a willing worker, not a captive. We needed someone dependable, and I felt that if this man believed it worth his while to join us, we would be able to trust him.

They must have thought him wonderfully brave the next day. On the block, before upturned white faces like frog spawn, peering up at him, he stood there smiling like a missionary with four aces. It was over in the space of a minute, only a stepping stone from one life to the next, crossed in the blink of an eye.

Seven hundred dollars bid and accepted in the span of ten heartbeats, and then the auctioneer moved on to the next lot, and we went out. As we counted out the gold pieces for the cashier, and signed the account book, Lewis Ford was looking a little askance at the whole procedure.

"So you're certain of this fellow, Newton?"

"Well, as much as one can be, I suppose," I said. "I talked at length with him last evening. Of course I did not explain the particulars of the work to him. That would have been most imprudent."

Lewis Ford grunted. "Well, he has the back for it, I grant you that. And, as you say, perhaps the temperament as well. But has he the stomach for it? After our experience with Clegg, that's what I wonder."

"Well, *I* would, Dr. Ford. If my choice in life was the work we have in store for this fellow or a short, hard life in the cane fields further south, by God, I would have the stomach for it."

"Indeed. Well, I defer to your judgment. I don't suppose what we're asking of him is much worse than what we do for a living, after all."

"We'll be serving the same master, anyhow," I said. "The college, you know, and the greater good of medicine."

"What is the fellow's name, do you know?"

I nodded. "He told me. It is Grandison. Grandison Harris."

"Odd name. I mean they *have* odd names, of course. Xerxes and Thessalonians, and all that sort of thing. People will give slaves and horses the most absurd appellations, but I wouldn't have taken Grandison for a slave name, would you?"

I shrugged. "Called after the family name of his original owner, I should think. And judging by the lightness of his skin, there's some might say he's entitled to it."

Grandison Harris had never been on a train before, and his interest in this new experience seemed to diminish what regrets he might have about leaving his home in Charleston. When the train pulled out of the depot, he leaned out the window of the car and half stood until he could see between the houses and over the people all the way to the bay—a stand of water as big as all creation, it looked from here. Water that flowed into the sky itself where the other shore ought to be. The glare of the afternoon sun on the water was fierce, but he kept on twisting his head and looking at the diminishing city and the expanse of blue.

"You'll hurt your eyes staring out at the sun like that," I said.

He half turned and smiled. "Well, sir, Doctor," he said, "I mean to set this place in my memory like dye in new-wove cloth. My eyes may water a little, but I reckon that's all right, for dyes are sot in salt. Tears will fix the memories to my mind to where they'll never come out."

After that we were each left alone with our thoughts for many miles, to watch the unfamiliar landscapes slide past the railway carriage, or to doze in relief that, although the future might be terrible, at least this day was over.

Instead of the sea, the town of Augusta had the big Savannah River running along beside it, garlanded in willows, dividing South Carolina from the state of Georgia. From the depot in Hamburg they took a carriage over the river into town, but it was dark by then, and he couldn't see much of the new place except for the twinkling lights in the buildings. Wasn't as big as Charleston, though. They boarded him for the night with a freed woman who took in lodgers, saying that they would come to fetch him in the morning for work.

For a moment in the lamplight of the parlor, he had taken her for a white woman, this haughty lady with hair the brown of new leather and green eyes that met every-body's gaze without a speck of deference. Dr. Newton took off his hat to her when they went in, and he shook her hand and made a little bow when he took his leave.

When he was alone with this strange landlady, he stared at her in the lamplight and said, "Madame, you are a red bone, not?"

She shrugged. "I am a free person of color. Mostly white, but not all. They've told you my name is Alethea Taylor. I'll thank you to call me Miz Taylor."

"You sure look white," he said. *Act it, too,* he thought.

She nodded. "My mama was half-caste and my daddy was white. So was my husband, whose name I ought to have. But it was Butts, so maybe I don't mind so much."

She smiled at that and he smiled back.

"We married up in Carolina where I was born. It's legal up there. I was given schooling as well. So don't think this house is any low-class place, because it isn't. We have standards."

The new lodger looked around at the tidy little parlor with its worn but elegant mahogany settee and a faded turkey carpet. A book shelf stood beside the fireplace, with a big leather Bible on top in pride of place. "Your white husband lives here, too?" he asked.

"Of course not." Her face told him that the question was foolish. "He was rich enough to buy up this whole town, Mr. Butts was. But he's dead now. Set me and our children free, though, when he passed. Seven young'uns we had. So now I do fine sewing for the town ladies, and my boys work to keep us fed. Taking in a lodger helps us along, too. Though I'm particular about who I'll accept. Took you as a favor to Dr. George Newton. Would you tell me your name again?"

"Grandison Harris," he said. "I guess the doctors told you: I'm the porter at the college."

She gave him a scornful look. " 'Course you are. Dr. Newton's uncle Tuttle is my guardian, so I know all about the college."

"Guardian?"

"Here in Georgia, freed folk have to have white guardians."

"What for?"

She shrugged. "To protect us from other white men, I suppose. But Mr. Isaac Tuttle is a good man. I can trust him."

He watched her face for some sign that this Tuttle was more to her than a disinterested legal guardian, but she seemed to mean no more than what she said. It made no difference to him, though. Who she shared her bed with was none of his business, and never would be. She had made her opinion of him plain. He was a slave, and she was a free woman, his landlady, and a friend of his owners. You couldn't cross that gulf on a steamboat.

"It's late," she said, "But I expect you are hungry as well as tired. I can get you a plate of beans if you'd care to eat."

"No, ma'am, I'm good 'til morning. Long day."

She nodded, and her expression softened. "Well, it's over now. You've landed on your feet."

"The college—It's a good place, then?" he asked.

"Hard work," she said. She paused as if she wanted to say more, but then she shook her head. "Better than the big farms, anyhow. Dr. George is a good man. Lives more in his books than in the world, but he means well. Those doctors are all right. They treat sick black folks, same as white. You will be all right with them if you do your job. They won't beat you to show they're better than you." She smiled. "Doctors think they are better than most everybody else, anyhow, so they don't feel the need to go proving it with a bull whip."

"That's good to hear."

"Well, just you mind how *you* treat *them*," she said. "You look like you wouldn't be above a little sharp practice, and those doctors can be downright simple. Oh, they know a lot about doctoring and a lot about books, but they're not very smart about people. They don't expect to be lied to. So you take care to be straight with them so that you can keep this good place."

He followed her meekly to a clean but spartan room. A red rag quilt covered the bed, and a chipped white pitcher and basin stood on a small pine table next to a cane-seat chair. Compared to the faded splendor of Miz Taylor's parlor, the room was almost a prison cell, but he was glad enough to have it. Better here with a family than in some makeshift room at the medical college. He wasn't sure whether the doctors kept sick people around the place, but he didn't like the thought of sleeping there all the same. In a place of death. The best thing about this small bare room was what it did *not* contain: no shackles, no lock on the door or barred window. He was a boarder in a freedman's house.

He turned to the woman, who stood on the threshold holding the lamp.

"Aren't they afraid I'll run off?" he asked.

She sighed. "I told you. They don't have good sense about people. I reckon they figure you'd be worse off running than staying here. You know what happens to runaways."

He nodded. He had seen things in Charleston, heard stories about brandings and toes lopped off. And of course the story of Denmark Vesey, whose rebellion had consisted mostly of talk, was never far from the surface of any talk about running or disobedience.

She set the lamp beside the basin. "I'll tell you what's the truth, Mr. Harris. If you give satisfaction at the college—do your work and don't steal, or leastways don't get caught at it—those doctors won't care about what you do the rest of the time. They won't remember to. They don't want to have to take care of a servant as if he were a pet dog. All they want is a job done with as few ructions as possible, and the less trouble you give them, the happier they'll be. You do your job well, you'll become invisible. Come and go as you please. You'll be a freedman in all but name. That's what I think. And I know the doctors, you see?"

"I won't give them no trouble," he said.

"See you don't. Can you read, Mr. Harris?"

He shook his head. There had been no call for it, and the

old miss in Charleston wasn't averse to her folks getting book learning, but she had needed him to work.

"Well," she said, "I school my young'uns every evening. If you would like to join us, one of my girls can start by teaching you your letters."

"I thank you."

She nodded and turned to leave. "Reading is a good skill," she said as she closed the door. "You can write out your own passes."

He had seen fine buildings in Charleston, but even so, the Medical College on Telfair Street was a sight to behold. A white temple, it was, with four stone columns holding up the portico and a round dome atop the roof, grand as a cathedral, it was. You stepped inside to an open space that stretched all the way up to the dome, with staircases curving up the sides that led to the upper floor rooms. The wonder of it wore off before long, but it was grand while it lasted. Soon enough the architectural splendor failed to register, and all he saw were floors that needed mopping and refuse bins that stank.

For the first couple of days he chopped firewood, and fetched pails of water when they needed them.

"Just until you are settled in," Dr. Newton had said. "Then we will have a talk about why you are here."

He didn't see much of the doctors during the couple of days they gave him to get acquainted with his new surroundings. Perhaps they were busy with more pressing matters, and, remembering Alethea Taylor's advice about giving no trouble, he got on with his work and bothered no one. At last, though, clad in one of the doctors' clean cast-off suits, he was summoned into the presence, a little shy before the all-powerful strangers, but not much afraid, for they had paid too much good money for him to waste it by harming him.

For a night or two he had woken up in the dark, having dreamed that the doctors were going to cut him open alive, but this notion was so patently foolish that he did not even mention it to his landlady, whose scorn would have been withering.

George Newton was sitting behind his big desk, tapping his fingers together, looking as if his collar were too tight. "Now Grandison," he began, "you have settled in well? Good. You seem to be a good worker, which is gratifying. So now I think we can discuss that other task that your duties entail."

He paused, perhaps to wait for a question, but he saw only respectful interest in the man's face. "Well, then . . . This is a place where men are taught to be doctors. And also to be surgeons. A grim task, that: the cutting open of living beings. Regrettably necessary. A generation ago there was an English surgeon who would vomit before every operation he performed. Do you know why?" The listener shook his head.

"Because the patient is awake for the operation, and because the pain is so terrible that many die of it. We lose half the people on whom we operate, even if we do everything right. They die of shock, of heart failure, perhaps, from the pain. But despite these losses, we are learning. We *must* learn. We must help more people, and lessen the torture of doing so. This brings me to your function here at the college." He paused and tapped his pen, waiting in case the new servant ventured a question, but the silence stretched on. At last he said, "It was another English surgeon who said, *we must mutilate the dead in order not to mutilate the living.*" Another pause. "What he meant was that we physicians must learn our way around the human body, and we must practice our surgical skills. It is better to practice those skills upon a dead body rather than a living one. Do you see the sense of that?"

He swallowed hard, but finally managed to nod. "Yes, sir."

George Newton smiled. "Well, if you *do* understand that, Grandison, then I wish you were the governor of Georgia, because *he* doesn't. The practice is against the law in this state—indeed, in all states—to use cadavers for medical study. People don't want us defiling the dead, they say— so, instead, out of ignorance, we defile the living. And that cannot be permitted. We must make use of the dead to help the living."

"Yes, sir," he said. The doctor still seemed lost in thought, so he added encouragingly, "It's all right with me, sir."

Again the smile. "Well, thank you, Grandison. I'm glad to have your permission, anyhow. But I'm afraid we will need more than that. Tell me, do you believe that the spirits of the dead linger in the graveyard? Object to being disturbed? That they'd try to harm anyone working on their remains?"

He tried to picture dead people loitering around the halls of the college, waiting for their bodies to be returned. This was a place of death. He didn't know whether to smile or weep. Best not to think of it at all, he decided. "They are gone, ain't they?" he said at last. "Dead. Gone to glory. They're not sitting around waiting for Judgment Day in the grave, are they?"

Another doctor sighed. "Well, Grandison, to tell you the truth, I don't know where the souls of the dead are. That is something we don't teach in medical college. However, I don't believe they're sitting out there in the graveyard, tied to their decaying remains. I think we can be sure of that."

"And you need the dead folks to learn doctoring on?"

Dr. Ford nodded. "Each medical student should have a cadaver to work on, so that he can learn his trade without killing anyone in the learning process. That seems a sufficiently noble reason to rob graves, doesn't it?"

He considered it, more to forestall the rest of the conversation than anything else. "You could ask folks before they dies," he said. "Tell them how it is, and get them to sign a paper for the judge."

"But since the use of cadavers is against the law, no judge would honor such a paper, even if people could be persuaded to sign it, which most would not. I wish there were easy answers, but there aren't. You know what we must ask of you."

"You want me to bring you dead folks? Out the graveyard?"

"Yes. There is a cemetery on Watkins Street, not half a mile from here, so the journey would not be long. You must go at night, of course."

He stood quite still for some time before he spoke. It was always best to let white folks think you took everything calmly and agreed with them on every particular. To object that such a deed would frighten or disgust him would make no difference. The doctor would dismiss his qualms as fear or superstition. The doctors had explained the matter to him, when they could have simply given him an order. That was something, anyhow. At last he nodded. The matter was settled, and the only considerations now were practical ones. "If I get caught, what then?"

"I don't suppose you will *get caught,* as you put it, if you are the least bit clever about it, but even if you should, remember that slaves are not prosecuted for any crime. They are considered property and therefore not subject to prosecution. The authorities simply hand them back over to their masters." Newton smiled. "And you don't suppose that *we* would punish you for it, do you?"

The others nodded in agreement, and the matter was settled.

He was given a lantern and a shovel, and a horse-drawn cart. Dr. Newton had written out a pass, saying that the bearer, Grandison Harris, servant of the medical college, was allowed to be abroad that night to pick up supplies for the doctors. "I doubt very much that the city's watchmen can read," Newton had told him. "Just keep this pass until it wears out, and then one of us will write you a new one."

He kept the pass in his jacket pocket, ready to produce if anyone challenged him, but he had met no one on his journey from Telfair Street to the burying ground. It was well after midnight, and the sliver of moon had been swallowed by clouds, so he made his way in darkness. Augusta was a smaller place than Charleston. He had walked around its few streets until he knew it by day and by night, and he had been especially careful of the route to Cedar Grove, where the town buried its slaves and freedmen. Now he could navigate the streets without the help of the lantern. Only the horse's footfalls broke the silence. Nearer to the town center, perhaps, people might still be out drinking and wagering at cards, but no sounds of merriment reached him here on the outskirts of town. He would have been glad of the sound of laughter and music, but the silence blanketed everything, and he did not dare to whistle to take his mind off his errand.

Do you want me to dig up just any old grave? he had asked the doctor.

No. There were rules. A body rots quick. Well, he knew that. Look at a dead cat in the road, rippling with maggots. After two, three days, you'd hardly know what it was. *Three days buried and no more,* the doctor told him. *After that, there's no point in bringing the corpse back up; it's too far gone to teach us anything. Look for a newly-dug grave,* Newton told him. Flowers still fresh on a mound of newly-spaded earth. *Soon,* he said, *you will get to know people about the town, and you will hear about deaths as they happen. Then you can be ready. This time, though, just do the best you can.*

He knew where he was going. He had walked in the grave-yard that afternoon, and found just such a burial plot a few paces west of the gate: a mound of brown dirt, encir-cled by clam shells, and strewn across it a scattering of black-eyed susans and magnolia flowers, wilting in the Georgia sun, but newly placed there.

He wondered whose grave it was. No mourners were there when he found it. Had there been, he would have hesitated to inquire, for fear of being remembered if the theft were ever discovered. There was no marker to tell him, either, even if he had been able to read. The final resting place of a slave—no carved stone. Here and there, crude wooden crosses tilted in the grass, but they told him nothing.

He reached the cemetery gate. Before he began to retrace his steps to the new grave, he lit the lantern. No one would venture near a burying ground so late at night, he thought, and although he had paced off the steps to the grave, he would need the light for the task ahead.

Thirty paces with his back to the gates, then ten paces right. He saw the white shape of shells outlining the mound of earth, and smelled the musk of decaying magnolia. He stood there a long time staring down at the flower-strewn grave, a colorless shape in the dimness. All through the long afternoon he had thought it out, while he mopped the classroom floors and emptied the waste bins, and waited for nightfall. His safety lay in concealment: No one must suspect that a grave had been disturbed. No one would look for a grave robber if they found no trace of the theft. The doctor had told him over and over that slaves were not jailed for committing a crime, but he did not trust laws. Public outrage over this act might send him to the end of a rope before anyone from the college could intervene. Best not to get caught.

He would memorize the look of the burial plot: the position of the shells encircling the mound, and how the flowers were placed, so that when he had finished his work he could replace it all exactly as it had been before.

Only when he was sure that he remembered the pattern of the grave did he thrust his shovel into the soft earth. He flinched when he heard the rasp of metal against soil, and felt the blade connect with the freshly-spaded dirt. The silence came flowing back. What had he expected? A scream of outrage from beneath the mound? When he had first contemplated the task before him, he had thought he could endure it by thinking only of the physical nature of the work: It is like digging a trench, he would tell himself. Like spading a garden. It is just another senseless task thought up by the white people to keep you occupied. But here in the faint lantern light of a burying ground, he saw that such pretenses would not work. The removing of dirt from a newly-filled hole was the least of it. He must violate consecrated ground, touch a corpse, and carry it away in darkness to be mutilated. He could not pretend otherwise.

All right, then. If the spirits of the dead hovered outside the lantern light, watching him work, so be it. Let them see. Let them hear his side of it, and judge him by that.

"Don't you be looking all squinty-eyed at me," he said to the darkness as he worked. "Wasn't my doing. You all know the white folks sent me out here. Say they need to study some more on your innards."

The shovel swished in the soft earth, and for a moment a curve of moon shimmered from behind a cloud, and then it was gone. He was glad of that. He fancied that he could make out human shapes in the shadows beneath the trees. Darkness was better. "You all long dead ones don't have no quarrel with me," he said, more loudly now. "Doctors don't want you if you gone ripe. You all like fish—after three days, you ain't good for nothing except fertilizer."

He worked on in the stillness, making a rhythm of entrenchment. The silence seemed to take a step back, giving him breathing room as he worked. Perhaps two hours now before cock crow.

He struck wood sooner than he had expected to. Six feet under, people always said. But it wasn't. Three feet, more like. Just enough to cover the box and then some for top soil. Deep enough, he supposed, since the pine boards would rot and the worms would take care of the rest.

He didn't need to bring up the coffin itself. That would disturb too much earth, and the doctors had no use for the coffin, anyhow. Dr. Newton told him that. It might be stealing to take a coffin, he had said. Wooden boxes have a monetary value. Dead bodies, none.

He stepped into the hole, and pushed the dirt away from the top of the box. The smell of wet soil made him dizzy, and he willed himself not to feel for worms in the clods of earth. He did not know whose grave this was. They had not told him, or perhaps they didn't know.

"You didn't want to be down there anyhow," he said to the box. "Salted away in the wet ground. You didn't want to end up shut away in the dark. I came to bring you back. If the angels have got you first, then you won't care, and if they didn't, then at least you won't be alone in the dark any more."

He took the point of the shovel and stove in the box lid, pulling back when he heard the wood splinter, so that he would not smash what lay beneath it. On the ground beside the grave, he had placed a white sack, big enough to carry away the contents of the box. He pulled it down into the hole, and cleared away splinters of wood from the broken box, revealing a face, inches from his own.

Its eyes were closed. Perhaps—this first time—if they had been open and staring up at him, he would have dropped the shovel and run from the graveyard. Let them sell him south rather than to return to such terrors. But the eyes were shut. And the face in repose was an old woman, scrawny and grizzled, lying with her hands crossed over her breast, and an expression of weary resignation toward whatever came next.

He pulled the body out through the hole in the coffin lid, trying to touch the shroud rather than the flesh of the dead woman. She was heavier than he had expected from the look of her frail body, and the dead weight proved awkward to move, but his nerves made him hurry, and to finish the thing without stopping for breath: only get her into the sack and be done with it.

He wondered if the spirit of the old woman knew what was happening to her remains, and if she cared. He was careful not to look too long at the shadows and pools of darkness around trees and gravestones, for fear that they would coalesce into human shapes with burning eyes.

"Bet you ain't even surprised," he said to the shrouded form, as he drew the string tight across the mouth of the sack. "Bet you didn't believe in that business about eternal rest, no more'n the pigs would. Gonna get the last drop of use out you, same as pigs. But never mind. At least it ain't alone in the dark."

She lay there silent in the white sack while he spent precious long minutes refilling the hole, smoothing the mound, and placing the shells and flowers back exactly as he had found them.

He never found out who the old woman was, never asked. He had trundled the body back to the porter's entrance of the medical college, and steeped her in the alcohol they'd given him the money to buy as a preservative. Presently, when the body was cured and the class was ready, the old woman was carried upstairs to perform her last act of servitude. He never saw her again—at least not to recognize. He supposed that he had seen remnants of her, discarded in bits and pieces as the cutting and the probing progressed. That which remained, he put in jars of whiskey for further study or scattered in the cellar of the building, dusting it over with quicklime to contain the smell. What came out of the classes was scarcely recognizable as human, and he never tried to work out whose remains he was disposing of in a resting place less consecrated than the place from which he had taken them.

"Well, I suppose the first one is always the worst," said Dr. Newton the next day when he had reported his success in securing a body for the anatomy class. He had nodded in agreement, and pocketed the coins that the doctor gave him, mustering up a feeble smile in response to the pat on the back and the hearty congratulations on a job well done.

The doctor had been wrong, though. The first one was not the worst. There were terrors in the unfamiliar graveyard, that was true, and the strange feel of dead flesh in his hands had sent him reeling into the bushes to be sick, so that even he had believed that the first time was as bad as it could get, but later he came to realize that there were other horrors to take the place of the first ones. That first body was just a lump of flesh, nothing to him but an unpleasant chore to be got over with as quick as he could. And he would have liked for them all to be that way, but he had a quota to fill, and to do that he had to mingle with the folks in Augusta, so that he could hear talk about who was ailing and who wasn't likely to get well.

He joined the Springfield Baptist Church, went to services, learned folks' names, and passed the time of day with them if he happened to be out and about. Augusta wasn't such a big town that a few months wouldn't make you acquainted with almost the whole of it. He told people that he was the porter up to the medical college, which was true enough as far as it went, and no one seemed to think anything more about him. Field hands would have been surprised by how much freedom you could have if you were a town servant in a good place. There were dances and picnics, camp meetings and weddings. He began to enjoy this new society so much that he nearly forgot that they would see him as the fox in the henhouse if they had known why he was set among them.

Fanny, Miz Taylor's eldest girl, made sport of him because of his interest in the community. "I declare, Mister Harris," she would say, laughing, "You are worse than two old ladies for wanting to know all the goings-on, aren't you?"

"I take an interest," he said.

She shook her head. "Who's sick? Who's in the family way? Who's about to pass?—Gossip! I'd rather talk about books!" Miss Fanny, with her peach-gold cheeks and clusters of chestnut curls, was a pretty twelve-year-old. She and her young sister Nannie were soon to be sent back to South Carolina for schooling, so she had no time for the troubles of the old folks in dull old Augusta.

When she thought he was out of earshot, Fanny's mother reproved her for her teasing. "Mary Frances," she said. "You should not poke fun at our lodger for taking an interest in the doings of the town. Do you not think he might be lonely, with no family here, and his wife back in Charleston? It is our Christian duty to be kind to him."

"Oh, *duty,* mama!"

"And, Fanny, remember that a lady is always kind."

But he had not minded Miss Fanny's teasing. To be thought a nosey "old lady" was better than to be suspected of what he really was. But in the few months before she left for school, Miss Fanny had made an effort to treat him with courtesy. She was well on her way to being a lady, with her mother's beauty and her father's white skin. He wondered what would become of her.

He was in the graveyard again, this time in the cold drizzle of a February night. He barely needed a lantern anymore to find his way to a grave, so accustomed had he become to the terrain of that hallowed field. And this time he would try to proceed without the light, not from fear of discovery but because he would rather not see the face of the corpse. Cheney Youngblood, a soft-spoken young woman whose sweet serenity made her beautiful, had gone to death with quiet resignation on Saturday night. It had been her first child, and when the birthing went wrong, the midwife took to drink and wouldn't do more than cry and say it weren't her fault. At last Miz Taylor was sent for, and she had dispatched young Jimmie to fetch Dr. Newton. He had come readily enough, but by then the girl had been so weak that nothing could have saved her. "I'd have to cut her open, Alethea," Dr. Newton had said. "And she'd never live through that, and I think the baby is dead already. Why give her more pain when there's nothing to be gained from it?"

At dawn the next morning he had just been going out the door to light the fires at the college when Alethea Taylor came home, red-eyed and disheveled from her long night's vigil. "It's over," she told him, and went inside without another word.

The funeral had been held the next afternoon. Cheney Youngblood in her best dress had been laid to rest in a plain pine box, her baby still unborn. He had stood there before the flower-strewn grave with the rest of the mourners, and he'd joined in the singing and in the prayers for her salvation. And when the minister said, *Rest in peace,* he had said "Amen" with the rest of them. But he knew better.

Three-quarters of an hour in silence, while the spadefuls of earth fell rhythmically beside the path. He would not sing. He could not pray. And he tried not to look at the shadows that seemed to grow from the branches of the nearby azaleas. At last he felt the unyielding wood against his spade, and with hardly a pause for thought, he smashed the lid, and knelt to remove the contents of the box. There had been no shroud for Cheney Youngblood, but the night was too dark for him to see her upturned face, and he was glad.

"Now, Cheney, I'm sorry about this," he whispered, as he readied the sack. "You must be in everlasting sorry now that you ever let a man touch you, and here I am seeing that you will get more of the same. I just hope you can teach these fool doctors something about babies, Cheney. So's maybe if they see what went wrong, they can help the next one down the road."

He stood at the head of the coffin, gripping her by the shoulders, and pulled until the flaccid body emerged from the box. Fix his grip beneath her dangling arms, and it would be the act of a moment to hoist the body onto the earth beside the grave, and then into the sack. He did so, and she was free of the coffin, but not free.

Attached by a cord.

He stood there unmoving in the stillness, listening. Nothing.

He lit the lamp, and held it up so that he could see inside the box.

The child lay there, its eyes closed, fists curled, still attached to its mother's body by the cord.

His hand was shaking as he set down the lantern on the edge of the grave, and reached down for the child. After so much death, could he possibly restore to life . . . He took out his knife, but when he lifted the cord, it was withered and cold—like a pumpkin vine in winter.

Dr. Newton sat before the fire in his study, clad in a dressing gown and slippers. First light was a good hour away, but he had made no complaint about being awakened by the trembling man who had pounded on his door in the dead of night, and, when the doctor answered, had held out a sad little bundle.

He was sitting now in a chair near the fire, still shaking, still silent.

Dr. Newton sighed, poured out another glass of whiskey, and held it out to his visitor. "You could not have saved it, Grandison," he said again. "It did not live."

The resurrection man shook his head. "I went to the burying, Doctor. I was there. I saw. Cheney died trying to birth that baby, but she never did. She was big with child when they put her in the ground."

"And you think the baby birthed itself there in the coffin and died in the night?"

He took a gulp of whiskey, and shuddered. "Yes."

"No." Newton was silent for a moment, choosing his words carefully. "I saw a man hanged once. I was in medical school in those days, and we were given the body for study. When we undressed the poor fellow in the dissecting room, we found that he had soiled himself in his death agonies. The professor explained to us that when the body dies, all its muscles relax. The bowels are voided . . . And, I think, the muscles that govern the birth process must also relax, and the gases build up as the body decays, so that an infant in the birth canal is released in death."

"And it died."

"No. It never lived. It never drew breath. It died when its mother did, not later in the coffin when it was expelled. But it does you credit that you tried to save it."

"I thought the baby had got buried alive." The doctor shook his head, and Grandison said, "But people do get buried alive sometimes, don't they?"

Newton hesitated, choosing his words carefully. "It has happened," he said at last. "I have never seen it, mind you. But one of my medical professors in Paris told the tale of a learned man in medieval times who was being considered for sainthood. When the church fathers dug him up, to see if his body was in that uncorrupted state that denotes sanctity, they found the poor soul lying in the coffin on his back, splinters under his fingernails and a grimace of agony frozen on his withered features." He sighed. "To add insult to injury, they denied the fellow sainthood on the grounds that he seemed to be in no hurry to meet his Maker."

They looked at each other and smiled. It was a grim story, but not so terrible as the sight of a dead child wrapped in its mother's winding sheet. Besides, first light had just begun to gray the trees and the lawn outside. That night was over.

Cheney Youngblood had been early on, though. And he was sorry for her, because she was young and kindly, and he had thought her child had lived, however briefly. A year or so after that—it was hard to remember after so long a time, with no records kept—a steaming summer brought yellow fever into Augusta, and many died, burning in their delirium and crying for water. Day after day wagons stacked with coffins trundled down Telfair Street, bound for the two cemeteries, black and white. The old people and the babies died first, and here and there someone already sick or weakened by other ailments succumbed as well. New graves sprouted like skunk cabbage across the green expanse of the burying field.

Now he could dig and hoist with barely a thought to spare for the humans remains that passed through his hands. By now there had been too many dark nights, and too many still forms to move him to fear or pity. His shovel bit into the earth, and his shoulders heaved as he tossed aside the covering soil, but his mind these days ranged elsewhere.

"I want to go home," he told George Newton one night, after he had asked for the supplies he needed.

The doctor looked up, surprised and then thoughtful. "Home, Grandison?"

His answer was roundabout. "I do good work, do I not, doctor? Bring you good subjects for the classes, without causing you any trouble. Don't get drunk. Don't get caught."

"Yes. I grant you all that, but where is home, Grandison?"

"I have a wife back in Charleston."

Dr. Newton considered it. "You are lonely? I know that sometimes when people are separated by circumstance, they find other mates. I wonder if you have given any thought to that—or perhaps she—"

"We were married legal," he said. "I do good work here. Y'all trust me."

"Yes. Yes, we do. And you want to go back to Charleston to see your wife?"

He nodded. No use in arguing about it until the doctor thought it out.

At last Newton said, "Well, I suppose it might be managed. We could buy you a train ticket. Twelve dollars is not such a great sum, divided by the seven of us who are faculty members." He tapped his fingers together as he worked it out. "Yes, considered that way, the cost seems little enough, to ensure the diligence of a skilled and steady worker. I think I can get the other doctors to go along. You would have to carry a pass, stating that you have permission to make the journey alone, but that is easily managed."

"Yes. I'd like to go soon, please." He was good at his job for just this reason, so that it would be easier to keep him happy than to replace him.

Not everyone could do his job. The free man who was his predecessor had subsided into a rum-soaked heap; even now he could be seen shambling along Bay Street, trying to beg or gamble up enough money to drown the nightmares.

Grandison Harris had no dreams.

"Excuse me, Dr. Newton, but it's time for my train trip again, and Dr. Eve said it was your turn to pay."

"Hmm . . . what? Already?"

"Been four weeks." He paused for a moment, taking in the rumpled figure elbow-deep in papers at his desk. "I know you've had other things on your mind, sir. I'm sorry to hear about your uncle's passing."

"Oh, yes, thank you, Grandison." George Newton ran a hand through his hair, and sighed. "Well, it wasn't a shock, you know. He was a dear old fellow, but getting up in years, you know. No, it isn't so much that. It's the chaos he's left me."

"Chaos?"

"The mess. In his will my uncle left instructions that his house be converted to use as an orphanage, which is very commendable, I'm sure, but he had a houseful of family retainers, you know. And with the dismantling of his household on Walker Street, they have all moved in with me on Greene Street. I can't walk for people. Eleven of them! Women. Children. Noise. Someone tugging at my sleeve every time I turn around. And the Tuttle family heirlooms, besides. It's bedlam. And Henry, my valet, is at his wit's end. He's getting on in years, you know, and accustomed to having only me to look after. I would not dream of turning them out, of course, but . . ."

Grandison nodded. Poor white folks often thought that servants solved all the problems rich people could ever have, but he could see how they could be problems as well. They had to be fed, clothed, looked after when they got sick. It would be one thing if Dr. George had a wife and a busy household already going—then maybe a few extra folks wouldn't make much difference, but for a bachelor of forty-five used to nobody's company but his own, this sudden crowd of dependents might prove a maddening distraction. It would never occur to George Newton to sell his uncle's slaves, either. That was to his credit. Grandison thought that things ought to be made easier for them so he wouldn't be tempted to sell those folks to get some peace. He considered the situation, trying to think of a way to lighten the load. He said, "Have you thought about asking Miz Alethea if she can help you sort it out, Doctor?"

"Alethea Taylor? Well, I am her guardian now, I know." Newton smiled. "Is she also to be mine?"

"You know she does have seven young'uns. She's used to a house full. Maybe she could set things in order for you."

George Newton turned the idea over in his mind. Women were better at managing a household and seeing to people's needs. He had more pressing matters to contend with here at the medical school. He reached into his pocket and pulled out a roll of greenbacks. "Well, we must get you to Charleston," he said. "Twelve dollars for train fare, isn't it? And, thanks. I believe I will take your advice and ask Alethea to help me."

George Newton's problems went out of his head as soon as the door shut behind him. He went off to the depot to wait for the train, and he wanted no thought of Augusta to dampen his visit to Rachel.

Three days later he walked into Alethea Taylor's parlor near suppertime, and found that one of the family was missing. "Where's Miss Mary Frances?" he asked as they settled around the big table.

Young Joseph waved a drumstick and said, "Oh, Mama sent her over to Dr. George's house. You know how he's been since Mr. Turtle passed. People just running all over him, asking for things right and left. And Mr. George he can't say no to anybody, and he has about as much common sense as a day-old chick. He asked Mama to come help him, but she's too busy with her sewing work. So we sent Fanny instead."

Jane, who was ten, said, "Mama figured Fanny would put a stop to that nonsense. She'll sort them all out, that's certain. Ever since she got back from that school in South Carolina she's been bossing all of us something fierce, so I'm glad she's gone over there. It'll give us a rest."

"But she's what—seventeen?"

Joseph laughed. "Sixteen going-on-thirty," he said. "Those folks at Newton's will think a hurricane hit 'em. Fanny's got enough sand to take on the lot of them, and what's more she won't need a pass to go there, either."

Harris nodded. No, she wouldn't need a pass. Fanny Taylor was a gray-eyed beauty, whiter than some of the French Creole belles he'd seen in Charleston. With her light skin, her education and her poise, she could go anywhere unchallenged, and she had the same fire and steel as Miss Alethea, so he didn't think she'd be getting any back talk from the Newton household.

"She's living over there now?"

Jim laughed. "No-oo, sir! Mama wouldn't sit still for that." He glanced at his mother to see if it was safe to say more, but her expression was not encouraging.

"She'll be home directly," said Anna. "She goes first thing in the morning and she comes home after dinner time."

Miss Alethea spoke up then. "Children, where are your manners? Pass Mr. Harris those fresh biscuits and some gravy, and let him talk for once. Hand round the chicken, Jim. Mr. Harris, how was your journey?"

"The day was fine for a train ride," he said, careful to swallow the last bit of chicken before he spoke. The Taylors were sticklers for table manners. "Though we did have to stop once for some cows had got out and would not leave the track."

Miss Alethea was not interested in cows. "And your wife, Mr. Harris? I hope you found her well?"

"She's well enough." He hesitated. "She is with child."

Miss Alethea glanced at her own brood, and managed to smile. "Why, don't say that news with such a heavy heart,

Mr. Harris. This will be your first born, won't it! You should be joyful!"

He knew it was his child. The old miss would never permit any goings-on in her house. Not that he thought Rachel would have countenanced it anyhow. But a child was one more millstone of Charleston to burden him. He couldn't be with his child, couldn't protect it. And the old missus professed to be delighted at this new addition to the household, but he was afraid that a baby on the premises would be more annoying to her than she anticipated. He thought of Dr. George's fractious household. Might the old missus part with Rachel and the infant to restore her house to its former peacefulness? Was it any wonder that he was worried?

Miss Alethea gave her children a look, and one by one they left the table, as if a command had been spoken aloud. When the two of them were alone, she said, "It's not right to separate a husband from his wife. I don't know what Dr. George was thinking when he brought you here to begin with."

"No, I asked him to. It seemed for the best. And my Rachel wasn't to be sold, so there wasn't any question of bringing her, too."

"Be that as it may, you have been here now, what? Three years? It is high time that Medical College did something about your situation. And a baby on the way as well. Yes, they must see about that."

"I suppose the doctors thought—"

"I know what they thought. They thought what all you men think—that you'd replace your wife and be glad of the chance. Folks said that about Mr. Butts, too, but they were wrong. Seven children we had, and he stayed with me until the day he died. Those doctors must see by now that you have not deserted your wife. You going so faithful on the train to see her every chance you get. Well, it's early days still. The baby not born yet, and many a slip, as they say. Let us wait and see if all goes well, and if it does, one day we will speak to Dr. George about it."

The anatomy classes did not often want babies. He was glad of that. He thought he might take to drink as old Clegg had done if he'd had to lift shrouded infants out of the ground during the months that he waited for his own child to be born in Charleston.

Women died in childbirth. No one knew better than he. The men he pulled from their shrouds in Cedar Grove were either old husks of humanity, worn out by work and weariness at a great age, or else young fools who lost a fight, or died of carelessness, their own or someone else's. But the women . . . It was indeed the curse of Eve. Sometimes the women died old, too, of course. Miss Alethea herself had borne seven babies, and would live to make old bones. She came of sturdy stock. But he saw many a young woman put into the clay before her time, with her killer wrapped in swaddling cloths and placed in her arms.

And the doctors did want those young mothers. Their musculature was better for study than the stringy sinews of old folks, Dr. Newton had told him. "A pregnant woman will make a good subject," he said, examining the body Grandison had brought in just before dawn. "Midwives see to all the normal births, of course, but when something goes wrong, they'll call in a doctor. When we attend a birth, it's always a bad sign. We need to know all we can."

"But why does birthing kill them?" Grandison had

asked. It was when he'd first learned about Rachel, and he wondered if the doctors here had some new sliver of knowledge that might save her, if it came to that. Surely this long procession of corpses had amounted to something.

George Newton thought the matter over carefully while he examined the swollen form of the young woman on the table before them. In the emptiness of death she looked too young to have borne a child. Well, she did not bear it. It remained inside her, a last secret to take away with her. Grandison stared at her, trying to remember her as a living being. He must have seen her among the crowds at the city market, perhaps, or laughing among the women on the lawn outside the church. But he could not place her. Whoever she had been was gone, and he was glad that he could summon no memory to call her back. It was easier to think of the bodies as so much cordwood to be gathered for the medical school. Had it not been for her swollen belly, he would not have given her a thought.

At last Dr. Newton said, "Why do they die? Now that's a question for the good Reverend Wilson over at the Presbyterian church across the street. He would tell you that their dying was the will of God, and the fulfillment of the curse on Eve for eating the apple, or some such nonsense as that. But I think . . ." He paused for a moment, staring at the flame of his match as if he'd forgotten the question.

"Yes, doctor? Why do you think they die?"

"Well, Grandison, I spent my boyhood watching the barn cats give birth and the hounds drop litters often at a time, and the hogs farrow a slew of piglets. And you know, those mothers never seemed to feel any pain in those birthings. But women are different. It kills some and half kills the rest.

And I asked myself why, same as you have, and I wondered if we could find something other than God to blame for it."

"Did you? Find something to blame besides God?"

Dr. Newton smiled. "Ourselves, I guess. The problem in childbirth is the baby's head. The rest of that little body slides through pretty well, but it's the head that gets caught and causes the problems. I suppose we need those big heads because our brains are bigger than a dog's or a pig's, but perhaps over the eons our heads have outgrown our bodies."

He thought it over. "But there's nothing I can do about that," he said, "I can't help Rachel."

The doctor nodded. "I know," he said. "Perhaps in this case Reverend Wilson would be more help to you than we doctors are. He would prescribe prayer, and I have nothing better to offer."

Newton turned to go, but another thought occurred to him. "Grandison, why don't you come in to class today?" He nodded toward the girl's swollen body. "She will be our subject today. Perhaps you'll feel better if you understood the process."

Grandison almost smiled. It would never occur to the studious bachelor that a man with a pregnant wife might be appalled by such a sight. Dr. George considered learning a cure in itself. Grandison did not think that was the case, but since learning was often useful for its own sake, he would not refuse the offer. And he would take care not to show disgust or fear, because that might prevent other offers to learn from coming his way. Doctoring would be a good skill to know. He had seen enough of death to want to fight back.

He had watched while the doctors cut open the blank-faced woman, and now he knew that the womb looked like a jellyfish from the Charleston docks, and that the birth canal made him think of a snake swallowing a baby rabbit, but the knowledge did nothing to allay his fears about Rachel's confinement. It was all right, though, in the end. Whether the prayers accomplished their object or whether his wife's sturdy body and rude good health had been her salvation, the child was safely delivered, and mother and baby thrived. He called that first son "George," in honor of Dr. Newton, hoping the gesture would make the old bachelor feel benevolent toward Rachel and the boy.

After that he got into the habit of sitting in on the medical classes when he could spare the time from his other duties. Apart from the big words the doctors used, the learning didn't seem too difficult. Once you learned what the organs looked like and how to find them in the body, the rest followed logically. They were surprised to learn that he could read—his lessons with the Taylor children had served him well. After a while, no one took any notice of him at all in the anatomy classes, and presently the doctors grew accustomed to calling on him to assist them in the demonstrations. He was quiet and competent, and they noticed his helpfulness, rather than the fact that he, too, was learning medicine.

He had been in Augusta four years. By now he was as accustomed to the rhythm of the academic year as he had once been attuned to the seasonal cadence of the farm. He had taken Alethea Taylor's advice and made himself quietly indispensable, so that at work the doctors scarcely had to give him a thought, except to hand over money for whatever supplies he needed for the task at hand or for his personal use. No one ever questioned his demands for money these days. They simply handed over whatever he asked for, and went back to what they had been doing before he had interrupted.

Sixteen bodies per term for the anatomy class. He could read well now, thanks to the Taylor daughters, although they would be shocked if they knew that he found this skill most useful in reading the death notices in the *Chronicle*. When there were not enough bodies available in the county to meet this need, Grandison was authorized to purchase what he needed. A ten-dollar gold piece for each subject. Two hundred gallons of whiskey purchases each year for the preservation of whole corpses or of whatever organs of interest the doctors wished to keep for further study, and if he bought a bit more spirits than that amount, no one seemed to notice. It never went to waste.

He tapped on the door of George Newton's office. "Morning, Dr. George. It's train time again."

The doctor looked up as if he had forgotten where he was. "Train time?—Oh, yes, of course. Your family. Sit down, Grandison. Perhaps we should talk."

He forced himself to keep smiling, because it didn't do any good to argue with a man who could break your life in two. He wasn't often asked to sit down when he talked to the doctors, and he made no move toward the chair. He assumed an expression of anxious concern. "Is there anything I can help you with, Dr. George?" he said.

The doctor tapped his pen against the ledger. "It's just

that I've been thinking, you know. Twelve dollars a month for train fare, for you to go and see your wife."

"And child," said Grandison, keeping his voice steady.

"Yes, of course. Well, I was thinking about it, and I'll have to talk it over with the rest of the faculty—"

I could take a second job, he was thinking. *Maybe earn the money for train fare myself . . .*

But Dr. George said, "I shall persuade them to purchase your family."

It took him a moment to sort out the words, so contrary were they to the ones he had anticipated. He had to bite back the protests that had risen in his throat. "Buy Rachel and George?"

The doctor smiled. "Oh, yes. I shall explain that we could save enough money in train fare to justify the purchase price within a few years. It does make fiscal sense. Besides, I have lately come to realize how much you must miss them."

Grandison turned these words over in his mind. If one of the cadavers had got up from the dissecting table and walked away, he could not have been more surprised. He never mentioned his wife and son except to respond with a vague pleasantry on the rare occasion that someone asked after them. Why had the doctor suddenly taken this charitable notion? Why not when the baby was first born? Dr. George was a kind man, in an absent-minded sort of way, but he hardly noticed his own feelings, let alone anybody else's. Grandison stood with his back to the door, the smile still frozen to his lips, wondering what had come over the man.

George Newton rubbed his forehead and sighed. He started to speak, and then shook his head. He began again, "It may be a few months before we can find the money, mind you. It should take about thirteen hundred dollars to buy both your wife and son. That should do it, surely. I'll write to your wife's mistress in Charleston to negotiate the purchase."

Grandison nodded. "Thank you," he whispered. The joy would come later, when the news had sunk in. Just now he was still wondering what had come over Dr. George.

"I'm going to be moving out one of these days," he told Alethea Taylor that night after supper.

She sat in her straight-backed chair closest to the lamp, embroidering a baby dress. "You'll be needing to find a place for your family to live," she said, still intent upon her work.

He laughed. "The world can't keep nothing from you, Miz Taylor. Dr. George told you?"

"Fanny told me." She set the baby dress down on the lamp table, and wiped her eyes. "She's been after George to bring them here, and he promised he would see to it."

"I wondered what put it into his head. Saying he was going to buy them, right out of the blue, without me saying a word about it. I can't make out what's come over him."

She made no reply, but her frown deepened as she went on with her sewing.

"I don't suppose you know what this is all about?"

She wiped her eyes on the hem of the cloth. "Yes. I know. I may as well tell you. Dr. George and Fanny are—well, man and wife, I would say, though the state of Georgia won't countenance it. Fanny has a baby coming soon."

He was silent for a bit, thinking out what to say. Dr. George was in his forties, and looked every minute of it. Fanny was a slender and beautiful sixteen. He knew how it would sound to a stranger, but he had known Dr. George five years now, and for all the physician's wealth and prominence, he couldn't help seeing him as a gray-haired mole, peering out at the world from his book-lined burrow, while the graceful Fanny seemed equal to anything. He knew—he *knew*—of light-skinned women forced to become their owners' mistresses, but Fanny was free, and besides he couldn't see her mother allowing such a thing to happen. Miss Alethea did not have all the rights of a white woman, though you'd take her for one to look at her, but still, there were some laws to protect free people of color. Through her dress-making business, Miss Alethea had enough friends among her lady clientele that if she'd asked, some lady's lawyer husband would have intervened. The white ladies hated the idea of their menfolk taking colored mistresses, and they'd jump at the chance to put a stop to it. Someone would have been outraged by such a tale, and they would have been eager to save Miss Alethea's young daughter from a wicked seducer. But . . . *Dr. George?* He couldn't see it. Why, for all his coolness in cutting up the dead, when it came to dealing with live folks, Dr. George wouldn't say boo to a goose.

"He didn't . . . force her?" he asked, looking away as he said it. But when he looked back and saw Miss Alethea's expression, his lips twitched, and then they both began to laugh in spite of it all.

Miss Alethea shook her head. "*Force? Dr. George?* Oh, my. I can't even think it was his idea, Mr. Harris. You know how he is."

"Well, is Miss Fanny happy?" he said at last.

"Humph. Sixteen years old and a rich white doctor

thinks she hung the moon. What do you think?" She sighed. "When a man falls in love for the first time when he's past forty, it hits him hard. Seems like he's taken leave of his senses."

"Oh. Well," he cast about for some word of comfort, and settled on, "I won't tell anybody."

She stabbed her needle at the cloth. "Shout it from the rooftops if you feel like it, Mr. Harris. It's not as if *they're* keeping it a secret. He wants to marry her."

He smiled. "Anybody would, Miss Alethea. Mary Frances is a beautiful girl."

"You misunderstand, Mr. Harris. I'm saying that he *means* to marry her."

"And stay here? And let folks know about it?"

She nodded. "I'm saying. Live as man and wife, right there on Greene Street."

Now he realized why George Newton had suddenly understood the pain of his separation from Rachel, but he felt that the doctor's newfound wisdom had come at the price of folly. St. Paul's seeing the light on the road to Damascus might have been a blessed miracle, but Dr. George's light was more likely to be a thunderbolt. "He can't do that," he said. "Set her up as his wife."

"Not without losing his position he can't." The needle stabbed again. "Don't you think I've told them that?"

"And what did he say?"

"He's going to resign from the medical school, that's what. Says he has money enough. Going to continue his work in a laboratory at home. Huh!" She shook her head at the folly of it.

He thought about it. Perhaps in Charleston such a thing

might work. Down in the islands, certainly. Martinique. Everybody knew that the French . . . But *here?*

"I even asked him, Mr. Harris, I said straight out, *Do you remember Richard Mentor Johnson?*" His expression told her that he did not remember, either. But she did. "Richard Mentor Johnson of Kentucky. He was the vice president of the United States, back when I was a girl. Under President Van Buren. Folks said that he had killed the Indian chief Tecumseh, which they thought made him a hero. But then he had also married a woman of color, and when word of that got out, they tried to run him out of office on account of it. When his first term was over, he gave up and went home to Kentucky. And, do you know, Mr. Johnson's wife wasn't even alive by that time. She had died before he ever went to Washington to be vice president. Just the memory of her was enough to ruin him. Now, how well does Dr. George think he will fare in Georgia with a *live* colored wife in his house?"

"But Miss Fanny—to look at her—"

"I know. She's whiter to look at than some of the doctors' wives, but that makes no difference. This is a small town, Mr. Harris. Everybody knows everybody. Fanny can't pass in Augusta, and they both say they've no mind to go elsewhere."

He thought he had made all the proper expressions of sympathy and commiseration, but he was thinking just as much about the effect that Dr. George's folly would have on him. Would this change of heart mean no more robbing Cedar Grove? Or in his madness would the doctor insist on obtaining an equal number of bodies from the white burying ground? Equality was a fine thing, but not if it got him hanged by a white lynch mob.

* * *

He swept the upstairs hall four times that morning, waiting for Dr. George to be alone in his office. Finally the last visitor left, and he tapped on the door quickly before anyone else could turn up. "Excuse me, Dr. George. We're getting low on supplies for the anatomy classes," he said.

He always said "supplies" instead of "bodies" even when they were alone, just in case anyone happened to overhear.

Dr. George gave him a puzzled frown. "Supplies? Oh— oh, I see. Not filled our quota yet? Well, are there any fresh ones to be had?"

"A burying today," he said. "Little boy fell off a barn roof. I just wondered if you wanted me to take him."

"Yes, I suppose so. He's needed. Though we could use a yellow fever victim if you hear of one. Must teach the Southern diseases, you know. Medical schools up north don't know a thing about them." Dr. George looked up. "Why did you ask about this boy in particular? Do you know him?"

That didn't matter. He had known them all for years now. Some he minded about more than others, but all of them had long ceased to be merely lumps of clay in his hands. "It's all right," he said. "I don't mind bringing him in. I just wondered what you wanted me to do, and if there's to be a new dean—"

The doctor leaned back in his chair and sighed. "Yes, I see, Grandison. You have heard."

"Yes."

"It's true that I am resigning the post of dean. I felt that it was better for the college if I did so." He picked up a sheaf of papers from his desk and held it out with a bemused smile. "But it seems that I shall be staying on as Emeritus Professor of Anatomy, after all. This is a petition, signed by all of the students and faculty, asking that I stay. And the Board of Trustees has acceded to their request."

"Do they know?"

"About Fanny? They do. They profess not to care. I suppose when one is a doctor, one sees how little difference there really is between the races. Just a thin layer of skin, that's all, and then it's all the same underneath. Whatever the reason, they insist that I stay on in some capacity, and I shall."

"So nothing will change? For me, I mean?"

George Newton shook his head. "We still must have bodies, and the only safe place to obtain them is from Cedar Grove. That has not changed. And I fancy that I shall still have enough influence to bring your family to Augusta. I do not intend to shirk my duty, so you may go and see to yours."

Madison Newton was born on the last day of February, red-faced, fair-haired, and hazel-eyed, looking like a squashed cabbage leaf, but a white one, after all.

"It's a fine baby," he had said to Fanny, when she brought the baby to her mother's house on a mild day in March.

Fanny switched the blanket back into place, so that only the infant's nose peeped out. "People only want to look at him to see what color he is," she said. "What do they expect? He had sixteen great-great grandparents, same as everybody, and only one of them was colored. All the rest of him from then on down is white. Of course, that doesn't change what he is to most folks' way of thinking."

He had kept smiling and said the plain truth: that the infant was a fortunate child, but he had been angry, and his annoyance had not left him. That night in Cedar Grove in a fine mist of rain, he dug as if he could inflict an injury upon the earth itself, "I reckon Miss Fanny is whiter in her head than she is on her face," he said to the darkness, thrusting the shovel deep into the ground. "Feeling sorry for a light-eyed baby born free, his daddy a rich white doctor. I guess pretty Miss Fanny wants the moon, even when it's raining."

He spared hardly a thought for the man in the box below. Some drunken laborer from the docks, hit too hard over the head in a brawl. He had even forgotten the name. An easy task tonight. No shells or flowers decorated this grave site. The dead man had been shunted into the ground without grief or ceremony. Just as well take him to the doctors, where he could do some good for once. His thoughts returned to his grievance. Spoiled Miss Fanny had never given a thought to his baby when she was complaining about her own son's lot in life. How would she have liked to be Rachel—separated from her husband, and left to raise a child without him, knowing that at any time old missus might take a notion to sell that child, and nothing could be done to stop it.

He brushed the dirt from the pine box, and stove in the lid with his shovel point. Miss Fanny Taylor didn't know what trouble was, complaining about—

A sound.

Something like a moan, coming from inside the smashed coffin. He forgot about Fanny and her baby, as he knelt in the loose dirt of the open grave, pressing his ear close to the lid of the box. He held his breath, straining to hear a repetition of the sound. In the stillness, with all his thoughts focused on the dark opening before him, he realized that something else was wrong with the grave site. The smell was wrong. The sickly sweet smell of newly decaying flesh should have been coming from the box, but it wasn't. Neither was the stench of voided bowels, the last letting-go of the dead. All he smelled was rotgut whiskey.

He gripped the corpse under the armpits and pulled it out of the grave, but instead of sacking it up, he laid the body out on the damp grass. It groaned.

He had heard such sounds from a corpse before. The first time it happened, he had been unloading a sack from the wagon into the store room at the medical college. He had dropped the sack and gone running to Dr. George, shouting that the deader from the burying ground had come back to life.

George Newton had smiled for an instant, but without a word of argument, he'd followed the porter back to the store room and examined the sacked-up body. He had felt the wrist and neck for a pulse, and even leaned into the dead face to check for breath, but Grandison could tell from his calm and deliberate movements that he knew what he would find. "The subject is dead," he said, standing up, and brushing traces of dirt from his trousers.

"It just died then. I heard it moan."

Dr. George smiled gently. "Yes, I believe you did, Grandison, but it was dead all the same."

"A ghost then?"

"No. Merely a natural process. When the body dies, there is still air trapped within the lungs. Sometimes when that air leaves the lungs it makes a moaning sound. Terrifying, I know. I heard it once myself in my student days, but it is only a remnant of life, not life itself. This poor soul has been dead at least a day."

He never forgot that sound, though in all the bodies that had passed through his hands on the way to the dissecting table, he had never heard it since.

The sound coming now from the man stretched out on the grass was different. And it changed—low and rumbling at first, and then louder. He knelt beside the groaning man and shook his shoulder.

"Hey!" he said. "Hey, now—" His voice was hoarse and unnaturally loud in the still darkness of Cedar Grove. *What can you say to a dead man?*

The groan changed to a cough, and then the man rolled over and vomited into the mound of spaded earth.

He sighed, and edged away a few feet. He had seen worse. Smelled worse. But finding a live body in the graveyard complicated matters. He sat quietly, turning the possibilities over in his mind, until the retching turned to sobbing.

"You're all right," he said, without turning around.

"This is the graveyard. Badger Benson done killed me?"

"I guess he tried. But you woke up. Who are you, anyhow?"

"I was fixing to ask you that. How did you come to find me down in the ground? You don't look like no angel."

He smiled. "Might be yours, though. You slave or free, boy?"

"Belong to Mr. Johnson. Work on his boat."

"Thought so. Well, you want to go back to Mr. Johnson, do you?"

The man stretched and kicked his legs, stiff from his interment. "I dunno," he said. "Why you ask me that?"

" 'Cause you were dead, boy, as far as anybody knows. They buried you this morning. Now if you was to go back to your master, there'd be people asking me questions

about how I come to find you, and they'd take you back
to Johnson's, and you'd still be a slave, and like as not
I'd be in trouble for digging you up. But if you just lit out
of here and never came back, why nobody would ever
even know you were gone and that this grave was empty.
You're dead. You don't let 'em find out any different, and
they'll never even know to hunt for you."

The man rubbed the bruise on the back of his head.
"Now how did you come to find me?"

Grandison stood up and retrieved the shovel. "This is
where the medical school gets the bodies to cut up for the
surgery classes. The doctors at the college were fixing to rip
you open. And they still can, I reckon, unless you light out of
here. Now, you tell me, boy, do you want to be dead again?"

The young man raised a hand as if to ward off a blow. "No.
No!—I understand you right enough. I got to get gone."

"And you don't go back for nothing. You don't tell
nobody goodbye. You are dead, and you leave it at that."

The young man stood up and took a few tentative steps
on still unsteady legs. "Where do I go then?"

Grandison shrugged. "If it was me, I would go west. Over
the mountains into Indian country. You go far enough,
there's places that don't hold with slavery. I'd go there."

The man turned to look at him. "Well, why don't you
then?" he said. "Why don't *you* go?"

"Don't worry about me. I'm not the one who's dead. Now
are you leaving or not?"

"Yeah. Leaving."

"You've got three hours before sunup." He handed the
shovel to the resurrected man. "Help me fill in your
grave, then."

Dr. George Newton—December 1859

It is just as well that I stepped down as dean of the medical college. I haven't much time to wind up my affairs, and the fact that Ignatius Garvin is ably discharging my former duties leaves me with one less thing to worry about. If I can leave my dear Fanny and the babies safely provided for, I may leave this world without much regret. I wish I could have seen my boy grow up . . . wish I could have grown old with my dearest wife . . . And I wish that God had seen fit to send me an easier death.

No one knows yet that I am dying, and it may yet be weeks before the disease carries me off, but I do not relish the thought of the time before me, for I know enough of this illness to tremble at the thought of what will come. I must not do away with myself, though. I must be brave, so as not to cause Fanny any more pain than she will feel at losing me so soon.

So many papers to sift through. Investments, deeds, instructions for the trustees—my life never felt so complicated. Soon the pain will begin, and it may render me incapable of making wise decisions to safeguard my little family. At least I have safeguarded the family of our faithful college servant, Grandison Harris. Thank God I was able to do that in time, for I had long promised him that I would bring his Rachel and her boy to Augusta, so I did a few months back. I am not yet fifty, sound in body and mind, and newly married. I thought I had many years to do good works and to continue my medical research. I suppose that even a physician must think that he will never face death. Perhaps we would go mad if we tried to live thinking otherwise.

I wonder how it happened. People will say it was the buggy

accident just before Christmas, and perhaps it was. That gelding is a nervous horse, not at all to be depended upon in busy streets of barking dogs and milling crowds. I must remember to tell Henry to sell the animal, for I would not like to think of Fanny coming to harm if the beast became spooked again. I was shaken and bruised when he dumped me out of the carriage and into the mud, but did I sustain any cuts during the fall? I do not remember any blood.

Dr. Eve came to look me over, and he pronounced me fit enough, with no bones broken, and no internal injuries. He was right as far as it went. My fellow physicians all stopped by to wish us good cheer at Christmas, and to pay their respects to their injured friend. They did not bring their wives, of course. No respectable white woman accepts the hospitality of this house, for it is supposed that Fanny's presence taints the household. We are not, after all, legally married in the eyes of the law here. Fanny professes not to care. *Dull old biddies,* anyhow, she declares. But she has certainly charmed the gentlemen, who consider me a lucky man. And so I was, until this tragedy struck—though none of those learned doctors suspected it.

I wish that I had not. I wish that I could go innocently into the throes of this final illness, as would a child who had stepped on a rusty nail, not knowing what horrors lay before me. But I am a trained physician. I do know. And the very word clutches at my throat with cold fingers.

Tetanus.

Oh, I know too much, indeed. Too much—and not enough. I have seen people die of this. The muscles stretch and spasm, in the control of the ailment rather than the patient, an agonizing distension such as prisoners must

have felt upon the rack in olden days. The body is tortured
by pain beyond imagining, but beyond these physical tor-
ments, the patient's mind remains clear and unaffected. I
doubt that the clarity is a blessing. Delirium or madness
might prove a release from the agony, yet even that is
denied to the sufferer. And there is no cure. Nothing can
stop the progression of this disease, and nothing can
reverse its effects. I have, perhaps, a week before the end,
and I am sure that by then I will not dread death, but
rather welcome it as a blessed deliverance.

Best not to dwell on it. It will engulf me soon enough. I
must send for James Hope. I can trust him. As the owner
of the cotton mill, he will be an eminently respectable
guardian for my wife's business interests, and since James
is a Scotsman by birth, and not bound by the old Southern
traditions of race and caste, he will see Fanny as the gen-
tlewoman that she is. He treats her with all the courtly
gentility he would show to a duchess, and that endears him
to both of us. Yes, I must tell James what has happened, and
how soon he must pick up where I am forced to leave off.

My poor Fanny! To be left a widow with two babies, and
she is not yet twenty. I worry more over her fate than I do
my own. At least mine will be quick, but Fanny has
another forty years to suffer if the world is unkind to her.
I wish that the magnitude of my suffering could be charged
against any sorrow God had intended for her. I must speak
to James Hope. How aptly named he is! I must entrust my
little family to him.

It was nearly Christmas, and Rachel had made a pound
cake for the Newtons. He was to take it around to Greene

Street that afternoon, when he could manage to get away from his duties. Grandison looked at the cake, and thought that Dr. George might prefer a specimen from the medical school supply for his home laboratory, but he supposed that such a gesture would not be proper for the season. Rachel would know best what people expected on social occasions. She talked to people, and visited with her new friends at church, while he hung back, dreading the prospect of talking to people that he might be seeing again some day.

He took the cake to the Newton house, and tapped on the back door, half expecting it to open before his hand touched the wood. He waited a minute, and then another, but no one came. He knocked again, harder this time, wondering at the delay. As many servants as the Newtons had, that door ought to open as soon as his foot hit the porch. What was keeping them so busy?

Finally, after the third and loudest spate of knocking, Fanny herself opened the door. He smiled and held out his paper-wrapped Christmas offering, but the sight of her made him take a step backward. His words of greeting stuck in his throat. She was big-bellied with child again, he knew that. She looked as if it could come at any moment, but what shocked him was how ill she looked, as if she had not eaten or slept for a week. She stared out at him, hollow-eyed and trembling, her face blank with weariness. For a moment he wondered if she recognized him.

"My Rachel made y'all a pound cake. For Christmas," he said.

She nodded, and stepped back from the door to admit him to the kitchen. "Put it on the table," she said.

He set down the cake. The house was unnaturally quiet.

He listened for sounds of baby Madison playing, or the bustle of the servants, who should have been making the house ready for the holiday, but all was still. He looked back at Fanny, who was staring down at the parcel as if she had never seen one before, as if she had forgotten how it got there, perhaps.

"Are you all right?" he asked. "Shall I fetch Miss Alethea for you?"

Fanny shook her head. "She's been already. She took Madison so that I can stay with George," she whispered. "And I've sent most of the others around there, too. Henry stayed here, of course. He won't leave George."

Something was the matter with Dr. George, then. It must be bad. Fanny looked half dead herself. "Shall I go for Dr. Eve?" he asked.

"He was here this morning. So was Dr. Garvin. Wasn't a bit of use. George told me that from the beginning, but I wouldn't have it. I thought with all those highfalutin doctors somebody would be able to help him, but they can't. They can't."

"Is he took bad?"

"He's dying. It's the lockjaw. You know what that is?"

He nodded. Tetanus. Oh, yes. They had covered it in one of the medical classes, but not to consider a course of treatment. Only to review the terrible symptoms and to hope they never saw them. He shivered. "Are they sure?"

"George is sure. Diagnosed himself. And the others concur. I was the only one who wouldn't believe it. I do now, though. I sit with him as long as I can. Hour after hour. Watch him fighting the pain. Fighting the urge to scream. And then I go and throw up, and I sit with him some more."

"I could spell you a while."

"No!" She said it so harshly that he took a step back in surprise. She took a deep breath, and seemed to swallow her anger. "No, thank you very kindly, Mr. Harris, but I will not let you see him."

"But if Dr. George is dying—"

"That's exactly why. Don't you think I know what you do over there at the medical college? Porter, they call you. *Porter.* I know what your real duties are, Mr. Harris. Known for a long time. And that's fine. I know doctors have to learn somehow, and that nothing about doctoring is pretty or easy. But you are not going to practice your trade in this house. You are not going to take my husband's body, do you hear?"

He said softly, "I only wanted to help you out, and maybe to tell him good-bye."

"So you say. But he is weak now. Half out of his mind with the pain, and he'd promise anything. He might even suggest it himself, out of some crazy sense of duty to the medical college, but I won't have it. My husband is going to have a proper burial, Mr. Harris. He has suffered enough."

It doesn't hurt, he wanted to tell her. *You don't feel it if you're dead.* He did not bother to speak the words. He knew whose pain Fanny was thinking of, and that whatever Dr. George's wishes might be, it was the living who mattered, not the dead. Best to soothe her quickly and with as little argument as possible. He did not think that the other doctors would accept George Newton's body anyhow. That would be bringing death too close into the fold, and he was glad that he would not be required to carry out that task. Let the doctor lie in consecrated ground: There were bodies enough to be had in Augusta.

"I'll go now, Miss Fanny," he said, putting on his best

white folks manners, if it would give her any comfort. "But I think one of the doctors should come back and take a look at you." He nodded toward her distended belly. "And we will pray for the both of you, my Rachel and I. Pray that he gets through this." It was a lie. He never prayed, but if he did, it would be for Dr. George's death to come swiftly—the only kindness that could be hoped for in a case of tetanus.

Dr. George died after the new year in 1860. The illness had lasted only two weeks, but the progress of the disease was so terrible that it had begun to seem like months to those who could do nothing but wait for his release from the pain. Grandison joined the crowd at the doctor's funeral, though he took care to keep clear of Fanny, for fear of upsetting her again. In her grief she might shout out things that should not be said aloud in Augusta's polite society. The doctors knew his business, of course, but not the rest of the town. He reckoned that most of Augusta would have been at the funeral if it weren't for the fact of the doctor's awkward marriage arrangements. As it was, though, his fellow physicians, the students, and most of the town's businessmen came to pay their respects, while their wives and daughters stayed home, professing themselves too delicate to endure the sight of the doctor's redbone widow. Not that you could see an inch of her skin, whatever its color, for she was swathed from head to foot in black widow's weeds and veils, leaning on the arm of Mr. James Hope, as if he were the spar of her sinking ship.

"Left a widow at eighteen," said Miss Alethea, regal in her black dress, her eyes red from tears of her own. "I had hoped for better for my girl."

He nodded. "She will be all right," he said. "Dr. George would have seen to that."

Miss Alethea gave him the look usually reserved for one of her children talking foolishness. "She's back home again, you know. Dr. George was too clouded at the last to do justice to a will, and Mr. James Hope had to sell the house on Greene Street. He vows to see her settled in a new place, though, over on Ellis, just a block from Broad Street. Having it built. There's all Dr. George's people to be thought of, you know, and the Tuttle folks, as well. Fanny has to have a house of her own, but I'm glad to have her by me for now, for the new baby is due any day—if it lives through her grief. We must pray for her, Mr. Harris."

Grandison looked past her at the tall, fair-haired Scotsman, who was still hovering protectively beside the pregnant young widow, and wondered if the prayer had already been answered.

The cellar was paved with bones now. Each term when the anatomy class had finished with its solemn duties of dissection, the residue was brought to him to be disposed of. He could hardly rebury the remains in any public place or discard them where they might be recognized for what they were. The only alternative was to layer them in quicklime in the basement on Telfair Street. How many hundred had it been now? He had lost count. Mercifully the faces and the memories of the subjects' resurrection were fading with the familiarity of the task, but sometimes he wondered if the basement resounded with cries he could not hear, and if that was why the building's cat refused to set foot down there. The quicklime finished taking away the flesh and masked the smell, but he wondered what part of the owners remained, and if that *great getting up in the morning* that the preacher spoke of was really going to come to pass on Judgment Day. And who would have to answer for the monstrous confusion and scramble of bones that must follow? Himself? Dr. George? The students who carved up the cadavers? Sometimes as he scattered the quicklime over a new batch of discarded bones, he mused on Dr. George peering over the wrought iron fence of white folks' heaven at an angry crowd of colored angels shaking their fists at him.

"Better the dead than the living, though," he would tell himself.

Sometimes on an afternoon walk to Cedar Grove, he would go across to the white burying ground to pay his respects to Dr. George, lying there undisturbed in his grave, and sometimes he would pass the time of day with the grassy mound, as if the doctor could still hear him. "Miss Mary Frances finally birthed that baby," he said one winter day, picking the brown stems of dead flowers off the grave. "Had a little girl the other day. Named her Georgia Frances, but everybody calls her Cissie, and I think that's the name that's going to stick. She's a likely little thing, pale as a Georgia peach. And Mr. James Hope is building her that house on Ellis like he promised, and she's talking about having her sister Nannie and young Jimmie move in along with her. I thought maybe Mr. James Hope would be moving in, too, the way he dotes on her, but he's talking about selling the factory here and going back to New York where his family is, so I don't think you need to linger on here if you are, sir. I think everything is going to be all right."

*   *   *

Dr. George hadn't been gone hardly more than two years when the war came, and that changed everything. Didn't look like it would at first, though. For the rest of the country, the war began in April in Charleston, when Fort Sumpter fell, but Georgia had seceded in January, leaving Augusta worried about the arsenal on the hill, occupied by federal troops. Governor Joe Brown himself came to town to demand the surrender of the arsenal, and the town was treated to a fine show of military parades in the drizzling rain. Governor Brown himself stood on the porch of the Planters Hotel to watch the festivities, but Captain Elzey, who was in command of the eighty-two men at the arsenal, declined to surrender it. He changed his mind a day or so later when eight hundred soldiers and two brigadier generals turned up in the rain to show the arsenal they meant business. Then Captain Elzey sent for the governor to talk things over, and by noon the arsenal and its contents had been handed over to the sovereign State of Georgia, without a shot fired. That, and a lot of worrying, was pretty much all that happened to Augusta for the duration of the war.

When the shooting actually started in Charleston, he was glad that Rachel and the boy were safe in Augusta, instead of being caught in the middle of a war, though personally he would have liked to see the battle for the novelty of it. Everybody said the war was only going to last a few weeks, and he hated to have missed getting a glimpse of it.

Folks were optimistic, but they were making preparations anyhow. Two weeks after Fort Sumpter, Augusta organized a local company of home guards, the Silver Grays, composed mostly of men too old to fight in the reg-

ular army. Mr. James Hope came back from New York City
to stand with the Confederacy and got himself chosen
second member of the company, after Rev. Joseph Wilson,
who was the first. Rev. Wilson's boy Tommy and little
Madison Newton were the same age, and they sometimes
played together on the lawn of the Presbyterian church,
across the road from the college. Sometimes the two of
them would come over and pepper him with questions
about bodies and sick folks, and he often thought that
you'd have to know which boy was which to tell which one
wasn't the white child. Fanny kept young Madison as clean
and well-dressed as any quality child in Augusta.

The months went by, and the war showed no signs of
letting up. One by one the medical students drifted away
to enlist in regiments back home.

"I don't suppose you'll have to worry about procuring any
more cadavers for classes, Grandison," Dr. Garvin told him.

"No, sir," he said. "I've heard a lot of the students are
fixing to quit and join up."

Dr. Garvin scowled. "I expect they will, but even if the
school stays open, this war will produce enough cadavers
to supply a thousand medical schools before it's over."

There wasn't any fighting in Augusta, but they saw their
share of casualties anyhow. A year into the war, the
wounded began arriving by train from distant battlefields,
and the medical school suspended operation in favor of setting up hospitals to treat the wounded. The City Hotel and
the Academy of Richmond County were turned into hospitals in '62 to accommodate the tide of injured soldiers
flowing into the city from far off places with unfamiliar

names, like Manassas and Shiloh. Many of the faculty members had gone off to serve in the war as well. Dr. Campbell
was in Virginia with the Georgia Hospital Association, seeing
to the state's wounded up there; Dr. Miller and Dr. Ford
were serving with the Confederate forces at different places
up in Virginia, and Dr. Jones was somewhere on the Georgia
coast contributing his medical skills to the war effort.

Grandison worked in one of the hospitals, assisting the
doctors at first, but as the number of casualties strained
their ability to treat them, he took on more and more
duties to fill the gap.

"I don't see why you are working so hard to patch those
Rebels up," one of the porters said to him one day, when
he went looking for a roll of clean bandages. "The Federals
say they are going to end slavery, and here you are helping
the enemy."

He shrugged. "I don't see any Federals in Augusta, do
you? I don't see any army coming here to hand me my
freedom. So meanwhile I do what I'm supposed to do,
and we'll see what transpires when the war is over."
Besides, he thought, it was one thing to wish the Confederacy to perdition, and quite another to ignore the
suffering of a single boy soldier who couldn't even grow
a proper beard yet.

Sometimes he wondered what had happened to the man
he "resurrected" who wasn't dead—whether the fellow had
made it to some free state beyond the mountains, and
whether that had made any difference.

He didn't know if freedom was coming, or what it would
feel like, but for the here and now there was enough work
for ten of him. So he stitched, and bandaged, and dressed

wounds. *I've handled dead people,* he told himself. *This isn't any worse than that.*

But of course it was.

The boy was a South Carolina soldier, eighteen or so, with copper-colored hair and a sunny nature that not even a gaping leg wound could dampen. The pet of the ward, he was, and he seemed to be healing up nicely what with all the rest and the mothering from Augusta's lady hospital visitors. The nurses were already talking about the preparations to send him home.

Grandison was walking down the hall that morning, when one of the other patients came hobbling out into the hall and clutched at his coat sleeve. "You got to come now!" the man said. "Little Will just started bleeding a gusher."

He hurried into the ward past the crippled soldier and pushed his way through the patients clustered around the young man's cot. A blood-soaked sheet was pulled back revealing a skinny white leg with a spike of bone protruding through the skin. Jets of dark blood erupted from the bone splinter's puncture. Without a word Grandison sat down beside the boy and closed his fingers over the ruptured skin.

"I just tried to walk to the piss pot," the boy said. He sounded close to passing out. "I got so tired of having to be helped all the time. I felt fine. I just wanted to walk as far as the wall."

He nodded. The mending thigh bone had snapped under the boy's weight, severing a leg artery as the splintered bone slid out of place. The men crowded around the bed murmured among themselves, but no one spoke to the boy.

"Shall I fetch the surgeon?" one of the patients asked Grandison.

He shook his head. "Surgeon's amputating this morning. Wouldn't do no good to call him anyhow."

The boy looked up at him. "Can you stop it, sir?"

He looked away, knowing that the *sir* was for his medical skills and not for himself, but touched by it all the same. The red-haired boy had a good heart. He was a great favorite with his older and sadder comrades.

"Get a needle?" somebody said. "Sew it back in?"

He kept his fingers clamped tight over the wound, but he couldn't stay there forever. He wanted to say: *Y'all ever see a calf killed? Butcher takes a sharp knife and slits that cord in his throat, and he bleeds out in—what? A minute? Two?* It was the same here. The severed artery was not in the neck, no, but the outcome would be the same—and it was just as inevitable.

"But I feel all right," said the boy. "No pain."

He ignored the crowd around the bed and looked straight into the brown eyes of the red-haired boy. "Your artery's cut in two," he said. "Can't nothing remedy that."

"Can you stop the bleeding?"

He nodded toward his fingers pressed against the pale white skin. The warmth of the flesh made him want to pull away. He took a deep breath. "I have stopped it," he said, nodding toward his hand stanching the wound. "But all the time you've got is until I let go."

The boy stared at him for a moment while the words sunk in. Then he nodded. "I see," he said. "Can you hold on a couple minutes? Let me say a prayer."

Somebody said, "I got paper here, Will. You ought to tell your folks good-bye. I'll write it down."

The boy looked the question at Grandison, who glanced down at his hand. "Go ahead," he said. "I can hold it."

In a faltering voice the boy spoke the words of farewell to his parents. He sounded calm, but puzzled, as if it were happening to someone else. That was just as well. Fear wouldn't change anything, and it was contagious. They didn't need a panic in the ward. The room was silent as the boy's voice rose and fell. Grandison turned away from the tear-stained faces to stare at a fly speck on the wall, wishing that he could be elsewhere while this lull before dying dragged on. These last minutes of life should not be witnessed by strangers.

The letter ended, and a few minutes after that the prayers, ending with a whispered amen as the last words of the Lord's Prayer trailed off into sobs.

He looked at the boy's sallow face, and saw in it a serenity shared by no one else in the room. "All right?" he said.

The boy nodded, and Grandison took his hand away.

A minute later the boy was dead. Around the bedstead the soldiers wept, and Grandison covered the still form with the sheet and went back to his duties. He had intended to go to the death room later to talk to the boy, to tell him that death was a release from worse horrors and to wish him peace, but there were so many wounded, and so much to be done that he never went.

The war came to Augusta on stretchers and in the form of food shortages and lack of mercantile goods—but never on horseback with flags flying and the sound of bugles. Augusta thought it would, of course. When Sherman marched to the sea by way of Savannah, troops crowded into the city to defend it, and the city fathers piled up bales of cotton, ready to torch them and the rest of the town with it to keep the powder works and the arsenal out of Union hands, but Sherman ignored them and pushed on north into South Carolina.

Three months later the war ended, and federal troops did come to occupy the city.

"I am a throne, Grandison!" Tommy Wilson announced one May morning. "And Madison here, he's only a dominion."

"That's fine," he said without a glance at the two boys. He was cleaning out the little work room at the college on Telfair Street. It had been his headquarters and his storage room for thirteen years now, but the war was over and he was free. It was time to be his own master now somewhere else. He thought he might cross the river to Hamburg. Folks said that the Yankees over there were putting freed-men into jobs to replace the white men. He would have to see.

Tommy Wilson's words suddenly took shape in his mind. "A throne?" he said. "I thought a throne was a king's chair."

"Well, a throne can be that," said Tommy, with the air of one who is determined to be scrupulously fair. "But it's also a rank of angels. We're playing angels, me and Madison. We're going to go out and convert the heathens."

"Well, that's a fine thing, boys. You go and—*what* heathens?"

"The soldiers," said Madison.

Tommy nodded. "They misbehave something awful, you know. They drink and fight and take the Lord's name in vain."

"And by God we're gonna fix 'em," said Madison.

"Does your father know where you are?"

Tommy nodded. "He said I could play outside."

Madison Newton shrugged. "Mr. Hope don't care where I go. He's living up at my house now, but he's not my daddy.

He says he's gonna take Momma and their new babies up north with him, but me and Cissie can't go."

Grandison nodded. Fanny Newton was now called Fanny Hope, and she had two more babies with magnolia skin and light eyes. He wondered what would become of Dr. George's two children.

"Don't you go bothering the soldiers now," he told the boys. "They might shoot the both of you."

Tommy Wilson grinned happily. "Then we shall be angels for real."

"Do we call you *judge* now, Mr. Harris?" Either the war or the worry of family had turned Miss Alethea into an old woman. Her hair was nearly white now, and she peered up at him now through the thick lenses of rimless spectacles.

He had taken his family to live across the river in South Carolina, but he still came back to Augusta on the occasional errand. That morning he had met Miss Alethea as she hobbled along Broad Street, shopping basket on her arm, bound for the market. He smiled and gave her a courtly bow. "Why, you may call me judge if it pleases you, ma'am," he said. "But I don't expect I'll be seeing you in court, Miss Alethea. I'll be happy to carry your shopping basket in exchange for news of your fine family. How have you been?"

"Oh, tolerable," she said with a sigh. "My eyes aren't what they used to be—fine sewing in a bad light, you know. The boys are doing all right these days, grown and gone you know. But I do have young Madison and Cissie staying with me now. Mr. James Hope has taken their mother off to New York with him. Their little girls, too. You know they named the youngest after me? Little Alethea." She sighed. "I do miss them. But tell me about you, Mr. Harris. A judge now, under the new Reconstruction government! What's that like?"

He shrugged. "I don't do big law. Just little matters. Fighting drunks. Disturbing the peace. Stealing trifling things—chickens, not horses." They both smiled. "But when I come into the court, they all have to stand up and show me respect. I do like that. I expect Fanny—er, Mrs. Hope—knows what I mean, being up there in New York and all."

The old woman sighed. "She hates it up there—would you credit it? Poor James Hope is beside himself with worry. Thought he was handing her heaven on a plate, I reckon. Come north where there's been no slaves for fifty years, and maybe where nobody knows that Fanny is a woman of color anyhow. Be really free." She shook her head. "Don't you suppose he expected her to thank God for her deliverance and never want to come back."

"I did suppose it," he said.

"So did the Hopes. But she's homesick and will not be swayed. Why, what do you suppose Mr. James Hope did? He took Fanny to meet with Frederick Douglass. The great man himself! As if Mr. Douglass didn't have better things to do than to try to talk sense into a little Georgia girl. He did his best, though, to convince her to stay. She'll have none of it."

"Do you hear from her, Miz Alethea?"

She nodded. "Regular as clockwork. In every letter she sounds heartbroken. She misses me and her brothers and sisters. Misses Madison and Cissie something fierce. She says she hates northern food. Hates the cold weather and that ugly city full of more poor folks and wickedness than there is in all of Georgia. Fanny has her heart set on coming home."

"But if she stays up there, she could live white, and her children could be white folks."

Alethea Taylor stared. "Why would she want to do that, Mr. Harris?"

She already knew the answer to that, of course, but stating the truth out loud would only incur her wrath, so he held his peace, and wished them all well.

A year later, James and Fanny Hope did return to take up residence in Augusta, and perhaps it was best that they had, for Miz Alethea died before another year was out. At least she got to be reunited with her family again, and he was glad of that.

He did not go to the burying. They laid her to rest in Cedar Grove, and he forced himself to go for the sake of their long acquaintance. At least she would rest in peace. He alone was sure of that.

He wished that she had lived to see her new grandson, who was born exactly a year after his parents returned from the North. The Hopes named the boy John, and he was as blond and blue-eyed as any little Scotsman.

Privately Grandison had thought Fanny had been crazy to come back south when she could have passed in New York and dissolved her children's heritage in the tide of immigrants. But before the end of the decade, he knew he had come round to her way of thinking, for he quit his post of judge in South Carolina, and went back over the river to work at the medical school. Perhaps there were people talking behind his back then, calling him a graven fool, as he had once thought Fanny Hope, but now he had learned the hard way. For all the promises of the Reconstruction men, he got no respect as a judge. The job was a sham whose purpose was not to honor him or his people, but to shame the defeated Rebels. He grew tired of being stared at by strangers whose hatred burned through their feigned respect, and as the days went by, he found himself remembering the medical school with fondness.

He had been good at his job, and the doctors had respected his skills. Sometimes he even thought they forgot about his color. Dr. George had said something once about the difference being a thin layer of skin, and then underneath it was all the same. Many of the faculty had left during the war, but one by one they were coming back now to take up their old jobs at the medical college, and he knew that he was wishing he could join them as well.

He was wearing his white linen suit, a string tie, and his good black shoes. He stood in front of the desk of Dr. Louis Dugas, hat in hand, waiting for an answer.

Dugas, a sleek; clean-shaven man who looked every inch a French aristocrat, had taken over as dean of the college during the war years. In his youth he had studied in Paris, as Dr. George had, and it was Dugas who had traveled to Europe to purchase books for Augusta's medical library. It was said that he had dined with Lafayette himself. Now he looked puzzled. Fixing his glittering black eyes on Harris's face in a long-nosed stare, he said, "Just let me see if I understand you, my good man. You wish to leave a judiciary position across the river and come back here to work as a porter."

Grandison inclined his head. "I do, sir."

"Well, I don't wish to disparage the virtues of manual labor, as I am sure that the occupation of porter is an honorable and certainly a necessary one, but could you just tell me why it is that you wish to abandon your exalted legal position for such a job?"

He had been ready for this logical question, and he knew better than to tell the whole truth. The law had taught him that, at least. Best not to speak of the growing anger of defeated white men suddenly demoted to second-class citizens by contemptuous strangers. He'd heard tales of a secret society that was planning to fight back at the conquerors and whoever was allied with them. But as much as the rage of the locals made him uneasy, the patronizing scorn of his federal overseers kindled his own anger. They treated him like a simpleton, and he came to realize that he was merely a pawn in a game between the white men, valued by neither side. It would be one thing to have received a university education and then to have won the job because one was qualified to do it. Surely they could have found such a qualified man of color in the North, and if not, why not? But to be handed the job only as a calculated insult to others—that made a mockery of his intelligence and skills. At least the doctors had respected him for his work and valued what he did. Fifteen years he'd spent with them.

Best not to speak of personal advantage—of the times in the past when he had prevailed upon one or another of the doctors to treat some ailing neighbor or an injured child who might otherwise have died. The community needed a conduit to the people in power—he could do more good there than sentencing his folks to chain gangs across the river.

Best not to say that he had come to understand the practice of medicine and that, even as he approached his fiftieth year, he wanted to know more.

At last he said simply, "I reckon I miss y'all, Dr. Dugas."

Louis Dugas gave him a cold smile that said that he himself would never put sentiment before other considerations, but loyalty to oneself is a hard fault to criticize in a supplicant. "Even with the procuring of the bodies for the dissection table? You are willing to perform that task again as before?"

We must mutilate the dead so that we do not mutilate the living. He must believe that above all.

He nodded. "Yes, sir."

"Very well then. Of course we must pay you now. The rate is eight dollars per month, I believe. Give your notice to the South Carolina court and you may resume your post here."

And it was done. What he had entered into by compulsion as a slave so many years before, he now came to of his own volition as a free man. He would return to the cart and the lantern and the shovel and begin again.

Well, all that was a long time ago. It is a new century now, and much has changed, not all of it for the better.

He steps out into the night air. The queasy medical student has tottered away to his rooms, and now the building can be locked again for the night. He still has his key, and he will do it himself, although his son George is the official porter now at the medical college—not as good as he himself once was, but what of that? Wasn't the faculty now packed with pale shadows—the nephews and grandsons of the original doctors? A new century, not a patch on the old one for all its motorcars and newfangled gadgets.

He will walk home down Ellis Street, past the house where James and Fanny Hope had raised their brood of youngsters. One of the Hope daughters lived there now, but that was a rarity these days. There was a colored quarter in Augusta now, not like the old days when people lived all mixed together and had thought nothing about it.

James and Fanny Hope had enjoyed eight years in that house on Ellis Street, before a stroke carried him off in 1876. They had let his white kinfolk take him back to New York for burying. Better to have him far away, Fanny Hope had said, than separated from us by a cemetery wall here in Augusta.

Fanny raised her brood of eight alone, and they did her credit. She had lived three years into the twentieth century, long enough to see her offspring graduate from colleges and go on to fine careers. Little blue-eyed John Hope was the best of them, folks said. He had attended Brown University up north, and now he was president of a college in Atlanta. So was little Tommy Wilson, the white preacher's son, who now went by his middle name of Woodrow, and was a "throne" at Princeton College up north. You never could tell about a child, how it would turn out.

Though he never told anyone, Grandison had hoped that Dr. George's son Madison might be the outstanding one of Fanny's children, but he had been content to work at low wage jobs in Augusta and to care for his aging mother. He and Dr. George had that in common—neither of the sons had surpassed them.

Funny to think that he had outlived the beautiful Fanny Hope. In his mind she is still a poised and gentle young girl, and sometimes he regrets that he did not go to her burying in Cedar Grove. The dead rested in peace there now, for the state had legalized the procuring of cadavers by the medical schools some twenty years back, but around that time, rumors had surfaced in the community about grave robbing. Where had the doctors got the bodies all those years for their dissecting classes? Cedar Grove, of course. There was talk of a riot. Augusta had an undertaker now for people of color. The elegant Mr. Dent, with his fancy black oak hearse with the glass panels, and the plumed horses to draw it along in style. Had John or Julia Dent started those rumors to persuade people to be embalmed so the doctors wouldn't get you? There had been sharp looks and angry mutterings at the time, for everyone knew who had been porter at the medical college for all these years, but he was an old man by then, a wiry pillar of dignity in his white suit, and so they let him alone, but he did not go to buryings any more.

The night air is cool, and he takes a deep breath, savoring the smell of flowers borne on the wind. He hears no voices in the wind, and dreams no dreams of dead folks reproaching him for what he has done. In a little while, a few months or years at most, for he is nearly ninety, he too will be laid to rest in Cedar Grove among the empty grave sites, secret monuments to his work. He is done with this world, with its new machines and the new gulf between the races. Sometimes he wonders if there are two heavens, so that Fanny Hope will be forever separated from her husbands by some celestial fence, but he rather hopes that there is no hereafter at all. It would be simpler so. And in all his dissecting he has never found a soul.

He smiles on the dark street, remembering a young minister who had once tried to persuade him to attend a funeral. "Come now, Mr. Harris," the earnest preacher had said. "There is nothing to fear in a cemetery. Surely those bodies are simply the discarded husks of our departed spirits. Surely the dead are no longer there."

Bibliography

Allen, Lane. "Grandison Harris, Sr.: Slave, Resurrectionist and Judge." Athens, GA: *Bulletin of the Georgia Academy of Science,* 34:192–199.

Ball, James M. *The Body Snatchers.* New York: Dorset Press, 1989.

Blakely, Robert L., and Judith M. Harrington. *Bones in the Basement: Post Mortem Racism in Nineteenth Century Medical Training.* Washington, DC: Smithsonian Institution, 1997.

Burr, Virginia Ingraham, ed. *The Secret Eye: The Journal of Ella Gertrude Clanton Thomas, 1848–1889.* Chapel Hill, NC: UNC Press, 1990.

Cashin, Edward J. *Old Springfield: Race and Religion in Augusta, Georgia.* Augusta, GA: The Springfield Village Park Assoc. 1995.

Corley, Florence Fleming. *Confederate City: Augusta, Georgia 1860–1865.* Columbia, SC: The USC Press; Rpt. Spartanburg, SC: The Reprint Company, 1995.

Davis, Robert S. *Georgia Black Book: Morbid Macabre and Disgusting Records of Genealogical Value.* Greenville, SC: Southern Historical Press, 1982.

Fido, Martin. *Body Snatchers: A History of the Resurrectionists.* London: Weidenfeld & Nicolson, 1988.

Fisher, John Michael. Fisher & Watkins Funeral Home, Danville, VA. Personal Interview, March 2003.

Kirby, Bill. *The Place We Call Home: A Collection of Articles About Local History from the Augusta Chronicle.* Augusta, GA: *The Augusta Chronicle,* 1995.

Lee, Joseph M. III. *Images of America: Augusta and Summerville.* Charleston, SC: Arcadia Publishing, 2000.

Spalding, Phinizy. *The History of the Medical College of*

Georgia, Athens, GA: The University of Georgia Press, 1997.

Torrence, Ridgely. *The Story of John Hope.* New York: Macmillan, 1948.

United States Census Records: Richmond County, GA: 1850; 1860; 1870; 1880; 1990.

The Temptation
of King David

Brendan DuBois

Brendan DuBois is a former newspaper reporter who lives in New Hampshire. His novels, *Dead Sand, Black Tide, Shattered Shell, Killer Waves, Buried Dreams*, and the recently published *Primary Storm* all feature continuing character Lewis Cole. DuBois has also written *Betrayed, Resurrection Day, Final Winter,* and *6 Days,* in addition to publishing two short story collections, *The Dark Snow and Other Mysteries* and *Tales from the Dark Woods*. His short stories have appeared in *EQMM, AHMM,* and numerous mystery and science fiction anthologies.

It started the night they were conducting surveillance from the rooftop of the Red Palm Hotel in the South Beach area of Miami Beach. David Santiago yawned as he looked through the tripod-mounted nightvision scope at the tiny bodega below them, about a block away from their vantage point. So far it had been a quiet night, and the mysterious white van with *Cuba. Sí, Castro No* bumper stickers hadn't shown up yet. Supposedly the van was carrying a couple of characters who were involved in a local crystal meth distribution ring. David was the head of the Miami office of the Drug Enforcement Agency and really shouldn't be out here tonight, but he liked being with his troops in the field, and his troops seemed to enjoy having him with them on occasion. Too many guys, once they got high up the ladder of management, forgot what it was like to be out on the streets. David promised never to forget, and this meant sometimes he had to work on these mean streets. And his men and women never forgot he was sometimes still out there with them, which is why his division had such a high conviction rate.

But try telling that to Michelle Santiago, home alone yet again. For her, her husband's position was a tool to get invitations to parties and charity events, to be seen in public with the mayor and commissioners from the county. She didn't care much for what he did, day in and day out, so long as she could use his position for her own private little joy. And lately she had been vocal in telling him how little joy he seemed to be bringing into her life. Too much work and not enough time for her and her precious events.

He sat back to ease the strain on his muscles, looked over to his companion for the night. Harry Cruz, a young up-and-comer, just over a year in the DEA after spending some time with the Miami–Dade County sheriff's office. He was young, he was tough, he was brash, and in some ways, reminded David just a bit of what he had been like, years ago, when he felt like he could take on anybody and anything out there on the streets.

But not tonight. He was too tired.

Harry said, "Quiet night, *jefe.*"

"That it is."

They were sitting on small lawn chairs with their cop gear at their feet. They had been up on the rooftop for three hours, sitting and waiting, spelling each other for quick catnaps or quick visits behind one of the hotel's air conditioning units, where plastic jugs served as handy latrines. The glamor of surveillance work, David thought. No bathroom, poor food and drink, and aching backs. Somehow those little details never made it into the movies or the TV shows.

Harry yawned and David said quietly, "You cut that crap out, or we'll both be sleeping up here. And that white van will get away."

"So what if it does?" Harry said. "There'll just be another like it, a week from now, a month from now."

David leaned forward, looked into the nightvision scope. Some street people were out in front of the store, talking and joking, listening to music from the store's speakers, gathering for some fun, maybe a bit of folding money being passed around for some recreational narcotics, but so what? He and Harry were after a bigger score.

He said, "You're too young to be this cynical."

"Maybe so, *jefe,* but I'm thinking of moving out in a while."

"Where to?"

"Don't know. CIA's been sniffing around, recruiting. Maybe I'll give them a call."

"What for?"

"You know. Nobody gives a crap about the War on Drugs. It's all about the War on Terror. The War on Drugs been forgotten."

David leaned back, rubbed at his lower back. "War on

Terror's a stupid phrase. Terror's a tactic. Not an opponent. It's like after Pearl Harbor, FDR declared war on carrier-based aircraft. Least they could do is get the words straight."

Harry laughed. "Whatever you do call it, that's where the money's at, that's where the action is. No offense, *jefe,* sitting up on my ass at a Miami hotel isn't where it's at."

"That's where we are now, babe, so get used to it."

Another laugh. "Wish I was home. Wish I was home with Carla, my little sheba. Keeping her company. Hey, you know, you can see our condo from here. You know that? Spotted it when we first got up here, after we went through the access door."

It felt like a little cool breeze was tickling at the back of David's neck when Harry mentioned his wife, though it was impossible. They were in Miami. No such animal as a cool breeze existed. He knew what he should do. He should keep his mouth shut. Should get back to the nightvision scope. Get back to waiting for that white van so they could get a license plate number, begin the usual and customary task of tracing the van, who owned it, who drove it, all that good stuff that went into making a solid case.

He knew what he should do.

So he said, "Really? Your condo?"

"Sure," Harry said. "Right to the south. Can't miss it, it's next to the causeway. We get up here again tomorrow night, I'll make sure Carla gives us a wave 'fore she gets to bed."

He laughed, and David said nothing.

Just let the little cool breeze play at the back of his neck.

He went back to the nightvision scope.

Waited.

*   *   *

And when he figured he had waited long enough, he pulled back from the nightvision scope and said, "Hey. You want to take a snooze?"

Harry yawned. "Christ, yes, *jefe*. You sure you'll be okay?"

"Yeah, I'm fine. Us oldsters, we take our afternoon naps, we get charged up, we don't need all that sacktime."

"*Jefe,* that'd be great. Look, I'll be over there by the ventilation ducts. You wake me if you need anything."

David said, "You can count on it."

So Harry got up, stretching his young and muscular body, and then went over to a low ventilation duct system. On the ground was a thin air mattress and a blanket, and he stretched out and pulled the blanket up. David watched him and then went back to the surveillance. Nothing was out of sorts. The same music, the same lights, the same people, probably. All down there, living and laughing and loving, while he was up here, an observer, watching, waiting, all alone.

He waited some more.

Harry moved some on the mattress. David bent down to the scope, began adjusting the focus again, and—

Snores.

The snoring had started. He sat up, looked over at the wrapped-up figure of his subordinate. Snoring the sleep of the loyal, the sleep of the peaceful, sleeping the sleep of the loved.

David moved back, went to the gear, picked up a pair of surplus navy binoculars—real powerful stuff, worth almost a thousand bucks on the open market—and then left his post. He walked quickly and carefully, heading to where they had first come up on the roof. There. The access door, and the south was over there, and—

He stood at the corner of the building, looking to the

causeway, seeing the condo where Harry and his Carla lived. Harry was right. It was easy to spot, next to the causeway, standing all alone in its lit splendor, as traffic moved by, as boats maneuvered in Biscayne Bay, as jets made their approach to the airport off to the west.

The binoculars were heavy in his hands. We could leave right now, he thought. Go back to where we were. Nobody will know, nothing bad will have happened. Could leave right now.

His arms came up, the binoculars were now at his eyes. His mouth was quite dry.

Just for a second, he thought. Just for a second.

The lights of the building snapped into view, making his head tilt back for a moment. He focused in on the individual floors. He remembered what Harry had told him, months ago. They lived on the top floor of their building. Harry's wife was worried about getting down to the street in case there was a fire. She was always worried about that. So—top floor.

He made a quick scan. Looked like there were three units visible on the top floor, each with their own balcony. Walls separated each balcony, giving the occupants an illusion of privacy. It looked like two of the units were dark. Which left the one on the left, the lit one, the one with—

Movement.

His hands tightened on the binoculars. He loved this feeling, had always loved it, during the countless hours of surveillance he had performed over the years. David had never had any interest in hunting animals—hunting down humans had always been more challenging and rewarding—but he always thought that the instant some-body appeared in his binoculars, the thrill must be like that of a hunter, finally spotting his prey.

Just like now.

God, look at that. . . .

He willed his hands to keep still as the image of Harry's wife Carla came into view in the binoculars. The condo unit had large windows and it was easy enough to look in and see Carla moving around. He could just make out her head and bare shoulders; furniture inside the condo blocked the view of the rest of her body. It looked like she was in the kitchen. He watched and watched, entranced. He had met Carla a few times earlier at after-hours functions for the Miami DEA office, and she stood out from all the other wives. She had light brown skin, a flashing white smile, raven hair down to her shoulders, and an old-fashioned hourglass figure. Harry had never been interested in the skin-and-bones, waiflike look that had lately taken South Beach and its beach colonies by storm, including his so-called better half. He had always liked women who, damn it, looked like women, and Carla Cruz was definitely all woman. In those after-hours events, she had always dressed a bit more stylish than the other wives, showing just that much more cleavage, that much more leg, that much more energy, like every hope and desire in one beautiful package—

Oh my.

His mouth was dry.

Carla had come out into a living room area, sipping a drink, holding a towel wrapped around her body. Must have just gotten out of the shower. She came out to the balcony, shook her head, and then put the drink down on a railing. She then took off the towel and rubbed her hair vigorously, and then wrapped the towel around her head and stood there in the night air, completely nude.

The binoculars were now trembling slightly in his hands. There was enough ambient light from the streetlights and other buildings to get a great view of that body, that body that made him catch his breath. In the odd light her skin looked polished, smooth, flawless . . . and he looked up to her face, her strong and confident and beautiful face, this wonderful woman standing nude outside on her balcony, secure in who she was, in what she was doing.

And not minding at all that she might be watched, by one of the thousands of people within viewing distance.

He watched and his hands cramped as they firmed up on the binoculars. He was no innocent, no pure-driven country boy. He had traveled the world and had been married to Michelle for more than a decade, and the thought of seeing a naked woman, well, so what? But now . . . it was different. It was like the time when he was twelve, growing up in a suburb of San Diego, and that brief flash all those years ago of seeing the woman next door, young Mrs. Concetta, seeing her sunbath topless out in her backyard . . . he remembered that sheer wave of excitement and pleasure that surged through him back then, that was surging through him now. . . .

Like a little boy he was, not the head of his section, not the *jefe,* not the king of all he surveyed.

Just a horny little boy.

He licked his dry lips and with a flash of a smile, young Carla Cruz picked up her glass and went back into her condo.

The lights went off shortly thereafter.

But still David waited.

Maybe she would come back.

Maybe the lights would come back on again.

Maybe.

And it was the cough of young Harry Cruz, back there on the stakeout, that finally broke him free.

He had no idea of how long he had been out there, but he felt that flush of embarrassment that came from screwing up on the job. What a rookie mistake. Harry was moving about some on the mattress pad and David went to the nightvision scope, bent down to look at it. His hands went cold at what he saw. A white van, moving away from the bodega. There were bumper stickers on the rear—he didn't have to read them to know what they were—and before he could get a glimpse of the license plate number, the one they had been seeking for so long, the van turned a corner and disappeared.

David stood up. His legs were shaking. They were shaking hard.

Had he been seen?

He looked over to Harry, now sitting up, rubbing at his face.

David stayed quiet. He waited.

"Hey," Harry said. "Anything going on, *jefe?*"

Hell of a question. While you were sleeping, he thought, I lusted after your wife. And I screwed the pooch: that damn van came by and I missed it, while I was ogling your little sheba like a horny teenage boy. All these days and weeks of prep work have been wasted. All because of that woman you married, that woman I desire . . . because I was here, where I could see her.

"No," he finally answered. "Nothings going on."

*   *   *

When the sky started lightening up in the east, they packed up their gear and went silently back into the hotel, into the elevator and down into the parking area. On the drive back to their office, at 8400 NW 53rd Street, in an old Ford LTD that belched smoke and bucked each time they started up after stopping at a red light, he said to Harry, "Any other reasons you want to get out of DEA, get working with the CIA?"

Harry yawned, "You know what I said back there, that's all. Looking for a bit of excitement, that's all. Trying to stop drugs is a losing proposition. Locking up bad guys who want to knock down buildings, that's more my speed."

"Yeah." David kept quiet and sensed something was bothering Harry. He was right. He didn't have to wait long.

"*Jefe?*"

"Yeah?"

"You're not going to tell God on me, will you?"

He hoped his younger companion couldn't see the smile. God was the nickname for their supposed overseer, an assistant attorney general from the Justice Department named George O'Toole Dunfey—who knew why an Irishman had been sent to oversee the drug importing hub for Latin America?—and it was a nickname never shared with anyone outside of the office. He was a stickler for protocol, for details, and for loyalty to the DEA and the Justice Department.

"No, Harry, you don't have to worry about God. Your secret's safe with me."

Harry sounded relieved. "Thanks, *jefe*. And thanks again for coming out with me tonight. Means a lot . . . to me and the other guys, knowing you're out here, backing us up."

"No problem."

"And *jefe* . . . if you've got any secrets to share, you can tell me, too."

A vision of Harry's nude wife, smiling, drink in her hand, beckoning . . .

The hell he would. The hell he would share something like that.

"You got it, Harry. You got it."

It was still early in the morning in their offices and David resisted the urge to drink a couple of cups of coffee while writing up an interim report on their overnight surveillance. Any coffee would just keep him up, and he wanted to sleep long and hard later on, so no caffeine in the system. Nope. Just write up the report and head home to Michelle and her cold and silent stares.

He was almost done typing when he thought a glass of water would at least rehydrate him. He walked out of his office, into the maze of cubicles before him. He walked by the little cube that had a HARRY CRUZ nameplate outside. He stopped. The lights in the cubicle were off. Harry had gone home, gone home to his lovely wife.

The flash of jealousy surprised him.

And so was what he did next.

He stepped into the cube, got around Harry's desk, and looked at the photos lined up next to the computer terminal. His legs felt tired, wobbly. There were three photos in frames, in a neat row. One showed a much younger Harry with his family. No big deal. The other was Harry and Carla, on their wedding day. Harry had on a tuxedo and his wife, Carla, was in a wedding gown . . . but what a wedding gown. It was strapless and her full bosom was straining against the white satin fabric, and that familiar smile was nice and wide. Beside that photo was one that might have been from their honeymoon. Harry in T-shirt and shorts, Carla in same, another big smile, the both of them standing on a beach, palm trees in the back.

He looked up and around. The office was still quiet. He went back to staring at Carla. Such a beautiful woman. He wondered if Harry was now back at home with her. Wondered if he woke her up when he got home. Wondered if he was just at this minute sliding into bed with her, a warm bed, her freshly washed and perfumed body, . . .

David swallowed, moved away from the desk, looked once more at the photos.

Something was odd.

He went back to the desk.

The third photo, the beach photo, there was something sticking out from behind it. He stood there just for a moment. He should leave. Should go back to his office, get his stuff, go home and get some blessed sleep.

It looked like the edge of another photo.

He shouldn't.

He moved his hand, grasped the visible edge, pulled out the paper, saw that it was indeed photo stock.

And a photo of Carla.

"Oh Lord," he whispered.

Carla was wearing a bathing suit, but really, the amount of fabric in the white suit could probably fit comfortably in a coffee cup. She was standing in the water, turned, smiling at the camera. The suit was wet and translucent. The bottom was a thong, and the tiny white fabric made the tanned flesh look even that much darker. And the top . . . it barely held in her breasts, and nothing was left to the imagination. Nothing. If anything, this photo was a hundred times more erotic than the memories of what he had seen on the rooftop, a few hours ago.

Another look around the office. Still empty.

From Harry's wastebasket, he picked up a discarded section of the previous day's *Miami Herald,* slipped the photo in, and went out into the common area of the office. There was a variety of tech gear there, including DVD and VHS tape players, and there was also a scanner, for scanning mug shots, driver license photos, surveillance photos, and so on.

This definitely was a "so on."

He put the newspaper down.

The photo went into the scanner, he saw the flashing tube of light slide back and forth, and with a few keystrokes the scanned photo was converted to a digital file and sent to his computer.

Voices, out in the main hallway.

The photo went back into the folded-over newspaper, and he walked around the corner and—

Right in front of God Himself, George O'Toole Dunfey, dressed in a dark gray suit, white shirt, and red power tie. Dunfey's green eyes narrowed as he spotted him in the hallway and said, "Going off shift?"

"Yes, I am," David said, knowing his voice sounded faint.

"How did it go last night?"

"A bust," he said.

"What next?"

"I plan to talk to my C.I. later today, try to squeeze more info out of him. Maybe we'll do another surveillance tonight. Or tomorrow night."

Dunfey nodded, his carefully trimmed red hair in place and perfect. "Very well. Though I don't understand, David, why you feel the need to get out on the street as often as you do."

He shrugged, feeling like the newspaper in his hand had grown to the size of a billboard. "The men and women . . .

they trust me, and part of that trust is remembering how it is, out on the streets."

Another judicious nod. "You've come very far and very fast here in Miami, David. I've read your personnel files. How you almost single-handedly took down a distribution network that was based in the Bahamas, that operated here and along the entire southern coast . . . you were here for just a short time when that happened, am I correct?"

"Yes." Man, would this guy ever shut up . . .

"Ah, yes," and a little smile traced itself upon Dunfey's lips. "There was a cargo ship involved. Named the *Goliath*. The newspapers had quite a time with that, David and the *Goliath*."

"Well, you know newspapers . . ."

Dunfey looked at David's hands and said, "Speaking of newspapers . . . the *Herald?*"

"Yes"

"Can I look at it?"

His heart seemed to seize up, like a water pump suddenly called upon to move molasses. He froze.

His boss waited, and said, "David?"

"It's . . . it's yesterday's copy. I was about ready to trash it."

"Oh. Well, I'm going to the coffee room, give it to me and I'll throw it out for you."

He moved the paper behind him. What would happen . . . God, the number of possibilities that existed right now for utter disaster and ruin.

"It's all right, there's an article in it I want to clip before I leave."

"I see." A firm, dismissive nod, and then, "Carry on," and

Dunfey left, the tone of voice he used leaving no more room for discussion. It was like Dunfey was no longer interested in the matters of mere mortals, and office jokesters—including himself!—said it was God speaking, and when God had spoken, it was time to scurry away.

Which is what he did.

The photo went back to Harry's desk, he went to his office and forwarded the digital photo to his home e-mail account, and then David thankfully, mercifully, went home.

Home was a condo unit that had seen better days, at the northern end of Miami's port. David unlocked the door, went inside and made sure all of the shades were closed. He was tired, he was buzzed, and all he wanted to do was to crawl into bed and go to sleep.

But his wife, Michelle, was there waiting.

She stood there, eyes flashing, wearing a simple white dress that fell below her knees, and sandals. Her blonde hair was cut short, almost as short as his, and her skin after a decade of marriage was now a leathery bronze. She was lean and muscular, nothing like the vision he had just seen, earlier that morning.

"So you're back," she said.

"Yep."

"Arrest anybody?"

"Nope."

She went around to the kitchen counter, picked up her purse and car keys. "I'm off to brunch at the club . . . and Tracy Ramirez, she's invited me up to Savannah for the weekend. All right?"

He was so tired. "Sure. That'd be fine."

"Good. I'll call you." Michelle walked by, brushed his cheek with her dry lips, and then she was gone.

Now he was really tired. He wanted to go to bed.

That's all he wanted to do.

Which he knew was a lie.

In a room designated as a spare bedroom, and which he had turned into an office some years ago, he went inside and sat down, almost missing the chair in his exhaustion. He switched on the computer and thought, just one look, that's all, just one look and we're off to bed.

Just one look.

He stared at the computer, as it laboriously booted itself up and went through all the self-checks and diagnostics, before the damn thing did what he wanted it to do. He moved the mouse about, double-clicked here and there, and went to his e-mail account.

There it was. The e-mail message sent from the office, an e-mail with an attached image file.

Dump it, a voice inside him said. Dump it and erase it and pretend you never sent it. Erase the file, get it off your computer and—

His hand moved of its own will. It made a series of mouse clicks.

There.

In all her glory, on his computer screen, in his private home . . .

Carla Cruz, smiling with her wet and translucent bathing suit, open and inviting, looking at the camera, looking out there . . .

Looking at him.

Looking at David Santiago.

Smiling and inviting him, David Santiago . . .

Just him.

He woke with a start. He was still in his office. His neck hurt from sleeping in his chair. He looked at his computer screen and the photo of another man's wife, and he refused to think anymore. David just closed up the computer file and stumbled off to bed, where his dreams were of warm water and wet fabric.

Later that night, in a section of Miami known—with some irony—as Liberty City, he wandered a series of deserted storefronts on Seventh Avenue, prepared and dressed for a night out on the town, such as it was. This part of Miami was the site of some serious rioting, more than twenty years earlier, and it had never really recovered. Most stores and restaurants were long gone, and those that remained were barely hanging on, selling bootleg DVDs, liquor, adult novelties and competing with the occasional tent-covered flea market. David wandered Seventh Avenue for a few minutes, and then went to one flea market, selling paperback books with their covers ripped off. He leaned up against a brick wall of a Winn-Dixie supermarket that had been closed for years, waiting and watching, until a tall, light-skinned male came by—Edgar Lee Chance, known to others here and there in Liberty City as Chancey, and known to David as his own personal C.I., Confidential Informant. David watched Chancey work the crowd around the bookstore for a bit, exchanging folded-up wads of money for little glassine plastic envelopes, and then Chancey looked over and David caught his eye. There was the briefest flash of recognition, and then Chancey loped down the street, his knee-length khaki shorts flapping in the breeze.

David waited for a minute or two, and then followed him.

And in a few minutes more, they were on the other side of the closed supermarket, by a collection of Dumpsters. Chancey scratched at his arms and said, "S'up?"

"Still looking for the van. Got any more info?"

A slow shake of the head. "Jus' what I said the other day. Stops every now and then at that bodega I was talking about. Don' know the license plate number, jus' the fact it's got those Castro stickers on it. You hasslin' me or somethin'?"

"No, no hassles, Chancey. Just remember the favors I've done for you, all right?"

Chancey grimaced. "Man, I know you got my sister popped and I'm glad and all that, but Christ, how long you gonna ride that favor for? Forever?"

Yes, Chancey's sister. A young woman with a taste for older men, cocaine, and a variety of other recreational pharmaceuticals. He had pulled some strings to get her loose from a Miami-Dade County sting operation involving a rented yacht and some Colombians looking for a good time, and had gotten Chancey's forced gratitude and information in return. He had known Chancey earlier from some minor-league distribution offenses, and was pleased to be able to use his sister's arrest for his own advantage. Chancey was rumored to have connections with some parts of a Colombian distribution network, but David had never pressed him on that, saving that little bit of information for later, when he could use it.

"Long as it takes. You find out anything more about the van, you call." Chancey nodded. "Sure. Yeah. Look, you're cuttin' into my business hours. All right?"

"Go on," David said, and Chancey moved out of sight, no doubt intent on grabbing his own piece of the American Dream. He stood there in the darkness, thinking about Chancey's sister. He had gotten her sprung loose without going through the proper channels and paperwork, but so what? That was what happened, out here in the streets. He gave Chancey another minute, and then headed out to Seventh Avenue.

And two young men were there, blocking his way.

"Goin' somewhere, meat?" the taller of the two asked.

"Yeah, I am," he said.

"Where that?" the shorter of the two replied.

He reached behind to his back, to the leather holster snug against his spine, and pulled out his government-issue 10-mm Glock pistol. He held the pistol out casually, so the two young men could see it with no difficulty.

"Home," David said. "I'm going home. You got a problem with that?"

They faded away, moving fast. He put the automatic pistol back in the holster and, yes, went home. To his empty and lonely home.

Office, the next day, struggling to make sense out of the new expense report forms, when there was a soft knock. He looked up and felt the heat surge right through him. Carla Cruz, standing right there, smiling at him. He could never remember Michelle ever coming to his office, but here was Carla, no doubt to see her man. She had on tight black slacks and a scoop-necked sleeveless white blouse that exposed a fair bit of lovely cleavage.

"Bother you for a moment, David?"

He tried to keep his voice even. "Bother away, Carla."

She stepped in, smile still there, seemingly lightening up the whole damn office. She came around and sat down next to him, said, "Funny thing is, I want to surprise Harry and maybe take him out to lunch. But his cubicle is empty. Do you know where he is?"

He had to think for a moment, because his brain was busily processing the beauty and eroticism of the woman before him, and he said, "Checking up on a vehicle in the motor pool. He should be back in a few minutes."

"Thanks," she said, getting up from the chair, giving him another lovely view of her cleavage, and she said, "Nice seeing you, David," and gave his wrist a squeeze.

She walked out. He stayed there.

She had touched him.

Right then and there.

And like the lovesick schoolboy he had apparently become, he raised up his wrist and gently sniffed there, trying to catch a bit of her scent.

Back on the roof of the Red Palm Hotel, he was conducting surveillance again. It was overcast, a thick cloud layer was moving in from the west, in the distance he saw distant flashes of lightning, and could hear the accompanying low grumbles long seconds later. Binoculars were in hands again, heavy as always, and he stood there, keeping an eye on what was out there.

It was late. He was tired.

And he was alone.

And he wasn't looking down on the street where the bodega was located, where the mysterious white van might arrive.

He was looking at the condo building, hundreds of yards away, and his hands ached and his knees ached, and his soul ached, for all the windows in the upper floor were dark. There was nothing to see. Was she gone? Was she out with her husband? If so, what were they doing? And what was she wearing? And did she remember how she had come into his office and had touched his arm?

There.

Dear Lord, the lights just came on.

His throat thickened, his breathing quickened, and he forced himself to keep his hands steady, for there was movement over there in the well-lit condo unit, he could see Harry and then Carla, who was laughing, going into the kitchen, and—

A crunch. A noise.

A light flashed and a voice said, "Freeze right there, pal! Freeze!"

He froze.

More crunching noises, as the man with the flashlight approached. "Turn real slow now, real slow."

He turned and lowered the binoculars and his heart was thumping so hard it felt like it would crack his ribs. Before him was a young man, twenties maybe, wearing a security guard's uniform and carrying a big flashlight with an attitude and a scrawny mustache. David said, "What's the problem?"

"Problem is, man, who the hell are you? What are you doing up here?"

Hand shaking, he pulled out his identification wallet, tossed it over to the guard. It fell to the rough surface and as the guard picked it up from the rooftop, David thought, man, if I was planning to do you harm, you could be dead now. A swift kick to the head and a quick punch to the throat, and you'd be—

The guard looked at the identification, looked up at David, and then looked back. "Oh."

"Yeah, oh," David said impatiently. "Understand now, kid? I'm up here on a surveillance, doing important work, and you're getting in my way."

The guard lowered his flashlight. "Sorry, I didn't know anything was supposed to be—"

David stepped forward and grabbed his identification back. "You're interfering in official DEA business. Get the hell out of here, all right? Shut off your damn flashlight and go away."

The guard quietly did just that, and when the young man started walking back to the stairway entrance, David turned quickly and raised up the binoculars.

Dark. The condo unit was dark.

He looked back at the figure of the security guard, walking away from him, and he knew right then and there that if he could get away with it, he would have that moron dead. Right now.

The condo unit was dark.

There was nothing to see.

Time to go back home.

Alone.

At work the next day, he was startled when Dunfey, a.k.a. God, stopped by and said, "See you David?"

"Sure." He got up and followed Dunfey to his corner office, briefly running his hand across his hair. Hadn't bothered to shower this morning, and had barely eaten breakfast. Michelle was still gone with her friend, up to

Savannah. The only high point of his day had been the quick look at the photo of Carla he had on his computer screen at home. He had allowed himself just a few minutes of gazing at that perfect woman before coming to work.

Now he followed Dunfey into his office, which had a marvelous view of the city. Two of the walls were glass, allowing the view, and the other two walls were ego walls, filled with plaques, framed certificates and photos of Dunfey with various political, military and religious leaders.

Except for the pope. There was a joke in the DEA that Dunfey didn't need a photo of the pope, since he was God and the pope worked for him, but that kind of joke didn't get repeated much when Dunfey was around.

Dunfey said, "I'll come straight to the point."

"All right," David said, hands suddenly feeling chilled, knowing that somehow he had been caught. That somebody in the Information Technology section had spied on the e-mail he had sent from work to his home computer, the e-mail with the attached picture file of Harry's wife, a single photo that was going to get him dismissed and humiliated and—

". . . a volunteer," Dunfey said.

"Excuse me?"

If Dunfey was irritated by being ignored, he didn't show it. He went on. "I said, David, that I've been in contact with our consulate in Medellin. There's a CIA op under way in the rural areas outside of the city, looking to penetrate a particular outfit. It's called *el Grupo* . . . the Group. Not a very original name, I know, but we're looking for a volunteer."

"What kind of volunteer?"

Dunfey picked up a pen from his desk, looked at it as if

to make sure it really was a pen, and carefully placed it back down in the same spot. "Someone young, someone strong, someone with a taste for . . . an exotic assignment. We're looking for someone to go undercover with *el Grupo*, someone who can blend in, someone who can take this type of dangerous assignment. I don't have to tell you what these type of people do to informers or undercover DEA agents. If he were to be discovered . . . we'd be lucky if there was enough left to identify at an autopsy. But the rewards could be tremendous."

"Of course."

"So. Volunteers. Do you know of anyone within your section who might want to take on this assignment?"

David didn't hesitate. "Harry Cruz."

Late that night, the phone rang. "Yeah?"

"David . . . it's Michelle."

"Oh . . . hi."

She sounded a bit drunk, as her words were slurred, but the words were clear enough so he could hear them.

"David . . . look, it's not working out anymore. You know it and I know it. So let's do the adult thing and just call it quits. All right? You've got this whole king-of-Miami trip going on and I just don't want to be part of it anymore. You'll hear from my lawyer next week. I'll be staying in Savannah with Tracy Ramirez in the meantime."

He had an idea that Michelle would want him to beg, would want him to reconsider, but he just rubbed at his tired eyes and said. "Sure."

And hung up the phone.

The going-away party for Harry took place two weeks later, in a small function room at a Hawaiian restaurant in Hialeah. There was a lot of forced laughs and jokes and Harry seemed to enjoy being the center going on. Harry was going right into the lion's den, right to where the risks and the fighting were the fiercest.

Harry had taken all the ribbing and the jokes with good humor, but David saw how Carla had been handling it, and he could tell she was frightened by her husband's new job. On this night she wore a simple black cocktail dress, high above the knees and with a nice expanse of tanned chest on display, and he went to her, before the party broke up.

"How are you, Carla?"

She smiled, her eyes filling. "Oh . . . I'm doing all right . . . it's just that . . . it's going to be a long time. Six months."

David said, "It'll go by fast. Just you see."

"I know . . . I know . . . it's just hard. Tell me . . . David . . . he's going to be all right? Won't he?"

"He'll be fine," David said. "Just you wait and see. He'll be fine."

She nodded and sniffed and he moved to her, and she came to him for a hug, a gentle squeeze, and her hair was in his face. Her soft scent was overpowering him, the sensation of her being in his arms made his heart race, he wondered how long he could hold her there and—

A tap on the shoulder.

"Hey! *Jefe,* you're trying to steal my wife, are you?"

David broke away, Carla laughing, her husband standing next to her, smiling widely, the self-confident smile of a strong and able young man, on his way to a dangerous assignment, his lovely wife waiting and waiting for him to return.

Caught. In a way, he had been caught, but he recovered and said, "You be careful out there, in the wilderness. I hear *el Grupo* plays for keeps."

Harry weaved a bit, slightly drunk, and he said, "Oh, I'll be the careful one. Just you see."

He squeezed his wife's shoulders. "See, I've got something important to come back to. Right?"

Carla was still smiling through her tears, and David said, "Yes, you sure do have something important to come back to, Harry. So watch yourself."

Harry laughed and then suddenly, his expression changed, and he leaned forward, still weaving slightly. "*Jefe* . . . you . . . you take care of Carla while I'm gone. Okay? If she needs anything, can she call you? Can she? You know . . . you know how we all feel about you, *jefe*. I just feel better, knowing you'll take care of her . . ."

"Yes," he said. "Absolutely."

The smile came back on Harry's strong face. "Thanks. Thanks, *jefe*."

David cleared his throat. "Don't mention it."

Alone again that night, David tried not to think of what kind of loving Carla might be giving her husband right now, right at this minute, before he headed out to Colombia. Odd fantasies and imaginations had been rattling around in his mind, ever since Harry asked him to take care of his wife. Of course. He imagined going over to see her at different times, when she was sunbathing or fresh out of the shower. Perhaps taking her out to dinner.

Maybe a weekend trip down to the Keys, to keep her occupied, keep her mind away from her absent husband. . . .

Something could happen, couldn't it?

A spark, an idle glance, a little too much wine with dinner, and if he was skilled and lucky, then that wonderful, hot, fleshy woman could be in his bed . . . God, how delightful that would be.

Wonderful fantasies.

Wonderful. Michelle gone and Carla here and . . .

And all drowned out by the harsh voice of reality. So what? A brief romp or two in the hay, and then Harry comes back. Harry comes back and he takes her back, and you're alone again, my friend, a pathetic man in his thirties who's now alone, after his wife of so many years has left him. . . .

Alone. Forever. And Carla would always be out of reach, always.

He turned on the light in his bedroom, noted the open door to his office. His computer was visible. A minute to get up, turn on the computer, and in a very few minutes later, he could be gazing at that stolen photo of Carla. Looking and looking, burning that image into his mind, that wonderful image that teased him and entranced him and excited him and—

For what?

For what?

A collection of computer programming, that's all that existed on his computer screen. Not the real thing. Not the real woman. No, the real woman was on the other side of town, with her husband, enjoying her man, and David would never have her.

All he had were the brief touches, the small conversations, and the stolen photo in his office.

He went to the nightstand, past a collection of magazines and paperback books. Found a well-creased and black leather bound book. His own Bible, given to him by his parents, years ago when he made the San Diego force. He hadn't picked it up in years and remembered his mom, whispering to him when she had given to him: "It's all in there, David. Any time you are troubled. It's all in there."

He hoped Mom was right.

He started leafing through the book, found a section about his namesake, the king of Israel, began reading the verses, and—

The temperature in the room seemed to rise, for he had suddenly become quite warm.

He could not believe the verses he was reading.

Could not believe it.

He reread them:

"And it came to pass in an eveningtide, that David arose from off his bed, and walked upon the roof of the king's house: and from the roof he saw a woman washing herself; and the woman was very beautiful to look upon.

"And David sent and inquired after the woman. And one said, Is not this Bathsheba, the daughter of Eliam, the wife of Uriah the Hittite?

"And David sent messengers and took her; and she came in unto him, and he lay with her . . ."

He went on through the elegant verses, now remembering the story:

"And it came to pass in the morning, that David wrote a letter to Joab, and sent it by the hand of Uriah.

"And he wrote in the letter, saying, Set ye Uriah in the forefront of the hottest battle, and retire ye from him, that he may be smitten and die."

He closed the with shaking hands. The Bible. Mom had been right. All the answers were right in there.

Back to Liberty City, a scorching hot day with haze hanging over everything like there was a series of burning trash dumps out on the city limits, their smoke drifting overhead. Back to the same stretch of Seventh Avenue, waiting and watching, knowing he didn't have long to wait. He may be a criminal and a thug and a low-life, but in all things, Chancey was a businessman, a pure capitalist. And Chancey knew that to make money and get ahead, he had to be on the street, where the business was.

Which is where he was this hazy day.

David walked by, gave him a glance, and even though Chancey looked pretty much ticked off, Chancey did break away from his open air market and make his way down the street. David waited, watched him go down the street, and felt just the briefest flash of something. Maybe he should turn around. Maybe he shouldn't go there. Maybe, maybe, maybe . . .

He went down the street and Chancey was near a Dumpster, leaning against a brick wall, arms crossed, and he said, "Look, man, I know you're diggin' about that white van, but I keep sayin', I'll tell you when I tell you, when I got somethin' to give you and—"

"Shut up," David said.

Chancey glowered and David stepped closer to the

young man and said, "I told you to shut up for a reason. Reason being, I've got something for you this time."

"What's that?" Chancey said, voice full of suspicion. "Don't like it when a man like you says he wants to do favors. Not natural."

David said, "Don't care if it's natural, don't care if it's made up. What I do care about it is the connections you have with some Colombians. There's serious weight there, right?"

Chancey had the look of a nine-year-old boy who was told that he was going to spend the night alone in a haunted house. "Man, that's it. Right there, it's over, you can take me in with what I got, you pull my sister in and send her away for ten years or twenty, 'cause that's it. What I got with the Colombians is never comin' out. Got that? Never. You pull some crap with some of these guys, you're dead, your family's dead, your nursery school teacher's dead, man, sorry, there's nothing you got that's worth that. So bring me in, forget it or change it."

David said, "You got me wrong, Chancey. I don't want anything from you and any Colombian connection you've got. I've got something for them."

"Say again?"

He glanced around, just making sure in that cop-sure way of doing things that they were alone. He said, "I've got some information, information I want you to give to the Colombians. All right?"

"Sure," Chancey said, shaking his head. "You're asking to set somebody up. Hell with that. I pass info along and some of their guys get capped, then I'm found a week later, down here, and my head's found a week after that, up on the beach. Not goin' to happen."

"You're right, it's not going to happen, because that's not what I'm doing," David said. "Look, here it is. There's a guy went out to Medellin today. He's going to be looking to slide into an organization called *el Grupo.* Got it? *El Grupo.* The guy's a narc. He's not to be trusted. All right?"

Now Chancey looked like a nine-year-old boy who just saw his parish priest draw a pentagram and light candles in service to Lucifer. "You . . . you want me to set up one of your guys? That's it?"

David kept his voice even and low. "What I want you to do is to pass along this information so it gets to an outfit in Medellin called *el Grupo.* That some guy is coming in to see them. Early thirties, muscular, short brown hair. He left Miami this morning on a ten A.M. flight to Bogota, with a connecting flight to Medellin, two hours later. He's a law enforcement agent. He's not to be trusted. Can you remember that?"

Chancey stepped away from the wall, "Man . . . that's the coldest thing I've ever heard . . . you know what they're going to do to him? Do you?"

"I don't care."

"Man must have ticked you off somethin' awful, you givin' him up like that."

"You just do it . . . and I'm sure you'll get a nice reward for it."

Chancey shook his head again. "Man, when they get ahold of him . . . he'll be beggin' for a bullet in the head before they're through. You know that, don't you? He'll be beggin' for a bullet in his head . . ."

David said, "Just do it, Chancey. Today."

There was the briefest of pauses, like the young drug dealer was struggling with what remained of his conscience, and David stood there, quiet, not wanting to say any more, not wanting to think anymore.

Chancey nodded, a quick gesture. "All right man, consider it done . . . but damn . . . you know, last year, I heard about this guy, he had his girlfriend fly up from Panama City, he was with her and all . . . and she was muleing for him. She swallowed all these balloons, filled with coke, all for her boyfriend and true man . . . and 'fore they got home, after they got here, one of those balloons in her gut, it let loose . . . poor girl died right there in his car . . . know what the dude did then?"

David said, "No, but I'm sure you're going to tell me."

"Yeah. Real true blue guy would take her to the nearest ER . . . but our hero, he drove her out on the Tamiami Highway, 'til he found a nice little remote turnoff . . . took her out there and got his knife . . . and gutted her, right there on the side of the road . . . so he could get his coke . . . a charmer, hunh? Left her bod there for the alligators to munch on. . . ."

David wanted to leave, wanted to leave this quick-talking fool, wanted to get away from this part of town, just wanted to leave.

"Yeah, great story. What's the point?"

Chancey looked amazed, like he couldn't believe David didn't understand. "Point is, man, I thought that was the coldest thing I ever heard."

A car horn blared nearby and then Chancey added, "Until today."

The phone rang and rang and rang and David woke up, pillow against his face, wondering what in hell was going on, and the phone rang and rang and his hand went out to the nightstand, fumbled around, until he grabbed the receiver and pulled it to his face and said, "Yeah. Santiago here."

A hiss of static. "Santiago? David Santiago?"

He rolled over on his back. "Yeah."

"Hold on, please."

Another hiss of static. He stared up at the dark ceiling. Another male voice came on the line. "Mister Santiago?"

"Yeah."

"Sir, this is Harold Doyle. I'm the night officer on duty at the American consulate in Medellin, Colombia. I'm afraid I have some very bad news for you."

He kept on staring at the dark and featureless ceiling. "Go ahead."

"Harry Cruz . . . he was on special assignment through your DEA office at the consulate. I'm afraid . . . he's dead, Mister Santiago. He's dead."

David rubbed at his eyes, took a breath.

And even though he knew the answer, he had to ask the question:

"How did it happen?"

The funeral services were held a week later, and David was in the front pew of the small Catholic church. Through all the proceedings, the prayers, the singing of the hymns, the gentle weeping among Harry's friends and coworkers, only one thing kept going through his mind: the stark beauty of Harry's widow, standing there in a lovely black dress, standing by the flag-draped coffin of her dead husband.

Dead because of David.

But now a widow.

All alone.

And through the prayers and the weeping and the singing of the hymns, David found he could not take his eyes off of her.

A week after the funeral, he had lunch with her, just to see how she was doing, and most of all, just to be alone with her, to know that there was nobody else out there now but him, and him alone.

They sat at a cafe on Bremont Street, enjoying the sunshine, the dishes having been cleared away, and he took her in, not even thinking of her dead husband, not even thinking of what she must be going through, only knowing that she was here now, available and desirable. The conversation had been light, about the weather and the latest political controversy involving the mayor, and it was like by unspoken agreement both had avoided the topic of Harry. Even in mourning she was desirable, the only offputting feature being that her eyes looked tired. She had on white shorts and a yellow knit top, and when he had paid the bill, he said, "Carla . . . I want to make sure you're all right."

She touched his forearm. "You've been such a dear, David. Thank you."

"Would . . . would you like to have dinner tonight?"

He waited, heart thumping along, wondering if he was moving too fast, if he had been spoiling it, what would he do if she said no. Another touch on the arm. "I'd love to," she said, smiling.

That night, riding the elevator up to her condo unit—her condo unit, nobody else's, all alone there. Her condo unit!—and in his hand, he carried a single rose. He had debated what to bring, what kind of flowers would be appropriate, and decided a single rose was enough. Not an overpowering bouquet, just a simple little flower. A little sign of affection, a little sign for big hopes for the future.

At the door to her condo unit he shivered from anticipation. He had seen her from outside the condo unit, looking in . . . and now he would be inside with her.

It was going to happen. Maybe not tonight, maybe not next week, but it was going to happen. . . .

He rang the bell. A muffled voice from inside, saying the door was unlocked, and the doorknob turned easily in his hand and he walked in, noting the bright lights and the fine furniture and the scent of Carla and a form coming out of the kitchen, and he was smiling and thinking of the right words to say . . .

And he froze.

Before him was George O'Toole Dunfey, a.k.a. God. David stood there, knowing how ridiculous he looked, rose in hand, but he could not move.

"David," Dunfey said.

"Yes."

Dunfey looked like he was trying to control his emotions, for his face seemed to quiver, like the nerve endings there were busy snapping back and forth. Dunfey took a deep breath and said, "Do you know why I'm here?"

"I . . . I'm not sure, I think it's—"

Dunfey said, "I'm here because of an internal investigation we've been conducting involving you and your street source, the man known as 'Chancey.' It seems some time ago, you did a favor for him, outside of normal channels and protocol. A favor involving his sister and some Colombians.

There was a thought that perhaps you were trading favors for something else besides information. And a while ago, when it seemed like nothing was going to pan out from this internal investigation, we were ready to stop it. Until . . ."

Dunfey turned to the kitchen, motioned with his left hand.

David dropped the rose on the floor.

Harry Cruz walked out, face red with anger, fists clenched at his side. He said one word, in a mixture of sorrow and hate and surprise: "*Jefe.*"

Dunfey said, "Until we saw what you did with Chancey and Harry's posting. Which led to fakery on our part, from the consulate phone call to the funeral. We wanted to know just why you did what you did . . . for what payment, what compensation. And David . . . I know what you think of me. I know what others in the office think of me. A straight-arrow prude who is a stickler for rules and procedures. A man to be joked about. Perhaps."

He seemed to try to control his emotions. "But at least I've never tried to kill a colleague for the purpose of seducing his wife."

Another movement of his hand. Two Miami-Dade County sheriff's deputies came out from the living room. Dunfey said, "You're now under arrest, David. You and your career are finished. And just in case you were wondering, Harry's wife, Carla, hates you, and will hate you for the rest of her life. And as for me . . ."

And without a trace of humor in his voice, his supervisor spoke up—and David could not reply—as Dunfey said:

"God has spoken."

Gustav Amlingmeyer, Holmes of the Range

Steve Hockensmith

Steve Hockensmith has worked as an entertainment reporter, covering pop culture and the film industry for *The Hollywood Reporter*, *The Chicago Tribune*, *The Fort Worth Star-Telegram*, *Newsday*, *Total Movie*, and other publications. He also served as editor of *The X-Files Official Magazine* and *Cinescape*. Hockensmith, who writes about mystery-solving cowboys Big Red and Old Red Amlingmeyer, found his first published mystery story, "Erie's Last Day," honored with the Short Mystery Fiction Society's Derringer Award. The story appeared in *Best American Mystery Stories 2001*. Hockensmith's story "Tricks" (a sequel to "Erie's Last Day") was nominated for a Shamus award, while "The Big Road" (yet another "Erie" follow-up) was nominated for a Shamus, a Macavity, and a Barry. He is a regular contributor to *EQMM* and *AHMM*. His first novel featuring The Amlingmeyer brothers, *Holmes on the Range*, was published in 2006, and his most recent novel, *On the Wrong Track*, came out earlier this year.

Harper's Weekly
Harper & Bros., Publishers
325 to 337 Pearl Street
Franklin Square
New York

Greetings to whichever Harper I have the pleasure of addressing!

First off, let me slather on a bit of butter by telling you how much I appreciate your family's fine magazine. Out here in Montana, a person can get to thinking the world isn't anything but grass, sky, and cow pies. *Harper's Weekly* is one of the ways we Westerners remind ourselves that there's still a thing called "civilization" out there and that supposedly we are a part of it. That's an important idea for folks to keep a rope on, I can assure you, for I've been to a few places where they didn't, and it was almost enough to get me believing all that science talk about men being nothing more than monkeys who traded in their tails for trousers.

As much as I admire your publication, however, I do have a notion as to how it could be improved. It has come to my attention in recent months that there are two kinds of stories much in demand by the reading public: yarns about cowboys and yarns about detectives. I know about the first because, until a few week's back, I was a working cowpuncher myself. Many's the time I've pulled out a copy of *Buffalo Bill Stories* or *Deadwood Dick Library* and tickled the boys in the bunkhouse by reading out the most outlandish bits of balderdash contained therein. Detective tales, on the other hand, I never troubled myself with until only recently, when my brother got himself a craving for them worse than a rummy craves rotgut. In the past two months, he's read dozens of the damned things—or, to be more accurate, he's *heard* dozens of them, because I do all the reading, my brother having discontinued his schooling before he could discover what follows A, B, and C.

It occurs to me that cowboys being popular and detectives being popular, a cowboy detective would be twice as popular as each. And I just happen to know one, for there are lessons to be learned from detective yarns, and my brother has put them to use. An account of how he's done so is what fills the next few pages—pages that I propose you reprint in *Harper's Weekly* under the title "Gustav Amlingmeyer, Holmes of the Range." (If that title is not to your liking, feel free to brand it with another. I'm also rather partial to "Old Red's Deadly Dilemma" myself.)

Gustav Amlingmeyer, as you might have guessed, is my brother, although those who know him by his Christian name are few and far between. It's much more common to hear him hailed by the handle "Old Red." This he earned both for his sunset-red head of hair and his midnight-black disposition. My name is Otto Amlingmeyer, though I've been rechristened "Big Red" because I've got the same hair as my elder brother but about a foot more of spine and leg beneath it.

It was only natural that Old Red and I should become cowboys, as we grew up with ample supplies of the profession's two most important requirements: poverty and desperation. Though droving is hardly the best way to go about ridding yourself of either, somehow we've managed to build up a small stake—though Old Red might argue with that "we." Like many a hand, I'm a man who likes to cut his wolf loose at the end of a trail, and no doubt wine, women, and song would claim every penny if the purse-strings were mine alone to draw tight or pull open. Gustav, on the other hand, manages to keep his wolf hogtied at all times, and he's insisted on squirreling away almost all of our pay.

"Pushin' other men's cows ain't gonna get us nowhere," he would tell me when I fussed over this. "We gotta save up and buy somethin' of our own if we wanna end up anything more than a couple of saddle bums."

I always assumed that the "something of our own" Gustav talked about would be a little ranch or farm somewhere. So you can imagine my dismay when my brother informed me we were going into the restauranting business. I was in a saloon here in Billings at the time, and though I was the one doing the drinking, I asked Old Red whether he was drunk or crazy, for surely it had to be one or the other.

"Nothin' crazy about cookin' for folks, little brother," he said. "People always need food."

I didn't bother asking him if he was joking, seeing as how he cracked a funny about as often as a coyote yodels "Onward, Christian Soldiers." "How much?" I asked instead.

"Two hundred."

That was nearly half what we had saved. I yelled out to the bartender to bring me some of his best whiskey, pronto, as soon enough I would not be able to afford it. Once the first shot was tickling my liver, I nodded at Old Red.

"All right," I said. "I'm ready. Tell me the rest."

And that he did. It seems he'd bumped into a fellow name of Starchy Baker who'd been one of the belly cheaters on a big West Texas roundup Gustav had ridden in '88. Starchy had tired of doing all his cooking out of the back of a chuck wagon, so he'd traded in his dutch oven for the real thing. He had himself a little lunch counter out near the stockyards, and there were always enough outfits coming through to keep his griddles hot. Only Starchy couldn't hardly keep up anymore on account of the rheumatoid arthritis that had driven him off the trail in the first place. It was getting worse now, and Starchy figured he needed a long soak in the Arkansas hot springs to uncurl his boogered-up bones.

"So you bought him out for two hundred dollars."

"He wanted three at first," Old Red said. "I haggled him down pretty good."

I tossed back another gulp of tonsil varnish. "We'll just see about that."

We walked out to the edge of town and Gustav showed me what two hundred dollars could buy a man in Billings: a rotting shack, twenty rickety chairs, a couple wobbly tables, and an ancient cast-iron stove.

"It ain't the looks that count. It's the location," Gustav said, probably just blowing back at me something Starchy had said to him.

"We'll, let's not forget another little certain something there, brother," I replied. "How about the damn *food!* You can hardly tell salt from pepper, and the last time I tried fixin' up any grub I nearly killed six men and a dog."

Now my brother's temper is a strange and unpredictable creature. Some days he might snarl at you for pouring your coffee too loud, other days you could tie the ends of his moustache together and he wouldn't say boo. This happened to be one of the latter kind of days, for he didn't take to screaming back at me or even raise his voice.

"You and me, we won't have to so much as crack an egg," he said. "Starchy had him an Irish gal that filled in from time to time. There's no reason we couldn't hire her on to do all the cookin'. All we'd have to do is take the orders, tote the food, and tally up the money."

That took some of the bite out of me. Old Red had thought it through fine enough. Still, I felt pretty strange about trading in my chaps for an apron.

"What do you say we fire up that oven and just shovel the rest of our money straight in?" I said. But Gustav was still feeling charitable, and be didn't take the bait.

Two days later, Starchy cleared out his gear, said his goodbyes, and left us to it. At last, the Amlingmeyer boys were respectable businessmen. Or at least we were as respectable as you can be when you're running around in a greasy apron fetching beans and bacon for cowboys. We had other customers, too—railroad men, soldiers, drifters who'd come into a charity nickel. We certainly weren't catering to the town's leading citizens, but Gustav and I didn't mind as long as folks paid for their food and ate it without getting into a fight.

Our clientele coming from the rougher classes, we did have a tussle on our hands every so often. Some Texas drover would get salty with a buffalo soldier, hot words would lead to flying fists, and lickety-split, grown men would be poking each other with forks and trying to spoon each other's eyes out. Now as I've got an uncommon amount of flesh to bring to bear, it at first fell to me to settle any dust-ups. But we quickly learned that imposing size was a less reliable peacemaker than questionable sanity. If I couldn't break up a fight quick enough to suit her, our cook would come flying out of the kitchen with a meat cleaver in her hand, a scream on her lips, and a bloodthirsty look in her eyes. She'd take to swinging that blade around, and everybody in the place would duck for cover. By the time she'd calmed down and headed back into the kitchen, we'd all of us forgotten who'd been punching who in the first place. Pretty soon, I didn't bother stepping into customers' tangles, as word spread that Starchy's Cafay was under the protection of Crazy Kathy McKenna, and all she had to do was lay hand on that cleaver to restore order.

Now you might think it would hurt business, people having the impression they could end up with cold steel in their belly along with their beef stew. But cowboys being cowboys, it was the best advertisement our little establishment could have. Fellows would come in straight off the trail and order up a batch of fried chicken just so they could sit there and gawk at Crazy Kathy. Every now and then a couple of them would try to get a rise out of her by playacting they were headed for a fracas, but I soon learned to spot our amateur thespians early on and would politely suggest they take their food and their foolishness outside.

Of course, there were some townsmen who didn't find all this a real tickle, and one of them would drop by from time to time to remind us that he still wasn't laughing. Seeing as he was the town marshal, we didn't have any choice but to listen.

"That dirty mick cook of yours ever hurts anybody, I'm holdin' you two responsible," he'd say. Then he'd grab him a couple of biscuits and walk out. He was a big, boulder-headed son of a mule name of Ben Nickles, and men who opened their mouths too wide in his presence often found a gun barrel where their teeth used to be. So we just nodded, said a silent goodbye to our biscuits, and then got back to work. Old Red would store up his curses until the restaurant was closed for the night, then he'd start pouring them out all over me.

"He's a disgrace to his badge," he'd say. "If there's a problem he can't solve with fists or guns, then that's a problem don't get solved at all. The man's all muscle, no method."

That last bit was considered by Gustav to be the ultimate insult to a lawman's skills. He'd made a study on "method" after stumbling upon accounts of one Sherlock Holmes of London, England. This Holmes fellow's sort of a gentleman layabout turned sleuth who solves crimes by means my brother describes as "observation and cogitation." Driving cattle's a true test for nerves and muscle, but you might as well deposit your brain in a bank before you hit the trail, for you won't be needing it until you get back. My brother being a man with little learning but much smarts, I believe drovering had become a kind of mental torture for him. His mind was dying of thirst, and this Sherlock Holmes was a cool drink of water. Whatever the explanation for it, my brother's fascination with Holmes drove him to snatch up every detective magazine he could lay hands on. Nick Carter, King Brady, Old Cap Collier, even Madge the Society Detective—we've read about them all. It didn't take long for Gustav to turn sour on these American crimebusters, though. All muscle, no method, he said. But we were stuck with them, as a yarn about Holmes is harder to find than a Mormon in a whorehouse. Gustav's only managed to rustle up two Holmes tales so far: one called "A Study in Scarlet," the other "The Red-Headed League." We end every day the same way, in the bed we share in the storeroom at the back of the shack, me reading out the story of Old Red's choice. I say a quiet prayer before we turn in that he won't ask to hear about Holmes, as I've read those two stories so many times the words are practically tattooed on my eyeballs.

Now let me warn you, spending the last waking hour of each day in the company of a dime-novel detective will do strange things to your sleep. My dreams are stuffed to bursting with black-caped kidnappers and bomb-lobbing radicals and skulking Chinamen with ruby-handled daggers hidden up their silky sleeves. It's almost a relief when Crazy Kathy barges in before the break of dawn to fire up the oven, making enough noise to wake the deaf and the dead alike.

Not long afterward our first customers bang on through the rickety door out front. Sometimes it's cowboys, sometimes it's railroaders. Either way, they want the same thing—coffee, biscuits, bacon, and eggs. When they start asking for beefsteak or beans, I know it's getting on toward noon. Every now and then some big-mouthed bull nurse will try to cut a shine on Crazy Kathy by calling out that he wants roast goose with oyster stuffing and he wants it now. If she's in a good mood, Kathy will ignore him. If she's not, she'll step out of the kitchen with that cleaver of hers and let the fellow know he's a catfish-faced son of a bitch and he's going to get beans.

For pure *mean,* we figured our cook was pretty near the hands-down champion of the plains. But eventually a customer came along who gave her a real run for her money. His name was Jack G. Johnson, and for two weeks solid he ate nothing but Crazy Kathy's cooking—breakfast, dinner, and supper. Why he did so was a mystery to us all, for he announced time and time again that it was the foulest hog slop he'd seen heaped on a plate since his days in the Confederate army. Of course, Kathy came out to challenge this notion the first time she heard it, but this Johnson fellow called her bluff.

"Get your ass back in that kitchen before I put my boot on it, you poxy Irish slattern," he growled at her. "And the next time you make me stew see to it you put some damn salt in it."

Every man in the place got set to jump when they heard that, for surely anyone slow on his toes was about to end up with old Jack's brains in his hair. But Crazy Kathy just sneered, spat at Johnson's feet—not *on* them, you understand, *at* them—and stomped off back to the griddle. It seemed Kathy had met her match, and those of us there to witness it could only gape in silent wonder. Johnson wasn't one to rest on his laurels, however.

"Hey, pimples," he said to an especially young puncher a couple chairs down from where he sat. "Stop your gawking and make yourself useful." He pointed at a salt shaker and snapped his fingers impatiently until it had been handed to him. Needless to say, the cowboy got no thanks.

Whereas Crazy Kathy added the kind of color our customers appreciate, no one appreciated Jack G. Johnson. Politics, religion, personal hygiene—no subject was taboo to him. He said men who wanted to keep Benjamin Harrison in the White House ought to have their heads examined, and men who wanted to put James Baird Weaver in Harrison's place ought to have their heads *removed*. Labor agitators should be shot on sight, but the real enemy were those Jew bankers in New York and the "mongrel races" flooding our shores from abroad. Sweep out the Chinese, the Irish, the Italians, the Poles, and the Russians—and exterminate the Indians down to the last suckling child while you're at it—and then this country might really stand for something again. Or so Johnson told us.

Every so often, there would be a fellow who agreed with every little thing he said, which seemed to annoy the man more than all those labor agitators and bankers and "mongrels" combined. He'd get to ripping into the poor chowderhead's crooked teeth or ratty clothes or big feet or some such thing, and before long his one potential ally would turn against him, and Johnson would be happy again.

But where Johnson's capacity for cussedness really took the prize was on the subject of Negroes and the Civil War. My brother and I hailing from Kansas and being of German stock, we have our own feelings on this matter. Gustav was born a year after the war ended, and I didn't mosey along until six years after him, but sometimes it felt like we were both of us at Chancellorsville and Gettysburg for all the talk we heard on it in our younger days. We were much aware that we'd lost three uncles, five cousins, and an aunt in the war. The uncles and one of the cousins died wearing blue. The others were cut down by rebel bushwhackers.

We'd also known a number of Negro cowboys over the years, for though you'll see nary a one in *Buffalo Bill Stories,* you'll find plenty working the trails. As with all men, some are good, some are bad. We didn't feel any hesitation about befriending the good, and one and all were welcome to spend their money in our little cookhouse.

But Johnson would get to fussing and cussing every time he found himself in the company of a Negro. And if he discovered you were a Union man—or, worse yet, a Union *veteran*—he'd lay into his Northern aggression, carpetbaggers, race mixers, and scoundrels speech. And if that didn't get a rise out of you, he'd wheel out the heavy artillery. The first time he did it, every customer in the place nearly emptied the stomachs they'd been trying to fill. Johnson had been storming away at Ricky Hess, a kid soda jerk who took his meals with us so he could hear the punchers blow some wind about life in the saddle. I think Ricky wanted to prove he had some eggs in his basket, for he was needling old Johnson right back, saying how Abraham Lincoln was a saint and your average Confederate soldier was nothing but a shoeless hillbilly fighting with a bent-barrel musket and a rusty butter knife.

"You want to see what the average Confederate soldier could do?" Johnson asked.

Ricky stiffened up and leaned back, getting himself set to dodge the old man's swing. But instead of throwing a punch, Johnson just smiled. His lips didn't stop at a simple grin though. They kept on going, pulling back until his whole face was stretched into an open-mouthed grimace, like he was screaming without making a sound.

And then the damnedest thing happened. Johnson's teeth began to *move*. They shifted to the right, shifted to the left, shifted to the right again, then wriggled themselves all the way free of his face. Johnson caught them in his hand as they fell and then held them up at Ricky. "You see these, boy?"

Ricky nodded, staring slack-jawed at Johnson as if the

man had just produced Jeff Davis from his mouth instead of a pair of dentures.

"Well, these ain't porcelain teeth. They're *Yankee* teeth, pulled from blue-bellies at Antietam." Johnson winked, and his pruned-up lips wormed themselves into another smile. "I do believe some of 'em weren't even dead yet. Those Northern boys weren't much in the way of soldiers, but I'll give 'em this much—they had some mighty fine choppers. These dentures were made for Major Dick Wheeler, my commanding officer, in eighteen sixty-two, and they served him well for twenty-four years. When he died, his widow was kind enough to give 'em to me. I had my son do 'em over to fit my mouth, and they've been chawin' up biscuits for me ever since." Johnson glanced around the room and, satisfied that he had everyone's full and utterly horrified attention, got to opening and closing those dentures so it looked like his hand had itself a working mouth.

"Glory, glory, Hallelujah," he sang. "Glory, glory, Hallelujah. Glory, glory, Hallelujah. His truth is marching on."

Ricky ran out of the place pale as a Klansman's sheet, Johnson cackling at him like some loco old squaw.

Now my brother typically adheres to a strict neutrality when it comes to customer disputes. "As long as folks can keep eatin', it ain't no business of ours," he'd say to me. But Gustav looked about ready to chuck that neutrality in favor of a public horsewhipping.

"Mr. Johnson," he said, and his voice sounded completely calm and respectful despite the words it was about to pronounce, "I'm advising you to keep those filthy things in your mouth when you're on my property or they're gonna end up . . ."

Well, the locale my brother suggested might offend delicate sensibilities, but it should suffice to say that depositing a pair of dentures there would be an unpleasant experience for all concerned.

Johnson didn't bat an eye. He just sucked in those teeth of his and got back to work on his chicken and dumplings. And come suppertime he was back again.

Gustav was glad enough to have the old man's money, if not his company. But I had to wonder why Johnson had to spend any money on grub at all. Certainly, he didn't come to Starchy's every day out of necessity. He had both an able-bodied daughter-in-law and a prosperous son, so home-cooking or a better class of restaurant were not beyond his reach. George J. Johnson, the son, was the top dentist around, the only competition in Billings being an opium-addled old quack name of Huggins who had the devil of a time convincing folks to call him "Painless" instead of "Brainless." As a result, Doc Johnson was doing enough business to make himself a real pillar of the community, the proof of which was his recent marriage to Elsa Mueller, the daughter of one of Billings's resident preachers (Lutheran, in this case) and a pillar in her own right as a leader of the town's growing temperance movement. Though it had been known that Doc Johnson was a Southerner, no one had known quite *how* Southern until Papa Johnson stepped off a train whistling "Dixie." The elder Johnson caused quite a stir, being as rude and hardheaded as his son was courtly and mild-mannered. The local tongue-flappers whispered that the old man had come West for his health, for he was a gnarled little lizard, and every day he seemed to turn more mottled and rashy-looking.

Now all this was but distant gossip for us no-accounts out on the edge of town until the day Johnson limped into Starchy's to plague us with his patronage. Despite the old man's constant complaints, *something* about our place agreed with him. He dragged himself in looking like a fellow not only at death's door but with one foot firmly inside the house. Within a few days, however, his color improved, his back straightened, and he was digging into Kathy's "hog slop" con mucho gusto. Some folks joked that Kathy's cooking had restorative properties and should be bottled as a patent elixir.

Others said Johnson would thrive in any environment in which he could make himself a nuisance. Either way, he quickly became our most loyal—and loathed—customer.

He minded Gustav's warning, though, keeping his dentures perched on his gums where they belonged. But from time to time he'd brag on his "little Yankee prisoners" and set them to squirming around so much behind his smile it looked like he kept a snake in there.

While Johnson was fixed to Starchy's tight as a tick, Ricky Hess we didn't see for a while. It took him a week to work up the nerve to come back. But when he did return, he did it big, striding in puffed up like a rooster and taking an empty seat to the left of the old man.

Johnson didn't notice at first, for he had already divided his forces on two fronts, firing affronts into the kitchen where Kathy was frying him up a steak while aiming the occasional barrage at the fellow to his right, a black puncher by the name of Feathers Purnell.

Though Ricky was trying to come off tough, I noticed him fiddling nervously with a salt shaker as I walked up to take his order.

"I'll have whatever he's havin'," he said, jerking a thumb at Johnson. When the old buzzard turned to point his beak at him, Hess gave him a hearty slap on the back. "How ya doin' today, reb? What's the latest news from Richmond?"

Johnson gave him a squint hot enough to bake a cake. "I'd thank you to keep your hands off me, you miserable little piss-puddle," he said.

I got set to haul myself over the counter and pull him and Ricky apart, but before either man could fire off a punch toward the other's face, Kathy stomped out of the kitchen and threw a plate down in front of Johnson.

"There's yer steak," she said. "May ya choke on it and catch the first coach to Hell."

Kathy's curse brought a smile to the old man's lips, and he turned away from Ricky and called after her, "If it tastes as bad as your cookin' usually does, chokin' to death will be sweet mercy."

Johnson snatched up his fork and knife, and for a second there everyone watching expected one or the other to end up in Ricky's throat. But the old man got to sawing away at his beef instead. He stuffed a big, bloody strip of it into his mouth, gave it a couple of chews, then winced and swallowed.

"Damn, woman," he said, bringing a hand up to rub the left side of his face. "I asked for steak, not fried rope." His cheeks bulged on one side, then the other, as his tongue probed around inside his mouth. He fished a finger in there and pulled out a small yellow sliver. "I've eaten shoe leather more tender than this. Ain't nothin' on this plate but gristle and bone."

But as much as he complained about that first bite, it didn't stop him from carrying on with a second and a third and so on. In-between chews he cheerfully badgered Kathy and Ricky and Feathers, squeezing off insults at each one in turn before starting around the circle again when he'd made a full rotation of it. Kathy and Feathers took it quiet, her busying herself with her cooking and him busying himself with his fried oysters. But young Hess sparred back, and whenever he and Johnson swallowed their last mouthfuls I figured we'd be right back where we started, with the two of them ready to throw around fists instead of harsh words.

After a few minutes, however, Johnson seemed to lose his taste for fighting and steak both. He went all quiet halfway through a remark about Feathers' mother and dropped his knife and fork on the countertop with a clatter that turned me around from the dirty plates I'd been handing to Gustav. Johnson had gone sweaty slick since the last time I'd glanced his way, and he proceeded to wrap his arms around his stomach and let out a moan like a motherless calf on a cold night.

"You all right, mister?" Feathers asked.

"Do I . . . look . . . all right?" Johnson gasped, managing to be nasty even when it appeared he hardly had the strength to stick out his tongue. He pushed his chair back and stood up, "I just . . . need to . . . go outside and . . ."

He didn't get anywhere near outside. After three wobbly steps, he swooned and hit the floor, managing to turn over a table and cover himself with other men's dinner in the process.

Feathers made it to him first, rolling Johnson over and brushing cornbread crumbs and beans off his face. The old man's eyes rolled back in his head, the lids fluttering, and a breathy whisper slipped through his trembling lips.

"What's he sayin'?" I asked.

Feathers leaned his ear in close. Then he put his hand up to Johnson's face again, this time wrapping the palm and fingers across the old man's eyes and nose and sort of giving a little squeeze. Then the cowboy stood up, a look on his face like the kind a fellow gets after taking a sip of rancid buttermilk. But he didn't say a thing.

Gustav piped up then. "Frank," he called out to one of our regulars, "go get Doc Snow. Anvil, I think you oughta fetch Doc Johnson. And quick, boys."

"You think he's dyin'?" I asked as Frank and Anvil darted out the door.

Gustav gave me one of those stares that tell me he's not altogether convinced he and I could come from the same bloodline.

Johnson took to heaving and purging after that, and soon he and the dirt floor around him were far from a pretty sight. As much as I might have cursed the man in my heart the past few weeks, it still stung to see him squirming like a gut-shot dog.

Now one thing you've got to understand about a town like Billings is, entertainment and spectacle are in mighty short supply. Not having an opera house, a music hall, a zoo garden, or any other modern place of amusement, folks out here have to make do with shootings, hangings, and fires. Misfortunes of all sorts being popular viewing, a man dropping a hammer on his foot is just about all you need to draw a crowd. So by the time Frank got back with Doc Snow, the two of them had to push their way through a swarm of spectators that had gathered around to witness the infamous Jack G. Johnson's final moments. Thanks to that crowd, Frank and the doctor missed those moments by about a minute, for when they finally wriggled past the last onlooker, Johnson was dead.

That didn't keep Doc Snow from hunkering down and giving the man's twisted-up corpse a good going over. Snow was an altogether overeducated, overmannered, and over-efficient fellow to have landed in a place like Billings without some trouble back East sending him our way. Folks viewed him as the gift horse you don't look in the mouth, however, so nobody asked too many questions about his past. They just listened to what he had to say and thanked the Lord they didn't have to get all their medical advice from strangers selling miracle cures off the back of medicine-show wagons.

So it hit the crowd like lightning when the town's one and only respected physician stood up, brushed off his frock coat, and announced, "This man was poisoned."

While everyone else was still sputtering out things like, "What?" and "Did he say 'poisoned'?" and "Hooo-whee! Murder!" Old Red was bending over the body asking the doc how he'd come by his conclusion.

"The symptoms," Snow said. "And you'll notice crescents of white on the fingernails and a whiff of garlic still on the tongue. All signs of *poudre de succession*."

Gustav looked up at Snow. "All signs of what, now?"

"Poudre de succession," Snow said again (and I'll admit right here I only know how to spell it out because I tracked him down this morning and asked him).

Before Snow could lay out for my brother and the rest of us rabble exactly what he was talking about, Anvil Hayes elbowed his way to the center of the room.

"Couldn't get Doc Johnson. He's out to the Lazy P pullin' teeth. Won't be back till tonight," Anvil said. "I told his wife the old man's sick, though." He looked down at the body, and I couldn't tell if the chagrin on his face was because Johnson had died or because he'd missed the dying.

Just then the crowd began to part like the Red Sea before Moses, and I knew before he even stepped into my sight that Billings's top lawman had arrived to irritate my brother with his enthusiastic application of muscle over method.

"Damn it all, is that man dead?" Marshal Nickles asked as he pushed past Anvil.

"As dead as the proverbial doornail," Dr. Snow replied.

"Doc said it was poison," I added, trying to be helpful. "Poo-drey dee zoo-zay-zion or some such."

"Arsenic," Snow finally explained.

That sent another lightning bolt through the place, and half the men there seemed compelled to shout out "Arsenic!" like it was "Hallelujah!" and they were at a tent revival. But none of them hollered louder than Nickles, who immediately whirled off toward the kitchen and backed Crazy Kathy up against the stove.

"All right," he said to her. "Let's go."

"What're ya talkin' about?" Kathy asked, a tremor of fear in her usually commanding voice. "Where would I be goin', then?"

"You're comin' with me to the jail, that's where you're goin'."

"Hold on there, Marshal," my brother said, following Nickles into the kitchen. "We don't know who slipped Johnson the poison. There ain't no proof it was Kathy."

"You shut your trap. And while you're at it, shut your

doors." Obviously pleased by the rare (for him) experience of making a clever remark, Nickles let his mouth tilt over into something that was half sneer, half smile. "I've warned you about lettin' this crazy Irish hag do your cookin'. Far as I'm concerned, you and your brother are practically murderers yourselves. So I'm orderin' you to close this fly-trap down till we can get this in front of a judge. And don't give me any back-talk about it. Just be glad you ain't under arrest . . . yet."

Then Nickles turned back to Kathy, locked a big paw on her wrist, and yanked her toward the door. She unraveled a string of curses on him that would make a soldier's ears bleed, but I saw terror in her eyes. The crowd moved back to let them through, then flowed in around them like quicksand, swallowing the two up and blocking our view.

I heard Gustav sigh and start rooting around for something in the kitchen. When he stepped out, he was strapping on his gun-belt.

"Better get yourself heeled, brother," he said to me. "We don't want poor Kathy runnin' into a lynchin' bee between here and the jail."

I dusted off my iron and strapped it on, wondering all the while if the mob wouldn't see fit to string us up, too, guns or no.

As it turned out, there was no need to fret about a lynching just yet. Quite the opposite; everyone seemed to take Johnson's murder as an excuse for a holiday, and Kathy wasn't in jail ten minutes before there were fellows outside selling boiled peanuts and ginger beer. Some folks even began spreading out blankets and getting down to picnics.

Gustav and I tried to get inside the jail to have a word

with Kathy, but one of Nickles's deputies encouraged us to amble along. As this encouragement came from the business end of a Winchester, we ambled. We could hear Kathy somewhere inside the jail, though, still telling Nickles his head was packed full of the stuff you pay a man a penny to shovel off a stable floor.

We sparked a good bit of commentary as we weaved our way through the throng, everybody trying to play Eddie Foy with cracks like, "Hey, boys! I hear the cookin' at your place is to die for!" and "Mind if I send my mother-in-law over for supper tonight?"

"Well, Old Red," I said once we'd escaped the jeers, "what do you think? The five o'clock or the eight-thirty?"

"The five o'clock or the eight-thirty *what?*"

"Train, brother. Five o'clock east, eight-thirty west. I vote for east, myself. From Miles City we can head all the way down to—"

Gustav gave me a look of disappointment and dismay he'd inherited from our mother. "We ain't goin' anywhere," he said. "Kathy needs our help."

"Oh, come now. There ain't no helpin' crazy folks. You know that. Hell, she probably did it."

"Well, then you just think of it as helpin' ourselves. It'd look mighty bad, us skeedaddlin' now. Like maybe Kathy had some help curling Johnson up. And what about Starchy's Cafay? We can't just walk away from that."

"I ain't sayin' we walk away. I'm sayin' we *run*. You heard those fellers back there. Starchy's ain't nothin' worth stickin' around for. The place was ruined the second Johnson hit the floor."

"We're stayin'," Gustav said, using the tone of voice that

told me he was pulling rank. There would be no more debate. The elder brother had spoken.

"All right. We stay. For now. But how in God's name are the two of us supposed to help Kathy?"

"It won't just be the two of us. We've got an important friend on our side." "Oh?"

I ruminated for a second on our friends in Billings, none of whom you could label "important." "Penniless," perhaps. Or "powerless." "Drunk," "rowdy," and "smelly" would also fit just fine on most. But there wasn't an "important" in the bunch.

"Just who are you thinkin' of?"

"Why, Mr. Sherlock Holmes, of course."

My brother gave me a sly little wink, and I took to wondering if crazy is something you can catch. After all, he'd spent a lot of time in the kitchen with Kathy. Maybe she'd given him a bad case of the locos.

Not that Gustav can't do up a fine display of detective-style thinking every so often. Mr. Holmes has this way of spinning little details into big "deductions," and my brother had taken a pretty fair whack at it on a few occasions. Then one day he pointed out a fellow slurping on some soup in Starchy's and told me he'd deduced that the man was a Hebrew butcher who'd served in the army and just returned from California. Turned out he was an Italian tailor two months off the boat from Europe, and he was as far west as he'd ever been in his life. My faith in my brother's grasp of "method" was never quite the same after that.

And anyway, even Holmes himself couldn't prove trees can sing, dogs have wings, and extra glue makes for tasty donuts. Kathy's innocence I saw as being much the same. I figured she'd walk free about the time I saw a flock of beagles flying south for the winter. Which meant Starchy's was finished, and so were we.

I was pulled free of these gloomy thoughts by an even gloomier sound—that of a woman weeping. It was Elsa Johnson, the old man's daughter-in-law. She was in our shabby little shack, looking about as out of place as a pearl on a plate of baked beans. Her white silk dress could just about blind you it was so gleaming clean. She was sitting with her back to the body, her slender shoulders shuddering slightly with delicate, ladylike grief. Doc Snow held one of her hands in his and whispered quiet comforts in her ear as Howard and Andrew Gould, the paunchy namesakes of Gould Brothers Funeral Parlor, hovered over the corpse like a couple of fat-bellied vultures in thirty-dollar suits. A simple wooden box lay near the corpse. It was just for toting stiffs, I assumed, being too plain for burying the father of an honorary member of the thriving merchant class.

We'd put on hats before running off after Nickles and Kathy, and I swiped mine off my head and elbowed Old Red to remind him to do the same.

"Ma'am," I said. "I would like to convey our most sincere condolences to you and your husband in this time of loss. If there's anything we can do to be of assistance, I just ask you to let us know and it will be done."

It was my thinking that a little honey could sweeten Mrs. Johnson's disposition towards us, which might help us sidestep reciprocations of a legal nature. But when that woman stood and turned to face us, she looked at me like I'd dumped a bucket of cold water on her head.

"You've already done enough," she said, her voice icy

calm despite the tears she'd been shedding just a moment before. She looked at the Gould brothers and nodded her head. "It's time we left."

"Hold on there, ma'am," Gustav said. "Someone needs to examine the body before it's moved."

"Excuse me?" If she'd looked at me like I'd been throwing water around, the glare she gave my brother suggested his bucket was full of vinegar—or worse. "That's how . . ."

I cringed, knowing the words "Sherlock Holmes would do it" were about to come from my brother's mouth. He seemed to sense what a damn dumb thing this would be to say, and he managed to get his lips pointed in a different direction before the damage could be done.

". . . police back East handle this kind of thing."

It was an improvement, but it still didn't get a warm reception.

"I don't care how 'police back East' do things. My husband's father is dead, and I will not have strangers pawing over his body."

She nodded at the Goulds again, then walked briskly into the kitchen and out the back door. Doc Snow was a step behind her fixing to catch her should she faint, I suppose. The Gould brothers followed, too, after loading up Jack G. Johnson with the dainty touch of a woman packing away fine china—which was a tad funny, seeing as he wasn't in any condition to complain, should you yank off his ears. Out back they slid the box up on a wagon, then proceeded to cart away the Johnsons, both living and dead.

Dr. Snow started to drift off after the wagon, but Gustav shouted out, "Doc!" and waved him back. He seemed a touch reluctant to step foot inside our humble establishment again, and he stopped just short of the door.

"That was rather indelicate, your request to the lady," he said to Gustav. The few times I'd run across him in the past, Snow had struck me as a rather stiff, crusty fellow, and now it looked like his contact with Mrs. Johnson had put even more starch in his collar.

"Ain't nothin' delicate about murder," my brother replied with such confidence and bravado you'd think he'd been a New York constable all his days instead of a farm boy, drover, and dishwasher. "Anyway, I thought you were a man of science."

Now a fair enough response would have been, "What do *you* know about being a 'man of science'? You can't even spell the words." Instead Snow blinked and kind of harrumphed and said, "I am."

"Good," Gustav said. "Then you can tell me if there's a test for arsenic."

Snow nodded. "The Marsh Test. It's simple enough. Through the application of heat one can convert arsenic into arsine gas, which can be precipitated on a surface such as a mirror or a porcelain dish as a—"

There was more, but I can't get it straight even after more talk with the doc. Suffice it to say the answer was indeed *"yes,"* and Gustav disappeared into the lunchroom and came back a moment later holding a plate topped with a half-eaten serving of steak and potatoes.

"You think you could apply all that hoo-ha you just talked up to this here chow?"

"Certainly."

Gustav held out the plate. "All right, then."

Snow took hold of the plate reluctantly, like he was being handed a bowl of scorpions. "This was Johnson's dinner?"

"That's right."

"I have to warn you—I'll feel obligated to report my findings to Marshal Nickles."

"That's what I'm countin' on," my brother said, sounding like he already knew what those findings would be and the test itself was practically beside the point. "When can you have an answer?"

"Tonight, maybe. Tomorrow morning at the latest."

"Good. I'll leave you to it."

As Snow went on his way, looking buffaloed to find himself walking across town with a plate of steak in his hand, I asked Gustav what exactly he expected this "Marsh Test" would prove.

"I've been practicin', brother," he replied. "Tryin' to shape myself into a real top-drawer observationalist, just like Mr. Holmes. And let me tell you—I was in the kitchen when Kathy was frying up that food for old man Johnson, and I didn't see her doctor it up with anything but salt and pepper."

"Yeah, you were in the kitchen, all right," I said. "Washin' dishes. You tellin' me you could scrub a pot and keep the eagle eye on Kathy at the same time?"

Though I half expected Old Red to take to barking at me for my lack of faith, he actually smiled and almost— *almost*—peeled off a chuckle.

"That's good, you askin' questions like that. I do believe you've picked up a thing or two from Mr. Holmes yourself," he said. "A first-class detective ain't gonna trust nobody's observations but his own."

"I ain't no detective," I said. "I'm a cowboy, and so are you. Now let's act like it and just saddle up, hit the trail, and forget this whole ugly . . ."

It was no use. He wasn't even listening to me anymore. He'd turned away and picked a frying pan up off the stove, and now he was staring into it like a sideshow Gypsy stares into her crystal ball.

"What do you see there?" he asked me, flipping the pan around and shoving it under my nose.

I shrugged. "Grease and gristle."

"That's right."

He clanged the pan back on the stovetop and snatched up a salt shaker from a shelf nearby.

"Every order of beef and taters Kathy did today got fried up in that pan—including a couple for fellers who moseyed in *after* Johnson." Gustav's words came out slow and quiet as he upended the shaker and sprinkled some salt in the palm of his left hand. "If she'd put any arsenic on the old man's food while it was cookin', we'd have ended up with more than one corpse clutterin' up the place."

He ran a finger over the granules in his hand, and I leaned in to get a closer look myself. Growing up, I had more experience with arsenic than with salt. The former we kept in ample supply to deal with rats and coyotes. The latter my mother guarded like it was gold dust, doling out about a pinch a year for the seasoning of food while hoarding the rest for pickling and preserving.

"Salt," I said.

"Salt," said my brother.

He clapped his hands clean then ran through the same business with the pepper.

"Pepper," I said.

"Pepper."

We spent the next half-hour peeking into every canister, prodding around all the corners, and poking away at anything that looked even the tiniest bit like arsenic powder. By the time we finished up, our hands were chalk-white with flour and sugar and baking soda, but there was no arsenic to be found.

"All right," Gustav said, wiping his hands clean on his trousers. "The food wasn't poisoned in the kitchen."

"I don't know. Kathy might still have the poison on her," I pointed out. "In one of her pockets, let's say. She could've slipped it out when the food was ready and sprinkled on a touch, before I took it to Johnson."

"Just sloppin' it over the top? 'Here's your steak, Mr. Johnson. Hope you like it extra *powdery*.' Even you would've noticed that."

"What do you mean, even me?"

But once again I was just giving my mouth muscles some exercise, for my brother had closed up his ears and moved on. He headed into the lunchroom and walked up to the chair in which Johnson had eaten his last supper.

"Ricky Hess," he said, pointing to the seat to the left of it. "Feathers Purnell." He pointed to the seat on the right.

"You think one of them did it?"

" 'It is a capital mistake to theorize before you have all the evidence,' " Gustav said. " 'It biases the judgment.' "

I recognized the quote right away, coming as it did from *A Study in Scarlet*, a story I've read so many times I'll still have bits and pieces of it bouncing around my skull if I live to be older than Noah.

"Well, before you go gettin' any ideas, I'll just point out that it's also a capital mistake to run around accusing people of murder," I replied. "Folks tend to take that kind of thing rather personal."

I may as well have been warning the sun not to come up in the morning. My brother just said, "Grab your scratch paper," and headed for the door. I followed, after snatching up the tattered old envelope and pencil I sometimes used to take orders when too many fellows got to shouting out their druthers at the same time.

I didn't need any of Mr. Holmes's method to figure out who Gustav was going to put the eyeball on first. When I caught up to him, he was headed for the stockyards over by the railroad depot. Feathers had been there for days helping the Triple T boys load up a herd of beeves bound for Chicago.

"So what am I supposed to do with this paper?" I asked Gustav.

"Write on it."

"My word, what a notion. You mean like . . ." I pulled out the pencil, gave the lead a lick, and began moving it over the envelope, " 'My . . . brother . . . is . . . a . . . horse's—"

"I can't very well take notes myself, now can I?" Old Red snapped, grumpy that he had to come right out and say it. "I need you to kind of . . . chronicle things."

My reading and writing were a gift from my elder siblings, as they worked extra hard so at least one member of the family—the baby, yours truly—could stay in school long enough to get some actual use out of it. I'm ever mindful of this, which is why I don't buck too hard when Gustav needs use of the skills he was too busy farming and driving cattle to collect for himself.

"I understand," I said. "I'll be like your Doc Watson."

Gustav gave me a hard look, and I knew I was being compared—none too favorably—to Dr. John Watson, the fellow who writes up Sherlock Holmes's adventures for the magazines.

"All you gotta do," my brother said, "is keep track of the clues."

"How am I supposed to know what they are?"

Gustav shook his head. "I'll let you know. Now button your lip. There's Dave Ryan."

Ryan was the Triple T's trail boss. He gave us a big grin as we approached and let us know he'd be eating his meals over at Blythe's Restaurant from now on. We took the joshing the only way we could—by shrugging and pretending to chuckle—and Gustav quickly moved things along to the point of our visit. Ryan told us where Feathers was and let us know it was all right to talk to him for a while . . . long as we didn't try to slip the man any food. We laughed again, thanked him, and walked away cussing him under our breath.

"You know, it's just gonna be more of the same long as we stay in Billings," I said to Gustav once we'd corked up our curses.

Old Red made a noise that might have meant "Ain't it a shame?" and might have meant "We'll just see about that" and might have meant "That corn on my toe sure is painin' me today." I didn't bother asking which, as he probably wouldn't have told me. Sometimes I think if words were water, my brother would be Death Valley.

We found Feathers with a couple other punchers, all of them using prod-poles to convince a group of bellowing beeves they ought to move on up into a cattle car. We got more japes thrown at us by the other two hands, but Feathers didn't even light up a smile. When we called him over for a parlay, he came slow and wary, like a dog approaches a man with meat in one hand and a switch in the other. That struck me funny, the relations between us being normally friendly, if not overly familiar.

"What do you want?" he asked us.

Though I'm usually the talker between the two of us, I decided to let Gustav have the honor of responding.

"Just wanted to ask you a few questions about what happened this afternoon," he said.

Feathers squinted at him. "Why ask *me* questions?"

"Cuz you were there."

"Lot a men were there."

"But you were up close."

"Not really."

"Well, you were the first one to get to Johnson when he fell. Looked like he even whispered something in your ear."

Feathers shook his head. "No words. Just noises. Like he was gasping for breath."

"But then after that I saw you kind of put your hand on him. Across his eyes. I thought maybe he'd already—"

"I don't know what you're talking about."

That stopped Gustav cold. He just stared at Feathers for a second, a little twitch kicking up around his eyes. When he spoke again, he sounded bona fide bewildered. "Now, Feathers," he said, "I saw you place your—"

"You're a damn liar. I never touched the man." Feathers began to back away from us, his eyes spitting fire. "Now you two just clear on out. I ain't got nothin' more to say to you."

He walked back to the cattle chute and grabbed up his prod-pole. Then he glanced back and gave us a look that said he was ready to use that big, mean stick on steer or man alike. That was enough to prod *us,* and we left.

"So," I said as we walked away, "you just let me know which clues I should be jottin' down and I'll—"

"Oh, shut up."

I don't always mind my brother when he gives me this little nugget of advice, but I did so now. I figured he was discovering detectiving isn't as easy as he'd made it out to be, and a man's got a right to be a mite tetchy when his daydreams get cut down and used for kindling.

But Gustav wasn't ready to light up that particular bonfire just yet. From the way he steered us through the streets, I reckoned our next stop would be C.V. Kramm Drug & Variety Store, where Ricky Hess spent his days jerking sodas. But as we passed by another store, Bragg & Company Dry Goods, Gustav froze up, spun on his heel, and marched inside.

We got a right warm welcome from Bragg and company. There were eight or nine people in the place, and they all greeted us with a smile. Several were even so kind as to point out exactly where the rat poison was stocked. I rode it out just fine, being accustomed to both making sport and being sported in turn. But Gustav's face turned almost as red as his hair, and the more folks pulled his leg the closer he got to kicking them with it.

"I'd like to have a word in private," he said to Mr. Bragg, a cheerful old backslapper with muttonchops so big they practically drooped out over his shoulders like a gray shawl.

"Why, certainly, Old Red," Bragg said, peering over my brother's head to wink at his customers. "There's something I'd like to ask you, as well."

Bragg stepped out from behind the counter and waved us back to a dark corner of the store.

"I'm wonderin' if Kathy McKenna, Ricky Hess, or Feathers Purnell have bought any arsenic off you in the last week or so," Gustav asked, his voice low once the three of us were circled up away from our audience.

The face under Bragg's carpet of whiskers turned mock serious. "I thought that's what you'd be asking," he said. "Well, I don't know this 'Feathers Purnell,' but I understand he's a Negro cowhand, and we haven't had any trade with the likes of that. As for Hess, I haven't had any business from him, either, though his aunt and uncle are regular customers. Kathy comes in often enough as well, but I can't recall selling her any arsenic recently. Which isn't to say she hasn't purchased any in the past. I'd be surprised if she hadn't."

"Oh? Why's that?"

Bragg chuckled. "Because it's easier to say who *hasn't* bought rat poison than who has. I can barely keep the stuff on the shelves."

Like most cow towns on a railroad line, Billings has rats like a dog has fleas. As even I could see, that meant mere possession of rat poison could hardly be considered a black mark against you. If it did, nearly everyone in town would be a candidate for the noose. Gustav seemed to come to the same conclusion as he thanked Bragg and turned to go. But Bragg reached out and snagged hold of his arm before he could take a step.

"Hold on. I've got a question for *you*, remember?"

My brother nodded curtly. "So ask it."

Bragg cleared his throat, then spoke in the loud, clear tone of voice men reserve for delivering either sermons or digs that are meant to be overheard.

"When you're on the stand, I'd appreciate it if you'd testify that you bought the poison here," he said. "That kind of word-of-mouth advertising can't be beat."

Gustav jerked his arm from Bragg's hand and stomped from the store, followed by both me and the guffaws that nipped at our heels. I pulled out my envelope and pencil again.

"Now what exactly should I write down? 'Nothing,' 'nada,' or 'nil'?"

My brother didn't break stride, just bolted once again toward C.V. Kramm Drug & Variety Store. I pocketed my note-taking gear and trailed along behind him. When we got to Kramm's, we found the fellow Gustav wanted to see hunched over a dime novel.

"Well, howdy there, pard," my brother said, taking a seat across from Ricky Hess and his gleaming brass soda fountain. Gustav's words had a casual, joshing quality about them I'd never heard him use before.

Ricky looked up and smiled. "Old Red! Big Red! What are you two doing here?"

At the sound of our nicknames, C.V. Kramm himself poked his head around the corner. He was in a back room, no doubt grinding up a treatment for vapors or shingles or some unpleasant thing. He took a short break from his important work to shoot us a hostile glare.

"Good day to you, Mr. Kramm," Gustav said with

uncommon cheer. "My brother and I thought it was about time we tried one of these here 'cola' drinks folks've been talkin' about."

Kramm couldn't quite muster a smile, but he did at least give us a nod. Then he was gone.

"I do believe your uncle doesn't care for us," Gustav whispered at Ricky.

The boy gave the back room a disdainful wave of his hand. "Awww, he doesn't like me going down to Starchy's."

Gustav winked. "Full of bad influences, huh?"

"So he says. Did you really want a cola?"

"Sure we do. Show us your stuff."

Ricky grinned and made a big show of scooping up our glasses, juggling them around, squirting in some syrup, and playing that soda fountain like it was a church organ. Gustav pretended to find the boy's display a right fascinating sight, but I saw his eyes flicker this way and that when Ricky was too caught up in his performance to notice.

"Here you are, fellers," Ricky said, sliding the glasses down smoothly onto the marble countertop. "Don't drink 'em too fast. They'll give you hiccups."

Though personally I can't see the sense in paying out good money for anything in a glass that won't get you drunk, both Old Red and I had sampled our share of fountain drinks over the years. Yet my brother took to smacking his lips over that cola like it was ribeye steak after a week on hardtack, so I did the same. There followed perhaps a minute of conversation on the unfortunate events at Starchy's, but my brother playacted like this topic was already a terrible bore and his only concern was finding us a new cook. He changed the subject by asking Ricky what he'd been reading when we came in.

"Oh, nothing," the boy replied bashfully.

I leaned over and took a peek at his magazine. " 'Jesse James and the Cheyenne Treasure,' " I read aloud.

"Jesse James?" Gustav sputtered in mid sip. He slapped his glass down and shook his head with fatherly disappointment. "I'm surprised at you, Ricky. Readin' one of them rags that make *Jesse James* out to be some kinda hero. The man was just a dirty reb thief and nothin' more."

"I know. But . . . well, I just—"

"Who's that feller up there?"

Leaning up against the long mirror behind Ricky were three portraits—Abraham Lincoln, U.S. Grant, and a middle-aged fellow in dress uniform I'd never laid eyes on before.

"That's my grandfather. Colonel D. L. Kramm. He was killed at Shiloh."

"Oh, was he now? Well, what do you think old Colonel Kramm would think of 'Jesse James and the Cheyenne Treasure'?"

"I . . . I don't know . . . he . . . I never . . ." Ricky began fiddling with an empty glass as he stammered, and something about the nervous fluttering of his fingers caught my eye and tickled my memory.

"Is that any way to honor your granpappy?" Gustav prodded Ricky. "Lookin' up to some mad-dog bush-whackin' murderer?"

"I do honor my grandfather. I do. I even—"

Gustav perked up so much at these words he practically took to floating above his chair. But at just that moment C.V. Kramm stepped out of the back room again and shouted for Ricky. He was holding a small package wrapped in brown paper.

"Take this over to Mrs. Gluck and come straight back with a dollar and two bits and not a penny less."

"Yes, sir." Ricky whipped off his white soda-jerk's apron, took the package, and gave us a halfhearted wave as he hurried out the door. He almost looked relieved to be escaping from us.

Instead of skulking back off to his pills and powders, Kramm took Ricky's position behind the soda fountain.

"I couldn't help overhearing some of your conversation," he said to us. "It's not so much Jesse James that boy idolizes. It's no-account saddle-tramp cowboys."

Gustav didn't even look at the man he was so lost in thought, so I took the liberty of answering for both of us.

"Oh, don't you fret, C.V. We was the same way when we was his age and just look how good we turned out! It's goin' on six weeks since I last shot a man in the back, and Old Red here hasn't rustled any cattle in months!"

"Drink up and get out."

My brother didn't bother to finish his cola, but I wasn't about to let Kramm kick me out without first getting my nickel's worth. So I threw my head back and drained the rest of my drink so fast I was hiccupping before I could even set the glass down.

"So, brother—what *hic* do you want me to *hic* chronicle for you *hic*?" I asked as we headed back toward Starchy's.

"If you want to 'chronicle' the fact that you're a flannel-headed fool, then go right ahead. Otherwise, don't bother."

"Now *hic* don't tell me we *hic* don't have any clues."

"Most likely we've already got all the clues we need." Gustav kicked at the dirt, and when he spoke again all the backbone was gone from his voice. "I just don't know what the hell they are."

"Well, *hic* I bet even Sherlock Holmes *hic*—"

"Otto."

"Yes *hic?*"

"Don't talk to me till you're over those damn hiccups."

"All *hic* right."

Hiccups being hiccups, of course, I couldn't keep quiet even though I wasn't saying a word. Gustav could only take it so long. Cursing "these infernal distractions" that cramped up his cogitations, he banished me from the restaurant practically the moment we arrived.

"Go on over to the jail and make sure that mob ain't gettin' restless. And don't come back until you've stopped making that blasted noise!"

As it turned out, the mob at the jail was nothing to worry about, as it had broken apart and drifted off when it became clear no necks were going to get stretched just yet. They'd be back tomorrow, though, when Kathy went before the justice of the peace for a hearing. If he said Yea, there would soon be a trial. If he said Nay, Kathy would be released—though that would hardly be a victory for her, as it was as likely as not that a makeshift Vigilance Committee would quickly decide a trial wasn't really all that necessary anyway. The oddsmakers had a Yea as an even money bet, as Thomas Fraser, Billings's justice of the peace, was known to be friendly with the Johnsons—so much so that Mrs. Fraser had been sipping tea with Mrs. Johnson when news reached them of the old man's death.

I learned all this from the deputy marshal who'd threatened us with lead poisoning when we'd asked to see Kathy
earlier in the day. He still wouldn't let me in to speak with
her, but he was a far more agreeable, talkative fellow
without a bloodthirsty crowd around to put him on edge.
Also I credit myself with having a way of putting folks at
ease, though my silk tongue was sorely tested by those
hiccups.

By the time I finally ambled back to Starchy's, both the
hiccups and the light of day had faded away. Old Red
seemed to have faded as well, for I found him in bed with
a pillow over his face.

"You asleep?" I asked.

"Nope," Gustav said, his voice muffled by burlap and
feathers. "You hiccuppin'?"

"Nope."

"Good. I need to talk to you."

I eased myself down onto a corner of the tattered soogan
we treat like a double bed. I'd been anticipating this talk
for hours. In fact, I'd already decided how to play it. If my
brother couldn't quite bring himself to give me a flat-out
apology for this whole restaurant fiasco, I'd be gracious
about it. All I cared about was putting it behind us. But I
was firmly opposed to sneaking out of town in the middle
of the night. We still had more than two hundred dollars in
the bank, and I didn't intend to leave Billings without it.

"I've been thinkin'," Gustav said from under his pillow.
"Thinkin' and thinkin' and thinkin' in circles. And I keep
endin' up in the same place."

"I understand," I said since he couldn't see me nodding
sympathetically.

"There's somethin' I've overlooked—somethin' Mr. Holmes would see that I don't. I need you to help me get a bead on it."

"I understand," I said again, though I wasn't entirely sure I did. This was not the talk I'd been hoping to have.

"Somehow somebody got that poison into Johnson a few minutes before he died. Now I wasn't out front at the time to see who was doin' what where. But you were. I need you to think hard—brain-bustin' hard, brother—and tell me everything you recollect from the time Johnson walked in to the time he keeled over."

"All right. But you gotta do somethin' for me first."

"What's that?"

"Well . . . do you think you could have this conversation without a pillow on your face?"

After a long, quiet moment, my brother brought up his hands and pressed them down on the pillow—and kept them there. "It helps me think," he said.

So I spent the next hour talking to a pillow and a pair of hands. I started out with what I'd seen before Johnson died. Then, just out of sheer momentum, maybe, I carried on through the rest of the day, laying out my impressions of our attempts at Sherlocking. I half expected to hear snoring coming out from under that pillow when I was finally done, so still were my brother's hands, but instead Gustav just said, "Thank you. You go on to sleep now." I was mighty tired by then, and I gave him no arguments. Soon I was the one doing the snoring.

Now one thing you learn when you're working the cattle trails is how to sleep light when you need to and heavy when you can. Since I no longer have any stampedes or rustlers to worry about, I can go as heavy as I please. So once I start catching my winks, almost nothing on earth can keep me from collecting all forty—not even Old Red sitting bolt upright and shouting, "Of course!" Or the sound of my brother jumping out of bed and banging around that restaurant like a bronc kicking his way out of a corral. Or the curses that soon followed. Or, a little later, what seemed to be the scuffing steps of a not particularly graceful man dancing a happy jig. All these noises came to me like echoes in my dreams, and when I awoke the next morning I could hardly be sure I'd really heard them at all.

I hefted myself out of bed and shuffled off in search of my brother, intending to round up a report on the night's happenings. I found him in the front room freshly shaved, dressed in his cleanest clothes, and sunny as a California July. Yet while he seemed uncommonly cheerful, he was no more chatty or charitable than usual.

"If you wanted explanations, you should've tracked 'em down yourself, cuz you saw all you needed to see to put you on the right trail," he said. "I ain't got time to walk you through it now. I need you to get busy makin' yourself presentable. You look worse than a sharecropper's scarecrow."

When I was shaved, combed, and dressed to Gustav's satisfaction, he finally let me know why we needed to dude ourselves up.

"While you were back in there sawin' logs, I was out arrangin' a little meetin' over to the Gould Brothers Funeral Parlor," he said. "It's set for quarter to nine. I need you to make sure Marshal Nickles and Judge Fraser are there."

"Now how am I supposed to do that? Ben Nickles would just as soon hang us as wave hello."

Gustav gave me a sly look of the sort that usually precedes a wink. "If you need to give Nickles a prod, you just tell him I've got Jack G. Johnson's *real* murderer hogtied and ready for a brand. And I don't care if the brand's his so long as justice is done. If that don't do it . . . well, I'm sure *you* can polish it up right with that slick talkin' you do."

It made sense to send me for Nickles and Fraser. I'm the talker. Gustav's the thinker. But looking at my brother then, I had to wonder if all that thinking hadn't overheated his head, like a fast horse that's been baked by a hard rider. After all, the man had taken to lying around with a pillow over his face.

"All right," I said reluctantly. "I'll try."

I found Nickles and Fraser in the judge's office. The hearing wasn't supposed to start until ten, but those two fellows looked so chummy I reckoned the judge wouldn't feel the need to hear a single word by that time. His decision would've been made hours before.

Now, if there's one thing in this tale in which I can take a personal kind of pride, it's this: Not only did I *try* to lure them over to the Goulds', I *succeeded.* As their minds were firmly closed to persuasion, I went by way of their hearts. Which is not to say that I appealed to their compassion, since I have my doubts as to whether Nickles has any to which one could appeal. Instead, I needled both men mercilessly, alluding to the ridicule and shame that would befall them should Old Red Amlingmeyer capture a culprit they were too stubborn to do anything about themselves. This fanned in them a tiny ember of doubt and a blazing fire of annoyance, and I believe they followed me primarily so they could later have the satisfaction of arresting me.

We arrived at the funeral parlor just a few minutes late. Howard Gould met us at the door, his round face sagging with strain, and he escorted us into the main viewing room mumbling about improprieties and irregularities. There were three men waiting for us. One of them was laid out in a beautiful maple-wood box. The other two were Doc Snow and my brother.

"I'm surprised to see you here, Dr. Snow," Judge Fraser said. He's a short, bushy-browed Scot with all of his clansmen's natural gift for ladling out scorn. "I hope you're not going to tell me you're mixed up in this nonsense."

Doc Snow's not the kind of fellow to brook much in the way of sass himself, and he responded first by dismissing Gould, then by brushing a bit of imaginary fluff off his sleeve, and finally by looking up at the judge as if he'd almost forgotten the man was there. "I am," he said.

"Damn it all!" Nickles exploded. "Somebody better get to explaining or Crazy Kathy's gonna have some company in her cell!"

Doc Snow looked at Gustav, so I looked at Gustav, so Nickles and Fraser looked at Gustav. Jack G. Johnson didn't look at anything but the insides of his eyelids.

My brother cleared his throat and pulled himself up to his full height, like a preacher getting set to rain down some fire and brimstone.

"All right," he said. "I can do the explainin'. But you gents might want to seat yourselves before I set into it. It's gonna take a good bit of talk to spool out.

"Now I don't know if any of you have heard of Mr. Sherlock Holmes of London, England. If you haven't, Marshal Nickles, I suggest you acquaint yourself with him at your earliest convenience. For when it comes to puzzle-bustin', he's the cock-a-doodle-doo. And he said somethin' once that I've been tryin' to keep in mind ever since I watched Johnson here cash in. 'In solving a problem of this sort, the grand thing is to be able to reason backward.'

"It occurs to me that layin' the blame on Kathy McKenna is reasonin' *forward*—and skippin' a few steps as you go along. It's true enough that she and Johnson weren't exactly cordial with each other. And it's also true that Kathy can be quite the wildcat when she's riled. But there's a big difference between breakin' up fights by wavin' a knife and seasonin' a man's vittles with arsenic. Poison is a sly, sneaky way to lay a person down, and there ain't much sly and sneaky about Crazy Kathy. If she'd taken a mind to kill Johnson, she wouldn't have plotted it out beforehand. She would've just grabbed up a blade and sunk it into the man's skull.

"But when you're known as 'Crazy Kathy,' I suppose people are liable to jump to conclusions. Even so, I would hope there would be some kind of search for what the experts call 'data' or 'clues' or 'evidence,' but I don't mean to call into question the abilities of anyone present, so I won't dwell on that now. I'll just move along by mentionin' the thought that struck me as I watched Kathy dragged away to the hoosegow: If someone were to slip a dose to Johnson, Starchy's would be the place to do it, as Crazy Kathy's reputation would ensure that the hand of the law would quickly fall on her.

"If, that is, the poison got noticed at all. I'm proud to say my brother and me haven't passed any bad meat or butter or eggs since we've been runnnin' Starchy's, but we all know it's easy enough to get doubled up on rotten grub you buy from someone else's kitchen. On top of that, Johnson was an old man, and not a very lit one at that to see him a couple weeks ago. If Doc Snow had been attendin' to sick folks outside town or tied up with some other business—or even if he'd just been a less book-smart and sharp-eyed feller than he is—we wouldn't be here talkin' about murder at all. We'd just figure the reaper finally caught up with the ornery old snake, and he'd be planted without a second thought or a single tear.

"So I got to thinkin', there's a slippery side to these goin's-on that folks aren't gettin' hold of. Havin' studied on Mr. Holmes's way of doin' things, I thought maybe I could. The way to start, I figured, was to cut the likeliest suspects out of the herd—'suspects' bein' detective lingo for folks you *suspect* might be guilty of somethin'. But I'm sure you already knew that, Marshal.

"Now there were really only two suspects to be had, far as I could see: Ricky Hess and a puncher name of Feathers Purnell. They were the fellers sittin' on either side of Johnson when he got that arsenic in him. The old man had given each of 'em a taste of his venom in the past, so maybe it wasn't no accident they were next to him when someone slipped him a taste of poison.

"I went to see both of 'em yesterday, and afterwards I had a devil of a time figurin' which one had done it, for I came away convinced it had to be one or the other. You see, Feathers was the first feller to try to help Johnson after he hit the floor. The old man whispered somethin' to him, somethin' he didn't seem to like at all. And then Feathers laid his hands on Johnson kinda peculiar-like—

though he called me a liar for sayin' so later, and I saw it all with my own eyes. And Ricky, he runs orders for his uncle. I've heard tell them druggists use arsenic in some of their medicines, so who's to say Ricky couldn't borrow himself a sample?

"Well, I set about to ruminatin' on all this last night, and damned if I didn't just about melt down my brain like so much candle wax. But I kept at it, and Mr. Holmes's advice about reasonin' backward finally gave me my first step ahead. I was thinkin' about Feathers puttin' his hands on Johnson's face the way he done. What's the use of such a thing? And why deny it? Johnson was already plenty sick, so it's not like Feathers needed to get any more poison in him by then. So maybe it was because of whatever Johnson said—not that it would make much sense for him to tell Feathers, 'I'm fadin' fast. Would you mind stretchin' your hands 'cross my face before the death rattle commences?' In fact, wouldn't he say just the opposite, seein' as how Feathers is a Negro and Johnson had made his hatred of that race plain time and time again?

"Once I hit upon that, I knew exactly what Feathers had heard and why he'd reacted the way he had. You see, the old man's last words on this earth were in keeping with all the nastiness he'd spread around before 'em. He'd said, 'Get your hands off me, nigger.' And Feathers decided to show the old bastard that his days abusin' black folk were over, so he gripped a hand right to Johnson's face. But this wouldn't go down too well with some—a Negro actin' in such a fashion with a dyin' white man, even one as hated as Johnson. So Feathers wisely decided to keep all this to himself.

"Now this didn't put Feathers in the clear, but it did

explain some of what needed explainin', and that freed me to concentrate on Ricky. He'd let the old man sorta run him out of Starchy's a week or so back, and when he finally showed his face again yesterday he seemed to be tryin' to live that down. I was back in the kitchen at the time, but I could hear him and Johnson tradin' stings somethin' fierce. Now though the boy was tryin' to act tough, he had him a touch of the jitters—or so it would seem from somethin' my brother told me. Like a lot of fellers, Ricky likes to get his hands to workin' when he's nervous. I noticed that when I was puttin' a little fire under his saddle-warmer yesterday. And it appears his fingers were plenty busy when he was ribbin' the old man, for Otto here saw Ricky piayin' with the salt shaker on the counter in front of him.

"I was lyin' down when I first got to cogitatin' on that salt shaker, but soon enough I hopped up and tried to work out a way to kick myself in the pants, for surely I'd been lookin' right over somethin' that was as hard to miss as a cougar in an outhouse. Johnson liked his food with a dash of pepper and a fistful of salt, and everyone around Starchy's knew it cuz he'd get to screamin' for the seasonings before the first bite even got off his plate. If there was somethin' you wanted on the man's food, here was a guaranteed way to get it there. When I realized this, I went chargin' out to the counter and grabbed up that salt shaker and turned it right over. And do you want to know what happened?

"The top came off. The whole thing emptied out in about two seconds. Ricky had been up to somethin' all right, but not murder. He'd been lookin' to catch Johnson with a trick boys have been pullin' since the day a shaker first put salt on food. Just to be sure, I spent a good amount of time sifting through that salt, and I assure you it was all crystals, no powder.

"Well, I sat there starin' at the mess I'd made for a good long while. I put the quirt to myself all night, and this was the best I could do. I was about to give up and go to sleep, but then I noticed somethin' else lyin' there on the counter where Johnson had been sittin'. A teeny yellow-brown ditty, not much different than a thousand other little things my brother and I sweep up and throw out every day. But it told me everything I needed to know. You see, I hadn't really been reasonin' backwards at all. I thought I knew the who, and I'd been tryin' to use that to get to the how. What I needed to do was go the other way. The how could tell me the who. And it did."

Out in the funeral home's foyer, chimes began to ring. It was nine o'clock, which meant my brother had been working his lips more than ten minutes straight. I wondered that those lips didn't drop right off, as sometimes a month went by without so many words passing between them. Exit unaccustomed as Gustav might have been to speechmaking, he had all of us there in his spell. Even Nickles seemed more than a little awestruck, when he piped up to ask, "What was it you saw?"

"That's a fair enough question, Marshal. But before I answer, I'd like Dr. Snow to tell you what he told me this mornin'." Gustav turned to Snow. "About Johnson's food."

Doc Snow nodded, then looked to Marshal Nickles and Judge Fraser. "There's a way to test for the presence of arsenic—the Marsh Test. Old Red asked me to try it on what was left of Johnson's food. I did, and it came up negative. I couldn't find the smallest trace of poison."

"But . . . but you said yourself Johnson died of arsenic poisoning!" Nickles blustered.

"That he did."

"But if it wasn't in his food—?"

I heard a door open in the front hall. Footsteps and low, murmuring voices followed. The sounds seemed to be some kind of signal for Gustav, for he quickly fished something out of his vest pocket and handed it to Nickles, and when he spoke again his words were running at a gallop.

"This is what I found on the counter, Marshal. Now what would you say that is?"

Nickles held up a small, dirty-yellow sliver no bigger than a pebble. I leaned forward to give it a stare and suddenly remembered the ugly little something Johnson had pulled from his mouth after his first bite of steak the day before.

"Looks like bone," Nickles said.

Gustav shook his head, then turned and walked to the casket that held Jack G. Johnson. What he did next knocked a gasp out of Nickles, Fraser, and myself—though our gasps were nothing compared to the *scream.* Howard Gould had opened the doors into the viewing room just as Old Red plunged a hand into Johnson's mouth, and the sight of my brother rooting around in there like a bear after honey set Mrs. George J. Johnson into a fit of hysterics. I glanced around to see her husband and Gould steering the woman into a chair as her head rolled back and her legs went all wobbly. Then a horrible *shlurp* kind of sound pulled me back in the other direction. What I saw there was my brother yanking the old man's dentures right off his gums.

Well, as you might imagine, there was quite an uproar,

with cries of outrage just about peeling the paper off the walls. But though Gustav was talking more slowly and softly than anyone else, his voice seemed to cut through, and before long folks were actually listening to it.

". . . chip of tooth, not bone," he was saying when everyone piped down enough for me to hear his words. He brought the dentures over to Nickles and Fraser and pointed at one of the Yankee teeth old Johnson used to brag on so much. "You can see the tooth it came from. It's been hollowed out. It's one of the big ones in the back, too. What do you call these, Mr. Johnson?"

Johnson had a fresh face of sun from his ride out into the country the day before, but even with the red there he somehow looked pale. "How dare you—"

"It's a molar," Doc Snow interrupted, looking so unruffled by this strange turn of events I had to figure (rightly, I learned later) that he'd helped my brother arrange them.

"Thank you, Doc. You think you could run that Marsh Test on this here 'molar'?"

Snow nodded, his eyes fixed on the Johnsons. "Certainly."

"Good. Though I don't know if it's even all that necessary, for if you gents take a good look, you'll see there's still some powder crammed up in there."

Both Fraser and Nickles took that good hard look, and once they did they shifted their glares over to young Johnson and his half-conscious wife.

"One thing I could never figure out about old man Johnson was why he kept comin' back to our place," Gustav said. "But you know, as much as he complained about the grub, it seemed to do him good. For if you'll recall, he had the color of a scabby toad a few weeks back, but he looked to be gettin' better with each passin' day. And I wonder now if that's because there was somethin' about Mrs. Johnson's cookin' that didn't agree with him—somethin' that sent him out lookin' for the cheapest food in town that wouldn't leave him feelin' sick as a dog. And if that certain somethin' couldn't be got to him through his food, well, maybe there was another way. It wouldn't be that hard to do if you had yourself a drill and a skill with teeth. You could fix it so your handiwork wouldn't show, then just wait for somethin' tough—like one of our ten-cent steaks, for instance—to pop off a bit of tooth and let the poison inside get to seepin' out. And doin' it roundabout like that had a big advantage, in that you could make sure you wasn't within a mile of the old man when he—"

Mrs. Johnson woke up enough then to start bawling and carrying on something awful. "God help us!" she sobbed. "The old man was a monster! A demon! He—!"

"Elsa!" her husband roared, leaping to his feet to tower over her. The woman's words choked to a stop with a weepy whimper. When he was satisfied that she would say no more, young Johnson turned to face us again.

"This disgusting spectacle has unhinged my wife," he said. "I'm going to take her home. If you insist on continuing with these hideous insinuations, you can call on me later. But now I'm leaving."

He and Gould helped Mrs. Johnson to her feet, and the three of them moved with slow, shuffling steps out of the room.

"You're gonna let 'em go?" I asked Nickles.

It was Fraser who answered. "They'll be dealt with in

due time," he said. "I see no reason not to allow them the opportunity to face this with dignity."

I thought back to the way Nickles had dragged Crazy Kathy off to jail and didn't recollect anything dignified about it. But I suppose pillars of the community have to be removed with special care. Or so think other pillars.

As it turned out, the Johnsons removed themselves, for when Marshal Nickles went to question them again an hour later they were both dead. There was no mystery as to the cause, as the tea cups and rat poison were left in plain view. What they hadn't seen fit to leave out, Nickles reported, was a letter of explanation—though of course the town was soon awash in rumors that this was a lie. The suicide note had been destroyed by Nickles and Fraser, folks whispered, as it revealed shocking improprieties old Johnson had taken with his daughter-in-law—improprieties her family wanted hushed up.

Gustav shrugged off such talk, saying he had no "data" with which to judge its merits. When I asked him about the *why* of Johnson's murder, he shrugged.

"Could be he really did take liberties with the lady. Could be his cussedness was bad for business. Could be he was an embarrassment for such fine, upstanding citizens," he said. "Could be he snored. Could be his feet smelled bad. Could be they just got sick of the old goat. All I know is, I've got dishes to wash."

And that he does—more than ever. For the Johnsons' misfortunes seem to have made ours. Though the appeal of it entirely escapes us, everyone else in Billings has gone out of their way to eat at least one meal at the scene of the town's most famous murder. Some even ask to sit in

Johnson's chair and order up exactly what he was chewing on when the arsenic did its work. We've been so busy, I've hardly had time to set this down on paper, which is why it heads out to you nearly three weeks after the fact.

I will now do my best to wait patiently for your response, though I'll admit that the thought of appearing in your publication has me wound so tight I could bust a spring. I certainly hope that you share my enthusiasm now that you've reached the end of my tale. I can't say whether your readers would embrace detective adventures of the sort experienced by Mr. Sherlock Holmes, but give them a native-born sleuth employing the same methods on our own Western plains, and they'll surely holler for more.

Sincerely,

O. A. Amlingmeyer
Billings, Montana
October 14, 1892

Wolf Woman Bay

Doug Allyn

Doug Allyn has written eight novels and over eighty novelettes and short stories. "Final Rites," his first published story, won the Robert L. Fish Memorial Award from the Mystery Writers of America in 1985. Allyn has also been honored with the Edgar Allen Poe Award for Best Short Story Mystery, two Derringer Awards for Novellas, the International Crime Readers' Award, and the Ellery Queen Readers' Award. His story in this anthology won the Ellery Queen Reader's award for 2005.

A sunny Saturday morning in Des Moines. Quiet little suburban neighborhood west of Pioneer Park, cookie-cutter split levels in muted pewter, clay, Prussian blue. Lawns mowed and raked. Kids playing soccer in the schoolyard.

The black Cadillac Escalade crawled slowly up the street. Brand-new. Smoked windows rolled up despite the heat, the heavy beat of rap music echoing across the sleep enclave like a warning drum.

Slowing in the middle of the block, the Caddy eased to the curb.

Two men got out. A mountain-sized Mohawk and a copper-skinned black man. Both around forty, black leather car coats, sunglasses. The Mohawk wearing a leather Kangol beret. Bad to the bone.

The black man was more compactly built but just as hard. Shaved head, Chinese characters tattooed on his neck, razor-cut goatee. Glancing at the name on the mailbox, he arched an eyebrow. "*Reverend* Alec Malley?"

"His marker doesn't say anything about a reverend. You sure this is the right place?"

"Address is right. Let's ask."

They sauntered up the steps. Moving easily. No hurry. On the porch, the front door stood wide open to the June morning. Canned laughter from a TV cartoon echoed from another room.

The black man rang the buzzer as the Mohawk moved to his right, giving him room.

"Got it, hon." A tall, slender guy, narrow-faced with thinning blond hair, answered the door. Barefoot, white T-shirt, pajama bottoms. His smile faded when he saw them.

"Hi. Are you Mr. Malley? Alec Malley?"

"I'm Reverend Malley. What can I do for you?"

"Mr. Malley, my name's Raven, this is Mr. Pachonka—"

"I know who you are. Let me alone," Malley snapped, slamming the door in their faces.

Shrugging, Raven pressed the buzzer again, holding it down this time. "Mr. Malley—"

The door exploded as a slug blew through it, slamming into Raven, kicking him backward off the porch.

Jerking an automatic from a shoulder holster, Pachonka backed quickly down the steps, covering the door. "Beau? How bad you hit?"

"I don't know. Can't feel my arm—" Both men ducked as a second gunshot echoed from the house.

"To hell with this," Pachonka snarled, charging back onto the porch, gun at the ready. The front door was ajar and he almost fired through it on reflex. Didn't, though. Stepped closer instead, nudging it open with his foot, sweeping up and down the gap with his weapon, two-hand hold.

Malley was down, leaning against the wall, a small nickel-plated revolver in his lap. Pachonka kept his gun on him but there was no need. Bullet hole in his temple, right eye bulging outward from the pressure. Blood and brains sprayed across the rose-petal wallpaper behind his head.

Easing warily inside, Pachonka knelt beside Malley, pressing a blunt fingertip against the carotid artery. Nothing. Gone.

A rustle to his right. Pachonka wheeled, raising his weapon to cover—a frightened woman in a fuzzy pink housecoat and bunny slippers. No makeup, her hair in curlers, holding a dripping spatula in her hand. Blood draining from her face when she saw him.

Pachonka's automatic didn't waver. "Step out where I can see you, lady. Is anyone else in the house?"

"My—my children. What's happened? Who are you?" And then she looked past him. And saw the late reverend's body.

* * *

Dan Shea slowed his pickup track to the posted limit as they neared the village. In the back country he drove with the hammer down. Never in small towns. Local hobby cops love writing tickets. What else have they got to do?

Wolf Woman Bay was like fifty other northern Michigan villages. Isolated, built around a rocky cove on the Lake Superior shoreline. Dying on the vine.

Pretty little place, though. Older houses, well maintained. Narrow streets lined with towering oaks and maples, leaves glowing red and gold in the pale October light.

"What kinda name is Wolf Woman?" Shea asked.

"Ojibwa," Puck said. "Anishnabeg. Stole their country, took the names right along with the land. Ever hear the story?"

"Another time, okay?"

"Fine, stay ignorant. Back in the big timber days, this town was famous for caskets."

"Why caskets?"

"Lot of black walnut in these hills back then. Since the wood doesn't rot, folks figured bodies would keep longer in a black walnut coffin."

"Do they?"

"How the hell would I know? Where's this job?"

"Right down on the harbor, the man said. Major remodel. Good money, maybe enough inside work to carry us till spring."

"Better be. It'll be a long winter, we don't find somethin' pretty quick. Thing is, I worked around here one winter when I was loggin'. Don't remember any houses near the harbor."

"How long ago was that?"

"Sometime after Korea. Mid 'fifties, maybe."

"Jesus, Puck, you really are older'n dirt." Shea grinned, turning right, cruising down a gently sloped main street lined with antique and curio shops, most of them already closed for the season.

Slowed as he approached the harbor. Not much to it. Paved parking lot, couple of cement ramps for lowering small boats into the water.

Not a home in sight. Only a ramshackle old warehouse crouching out over the water on ancient log pilings. Sagging wooden ramp leading out to it, windows boarded up. Eyeless. Weather-beaten sign over the door. Jastrow's Wholesale Fish.

"The job must be someplace else," Shea said, looking around. "Guy said he'd meet us here . . ." He broke off, his voice drowned by the rumbling thump of rap music. The black Cadillac Escalade pulled up alongside Shea's pickup, the heavy bass rattling his windows.

Raven and Pachonka climbed out. Leather car coats, shades. Raven's left arm was suspended in a blue shoulder sling under his coat.

"Who we got here?" Puck asked. "The freakin' Sopranos?"

Puck and Shea stepped out of the pickup. Both of them North-Country working class. Faded jeans, sweat-stained baseball caps, Carhartt vests, steel-toed boots. Faces rough and reddened from working in the wind. A matched set, blue-collar men, before and after, thirty years apart.

"Mr. Raven? I'm Dan Shea. This is my foreman, Puck Paquette."

"Beau Jean Raven," the black man said. "That's Tommy Pachonka." Nobody offered to shake hands. "So, what do you think? Is it doable?"

"Is what doable?" Shea asked. "You don't mean this old . . . fish house?"

"It looks rough, but that's how you guys earn your money, right? I have architectural drawings in the car. Would you like to check them over?"

"Why don't you just walk us through it first," Shea said doubtfully. "Might save time all around."

"Fine. Got a flashlight? Power's turned off in there."

Grabbing a lantern out of the glove box, Puck fell into step with Pachonka, following Shea and Raven across the ramp.

"For openers, you're gonna need a new ramp," Puck said, kicking at a loose timber. Pachonka glanced at him, but didn't reply.

The front door was padlocked and Raven's key didn't seem to fit. Annoyed, he reared back and kicked the door in, nearly tearing it off its hinges.

"And a new door," Puck added.

Inside, the building was musty, dusty, and dim. And huge. Puck played his light across the cobwebbed ceiling peak, two and a half stories above the rough wooden floor, massive wooden roof beams the size of tree trunks. Except for a couple of corner offices, the room was entirely open, no partitions.

"Floor's rock solid," Raven said, stamping his foot for emphasis. "They used to store ice blocks in here to preserve the fish, stacked it all the way to the ceiling. Must've weighed thirty, forty tons. The plans call for adding a second level in here, twelve feet up, steel beams bolted to the original building frame for support. The new upper level will be a loft, living quarters with a lot of light and a full view of the bay. Windows all around, skylights in the ceiling. With me so far?"

Shea nodded.

"The bedrooms and baths will be partitioned off, but I want everything else left open to the light. See that little door at the far peak? It leads to a tackle tower outside, built out over the water. It held the winch for lifting the ice blocks. I want that tower enlarged into an office, fourteen foot square, glass walls." He glanced the question at Shea.

"If they winched ice up from it, it should be solid enough for an addition."

"The ground floor will be partitioned," Raven continued. "Weight room, laundry room, storage room, a heated garage, and a workshop for my motorcycles. Still with me?"

"Sure you don't want one of them discos down here while we're at it?" Puck asked drily.

"I'll let you know. Can you do the job or not?"

"Maybe," Shea nodded, scanning the room. "What you've described is complicated but not impossible, Mr. Raven. Pretty damned expensive, though."

"The architects priced it out at two hundred and eighty thousand, give or take ten percent. Does that sound right to you?"

"I'd have to check their paperwork," Shea said, "but it's in the ballpark. Can you play ball in that park, Mr. Raven?"

"I have a little over two hundred thou in savings. I can finance the balance."

"That might be a problem. Loan officers don't like jobs like this."

"Our bank will cover it," Pachonka said.

"You fellas own a bank, do ya?" Puck asked.

"We work for one. Sort of. M.T.C.A. Mohawk Tribal Casino Administration, St. Regis, New York."

"You're a long way from home."

"Only me. Beau Jean is half Ojibwa, so Northern Michigan is home, I guess. He's sector boss for the Midwest. The Financial section will cover anything he needs."

"Must be nice," Puck said. "What kind of work you fellas do, exactly?"

"Collections," Pachonka said with a smile that never reached his eyes. "Write a bum check, cancel a credit card, scam a casino dealer, we'll be around to see you. Some white people shouldn't gamble."

"Some Mohawks shouldn't talk so much," Beau Jean said. "What else do you need to see, Mr. Shea?"

"We'll have to look under the building, check the support structure."

"Let's get to it, then."

Two people were waiting on the shore side of the ramp when they came out. A woman, late twenties, tweed sport coat and jeans, auburn hair cropped short. Pretty, in a tomboyish way. Her companion was taller, elderly, with thinning silver hair, sunken cheeks. Blue cardigan with a matching bow tie.

"Excuse me," the woman called, "we're looking for a Mr. Raven?"

"That would be me," Beau said, crossing the ramp with Pachonka at his shoulder. "What's up?"

If the woman was intimidated, it didn't show. "I'm Erin Mullaney and this is—"

"—Mr. Stegman," Beau finished for her. "Nice to see you again. Still running the supermarket on Montreal Street?"

"No, I'm retired now but—I'm sorry, have we met?"

"A few years back. Maybe thirty. You caught me stealing

comic books in your store, slapped me around pretty good. Called me some pretty ugly names. Funny you don't remember. I was the only black kid in town. And I definitely remember you."

Stegman started to shake his head, then hesitated, reading Beau Jean's face. "My God. Raven. You're Mary Raven's . . . boy."

"Mary Raven's pickaninny, you mean? That's what people used to call. me. Not politically correct nowadays, but I guess those were different times."

"I'm sorry. I—"

"No need to apologize, it, was a long time ago. Still, it seems like there ought to be some sort of . . . settlement." Reaching inside his coat, Beau took out his wallet, peeled off a bill, and held it out.

"Here, Mr. Stegman. Fifty bucks for all the times you *didn't* catch me stealing comic books."

"I don't want your money," Stegman said, reddening.

"Then give it to charity," Beau said, stuffing the bill in the older man's shirt pocket. "I always pay what I owe."

Crumpling the fifty, Stegman tossed it aside, then turned and stalked away. Erin started after him, then whirled to face Raven. "What the hell was that about?"

"History. His and mine. What can I do for you?"

She took a breath, visibly controlling her temper, face flushed, accenting her freckles. "I'm Erin Mullaney, I'm city manager here. The Bay Chamber of Commerce has been planning to convert this warehouse into a combination museum and community center. A magnet to draw people downtown."

"Nice idea. Why didn't you bid when the state put it up for auction?"

"We did, but—"

"—but you went lowball. Tried to grab it up for back taxes plus a dollar, right?"

"We didn't think anyone else wanted the place."

"You thought wrong. Sorry about that."

"Granted, bidding low was our mistake, but the council is prepared to make things right with you, Mr. Raven. We're willing to refund your bid and any expenses you've incurred plus a reasonable profit for your trouble—"

"Not interested."

"Let me finish, please!"

Surprisingly, Beau smiled. A good smile that softened his face. "Okay, sorry, Red. Go ahead on."

"The name is Erin Mullaney, not Red."

"I'm guessing the locals call you Red, right? They're big on nicknames around here. Or used to be."

"Not that I've noticed. There are a number of attractive vacation homes for sale in the area. If any of them interest you, the council can help you arrange financing."

"Very considerate. Of course, they made this offer before they knew who I was, right?"

"I don't see what difference that makes."

"Maybe none. Times change, maybe things are different now. We'll see."

"Then you'll consider the offer?"

"Nope. I don't need financing and I'm not interested in any other properties. I have the one I want."

"But why would you want this . . . dump? It's practically falling apart."

"I'm going to put it back together. As for the why part,

that's really none of your business, Red—*Miss* Mullaney. There is one thing you can do for me, though."

"What would that be?"

"This property is zoned commercial. I'll need a variance from the zoning board to convert it into a private residence. I'd appreciate it if you could arrange that for me."

"All things considered, the board might be reluctant to do you any favors, Mr. Raven."

"Then I'll manage without it. My attorney says one rental row-boat tied to the dock will qualify the site as commercial."

"You've already consulted an attorney? Why? Were you expecting trouble?"

"I'm just a careful guy, Miss Mullaney. Like a Boy Scout, you know? Be prepared? When you get careless in my line of work, bad things happen." He patted his sling.

"I wouldn't know. And I don't know what your problem is with Mr. Stegman, but—"

"I don't have a problem with old man Stegman or anybody else in this town."

"Then I wish you'd at least consider the council's offer."

"No deal. Sorry."

"So am I," Erin said, disappointed. "If you change your mind or want more information, here's my card. In the meantime, I'll ask about getting your variance."

"That's mighty white of you, miss."

"Just doing my job. By the way, how did you injure your arm?"

"I was just doing my job. And somebody shot me."

"Why am I not surprised?" Erin sighed. "Nice meeting you, Mr. Raven. Gentlemen. Welcome to Wolf Woman Bay."

* * *

Sloshing around in the muck, beneath the warehouse, Puck pulled a clasp knife out of his hip pocket, flicked it open, then stabbed upward into the support beam. The blade barely penetrated. Jerking it free, he tried another beam, then a third. At the far end of the warehouse, Shea was doing the same, methodically checking every piling. A dirty job. The beams were filthy, draped with cobwebs and grunge from decades of exposure.

"What do you think?" Shea asked when they met in the middle.

"I think that half-breed Ojibwa up there ain't no Boy Scout. Nor his pal. neither. Look like leg breakers to me."

"I meant about the building."

"I'm getting to that. Building looks okay, sort of. Been here a hundred freakin' years, oughta be good for another hundred."

"So why aren't we happy?"

"This ain't the original building, Danny. See them doubled up pilings under the east wall?"

"I wondered about those. Why are they so much heavier than the others?"

"Because they weren't designed to support a warehouse. They're trestles for a narrow-gauge railway. Timber train. I noticed some old photographs of a sawmill and a bay full of logs up in the office. Thought they were for pretty, you know? But now I'm guessing they're pictures of the original building. You don't run railroad tracks to a fish house. I think this place used to be a sawmill. Probably burned in the Great Fires."

"What fires?"

"*The* Great Fires, you young pup. Remember the Great Chicago Fire? Mrs. O'Leary's cow and all that crap? Michigan burned at the same time, only one helluva lot worse. Millions of acres went up, more than a thousand people died, maybe fifteen hundred, roasted alive. Pretty goddamn awful."

"Why did it burn?"

"Loggers. Like me and my dad and my granddad. Back when they cut the virgin timber they didn't clean nothin' up. Left the branches and slash to rot on the ground. After the loggers moved on, that slash dried out, turned into tinder. Lightning strike, careless campfire, it exploded like napalm. Lucky the whole damn country didn't burn down."

"Okay, there was a bad fire. So what?"

"Wasn't no timber left after the Fires so they didn't rebuild the sawmill. Built this fish house instead. On the original pilings."

"Even so, they're in great condition."

"You bet they are. They're at least a hundred years old and not a termite hole or dry rot on any of 'em. Know why? Because they're from the virgin forest around here. They're black walnut. Every damn one of 'em."

"My God," Shea said, glancing around. "How many are there? Twenty?"

"Twenty-four, all at least a foot thick. And nowadays they sell black walnut logs by the inch. I don't know what Raven paid for this wreck, but the timbers holdin' it up are worth six, eight thousand apiece. Too bad."

"Why? I don't . . . Ah." Shea nodded, getting it. "If we tell him, we can kiss our remodeling job goodbye. He'll tear this dump down, sell off the timbers, and walk away whistlin', a hundred grand ahead of the game."

"That's what he'll do, all right. *If* we tell him."

"Let me get this straight," Raven said. "You're saying this building's worth a lot of money?" They were in the fish-house office. Dusty desk, layout table. Yellowed photos on the wall beside crossed fish spears, an antique shotgun over the door, North-Country chic.

"The building isn't worth doodly, only the pilings that support it," Shea explained. "They're black walnut. When they built this place there was a lot of it around here but it's a rare wood now, used for veneers and fine furniture. Black walnut logs sell by the inch. This dump of a fish house is sitting on a hundred, maybe a hundred and fifty grand worth of timber, give or take."

"Wow. I only paid twenty-two for the place," Raven grinned, glancing at Pachonka. "Seventeen for back taxes plus a five-K bump."

"Looks like you got one helluva deal, Mr. Raven," Puck said. "Tear it down, take the money and run. You want to thumb your nose at this town, it's the perfect way to do it."

"Who said anything about thumbing my nose?"

"I just did. You've obviously got some kind of beef, that's why you lit into that Mr. Stegman, ain't it?"

"He slapped me around when I was a kid. Seeing him again . . . maybe I overreacted. But that's got nothing to do with building this house."

"Don't it?"

"No, Mr. Paquette, it doesn't. Now about these support logs. The only way to salvage them is to tear the building down?"

"The only practical way," Shea said. "You might be able to jack up the building, replace the beams with a concrete and steel framework, but it would take a year and eat up most of your profits."

"Are the beams sound the way they are?"

"Appear to be. They'll have to be inspected but they look rock solid."

"Good. Then it's nice to know they're valuable but it doesn't matter. If you want the remodeling job it's yours, Mr. Shea."

"Whoa up, Beau," Pachonka said. "The man just said you can clear a quick hundred grand."

"But only if I wreck the thing I came for," Raven said. "That wouldn't make much sense, would it?"

"You haven't been making sense since that cracker popped you in Iowa. You got nailed in the arm man, not the head. You need to start thinkin' straight."

"If you don't like it here, Chunk, the keys are in the Caddy. Take off."

"Not me," Pachonka snorted. "Wouldn't miss this for the world."

"What about you, Mr. Paquette? I get the feeling you don't like me much."

"Not much, no."

"Which half bothers you? The Ojibwa half or the black half?"

"Color's got nothin' to do with it, sonny. I've worked with Indians all my life and I soldiered with blacks in Korea. We all bleed red. But I do have a problem with you."

"What's that?"

"The chip on your shoulder. This is rough country up

here, Mr. Raven, with some pretty rough characters in it. If you're here lookin' for trouble, you're damn sure gonna find it. If it don't find you first."

Shea shook his head, kissing the job goodbye. But again Raven's smile surprised him.

"I'll bear that in mind, Mr. Paquette. Thanks for telling me about the logs, gentlemen. I know you didn't have to. So. Do you guys want the job or not?"

Two days later, the first trucks rolled in. Flatbeds carrying structural steel, fifty-foot H- and I-beams. Shea's work crew followed the steel in a ragtag convoy of work vans and pickup trucks. A gypsy construction gang, six men plus Puck and Danny. North-Country boys from around Valhalla. Woolly and rough around the edges. Hard workers who knew their trades.

Job one? Tearing out the ramp from the shore to the fish house, replacing it with twelve-inch I-beams, bolted to concrete pylons ashore and the ancient railroad trestle supports over the water.

A few locals stopped by to eye the construction and the crew. One old-timer complained about the stack of steel girders blocking access to the boat ramps. Most left without saying much, a rare thing in a part of the country where common courtesy is still common.

First official visitor? The village constable. Old enough to vote but not much more. Looked like a kid dressed up to play sheriff: tan uniform, brown jacket, oversized baseball cap. Adolescent acne. Found Shea, Puck, Raven, and Pachonka in the fish-house office, scanning the architectural drawings.

"Who's in charge here?"

"I'm Beau Jean Raven, it's my property. What can I do for you, Officer?"

"I'm Constable Chabot. Those men out front work for you?"

"They work for me," Shea said. "What's the problem?"

"Half the parking lot is still city property. Your men are taking up most of the slots."

"A few are still open and I haven't noticed anybody using them."

"Maybe they don't like the company. There's another lot up the street. Move some of those vehicles there, all right?"

"Sure. Anything else?"

"Nothing official, but some of the town folk are wondering about the boat ramps. You've got them blocked off. I understand they're on your property now, Mr. Raven, but they're the only access to the bay at this end of town. Are you going to keep them closed?"

"I haven't given it much thought."

"They have to stay blocked for now," Shea said. "It's a construction zone. What happens afterward is up to Mr. Raven."

"Who hasn't given it much thought. Okay, I'll pass that along. Meantime, keep the parking lot clear, understand?"

"No problem."

"You'd best think hard about keeping those ramps open for the locals," Puck said after the constable left.

"Why? There's another park with ramps at the far side of town. They still have free access to the bay."

"You're not seeing it the way they do. When we finish this remodel it'll be a showplace, a three-story home in the heart of the town shoreline. It'll have a great view of the bay, five miles out at least. And your house will be visible just as far. Man goes out to do a little fishing, get away from things. He looks up, first thing he sees will be your place. It's like you're making the bay your own private pond, Mr. Raven. Or is that the point?"

"The point is, I'm turning an eyesore into something special. It's got nothing to do with anybody but me."

"It ain't that simple. Look at these old pictures on the wall. The bay full of logs from one end to the other. Most of these folks came here then to work the timber. After the virgin forest was logged off and the Fires took the rest, they stuck it out, fished the lakes for a living. Now that's played out, too. But they still hang on, doing what they can to make a life in this country, raise their kids. An outsider comes in, buys up—"

"Outsider?" Raven snapped. "Mister, I've been gone awhile but I was born in this town. And you don't have to tell me squat about fishing. My mother worked in this building. Standing at a long table with a half-dozen other women, mostly Ojibwa, cleaning fish with big-ass scissors. Snip off the head, zip open the belly, scoop out the guts with your thumb. Her hands always ripped up by fish bones. Don't tell me how tough life is around here, pops. I know all about it.

"Know what a gutbucket man is? End of the day, all the fish heads and guts are dumped in a big tub. Somebody's gotta row that tub way the hell and gone out in the bay, dump it downwind, away from the town. The gutbucket man. Filthy job. Ojibwa job. My grandfather's job. Everybody else is headed home for supper, we're puttin' out in the bay with a stinkin' tub of fish guts. Gramps half drunk—" Raven broke off suddenly, turning away, massaging his injured shoulder.

"Look, I don't want anything from these people, but they've got no favors coming from me, either. I just want to wake up in my house, make a fresh cup of coffee, watch the sun climb out of the bay. If anybody's got a problem with that, tough rocks."

"It's not just their problem, Mr. Raven," Shea said, "it's yours, too."

"How so?"

"For openers, we aren't likely to get that commercial-zoning variance you want from the city council."

"I can manage without it."

"Sure you can. And if the local building inspector gives us trouble we can appeal his rulings to the state board, but it'll cost time and money. It'd be a lot simpler to make peace, try to get along."

"Hate to say it, but the cracker's making sense, Beau," Pachonka said. "Sooner you finish this dump, sooner we get back to real life. Do a deal."

Pausing in front of the old pictures of the bay, Beau shook his head. "Man. I wonder if it was this complicated a hundred years ago."

"It was worse," Puck said. "Loggin's a tough life."

"Yeah, I bet it was," Beau said, shrugging his leather coat on over his sling.

"Where you goin'?" Pachonka asked.

"To cut a damn deal."

"With that redhead?" Pachonka grinned. "Dirty job but somebody's gotta do it. Want company?"

"No."

"Didn't think so."

* * *

City hall was a Main Street storefront with a sign in the window. Wolf Woman Bay, Village Office. A bell jingled as Bean stepped in. Small room, knotty-pine paneling, a Formica counter. Erin Mullaney alone at her desk. White blouse, blue skirt. Prim as a nun. A pretty nun. Scowling over a spreadsheet. On seeing Beau, her frown deepened.

"Mr. Raven, what can the village do for you today?"

"What makes you think I need something?"

"Because you're not the kind of guy who drops by to shoot the breeze. What's the problem?"

"I don't have one, you do. The boat ramps on the harbor. I own them now. I'm told the locals want them kept open."

"It would be convenient. The public's always had the use of those ramps."

"Not anymore, sorry. I prefer to keep them private, but—" He held up his hand, stilling her objections. "—since the construction crew will be repaving the ramp to my building anyway, I can arrange to have them build new boat ramps on the public parking lot next-door. We can split the cost fifty-fifty: Does that sound fair?"

"More than fair," she said warily. "And in return you'd want . . . ?"

"Zero. Nada. Consider it a peace offering. All I want is to be left alone."

"Odd attitude for a guy building a house in the middle of a town park."

"Anything I do to that building will be an improvement. Hell, dynamite would be an improvement. So is it my building you don't like, or just me?"

"It has nothing to do with you. We had plans for that building. A museum, a gift shop for tourists—"

"Get over it. I have plans of my own."

"Plans for a home? Or for getting even?"

"Getting even? Whoa up, where's that coming from?"

"I've heard stories about, your childhood here—"

"These people don't know squat about my childhood. Know what they used to call me? Mary Raven's pickaninny. My dad was an airman from the base at K.I. Sawyer, killed in Vietnam. No other blacks here, so I was the town joke. After my mom got fed up and took off, I fought my way through foster care till I was old enough to enlist. Three tours in the Corps: Beirut, Iraq. Then a security job with the Mohawk Nation. All the time saving every damn dime so I could live where I want, the way I want."

"Even in a place where you're not welcome?"

"Lady, I collect gambling debts for a living. Nobody rolls out the welcome mat for me, but nobody runs me off, either. We can all get along or not, that's up to you people. Either way, I'm here to stay. Get used to it."

"Mr. Raven?"

He turned, his hand on the door. "What?"

"You're right. It's not your fault our plans for the fish house fell through. We should have worked harder to make them happen. As you did. Your offer to build new boat ramps is very generous. I'll take it to the council. But to be honest, I doubt they'll accept it. People are pretty upset."

"Whatever."

"But for what it's worth, not everyone's unhappy you're here."

"No?"

"No. You've made my job a little more complicated but at least it isn't boring. I'll let you know what the council decides."

"Right. Do that. And . . . thanks."

"No charge. Anything else?"

"Just one thing. Used to be a guy here named Tobias Gesh. He wrote to me when my grandfather died. Know him?"

"Old Toby? Sure. Still lives in the same place."

"Which is?"

"A cabin west of town on Old Reservation Road. The gravel ends about three miles out, but just keep going. Can't miss it. Figures you'd want to see him."

"Why?"

"Because the locals call Toby the last wild Indian. Of course, that was before you showed up. Have a nice day, Mr. Raven."

Mullaney was right, he couldn't miss it. But getting there wasn't easy.

After a mile or so, the dirt road narrowed to a two-rut trail barely wide enough for the Escalade. It took Beau nearly forty minutes to crawl back to Gesh's place in low gear.

Erin had called it a cabin but it wasn't, exactly. It was a Hogan, a traditional Ojibwa log hut, sod-roofed. Seemed such a natural part of the forest that it could have grown there like a wild mushroom amid the dark pines surrounding it. Cords of firewood were stacked neatly along one wall. Antlered deer skull nailed up over the door.

Stepping out of the black Cadillac, Beau tapped the horn. "Mr. Gesh?"

"Around back."

Following the voice, Beau circled the lodge. Old guy out back, seamed face dark as walnut, flannel shirt, jeans, moccasins, buckskin vest, shaggy mane of gray hair. Sitting on a stump, scraping the fat off a beaver hide with a bowie knife. Other furs stretched on hoops were drying in the sun. Muskrat, coyote.

"Mr. Gesh? I'm—"

"—Mary Raven's kid," the old man finished for him. "Heard you were in town. Pull up a stump, set yourself. Got anything to drink?"

"No, sir, sorry. Didn't know I was coming."

"Just as well. What can I do for ya?"

"For openers, I wanted to thank you for writing to me when my grandfather died. It meant a lot."

"But not enough to bring you back for his funeral."

"I was stationed in Beirut at the time, got your letter a couple of weeks late."

"Figured it was like that. Well, for what it's worth, Frank didn't feel no pain. Died like he lived, drunk as a skunk. Got trashed out of his skull one night, never woke up. For guys our generation, it was natural causes."

"What about his funeral? Do I owe anybody for that?"

"Nah, the tribe paid for it. They got plenty of casino money and it didn't amount to much anyway. Just me and a couple old-timers. Your grandfather didn't have many friends. From what I hear, you're not so different. Why'd you come back, anyway? Ain't no casinos around here."

"Maybe that's why. I'm done with casinos. Seen too much of the harm they can do."

"Never cared for 'em much myself," Gesh said, flicking a

dollop of fat off the blade of his knife. "Not natural for Native people to earn that way. Playin' white man's crazy games."

"Do you know if my grandfather ever heard from my mother? Where she went to? Anything at all?"

"No." He paused, frowning. "He never said nothin' about Mary one way or the other. But it wasn't like we was big pals. Just knew each other a long time. Are you tryin' to find her?"

"Why should I? She gave me up."

"That was pretty common back in them days. Before the casinos, the Anishnabeg people had nothin'. Whites made our kids cut their hair, educated 'em in white schools. Made 'em ashamed of what they were. Nobody wanted to be Ojibwa back then. Now everybody does. Even black guys."

"Is that how you see me?"

"You shave in a mirror every morning. What do you see?"

"I'm not sure anymore. When I was a soldier, I traveled, saw a lot of the world. Seems like I've been moving most of my life. I need a place of my own now. A place I belong."

"And you think you belong in Wolf Woman country?"

"I was born here."

"I was born in a hospital in Manistique. Don't figure I belong there."

"You know what I mean." Raven glanced around, taking in the woodland clearing, the scent of hides drying on hoops, woodsmoke rising from the hogan. Remembering other scenes like it. Hazy memories from long ago. In other lives.

"Yeah, I guess I know what you mean," the old man admitted, squinting up at him. "And I guess you got a right to come back here. But as far as belonging? If I was you, sonny, I wouldn't try puttin' that to no vote."

* * *

Fish-house office: Beau, Shea, and Puck.

"So?" Shea asked.

"I gave it a shot," Beau shrugged. "The lady doubts it'll fly."

"Like sendin' Attila the freakin' Hun to a tea dance," Puck groused. "Now what?"

"We'd best find out how tough they're going to make it," Shea said. "Pull two men off the ramp and dig out around a couple of the support pilings. I'll ask the county building inspector to check 'em. If he's gonna jack us around, we might as well know up front."

"And if he does?" Beau asked.

"Those supports may be a hundred years old but they'd hold up the Sears Tower. If he won't approve them, we can file a complaint with the Bureau of Construction Codes, ask for a state inspection. We'll win, but it'll take time."

"How much time?"

"Depends. Might take a month for the inspector to show up."

The next afternoon, Shea was installing headers for the new door when a white Chevy van pulled into the lot. Lanky older guy in coveralls and a painter's cap clambered out, carrying a clipboard.

"Mr. Shea? I'm Howard Donakowski, township building inspector. Understand you've got some supports you need checked."

"Right. Thanks for coming out so quickly." Shea tossed aside his wrench, waving Puck over. "They're down here."

"Do tell," Donakowski said sourly, following Puck and Shea down the bank into the soft sand beneath the fish house, now neatly raked. "Any idea how old these timbers are, Mr. Shea?"

"Older'n any of us, but in better shape," Puck answered.

"Speak for yourself," Donakowski grunted, kneeling down beside one of the two beams Puck had dug out, prodding the concrete base with a scratch awl, then jabbing the timber as he rose. "The bases are original Portland cement. Gotta be a hundred freakin' years old."

"Still rock-solid, though," Shea said.

"That one seems to be." Donakowsld conceded, crossing to the other, repeating the process. "You only dug out two. I count . . . twenty-four."

"We checked the others down to the ground, they're all in perfect shape. We'd replace 'em if they weren't."

"Damn straight you would. I wouldn't pass them otherwise," Donakowski finished filling out the check sheet. Signing it, he tore off the small green sticker at the bottom and gave it to Shea. "You're approved."

"Thanks," Shea said, surprised, checking the number on the sticker against the sheet, to be sure it was in order. "We appreciate it."

"You should. I'll tell you flat out, Mr. Shea. I don't like this project of yours. An outsider buyin' up the only dock this end of town to build a fancy condo? Lived here all my life, like the harbor just fine the way it is.

"If it was up to me, I'd chickenshit this job every step of the way. Make you dig out every damn one of those pilings, check every timber for plumb, exactly ninety degrees, you know the drill. But I've got my orders. Keep your work up to code, you won't have any problems with me. See you boys around."

"Right," Shea said, giving Puck a what-the-hell look. "Thanks for coming out."

"He didn't hassle you at all?" Raven said when they told him. "Why not? What's up with that?"

"The man said he had his orders," Puck shrugged. "Must be small-town politics involved. Same families probably been runnin' this place for a hundred years. Maybe you've got a friend here you don't know about."

"Not likely. Well, maybe one. So what does this mean to the project?"

"Katie bar the door." Puck grinned. "If we're gonna be inside before the snow flies, it's pedal to the metal from here on, full speed ahead."

As soon as the new ramp was complete, Shea backed the flatbed across it and unloaded the I-beams into the warehouse. Inside, the crew began bolting them together like an Erector set, stiffening the original structure and creating a support base for the new second floor.

On the roof, a three-man crew began stripping off the old shingles, leveling or replacing uneven boards, marking it off for skylights and modern shake-style architectural shingles. Shea was pushing the crew hard, ten-hour days, sometimes more.

No complaints. The men were used to the grind and happy to collect the overtime pay, knowing the first winter gales could sweep down anytime. Nobody wanted to be skating around on a roof or wrestling steel beams in the wind at ten below.

The first week blew past in a blur. Men cursing, riveting

the building's new steel skeleton into place, trash trucks dropping off dumpsters winch the roofers promptly filled, suppliers delivering materials for the first phase of construction: rough lumber, shingles, skylights for the roof, rolls of Tyvek insulation wrap to seal the building, prepping the walls for cedar siding.

Then? Trouble. Shea and Puck found it when they arrived at first light. Paint thrown against the side of the building, lumber stacks tipped over. *Nigger* spray-painted over the old Jastrow's Fish Wholesale sign.

The constable was already leaving when Raven and Chunk rolled in.

"What's all this?" Raven asked.

"Kids, according to the local junior G-man," Shea said.

"What kids?"

"He doesn't know," Puck said. "He's gonna look into it."

"How much damage?"

"Nothing serious. The paint they slopped around doesn't really hurt anything, we're re-siding the building anyway. I'll have my guys pick up the lumber and paint over the racial slur—"

"Leave it. It doesn't bother me."

"It bothers *me*," Puck said.

"Whatever. What do we do about this?"

"I'll move a cot into the office," Shea said. "Keep a man here at night."

"No need for that. I can sleep here."

"That's not a good idea, Mr. Raven. You've got a bum wing and I don't think kids did this."

"Neither do I. That's why I want to be here if they show up again. Don't worry about my arm."

"It's not just the arm," Puck said. "If they know you're here alone they may decide to have a go at you."

"Good. Let's get back to work. Winter's coming."

That afternoon, Raven was in the fish-house office scanning delivery lists when there was a knock on the door.

"Got a minute?" Erin Mullaney asked, stepping in. She was wearing a somber blue business suit and a look to match.

"What's up, Red?"

"I stopped to let you know about the council meeting last night. They didn't, grant your zoning variance. Sorry."

"Gee, what a surprise. No sweat, I'll have a rental boat tied to the dock by the end of the day."

"It may not be that simple."

"Why not?"

"We had a bigger turnout than usual last night and things got a little out of control," she said, avoiding his eyes. "A lot of people spoke against your project. They said a private home on the harbor will wreck the bay view and that the council should have stopped you. There were threats of a recall election. And some talk about taking more direct action."

"Okay."

"You don't seem concerned."

"Actually, I've already been notified. Somebody painted 'nigger' over my door last night."

"My God!"

"Hey, it's just a word. It's not the first time I've heard it."

"I can't believe what's happening to this town. Before I came here I worked in Detroit six years. There were so many problems, it was like shoveling smoke. Poverty, unemployment, politics. Coming up here was the answer to a prayer. Scenic little village dreaming on the lakeshore, no crime, no pollution. I thought I could really help improve people's lives."

"Maybe you will."

"Not after last night. When I brought up your offer to build new boat ramps I was shouted down."

"They weren't interested?"

"I never got the chance to find out. Mr. Stegman's oldest son runs a sawmill on the north shore of the bay. His crew was making most of the noise and they're a pretty rough lot. People were intimidated."

"Thanks for trying anyway. And for talking to Mr. Donakowski."

"Who?"

"The building inspector. He was here a few days ago and gave us a pass, though he wasn't too happy about it. I assumed you leaned on him."

"No, I haven't seen him."

Puck rapped on the door and stuck his head in. "Mr. Raven? You'd better get out here. We got visitors and they ain't the welcome wagon."

Raven started to follow, then turned back to Erin. "You'd best stay here."

"I'm not afraid of them."

"It's still better for you if they don't see you with me. Wait here, okay?" He hurried out without waiting for her answer.

Outside, the parking lot was filling with vehicles, SUVs and oversized pickups with contractor cabs and dual rear wheels. Engines roaring like a NASCAR practice lap, they formed up in a phalanx of Detroit iron facing the fish house.

Someone blared a horn, and in an instant the others followed suit, raising a thunderous din that echoed across Wolf Woman Bay like an L.A. gridlock.

On the fish-house deck, Puck glanced at Shea but neither man said anything. Overhead, the roofers quit working, eyeing the scene below.

Pachonka took a long look at the crush in the parking lot and shook his head, smiling.

"Guys, I think I hear my mama callin'. Have fun, Beau Jean. See ya."

"Right," Raven nodded as Chunk walked coolly to the Cadillac Escalade, climbed in, and drove off.

Gradually the din slackened, then halted altogether as the men began piling out of their vehicles. A rough dozen loggers, flannel shirts, canvas pants, hobnailed boots. No weapons in sight, but considering the odds, they didn't need any.

"Cedar savages," Puck said. "That's what the locals call 'em."

"An insult or a compliment?" Raven asked.

"Depends on who says it," the older man said grimly. "I wouldn't use it if I were you."

"But you could say it?"

"Hell, I'm one of 'em. You want me to talk to them?"

"No point, Mr. Paquette. They're not here for you."

"Which one of you clowns is Raven?" Big guy, a step in front of the rest. Burly, bearded, shaggy hair shot with gray. Tweed sport coat over faded jeans. A fashion plate compared to the others.

"That would be me." Beau Jean stepped onto the ramp, alone.

"I'm Rich Stegman, I own a sawmill on the north shore. I understand you gave my dad a hard time."

"I gave him fifty bucks. Figured I owed it. If you don't like it, give me a fifty back, we'll call it even."

"You always were a mouthy little punk. But you ain't a kid no more. I'd kick your ass for ya but it looks like somebody beat me to it. Or is that sling a city-boy thing, like carryin' a purse?"

"It's real enough. But I can put my other arm behind my back if it makes you nervous."

"Another time. And it'll have to be some other place. Because you're leaving."

"Not likely. I just got here."

"We know the city council offered to buy this dump, but we figure they're a bunch of politicians, so maybe they didn't explain the situation clear enough. That's why we put together this here citizen's committee. To make sure you understand how things are."

"I think I get the picture."

"No, you don't, or you'd already be gone. This is our town, Raven. Our bay. We don't want any houses here, especially when you're only building it to give everybody the finger."

"Not true. It'll be a nice place. I've offered to build the village new launching ramps—"

"Screw that. We don't want anything from you. But we're not chiselers. We took up a collection, came up with fifty grand. Cash money. You'd better take it while you can."

"Not interested."

"No reason he should be," Puck said, stepping onto the ramp, the decorator shotgun from the office cradled casually in his arms. "The building's worth two or three times that in salvage alone. Maybe more."

"What are you talking about?" Stegman demanded. "Who the hell are you?"

"My name's Dolph Paquette, Puck to my friends and everybody else. I'm a workin' man, like, you boys. Spent a couple winters loggin' these hills back in the day. I work construction now with Danny Shea. This is our job site. Know what we found here? The substructure holdin' up this old fish house is black walnut, timbers a foot thick. Or maybe you knew that already?"

"No," Stegman said, glancing uneasily at some of the others. "We didn't know anything about it. But if that's the problem, we can work something out—"

"We tried that," Puck said, cutting him off. "Me and Danny already told Mr. Raven he could make a bundle of money by tearin' down this rattrap and sellin' it for scrap. He said no. Just wants to build his house. So that's exactly what we're gonna do. Why don't you boys get on back to your jobs, let us get on with ours?"

"And if we don't?" One of the loggers stepped forward. Barrel chest, bow legs. Built like a bear in Carhartt coveralls. "You plan on using that shotgun, old man?"

"This? Nah, I found it in the office. Don't even know if it works. Some chickenshit weasel messed up our job site last night. If I knew who did it, I'd find out if this thing shoots or not. Wasn't you, was it?"

"Don't know a thing about it."

"Glad to hear it. Anybody else know who trashed our site? No? Good. We'll be addin' some crew in a few weeks. Any of you boys need work over the winter, come see me."

Puck turned and sauntered back toward the porch, giving Raven a "Come on" look. With a shrug, Raven started to follow.

"Wait a minute," Stegman said. "We're not finished."

"Sure we are," Raven said. "You made your offer, I'm not interested. Have a nice day."

"Hey, Raven! Hey, pickaninny!" the bear in the Carhartts yelled, pushing past Stegman. "Remember me? Tay Maggert? I used to jump your mama. Five bucks a hump."

"Really?" Raven said, facing him. "I'm surprised. You look like little boys would be more your speed."

"You sonovabitch!" Maggert roared, charging him, swinging wildly.

Raven held his ground, waiting. Ducking under a haymaker, he hinged upward, headbutting Maggert full in the face, lifting the big man off his feet, kicking his legs out from under him as he fell. Maggert hit the deck with a thud. Raven was on him like a cat, his knee jammed against Maggert's chest, fist cocked, ready to finish him.

No need. Maggert lay writhing on the ramp, blood gushing from his ruined face, his right leg twisted at an odd angle. Beau rose, facing Stegman. "How about it, sport? Wanna try your luck? Anybody else?"

Dead silence, except for Maggert's moaning.

"Take your friend and go," Raven said. "If you come back, better pack a lunch. You'll be in for a long day."

A few minutes after the parking lot cleared, Pachonka came rolling back in the black Escalade. Taking a rifle case out of the backseat, he came trotting up the ramp.

"Nice you could drop by," Puck said sourly. "Fun's over."

"I know, watched it from higher ground a few blocks up the street. Through a scope," he added, patting the gun case. "That was a pretty gutsy move with that old shotgun, pops. It's broken, you know."

"I thought it worked pretty well," Raven said drily. "Thanks for stepping in, Mr. Paquette."

"Didn't do it for you," Puck said. "If I'd known Cochise here had your back—ah hell, now what?"

Siren howling, strobes flashing, a village patrol car roared into the lot, screeching to a halt at the ramp. Constable Chabot scrambled out, tucking his nightstick into his belt.

"Mr. Raven, you're gonna have to come along with me."

"For what?"

"Assault, for openers. Tay Maggert's on his way to the hospital with a broken nose and his kneecap kicked halfway off."

"I was on my own property and he came at me. I just defended myself."

"Mr. Stegman tells it differently."

"I'll bet he does," Erin said, stepping out onto the deck. "But we all saw it and you work for the village, Constable, not for the Stegmans."

"There were a dozen loggers with him," Puck said. "If you don't wanna take our word for it, ask them. They may work for Stegman but I doubt they'll lie for him."

"I'll question them later. Right now, Mr. Raven's coming with me."

"I don't think so," Chunk said quietly. "You have no warrant and no cause to make an arrest. So maybe you'd better do like the man says and question the other witnesses.

Because nobody's going anyplace with you. Unless you think you can take me, too."

Pachonka's hands were in plain sight. There was no obvious threat and Chabot was armed. But he read Chunk's dead eyes. And that was enough.

"Maybe you're right," he said, swallowing. "I'll talk to the others, check out your story. But if I don't like the answers I get, I'll be back."

"I'll be here," Beau said.

"You two aren't fooling anybody, you know," Chabot said, "I ran your names through the Law Enforcement Intelligence Network. You've both been arrested a half-dozen times."

"Wrong," Pachonka corrected. "We've been detained for questioning a few times. Neither of us has ever been arrested for anything."

"That's a lot of questions."

"They must have liked our answers." Pachonka shrugged. "Because here we are."

"You were involved in a shooting a month ago in Iowa."

"Jesus, Constable, can you read your own damn reports? Beau was the *victim* in that shooting. We ring the guy's buzzer, he fires a round through the door that puts a hole in Beau, then blows his own brains out. How is that our fault?"

"Maybe it's not," Chabot conceded. "Maybe what happened here today wasn't, either. But you two aren't just innocent bystanders."

"Never said we were," Pachonka said.

"This isn't over," Puck said after the constable left. "Those boys came out on the short end today but they'll be back.

The way they see it, the bay is theirs. If we're gonna work here through the winter, we need to iron this out."

"I offered the town new ramps," Raven said. "They aren't interested. What else am I supposed to do?"

"Lemme think on that. Meantime, maybe you'd better think about seeing a doctor."

"I'm all right."

"No, you're not. You're bleedin' all over your damn shirt."

"Oh my God," Erin said. "Do you have a first-aid kit?"

"In my truck," Puck said. "I'll get it."

"Do you know what you're doing?" They were in the office, Raven watching as Erin quickly rifled through Shea's red emergency kit, taking stock.

"I'm a licensed practical nurse, paid my way through grad school working in the Samaritan Hospital E.R., Detroit. Take off your shirt and sit on that table."

Beau thought about cracking wise but the set of her mouth was so grim he passed. Eased out of his shirt instead. After wiping her hands down with disinfectant pads, Erin turned to face him. And hesitated, eyeing his tattoos. And his rock-solid frame.

"What?"

"You work out."

"Sometimes."

"A lot," she countered, peeling back the adhesive strips holding the surgical pad in place. "Most guys with tats like yours are fresh out of jail. My. Your wound is more like a gash than a puncture. What did he shoot you with?"

".38 Smith. Punching through the door deformed the slug, slowed it down."

"Lucky you," she said, dabbing up the blood oozing around the plastic clips that held the gash closed. "Looks like it hurt."

"Yes, ma'am."

"And why did the gentleman shoot you?"

"He didn't say. I suppose he was afraid."

"Of what you'd do to him?"

"We couldn't do anything to him. Some states don't recognize gambling debts at all and taking losers to court is bad publicity for the casinos."

"Then what can you do?"

"Realistically? All we can do is talk. Sit down with the guy, figure out his situation. If he wants to pay, we can work out an arrangement. If he doesn't, we can have him barred from every casino in the country. For most deadbeats, getting barred is a blessing."

"And it takes two guys like you and Pachonka to deliver this blessing?"

"Intimidation is part of our game," he admitted, meeting her eyes. "We want the deadbeats to pay. They owe the money to the Native people and compared to what's been stolen from us, it's spit in the ocean. When they win, we pay them. If they lose, we expect them to make it good. But if they welsh, we don't have all that many options."

"If that's true, why did he shoot you?"

"He gambled away money he'd embezzled from his church. He was facing disgrace and probably jail time. So he shot me and then killed himself. With his wife and kids in the next room eating Cheerios. Nice business I'm in."

"What he did wasn't your fault."

"Maybe not. But like the man said, I wasn't an innocent bystander, either."

"This isn't the first time you've been shot," she said, touching a scar on his rib cage.

"Actually, it is. That one was mortar fragment in Beirut. Got these two when our Hummer hit a mine in Iraq."

"And these?" she asked, frowning at a thin arc of keloids along his collarbone.

"Cigarette burns," he said evenly. "After my mom took off, I bounced around in foster homes. Some were pretty bad. Beirut was better."

"You're a beautiful man, Mr. Raven. These scars are . . . a crime."

"I didn't put them there."

"No. But I've got a feeling you earned most of them. The bleeding looks worse than it is. You tore one of your clamps loose, but the wound's still closed. The next time you're mad at somebody, try beating them at chess."

"I'll do that." As she straightened, he reached out, cupping her cheek with his palm, reading her eyes. She met his gaze just as openly. Curious. Unafraid.

"Is something happening with us?" he asked.

"I think so," she said quietly. "Can I ask you something?"

"Sure."

"Why did you come back? Really? From what I've heard, your childhood was miserable here. Why is this building so important to you?"

"You wouldn't understand."

"I definitely won't unless you tell me. Please. I want to know."

"All right, maybe I owe you that. When I got shot in Iowa, I was in the hospital for a week. Nothing to do but lie there. And think. What Maggert said about my mother—"

"That was vile."

"But it might be true. All I know about her is what I can remember from when I was six or seven. From the odds and ends I recall, I think she probably was a prostitute. And maybe a little slow, mentally, I mean. I know we were dirt poor because we were staying in the fish house with my grandfather. The gutbucket man.

"I guess it was pretty grim, but it didn't feel that way to me. I used to dream a lot. Had a little battery radio, and I'd hide up in the tackle tower, read comic books, listen to music. It was like my own private castle. I'd look out over the bay and daydream about the places I'd go someday, the things I'd do. And I was happy.

"I didn't understand racism. They'd call me pickaninny or red nigger and laugh, and because they were laughing I thought they liked me. That I'd done something clever. So I'd laugh too and play the fool. . . .

"Later, after my mom ran off and I got kicked around in foster care, I remembered this place as a special time in my life. Maybe the best time. Subscribed to the local paper, followed the high-school teams, birth announcements, obits. Wolf Woman Bay was like my . . . virtual hometown, I guess. The only one I had.

"So I'm laid up in that Iowa hospital, thinking. A man killed himself and nearly killed me. Didn't know who I was, didn't care. Shot me just for showing up. And I realized my life wasn't anything like I dreamed it would be. Nothing.

"I knew from the paper the old fish house was for sale. And I got this idea that if I could come back here, start over somehow, turn my old make-believe castle into a nice home, maybe I could start my life over, too. Do something better with it. Stop being a guy people shoot just for showing up. Pretty funny, considering how things are working out."

"It's not funny at all, it's a wonderful dream, Beau. Thank you for telling me."

"But?"

"I can't help it. I hate what your dream is doing to my town."

"I only want to build a house."

"I know, and you have every right to do it. . . . I just wish you could do it somewhere else."

"Sorry, but I can't. Thanks for patching me up."

"No problem, Mr. Raven. You'll be fine. Until the next time."

"Gonna live?" Pachonka asked, when Beau and Erin rejoined the others out front.

"For now."

"Good. Shea here is making a goodie run back to Valhalla to pick up some gear. I'm gonna catch a ride with him to the airport. I'll leave the Cadillac and the gun case with you. What do you want me to tell the boss?"

"Say I said hello."

"You're not coming back to work, are you?"

"I don't know. I'll be busy here awhile. Tell her I'll call in a week or so."

"Assuming you're still breathin'. Okay, I'll tell her. I'll see you, brother."

Beau nodded. "Hope so."

Pachonka swiveled in the seat, taking a long look back over the town as Shea's pickup climbed the shore road above Wolf Woman Bay. He caught Shea's glance as he turned back.

"What?"

"You tell me. I think your pal Raven's in a peck of trouble."

"So do I." Pachonka shrugged. "Might even get himself killed."

"And you're bailing out? I thought you two were friends."

"We are. Been together since the Corps. I got him the job collecting for the Mohawk Nation casinos and we work good together. But that's over. He's changed. Still tough enough for the work, but not mean enough. Not anymore."

"Looked mean enough to me. That logger outweighed him by forty pounds. He took him one-handed, put him in the hospital, and barely broke a sweat."

"Beau Jean's a bad-ass, no doubt about that. But he could've hurt that guy a lot worse. And he should have. A month ago he would have stomped him into dog meat. Put the fear of God in the others, maybe they let him alone."

"Why didn't he?"

"That thing in Iowa messed him up. It was pretty damn ugly, Beau on the sidewalk bleedin' out with the guy's kids screamin' we killed their daddy."

"Well, didn't you? I mean—"

"Mister, all we did was ring that prick's doorbell. It was the wrong he did that killed him. But if he hadn't blown his own dumb-ass brains out I damn sure would've done it for him. You have to pay what you owe in this life."

"I guess that's true."

"Damn straight it is. Only Beau doesn't see it that way now. Laid up too long. Too much thinkin' isn't healthy in our game. Especially for a guy like Beau. I don't even think he's strapped anymore."

"Strapped?"

"Packing a gun, man. We're licensed to carry everything but a freakin' bazooka. When that cracker came at him Beau never even made a move for a piece. That thing in Iowa's got him so messed up I think he'd rather take a bullet than kill anybody else, even to save his own life. Or mine. You can't help a man like that. He'll get himself killed, and anybody near him. You had half a brain, you'd bail out, too."

"Nobody's ever accused me of being smart."

"So you're sticking? Why? You only met Raven a few days ago. You don't owe him anything."

"Sure I do. He's my client, so we're in this thing together, like it or not. And I gave him my word."

Pachonka snorted. "No offense, Shea, but I'm Mohawk, full blood. You can probably guess what we figure a white man's promise is worth."

"I can't answer for anybody else. Only me."

"You want to throw in with Beau Jean, fine by me. I like white men who gamble. Good for my business. But take some advice. Don't lay too much on the line. Right now Beau's a real risky bet."

Neither man spoke the rest of the trip. But as Shea turned into the airport drive, Pachonka swiveled to face him.

"One last thing. My line of work, you get pretty good at reading people."

"I expect so."

"That bunch of crackers today? There was something wrong about them."

"How do you mean?"

"I'm not sure, that's what bothers me. They were definitely ticked off because Beau's an uppity half-breed building a nice house in their town. But there was more to it. Must have been a dozen of 'em, they could have stomped us all. Why didn't they? Why did they try to buy him off instead?"

"I don't know."

"Neither do I, and I don't like it. Know what's weird? I had the feeling they were afraid of him. Or afraid of something. Beau missed it 'cause he's all wrapped up in his dream house, so I'm telling you. Maybe that ol' hard-case partner of yours can figure what's up with those boys. He's practically one of 'em."

"I'll ask him."

"Do that," Pachonka said, climbing out, getting his flight bag out of the back. "Thanks for the lift, Mr. Shea. For what it's worth, Beau Jean's a bud so I appreciate you standing by him in this thing. Just don't stand too close."

The next morning, first light, Beau Raven came putting across the harbor in a small wooden motorboat. Idling down the outboard, he coasted to shore beside the fish house. Shea was on the roof with Puck, checking the new felt and the alignment of the first rows of shingles.

"Little late in the season for fishin'," Puck yelled. "Where'd you get that junker?"

"Bought it up the shore. We'll keep it tied up with a For Rent sign on it. A real small one—" He broke off, startled by a splash fifteen yards offshore.

"What the hell?" Splinters leapt out of the roof a few feet from Shea.

"Get down off there," Beau yelled. "Somebody's shooting!" The first echo of gunfire rolled across the water like distant thunder as Raven scrambled out of the boat. Shea was already dialing 911.

"Did you actually see anybody firing at you?" Constable Chabot asked doubtfully.

"Hell no," Shea said. "It was coming from the far side of the bay. Come on up top, I'll show you the damn bullet holes in the roof."

"Oh, I'm sure you've got a few dings up there. This is hunting country. We get stray-round complaints every year, nothing unusual about it."

"Balls," Puck said. "This wasn't no accident, son. He ranged us. First shot barely missed, next three didn't."

"I admit it might look like that, but it could just as easily have been some guy sighting in a rifle who overshot his backstop. And even if it wasn't, take a look at the far shore. Forty square miles of timber and only a few logging trails in and out. We'd never find anybody in there."

"Especially if you don't look," Beau said.

"Look, Mr. Raven, I got myself and two part-time officers to cover the whole township. Normally, we manage just fine. An occasional B and E in a vacation home, drunks on Saturday night. No real trouble. Until you and your Mohawk buddy showed up. Now it seems like every damn day there's some new hassle. So I'm sorry your building caught a few stray rounds—"

"Stray?" Puck echoed.

"That's how it's going in my report unless I get some indication that it's anything more."

"When one of my men stops a slug, you mean?" Shea asked.

"You knew what this job was when you took it, Mr. Shea," Chabot shrugged. "Maybe you should ask for combat pay. I'll look into this, but I wouldn't expect too much. Probably just a hunter."

"That kid had one thing right," Puck said after Chabot left. "He's not gonna find anything."

"What do we do?" Shea asked. "I can't keep men working with lead flying around."

"Give them the afternoon off," Beau said. Grabbing several short pieces of scrap one-by-two lath, he scrambled up the ladder to the roof with Shea right behind.

"Show me the bullet holes." Flicking open a butterfly knife, Raven quickly whittled down the ends of the lath into round dowels. Shea pointed out the gouges and Raven plugged a lath into each of them. When he'd finished, the three sticks pointed back across the bay like accusing fingers.

"There," Raven said. "He was somewhere just beyond that little notch. Probably fired from the beach. Must be twelve hundred yards. Pretty fair shooting. Know anybody around here who can shoot like that, Mr. Paquette?"

"Hit a building at twelve hundred yards? Around here, grab any six guys off the street, half of 'em could make that shot. As I recall, there's a logging road that goes through that area."

"Think you could find it?"

"You bet. And I believe I'll bring my old 30/30 deer rifle along. Just in case we run into any more stray rounds."

"What makes you think he fired from the beach?" Shea

asked. They were in Raven's Escalade, snaking along a rutted trail through the hills on the northern shore.

"The first shot splashed wide right. He corrected for windage with the next round so he must have seen the first one hit. To do that he'd need a decent scope and a clear view of the fish house. Had to be on the beach or just above it."

"It's a long shoreline."

"And a pretty one. Odd name, though."

"You don't know about the Wolf Woman?" Puck asked. "I thought you were Ojibwa."

"Half. I think my mom told me the Wolf Woman story but it's been a long time. Tell it."

"Story goes, back in the Ojibwa days, a woman lost her husband and went mad with grief. Tribal custom was to protect crazy people, but the woman was beautiful, and in her madness, she would dance naked, drive the young bucks wild. Naturally, this made the village wives unhappy, so one day while the men were off on a hunt, the women drove the madwoman into the forest.

"A pack of wolves found her there, dancing. But instead of ripping her apart, the boss wolf carried her back to his den, made her his mate. But her wolf pups were mad like their mother. Foaming at the mouth, attacking any man they met. To this day, you still see 'em in these hills, sometimes."

"Rabies," Shea said.

Raven nodded. "Every Ojibwa tale has a point. You see a wolf foaming at the mouth, you remember the story, get him before he gets you."

"Kinda like we're doing today," Puck agreed. "How will you know the spot?"

"When we can look back at the fish house and see the

tips of the three dowels I stuck in the bullet holes, we'll be there."

"You seem to know a fair amount about shooting at folks."

"It used to be my trade, Mr. Paquette. Like construction is yours. Rough guess, it's not far now."

Leaving the Caddy in the middle of the trail, they shouldered through wind-blasted clusters of jack pines down to the stony shore, then turned north along the beach. Coppery autumn light glittered off the gentle swells of the bay. With Puck carrying his ancient Winchester and Raven scanning the far shore with binoculars, they could have been a hunting party from the last century. Or the one before that.

"Right here," Beau said, lowering the binoculars. "All three rods are lined up. We must be near the place. See any signs?"

"Up there," Puck gestured with the rifle, trudging up the slope to an old stump at the edge of the tree line. Picking up an empty brass cartridge, he squinted at the base, then tossed it to Raven. "I can't read it. What is it?"

"Seven-millimeter Magnum." He sniffed it. "Fresh. Good eyes, Mr. Paquette."

"Yeah, but that's about all we're gonna get," Shea said. "The logging road is about forty yards farther on. The shooter parked there, came down through the trees same way we did."

"Probably used this stump for a shooting rest." Raven nodded. "It's a perfect spot. Which makes him a local, right? Only somebody familiar with the area would know it was here."

"Not necessarily," Puck said. "There are clearings like

this all over these hills. Black walnut stumps, most of them a hundred years old and more."

"How can you tell how old they are?"

"See the gouges across the top? Two-man crosscut saw. The scorch marks mean it was dropped before the Great Fires burned through here back at the turn of the century. This one was a big tree. Near two foot across. Won't see walnut that size again in this life."

"If it was cut a hundred years ago, why hasn't the forest grown over it?"

"Walnut sap is toxic, carries a poison called juglone. Kills bugs, grapevines, anything that might injure a tree. Gives it growing room. Nature's insurance policy. So our shooter didn't have to know about this particular stump, he could have stopped anywhere."

"Are there any tire tracks on the trail?"

"Not anymore," Shea said. "A skidder's been through here, a big log hauler. If there were any tracks, it wiped them out."

"Unless our guy was driving it," Puck countered. "I see more skidder tracks farther along the beach. Somebody must be logging near here."

"Logging what?" Shea asked. "There's nothing but second-growth poplar and scrub pine. Trash trees."

"Maybe we should ask," Beau said. "Didn't Stegman say he owned a sawmill on this shore?"

Stegman's Great Northern Custom Cutting was nowhere near as grand as its name. A backwoods sawmill housed in a converted cow barn with a half-dozen smaller out-buildings used for storing or seasoning lumber, an office housed in a squat, double-wide trailer. Several late-model pickup trucks in the parking lot. Some of the same trucks they'd seen at the fish house.

Puck wandered off to look over the operation. Beau and Shea trotted up the office steps, rapped, and stepped in.

Rich Stegman was alone behind a desk, blue chambray shirt, woollen vest. And an attitude.

"What the hell do you want? If you came to buy lumber, forget it. I'd burn it before I'd sell you a damn stick."

"Nice to see you, too," Beau said. "Somebody fired shots at my place this morning. Thought you might know something about it."

"You've got a ton of nerve, coming out here. Tay Maggert's still in the hospital. They have to operate on his knee."

"I'll send him a card. What about those shots?"

"We hear shots all the time. Poachers bang away at anything that moves in these woods. Probably just a stray round."

"These weren't strays. Somebody fired from the beach less than a mile from here. He used a stump for a rest and he was aiming directly at my place. We even found the brass he left behind. Seven-millimeter Magnum."

"A lot of guys hunt with that round. Common as dirt up here."

"Really? Do you own a seven-millimeter, Mr. Stegman?"

"I own three. This is gun country, Raven. NRA heaven. And like I said, seven-mils are—"

"—common as dirt, right. Why don't we step outside, Mr. Stegman?"

"Look, I don't want any trouble—"

"No trouble. I just want to show you something."

Rising warily, Stegman followed Beau and Shea out. Beau strode to the Escalade, pulled Puck's ancient 30/30 out of the backseat. Stegman paled, backing away.

"Relax, Mr. Stegman, I'm not here to shoot anybody. But I do need a likely target. How about that weather vane?"

"Hey, wait a minute—"

Racking the rifle one-handed, Beau shouldered it and fired, three times in as many seconds, punching holes through the copper rooster atop the barn. The third round blew it off the roof. The gunfire brought loggers charging out of the building in their goggles and hard-hats. But everyone froze when they saw Raven with the rifle.

"Sorry about your bird, Mr. Stegman. I'll admit, clocking a copper rooster is nothing to crow about, even one-handed. Weather vanes can't shoot back. But from now on, my building can. I was a sniper in the Marine Corps, trained to punch out a playing card at two thousand yards. A man's a much bigger target, even across a bay. Fair warning, the next weasel who uses my building for target practice will go home in a box."

"Why tell me?" Stegman blustered. "I told you I don't know anything about it."

"You're head of a citizen's committee, right? I'm counting on you to get the word out. Before somebody gets hurt. Send me a bill for the rooster."

"That was quite a show you put on back there," Puck said. They were in the Escalade, driving back to town.

"Let's hope it works."

"They got the message," Shea said. "They may not like you, Mr. Raven, but nobody wants to get killed over a building. If that guy this morning was really serious about hitting somebody he could have set up closer."

"How about you, Mr. Raven?" Puck asked. "Were you serious? About shooting back, I mean."

Raven glanced at him but didn't answer. Which was answer enough.

Shea turned to Puck. "Where were you, anyway?"

"Took a look around, talked to some of the guys. Used to work in a backwoods operation back in 'sixty-one. Fifty-inch buzz saw powered by a Ford 8N tractor. Stegman's got himself a real high-tech operation here. Brand new Poulan laser-guided blade. Can zip through sixty-inch oak or take your appendix out. Everybody tricked out in fancy respirator face masks. They look uncomfortable as hell but it must pay pretty good, judging from all that shiny Detroit iron in the parking lot."

"You don't miss much, do you, Mr. Paquette?" Beau said.

"Your line of work and mine have somethin' in common, Mr. Raven. Careless people ain't around long. Know what else I saw? Two skidders parked beside the barn. Engine was still warm on one of 'em. And I saw a dead owl. A snowy."

"Somebody shot a snowy?" Shea asked. "They're protected, aren't they?"

"Nobody shot this owl, it was just dead on a sawdust pile. Quite a few dead critters around. Mice and such."

"Stegman probably puts out rat poison and the owl ate the wrong rat."

"Could be." Puck nodded. "Damn shame, though. Snowies are beautiful birds. Not many of them left. Sons of bitches shouldn't leave their damned poison lying around like that."

Raven caught the edge in Puck's tone and glanced curiously at the older man. Puck was staring out the window, lost in thought.

So Beau let it pass. Which was a mistake.

By midafternoon, construction was back in full swing. Roofers were shingling and laying down new felt while the ironworkers continued assembling the structural beams inside.

Raven disappeared for a few hours. When he came back, he started toting boxes into the office.

"What's all this?" Shea asked.

"A cot, sleeping bag, a little space heater. I'm moving in for the duration."

"Sounds cozy," Puck said. "Want some company?"

"No. It's too dangerous now. I don't want anybody else getting hurt."

"Neither do I, Mr. Raven. That's why I'll be here, too. And the next time we have trouble, I'd better do the talking."

"Meaning what?"

"You're a scary fella, Mr. Raven. Stomped that logger into the hospital and blew away Stegman's weather vane onehanded. You've also got some baggage from growing up in this town. And kind of a short fuse. Bad combination."

"Maybe you're right," Beau admitted. "Fair enough, Mr. Paquette, the next time we get company, you can do the talking. Just be ready to duck."

"Sonny, I been ready to duck since the first day I met you."

Raven snapped awake. Listening. Checked the clock. One-forty hour's. Across the darkened office, Shea was snoring softly on his cot. Puck was in a chair by the window in his long johns, silver hair awry, watching a sliver of moon coasting like a galleon through the clouds over the bay.

"What's that noise?" Beau asked quietly.

"Engines, I think, somewhere across the water. Nothing to do with us."

"What kind of engines?"

"Couple of trucks, maybe a motorboat. And a skidder."

"You mean that big log hauler? Why would it be running at two in the morning? Do loggers work at night?"

"Never heard of any who did. Job's risky enough by daylight. Big trees droppin', chain saws ripping away an inch from your boots. Bit like your trade, Mr. Raven. On any given day you can come home from work in a bag. Even worse in the old days. All hand labor back then, double-bitted axes and saws. Bullwork. Cold, too. They only logged in the winter."

"Why?"

"Needed snow to skid the big timber out of the woods. Used horses to drag 'em to the nearest frozen stream. Come spring, the flood would carry the logs down to the bay. Thousands of 'em. Like that old picture over the layout table. Log rafts as far as you can see. Know when that was taken? May of eighteen ninety-six. Just before the Great Fire swept through. Burned the forest, the town, this old sawmill. Quarter of a million acres burned down to the ground that year. Three hundred dead. Before my time, of course, but my granddad said the land looked like Hiroshima after the bomb. Nothing but ashes for hundreds of miles. Railroad tracks twisted like pretzels, whole towns erased like they'd never existed."

"Must've been God-awful."

"Damn straight. But afterward, the people came back, the land came back. And a hundred years later, here we are."

"I get the feeling you're trying to tell me something, Mr. Paquette."

"Maybe one thing. A lot of folks around here are kin of the same families who burned out in 'ninety-six. Grandsons, granddaughters. Bad as those times were, they toughed it through, put things back together. Different breed than folks in the cities down below. Harder, maybe. But good people all the same. You give 'em time, I believe they'll come around."

"I've never been much on patience."

"I've noticed that," Puck said. "Go back to sleep, son. I've got the watch."

The wind woke Raven at first light. Whining and keening like the rabid wolves of the Wolf Woman tale. An early November gale, mild by north-country standards, dark waters rolling like a great beast shifting in its sleep, temperature dropping like someone opened a freezer door.

Raven found Puck at the rail, scanning the horizon with his binoculars.

"Nice little blow," the older man said. "Might see some early snow this year. Come on inside, I'll rustle us up some breakfast."

"What were you looking at?"

"Nothing. Just the storm."

"Mind if I look?" Taking the glasses from Puck, he scanned the horizon, slowed, then stopped cold. "Something's moving out there. What is that? An overturned boat?"

"Not likely. Not in this weather."

"Likely or not, it's there," Raven said, offering him the binoculars, "look for yourself."

"Son, I couldn't see that far if you gave me a damn telescope. But nobody in his right mind would be boatin' in a storm."

"Someone was out there last night. We heard them."

"We heard *some*thing, but sound can be tricky across the water. That engine noise could've been ten miles off."

"Or maybe somebody's in big trouble. Either way, I'm going to find out. Feel like a boat ride, Puck?"

"Hell no. Let it be, Mr. Raven. It's dangerous, it's none of our damn business, and there's nothing out there anyway."

"Isn't there?"

Beau kept the outboard throttled down, putt-putting slowly across the bay, sliding over the oily swells instead of trying to buck through them. Scattered rain squalls blew past every few minutes, cutting visibility, shadowing the far shore. Ten minutes into the run, even the fish house receded into a vague outline glimpsed through the drizzle.

He'd used a twisted pine on the far shore to fix the overturned boat's position but the thrust of the waves kept driving his small craft off course and he lost sight of the marker tree in the rain. Tried to correct by steering into the wind. Twenty minutes out he guessed he must be near the place but couldn't see anything.

Shifting the outboard motor to neutral, he rose slowly, keeping his knees relaxed, gliding over the waves like a surfer. Spotted the shape. Roughly forty meters off in the mist.

Not a boat. A log. Big sucker, maybe twenty feet long,

couple of feet thick, its stubby nose rising and falling with the swells. Something black and bulbous appeared to be lashed to it a third of the way along its length.

Squinting into the wind, Beau tried to get a better look— and a bullet ripped past his ear!

Reflex! Beau dove hard to the left, kicking the boat out from beneath him, hearing the crack of the rifle as he plunged into the waves.

Floundering beneath the surface, he felt the icy grip of the bay surging through his clothing, chilling him to the bone.

And clearing his head. Gunfire. And that was no stray round. Only missed him by an inch. He tried to remember which way he'd fallen, to orient himself. Couldn't think, running out of air . . . He surfaced, gasping, frantically looking around for the boat—*Damn!* It was already twenty yards away, drifting with the wind, motor idling. Leaving him exposed—

Sucking in a quick breath, he ducked under again, just as a second slug smacked into the surf over his head. Dove deeper, kicking hard, swimming with his free hand, trying' to catch up with the little boat. Couldn't.

Surfacing again, he gulped down air like a seal, then dove again. No shot. Hadn't showed himself long enough. But the shooter would be waiting the next time he surfaced, timing him. Had to get behind the damned boat!

Swam harder, desperately seeking the outline of the boat overhead. Finally spotted it. Too far. No! Not if he could hold on just a little longer . . . Ten seconds, twenty. His world was going red. Had to breathe!

Exploding out of the surf, he gagged down a mouthful of water instead of air. Coughing, flailing around—his fingertips brushed the boat.

Grabbing the gunwale, he hung on, hacking up lake water, clearing his lungs. Felt the boat jerk as a bullet punched through it, smashing out a fist-sized exit wound a foot from Beau's head.

Whoa! Couldn't stay here. Had to get aboard and make a run for it. If the shooter popped it at the waterline or trashed the motor he was dead meat out here. Could he haul himself over the gunwale with one hand? No choice. Had to. But even as he braced himself to try, he hesitated, his mind flashing to the images he'd glimpsed below when he was looking for the boat. He knew he only had seconds to get clear but . . . Damn it! Sucking in a deep breath, he let go of the gunwale, slipping beneath the waves again, swimming down and down into the dark, trying to make sense of what he'd seen.

Then he was kicking hard for the surface. Bursting out of the surf, clutching the rail, using his momentum to roll himself aboard. Felt a bolt of agony as he landed hard on his injured shoulder. Sweet Jesus!

Grabbing the steering arm, he cranked the throttle wide open, nearly throwing himself overboard again as the boat wheeled into the surf, bucking wildly through the waves, engine howling, charging headlong into the gathering storm.

"A log?" Shea said. "You went out in the middle of a blow to look at a damn log?"

"Didn't know what it was when I went out," Beau said, teeth chattering as he sipped scalding coffee. "Puck and I heard engine noise from across the bay last night. Thought it might be an over-turned boat. But it was only a log. Big one, though, twenty feet long, couple of feet in diameter. With a float attached to it."

"What kind of float?"

"Inner tubes, I think, to make it buoyant. Didn't get a close look at it. Somebody started shooting at me from the far shore and I had to bail out."

"Stegman?"

"Couldn't see, I ended up in the water. Between the mist and the surf he couldn't see me any better or I might not be here. Kept diving, got behind the boat, then made a run for it in the rain."

"You're lucky you made it back," Shea said.

"Funny, I don't feel very lucky. More disappointed. Because you're not surprised at what I found out there, are you Mr. Paquette? You knew what it was."

"No."

"What are you two talking about? What's out there?"

"Not just one log," Raven said. "Hundreds of them, maybe thousands. I couldn't see very far when I ducked under the water, but I could see enough. The bottom of the bay is littered with them."

"What logs?" Shea demanded. "From where?"

"The last cutting before the fire of 'ninety-six," Puck explained. "They were felled that winter, floated down to the bay in the spring, filled it from shore to shore like that picture in the office. They were there waiting to be cut when fire took the town and the sawmill. By the time folks moved back, the logs had settled to the bottom. No way to get them out in those days. Been down there ever since."

"Until now," Raven said.

"That's why Stegman's men wear respirators and animals

are dying near the sawdust piles." Shea nodded, getting it. "They're salvaging black walnut logs out of the bay. Did you know about this, Puck?"

"Not for certain. From the skidder tracks on the beach, the dead owl, Stegman's loggers driving new trucks, I guessed what might be going on."

"But you didn't warn me," Beau said.

"I told you it was none of your damn business and it's not," Puck said bluntly. "They may be outside the law, but it's a lousy law. Down in Lansing they claim every damn thing in the lakes belongs to the state. Easy to say when you've never swung an axe. Old-time loggers busted their backs puttin' those timbers into the bay and now their grandsons are takin' 'em out again. They aren't stealing anything that isn't already theirs. They aren't hurting anybody."

"Until they started shooting at me."

"To be honest, I never thought they'd go that far."

"Because they're all such fine people?"

"No, damn it, because it's stupid! Half the folks in town must know what Stegman and his loggers are doing. Nobody rats 'em out because they're local and they're risking their necks for every log they salvage. I can understand them trying to run you off to protect their living. But a killing would be crazy. It'd bring the state police down on 'em and their secret wouldn't last ten minutes. Folks won't lie to the law to cover a murder."

"Not even mine?"

"Hell no! You don't think much of these people, do you, Mr. Raven?"

"Let's just say we've had different life experiences. If your tan was a little darker, maybe you'd have a clue."

"Ever occur to you when you show up packing an attitude and an automatic, folks won't roll out no red carpet no matter what color you are?"

"What's wrong with my attitude, Paquette? Too uppity for you?"

"Put a lid on it, both of you!" Shea snapped. "We're all in the same crapper now and barking at each other won't help."

"Not exactly the same," Raven countered. "Nobody's shooting at you.

"They were yesterday and they might try again tomorrow unless we come up with something. Puck, if you had this thing figured, why the hell didn't you say so?"

"I thought Raven squared thing's away out at the sawmill. These guys are loggers, not gangsters. He put the fear of God into 'em. I figured they'd talk it over and try to cut a deal."

"What kind of a deal?" Raven asked.

"Your place has a perfect view of the bay. You'd spot their operation sooner or later and they know it. When running you off didn't work, I expected 'em to offer you a piece of the action to keep quiet. I never thought they'd try to kill you. It doesn't make sense."

"Maybe they're dumber than you think."

"No," Shea frowned, "he's right. Why risk murder when you can solve the problem for a few bucks? The constable took you for a lowlife because of your arrest record, and anything that kid knows, the Stegmans know, too. They should have tried to buy you off."

"Maybe they figured a bullet would be cheaper. Especially for a half-breed."

"I don't believe that," Puck said stubbornly. "I'm a logger, a cedar savage like those boys. I don't feel that way and don't think they do, either. We got no royalty up here, nobody gives a damn about your pedigree. A man's measured by what he does, not who his daddy was."

"Okay, Mr. Paquette, let's say your logger pals are all stand-up guys, not a racist prick in the bunch. I don't think so, but for the sake of argument, if the color of my skin isn't the problem, then what is?"

"I don't know," Puck said slowly. "The only thing that killing you would change is this house. It would go back to being a museum, the way they wanted in the first place."

"That can't be it," Shea argued. "Nobody shoots anybody over dinosaur bones or old arrowheads."

"But as a museum it would have stayed pretty much as it was," Puck mused. "Maybe it's something about the way we're remodeling it—"

"No, the trouble started even before they knew what my plans were."

"But they could have made things a lot tougher," Shea said "Why didn't they?"

"How do you mean?"

"That building inspector could have stopped us cold. If he'd condemned the supports, an appeal to the state would've taken months and cost a bundle. He even admitted he wanted to jack us around—"

"—but he had his orders," Raven finished. "You're right. If they're trying to run me out, why did Donakowski give us a pass?"

"It doesn't make sense," Puck said. "Unless . . ."

"What?"

"Maybe he wasn't giving us a break. Maybe he just didn't want us digging around those timbers."

"Why would he care?"

"I don't know. Unless there's something down there they don't want us to see?"

Raven eyed the older man a moment, then both men nodded.

"Dig them out," Raven said. "Every damned one of them."

They didn't have to. Shea pulled the men off their jobs, passed out shovels, and set them to digging. Intersecting circles around each support base beneath the building, four feet deep. At the sixth column, halfway back, one of the men called Shea over.

"Is this what we're looking for?" A bone angled up through the soil about thirty inches down. A femur. Possibly human.

"We'll need to see more of it to be sure," Shea said grimly. "But be very careful."

Using spoons and a whisk broom, they cleared away more soil, revealing a rib cage, still wrapped in a rotted blanket. And a cheap red plastic purse tucked beside the remains.

Shea fished it out gingerly, checked inside. A few loose coins, lipstick tube, a wallet with three dollars. And a thirty-five-year-old driver's license. A faded photo ID of a young dark-haired woman smiling shyly at the camera.

Mary Beth Raven.

Swallowing, Shea turned to hand the purse to Beau. But he was gone.

He found him in the inner office, his weapons case open on the display table. An AR-15 assault rifle, matte black. A blunt, Benelli Tactical pump shotgun with a rear pistol grip. Two Glock handguns, both automatics. Checking the retainer spring on a magazine, Beau slid it into the pistol butt and slammed it home.

"What are you going to do?" Shea asked.

"What I do best. Collect what's owed."

"From whom? You don't know who did this."

"The hell I don't—"

A hard rap on the door. Erin Mullaney stepped in.

"Puck called me, told me what you'd found. I'm so sorry—"

"We both know who's been pushing me since I got here," Beau continued, ignoring her. "That inspector who wanted to jack us around said he had his orders. I thought maybe Erin cut us a break but she didn't. I only know one other person in this town with enough juice to order an inspector to give us a pass."

Shoving the automatic into his belt in the small of his back, he picked up the short-barreled shotgun. Holding the slide, he racked the action one-handed, then began loading the magazine, pushing blunt red shells into the tube with a solid thunk.

"You can't really believe Mr. Stegman caused your mother's death," Erin said.

"I don't know. Neither do you. But I'm sure as hell going to ask him." He racked the shotgun again, chambering a round.

"With that?" Erin asked.

"Lady, it's a tool of my trade. Never shot anybody with it. Never had to. You'd be surprised how talkative people get when they're starin' down a barrel, seeing their future."

"If that young punk constable spots you with that thing, he'll panic and start shooting," Puck said.

"Then he'd better not miss."

"Or what?" Erin asked. "You'll kill him? You don't want that."

"Don't tell me what I want! That's my mother down there! Thrown away like garbage, all these years. I'm gonna settle up for that, so you'd better decide which side you're on."

"You know I'm with you," Erin said. "All the way. That's why I won't let you screw up like this. You had a gun in Iowa. It didn't solve anything there. It won't here, either. What do you want, Beau? To know the truth? Or just to get even?"

"Both," he said. But he left the shotgun in the case when he snapped it closed.

A handful of townspeople were already gathered in the parking lot as word of the discovery spread. Beau stalked out of the fish house amid a buzz of murmurs and whispers, but no one asked him anything. One look at his eyes and people stepped aside.

He started for his Cadillac, then veered off, leaving it, heading for Main Street. The town was only four blocks long and he knew exactly where he was going. Erin walked beside him with Shea and Puck only a step behind.

A few locals followed, more joining in as they marched through the village. Shopkeepers, retirees, curious, concerned. They'd grown to a fair-sized crowd by the time Raven's group arrived at a proper, white Victorian home at the end of the block. Trotting up the steps, Beau hammered on the door.

George Stegman opened it. Gray man in a gray cardigan

and reading glasses, holding a book that slipped from his fingers when he saw Raven and the crowd in the street behind him.

"What do you want?"

"We found my mother's body, Mr. Stegman. Buried under the fish house. What happened to her? How did she get there?"

Stegman paled, backing away, the bluish hue of his lips becoming darker by the moment. "Why do you—I don't know what you're talking about."

"Sure you do," Beau said, pushing the elderly man farther back into his living room with two fingertips. "This is your town, Mr. Stegman, you know everything that happens here. And you know about Mary Raven." Stegman's knees bumped against the sofa and he sat down.

"I make a living reading people, Mr. Stegman," Beau said softly, leaning over him, their faces only inches apart. "You've been carrying the truth like a cancer in your belly all these years. But it's worse since I came back, isn't it? Give it up. It'll take your pain away."

"I don't—" Stegman swallowed. "Look, I can give you money—" He coughed, trying to catch his breath. Didn't work. His coughing became a wrenching paroxysm, convulsing him. Then he stiffened, eyes rolling up, face going blue.

"No, you don't!" Beau roared, grabbing Stegman's shirt, pulling him upright. "Don't die on me, old man! You don't get off that easy!"

"Beau! Let, him go! You're killing him!" Erin shouted, pulling him off. Cradling Stegman in her arms, she eased him down on the sofa, wiping the foam from his mouth.

Beau loomed over her, eyes dark as a thunderhead.

"Back off!" Erin snapped. "Leave him to me. He can't tell you anything if he's dead!"

Beau straightened as the front door banged open and Constable Chabot burst in.

"What's going on here?"

"Mr. Stegman's having some kind of a seizure," Erin said. "Call an ambulance."

"What did you do to him?" Chabot demanded, pushing Beau backward.

"Nothing, yet."

"Damn it, I knew you'd be trouble—"

"Constable!" Erin roared. "Are you freaking deaf! This man's having a seizure! Now call an ambulance and give me a hand!"

"You stay put!" Chabot ordered, glaring at Beau. Yanking the cell phone from his utility belt, he hastily tapped 911 and reported the emergency. When he looked up, Raven was gone.

Puck trailed Raven back to the fish house. Found him kneeling beside the remains, trying to clear away the soil with his fingertips.

"There's no need to dig any farther, Mr. Raven. It's a crime scene now. The state police will be here in the morning. They'll see to it."

If Beau heard him, he gave no sign. Kept scraping away the soil.

"Mr. Raven—"

"Thirty years," Beau said quietly. "Alone down here in the dark. In this muck. Nobody even looked for her. Not the police. Or my grandfather. Not even me. I don't want to leave her this way another night, Mr. Paquette. Not another hour. But I can't dig very well with one hand. Will you help me? Please?"

"Sure," Puck said, kneeling beside him. "You bet."

It was nearly dusk when Erin got back from Valhalla. Beau was alone in the inner office. Sitting beside the layout table. A single candle the only light.

His leather coat was lovingly folded around the mortal remains of Mary Raven. It made a surprisingly small bundle.

"Where is everybody? I thought Shea and Paquette were staying here?"

"I sent them away. Wanted to be alone with . . . my mom." He nodded at the bundle. "How is Mr. Stegman?"

"He was alive when I left. They're medevacking him down to Ann Arbor by helicopter. I don't think he'll make it."

"Did he tell you anything?"

"Almost everything. We talked in the ambulance. He knows he's dying. Afraid to face final judgment, I guess. But . . . Please don't make me tell you, Beau. It's . . . ugly."

"It's all right," he said, reaching up, covering her hand with his. "It can't hurt her anymore. What happened?"

"There was a party. Rich Stegman and some of his crew were drunk, decided to . . . visit Mary. From what Stegman said, there was nothing unusual about that."

"I know what she was. Go on."

"Anyway, something went wrong. Maybe they were too drunk or there were too many, but Mary tried to stop them. She started screaming. And . . ." Erin took a ragged breath. "Somebody hit her with a bottle. Just to shut her up, Stegman said. But he must've hit her too hard.

"They tried to revive her, but couldn't. So Rich ran and

fetched his dad. Mr. Stegman said Mary was dead when he got there. So they buried her under the fish house. The next day Mr. Stegman told your grandfather she'd run away. Gave him money to take care of you—"

"Please. He paid him off to keep his mouth shut. My grandfather didn't give a damn about anything but his next bottle and Stegman knew it. Who hit my mother?"

"He said he doesn't know, Beau, and I think it might be true. He wasn't there. I'm sorry."

"It's okay. Thanks for trying. And thanks for backing me off the old man at his house. I was out of control. I don't know if you were trying to save my ass or his but you did the right thing."

"No charge. Actually I've grown rather fond of your ass. And the rest of you, too. Do you mind if I sit with you awhile?"

"No. I'd like that."

They sat without talking for a time, the only sound the rising wind whining and rustling around the old house.

"I remember the night it happened . . ." Beau spoke so quietly Erin wasn't sure if he was talking to her or himself. "She sent me away. To my hidey-hole up in the tackle tower. She'd done it before when she had a . . . visitor, you know? Boyfriends, she called them. But I woke up and . . . I heard her crying.

"Sometimes she made noises when she was with a man and . . . I didn't want to know about it. So I turned up my little radio. Pretended it was the Wolf Woman and her pups howling."

"Maybe it was only the wind. Like tonight."

"No. The bay was like glass. It wasn't the Wolf Woman. It was my mother. Screaming."

"You were only a kid, Beau. You couldn't have done anything."

"Maybe not. But I didn't try. I didn't even goddamn try."

"What will you do now?"

He chewed that one over a moment. "Nothing."

She glanced at him curiously.

"I won't have to do anything. They think I came back to get even. Like an avenging angel or something."

"Didn't you?"

"No. I didn't know about any of this. After I got decked in Iowa, I was just trying to find my old hidey-hole again. If they'd let me alone, I would have laid up here awhile, then moved on. None of this had to happen."

"And now?"

"I won't have to find them," he said, rising. "They'll be coming for me. You'd better go."

"Not a chance."

"I mean it. I can't do what I have to if you're—" He froze, listening. "Get over against the wall. Right now."

A single rap on the door. "Mr. Raven? It's me." Puck slid inside, closing the door behind him.

"I told you to stay out of this."

"We thought about it. Stopped at a bar up the street. Heard some talk. About burning this place and you along with it. Danny's trying to locate the constable. I thought you ought to know."

"Okay, you've told me. Thank you. Now I want you to take Miss Mullaney and go."

"It's too late for that," Puck said, over the rumble of pickup trucks pulling into the lot. "This is my building, too. I'm in."

"No, you're not. You stay inside and keep her safe, you

understand? And stay the hell away from the windows."

"*Raven!*" Rich Stegman yelled from the parking lot. "Come on out. Your time's up!"

Beau paused a moment to touch the small bundle on the table, then stepped through the door, closing it carefully behind him.

Outside, the fish house was awash in light, four pickup trucks in the lot, headlights and roof-rack halogens erasing the night.

The same men as before, but not so many. Five loggers in a loose line. Armed, this time.

Stegman looked as if he'd just come from the mill: flannel shirt, jeans, and boots. Unshaven, haggard, red-eyed. Holding a rifle. An expensive one. Weatherby Mark V. Seven-millimeter Magnum. The others were carrying a mix of shotguns and rifles. Hunting guns.

"People tell me you roughed up my dad. Put him in the hospital. I'm gonna finish you for that." His words were slurred. He'd been drinking. Maybe all of them had.

"Is that why you're here? I thought it might be about the body under the fish house. Mary Raven."

"We don't know anything about that. You've been pushing people since the day you got here. Jumping my dad was way over the line."

"And your pals? Are they all here about your dad, too?"

"They're my backup. We know you're some kind of professional thug. Saw what you did to Tay Maggert. You wouldn't know what a fair fight is."

"Sure I do. And this isn't it. Because if you came to settle up for my mom, Stegman, you'd better send for more help. A lot more."

"What are you talking about? You're alone."

"No he ain't," Puck said, easing through the doorway behind Raven, moving to the end of the porch. Carrying Beau's shotgun.

"You're backing the wrong side, old man," Stegman said. "You're one of us."

"Been a logger most of my life," Puck agreed. "Cedar savage and proud of it. But I ain't no murderin' rapist, Stegman. And I'm not with you."

"You can't get all of us, not even with that thing."

"It won't matter," Erin said, stepping through the doorway, standing beside Beau. "They have Mary Raven's body now, Mr. Stegman. Your father has already told the police how she died and who was involved—"

"Hey, now hold on a damn minute!" one of the loggers said, lowering his rifle, backing away. "I had no part in that. I'm out."

"The rest of you best do the same," Puck said. "The police are on their way. You might get past what happened to Mary Raven. It was a long time ago. But only if you back off now. Lay 'em down, boys. Go home. It's over."

And it worked. After a moment's hesitation, a second logger backed away, then another.

"No!" Stegman roared, shouldering his rifle. "Damn you, Raven, I should have killed you the first day!"

Beau wheeled, pushing Erin aside, clawing for his pistol as gunfire exploded. Stegman's first shot went wild, whistling past Beau's head as his weapon came up, too late—then the shotgun's savage blast ripped into Stegman, smashing him to the pavement in a tangled heap, his rifle spinning out of his hands, clattering across the concrete.

A moment of stunned silence, then the loggers broke and ran. Scrambling into their pickups, tearing out of the lot as a police cruiser roared in, siren howling. Chabot and Dan Shea piled out. Shea hurried to the deck as the constable knelt beside Stegman, feeling for a pulse.

Nothing. Chabot rose, his hand on his gun butt. "You on the porch. Put that shotgun down. Now."

Puck seemed surprised he was still holding the stubby weapon. Lowering it to the deck, he backed away from it.

"Mr. Paquette—"

"Get the hell away from me, Raven. I'm done with you. None of this had to happen." Puck turned and walked unsteadily toward the end of the deck, staring blindly into the darkness over the bay.

Raven started after him but Shea grasped his arm. "Let him be. He's upset but he's a tough old bird. He'll feel different tomorrow."

"No, he's right," Beau said, helping Erin up. "Maybe I shouldn't have come back. But I'm not sorry. All these years, I thought she abandoned me. When my grandfather said she ran off, I didn't understand. She was my mom and I loved her. It didn't make sense. Now it does.

"But Puck's right, it's a high price to pay. Maybe too high. It's finished, Mr. Shea. Thank your men for their work, send me a bill."

"Hold on, Mr. Raven, we should talk about this. I'll admit I thought remodeling this place was nuts at first, but you were right. It can really be something special."

"Not to me. Not anymore."

"I understand that, but you can't just walk away from it, either. If we leave it half-finished it'll be ruined. This old building has stood a hundred years, it deserves better."

"So did Mary Raven. We're done here, Mr. Shea. Collect your crew and go. You're fired."

It took the state police most of the day to gather the evidence and complete their interviews. Four loggers were arrested in the death of Mary Raven. Puck would have to testify at the coroner's inquest but there were no formal charges against him. The county prosecutor ruled Stegman's death a justifiable homicide.

Shea tried talking to Raven again but it was no use. It was truly over for him. Finished.

First light the next morning, Puck and Shea packed up their gear and checked out of the motel. Their crew was already pulling out, a convoy of work vans and pickups, heading home to Valhalla.

And none too soon. The storm had been gathering strength during the night, the temperature dropping to zero like a rock as a fierce cold front moved in. In the hills above the village, the pines were already glistening Christmas white. Branches rimed with frost, unable to flex in the wind, were snapping like gunfire in the forest.

"Pull over," Puck said suddenly.

"What's wrong?" Shea asked, easing the truck onto the shoulder.

"Will you look at that," the old man breathed. From the roadside they had a panoramic view of the village and the hay beyond it.

A northern miracle.

Sometime during the night, the temperature and

winds had fallen together and worked their wintry magic.

Wolf Woman Bay had frozen over.

From the shore to the horizon, the surface was a single, glittering sheet of ice. White as a wedding gown, dusted with diamonds.

But not for long. Mountainous storm clouds were rolling in off the big lake, looming over the northern shore, marching inland, their shadows darkening the hills.

"Gonna be a serious blow," Shea said. "We're clearing out of here just in time."

"Not hardly," Puck growled. "Way late, if you ask me. Wish to God we'd never heard of this place."

In the heart of the village below there was a sudden flash, then another. A streak of flames raced along the porch of the fish house, climbing up the walls. In seconds the front of the building was engulfed. And even at that distance, they could see a single dark figure backing away from the blaze as the fire took hold.

"My God," Shea said, grabbing his cell phone, "he's torching his own damn building." Puck seized his wrist.

"Let it be, Danny. It's his house."

"But he's letting it burn!"

"What else can he do? Couldn't live there or give it back to the town. It's better this way. Finally over and done with."

"Maybe you're right. But that's one hell of an expensive gesture. And it's a damn shame."

Far below, Beau Raven stood like a stone, watching his dream burn down to the waterline. A few townspeople gathered but kept a wary distance. No one tried to stop him.

As if answering the madness in the village, the northern

gale unleashed its fury over the bay. Storm winds howled out of hills and across the ice, snow devils spinning wildly ahead, keening like a pack of ghost wolves.

The rising storm whipped the blazing fish house into an inferno. Sparks and cinders hurtling upward in a pillar of smoke, towering high above the bay.

Writhing and swirling in the wind.

Like a Wolf Woman.

Dancing.

Merely Hate

Ed McBain

Ed McBain's (1926–2005) first published work was *The Black-board Jungle,* written under the name of Evan Hunter, which was made into a motion picture. His 87th Precinct novels held a cap-tive audience through more than fifty novels, published from the early fifties to 2002. Under his McBain name, he also wrote a dozen Matthew Hope novels, and under his Evan Hunter name, he penned screenplays, teleplays, children's works, and short stories. Mystery Writers of America Award, 1957, for his short story "The Last Spin." He was awarded the Mystery Writers of America's Grand Master Award for lifetime achievement in 1986, and was the first American to receive the British Crime Writer's Association Cartier Diamond Dagger in 1998. He also was honored with the Frankfurt Original e-Book Award for Best Fiction in 2002. He passed away in July 2005 after a long and valiant battle with cancer.

A blue Star of David had been spray-painted on the wind-shield of the dead driver's taxi.

"This is pretty unusual," Monoghan said.

"The blue star?" Monroe asked.

"Well, that, too," Monoghan agreed.

The two homicide detectives flanked Carella like a pair of bookends. They were each wearing black suits, white shirts, and black ties, and they looked somewhat like mor-ticians, which was not a far cry from their actual calling. In this city, detectives from Homicide Division were over-seers of death, expected to serve in an advisory and super-visory capacity. The actual murder investigation was handled by the precinct that caught the squeal—in this case, the Eight-Seven.

"But I was referring to a cabbie getting killed," Monoghan explained. "Since they started using them plastic partitions . . . what, four, five years ago? . . . yellow-cab homicides have gone down to practically zip."

Except for tonight, Carella thought.

Tall and slender, standing in an easy slouch, Steve Carella looked like an athlete, which he wasn't. The blue star both-ered him. It bothered his partner, too. Meyer was hoping the blue star wasn't the start of something. In this city—in this world—things started too fast and took too long to end.

"Trip sheet looks routine," Monroe said, looking at the clipboard he'd recovered from the cab, glancing over the times and locations handwritten on the sheet. "Came on at midnight, last fare was dropped off at one-forty. When did you guys catch the squeal?"

Car four, in the Eight-Seven's Adam Sector, had dis-covered the cab parked at the curb on Ainsley Avenue at two-thirty in the morning. The driver was slumped over the wheel, a bullet hole at the base of his skull. Blood was running down the back of his neck, into his collar. Blue paint was running down his windshield. The uniforms had phoned the detective squadroom some five minutes later.

"We got to the scene at a quarter to three," Carella said.

"Here's the ME, looks like," Monoghan said.

Carl Blaney was getting out of a black sedan marked with the seal of the Medical Examiner's Office. Blaney was the only person Carella knew who had violet eyes. Then again, he didn't know Liz Taylor.

"What's this I see?" he asked, indicating the clipboard in Monroe's hand. "You been compromising the crime scene?"

"Told you," Monoghan said knowingly.

"It was in plain sight," Monroe explained.

"This the vic?" Blaney asked, striding over to the cab and looking in through the open window on the driver's side. It was a mild night at the beginning of May. Specta-tors who'd gathered on the sidewalk beyond the yellow crime scene tapes were in their shirt sleeves. The detec-tives in sport jackets and ties, Blaney and the homicide dicks in suits and ties, all looked particularly formal, as if they'd come to the wrong street party.

"MCU been here yet?" Blaney asked.

"We're waiting," Carella said.

Blaney was referring to the Mobile Crime Unit, which was called the CSI in some cities. Before they sanctified the scene, not even the ME was supposed to touch anything. Monroe felt this was another personal jab, just because he'd lifted the goddamn clipboard from the front seat. But he'd never liked Blaney, so fuck him.

"Why don't we tarry over a cup of coffee?" Blaney suggested, and without waiting for company, started walking toward an all-night diner across the street. This was a black neighborhood, and this stretch of turf was largely retail, with all of the shops closed at three-fifteen in the morning. The diner was the only place ablaze with illumination, although lights had come on in many of the tenements above the shuttered shops.

The sidewalk crowd parted to let Blaney through, as if he were a visiting dignitary come to restore order in Baghdad. Carella and Meyer ambled along after him. Monoghan and Monroe lingered near the taxi, where three or four blues stood around scratching their asses. Casually, Monroe tossed the clipboard through the open window and onto the front seat on the passenger side.

There were maybe half a dozen patrons in the diner when Blaney and the two detectives walked in. A man and a woman sitting in one of the booths were both black. The girl was wearing a purple silk dress and strappy high-heeled sandals. The man was wearing a beige linen suit with wide lapels. Carella and Meyer each figured them for a hooker and her pimp, which was profiling because for all they knew, the pair could have been a gainfully employed, happily married couple coming home from a late party. Everyone sitting on stools at the counter was black, too. So was the man behind it. They all knew this was the Law here, and the Law frequently spelled trouble in the hood, so they all fell silent when the three men took stools at the counter and ordered coffee.

"So how's the world treating you these days?" Blaney asked the detectives.

"Fine," Carella said briefly. He had come on at midnight, and it had already been a long night.

The counterman brought their coffees.

Bald and burly and blue-eyed, Meyer picked up his coffee cup, smiled across the counter, and asked, "How you doing?"

"Okay," the counterman said warily.

"When did you come to work tonight?"

"Midnight."

"Me, too," Meyer said. "Were you here an hour or so ago?"

"I was here, yessir."

"Did you see anything going down across the street?"

"Nossir."

"Hear a shot?"

"Nossir."

"See anyone approaching the cab there?"

"Nossir."

"Or getting out of the cab?"

"I was busy in here," the man said.

"What's your name?" Meyer asked.

"Whut's my name got to do with who got aced outside?"

"Nothing," Meyer said. "I have to ask."

"Deaven Brown," the counterman said.

"We've got a detective named Arthur Brown up the Eight-Seven," Meyer said, still smiling pleasantly.

"That right?" Brown said indifferently.

"Here's Mobile," Carella said, and all three men hastily downed their coffees and went outside again.

The chief tech was a Detective/First named Carlie . . .

"For Charles," he explained.

. . . Epworth. He didn't ask if anyone had touched anything, and Monroe didn't volunteer the information either. The MCU team went over the vehicle and the pavement surrounding it, dusting for prints, vacuuming for fibers and hair. On the cab's dashboard, there was a little black holder with three miniature American flags stuck in it like an open fan. In a plastic holder on the partition facing the back seat, there was the driver's pink hack license. The name to the right of the photograph was Khalid Aslam. It was almost four A.M. when Epworth said it would be okay to examine the corpse.

Blaney was thorough and swift.

Pending a more thorough examination at the morgue, he proclaimed cause of death to be a gunshot wound to the head—

Big surprise, Monroe thought, but did not say.

—and told the assembled detectives that they would have his written report by the end of the day. Epworth promised likewise, and one of the MCU team drove the taxi off to the police garage where it would be sealed as evidence. An ambulance carried off the stiff. The blues took down the CRIME SCENE tapes, and told everybody to go home, nothing to see here anymore, folks.

Meyer and Carella still had four hours to go before their shift ended.

"Khalid Aslam, Khalid Aslam," the man behind the computer said. "Must be a Muslim, don't you think?"

The offices of the License Bureau at the Taxi and Limousine Commission occupied two large rooms on the eighth floor of the old brick building on Emory Street all the way downtown. At five in the morning, there were only two people on duty, one of them a woman at another computer across the room. Lacking population, the place seemed cavernous.

"Most of the drivers nowadays are Muslims," the man said. His name was Lou Foderman, and he seemed to be close to retirement age, somewhere in his mid-sixties, Meyer guessed.

"Khalid Aslam, Khalid Aslam," he said again, still searching. "The names these people have. You know how many licensed yellow-cab drivers we have in this city?" he asked, not turning from the computer screen. "Forty-two thousand," he said, nodding. "Khalid Aslam, where are you hiding, Khalid Asiam? Ninety percent of them are immigrants, seventy percent from India, Pakistan, and Bangladesh. You want to bet Mr. Aslam here is from one of those countries? How much you wanna bet?"

Carella looked up at the wall clock.

It was five minutes past five.

"Back when *I* was driving a cab," Foderman said, "this was during the time of the Roman Empire, most of your cabbies were Jewish or Irish or Italian. We still got a couple of Jewish drivers around, but they're mostly from Israel or Russia. Irish and Italian, forget about it. You get in a cab nowadays, the driver's talking Farsi to some other guy on his cell phone, you think they're planning a terrorist attack. I wouldn't be surprised Mr. Aslam was talking on the phone to one of his pals, and the passenger shot him because he couldn't take it anymore, you said he was shot, correct?"

"He was shot, yes," Meyer said.

He looked up at the clock, too.

"Because he was babbling on the phone, I'll bet," Foderman said. "These camel jockeys think a taxi is a private phone booth, never mind the passenger. You ask them to please stop talking on the phone, they get insulted. We get more complaints here about drivers talking on the phone than anything else. Well, maybe playing the radio. They play their radios with all this string music from the Middle East, sitars, whatever they call them. Passengers are trying to have a decent conversation, the driver's either playing the radio or talking on the phone. You tell him please lower the radio, he gives you a look could kill you on the spot. Some of them even wear turbans and carry little daggers in their boots, Sikhs, they call themselves. 'All Singhs are Sikhs,'" Forderman quoted, " 'but not all Sikhs are Singhs,' that's an expression they have. Singhs is a family name. Or the other way around, I forget which. Maybe it's 'All Sikhs are Singhs,' who knows? Khalid Aslam, here he is. What do you want to know about him?"

Like more than thousands of other Muslim cab drivers in this city, Khalid Aslam was born in Bangladesh. Twelve years ago, he came to America with his wife and one child. According to his updated computer file, he now had three children and lived with his family at 3712 Locust Avenue in Majesta, a neighborhood that once—like the city's cab drivers—was almost exclusively Jewish, but which now was predominately Muslim.

Eastern Daylight Savings Time had gone into effect three weeks ago. This morning, the sun came up at six minutes to six. There was already heavy early-morning rush-hour traffic on the Majesta Bridge. Meyer was driving. Carella was riding shotgun.

"You detect a little bit of anti-Arab sentiment there?" Meyer asked.

"From Foderman, you mean?"

"Yeah. It bothers me to hear another Jew talk that way."

"Well, it bothers me, too," Carella said.

"Yeah, but you're not Jewish."

Someone behind them honked a horn.

"What's with him?" Meyer asked.

Carella turned to look.

"Truck in a hurry," he said.

"I have to tell you," Meyer said, "that blue star on the windshield bothers me. Aslam being Muslim. A bullet in the back of his head, and a Star of David on the windshield, that bothers me."

The truck driver honked again.

Meyer rolled down the window and threw him a finger. The truck driver honked again, a prolonged angry blast this time.

"Shall we give him a ticket?" Meyer asked jokingly.

"I think we should," Carella said.

"Why not? Violation of Section Two Twenty-One; Chapter Two, Subchapter Four, Noise Control."

"Maximum fine, eight hundred and seventy-five smackers," Carella said, nodding, enjoying this.

"Teach him to honk at cops," Meyer said.

The driver behind them kept honking his horn.

"So much hate in this city," Meyer said softly. "So much hate."

*   *   *

Shalah Aslam opened the door for them only after they had both held up their shields and ID cards to the three inches of space allowed by the night chain. She was wearing a blue woolen robe over a long white cotton nightgown. There was a puzzled look on her pale face. This was six-thirty in the morning, she had to know that two detectives on her doorstep at this hour meant something terrible had happened.

There was no diplomatic way to tell a woman that her husband had been murdered.

Standing in a hallway redolent of cooking smells, Carella told Shalah that someone had shot and killed her husband, and they would appreciate it if she could answer a few questions that might help them find whoever had done it. She asked them to come in. The apartment was very still. In contrast to the night before, the day had dawned far cold for May. There was a bleak chill to the Aslam dwelling. They followed her through the kitchen and into a small living room where the detectives sat on an upholstered sofa that probably had been made in the mountains of North Carolina. The blue robe Shalah Aslam was wearing most likely had been purchased at the Gap. But here on the mantel was a clock shaped in the form of a mosque, and there were beaded curtains leading to another part of the apartment, and there were the aromas of strange foods from other parts of the building, and the sounds of strange languages wafting up from the street through the open windows. They could have been some-where in downtown Dhakar.

"The children are still asleep," Shalah explained. "Benazir is only six months old. The two other girls don't catch their school bus until eight-fifteen. I usually wake them at seven."

She had not yet cried. Her pale narrow face seemed entirely placid, her dark brown eyes vacant. The shock had registered, but the emotions hadn't yet caught up.

"Khalid was worried that something like this might happen," she said. "Ever since 9/11. That's why he had those American flags in his taxi. To let passengers know he's American. He got his citizenship five years ago. He's American, same as you. We're all Americans."

They had not yet told her about the Star of David painted on her husband's windshield.

"Seven Bangladesh people died in the towers, you know," she said. "It is not as if we were not victims, too. Because we are Muslim, that does not make us terrorists. The terrorists on those planes were Saudi, you know. Not people from Bangladesh."

"Mrs. Aslam, when you say he was worried, did he ever say specifically . . . ?"

"Yes, because of what happened to some other drivers at Regal."

"Regal?"

"That's the company he works for. A Regal taxi was set on fire in Riverhead the very day the Americans went into Afghanistan. And another one parked in Calm's Point was vandalized the week after we invaded Iraq. So he was afraid something might happen to him as well."

"But he'd never received a specific death threat, had he? Or . . ."

"No."

". . . a threat of violence?"

"No, but the fear was always there. He has had rocks thrown at his taxi. He told me he was thinking of draping a small American flag over his hack license, to hide his picture and name. When passengers ask if he's Arab, he tells them he's from Bangladesh."

She was still talking about him in the present tense. It still hadn't sunk in.

"Most people don't even know where Bangladesh is. Do you know where Bangladesh is?" she asked Meyer.

"No, ma'am, I don't," Meyer said.

"Do you?" she asked Carella.

"No," Carella admitted.

"But they know to shoot my husband because he is from Bangladesh," she said, and burst into tears.

The two detectives sat opposite her clumsily, saying nothing.

"I'm sorry," she said.

She took a tiny, crochet-trimmed handkerchief from the pocket of the robe, dabbed at her eyes with it.

"Khalid was always so careful," she said. "He never picked up anyone wearing a ski cap," drying her cheeks now. "If he got sleepy, he parked in front of a twenty-four-hour gas station or a police precinct. He never picked up anyone who didn't look right. He didn't care what color a person was. If that person looked threatening, he wouldn't pick him up. He hid his money in his shoes, or in an ashtray, or in the pouch on the driver-side door. He kept only a few dollars in his wallet. He was a very careful man."

Meyer bit the bullet.

"Did your husband know any Jewish people?" he asked.

"No," she said. "Why?"

"Mama?" a child's voice asked.

A little girl in a white nightgown, six, seven years old, was standing in the doorway to one of the other rooms. Her dark eyes were big and round in a puzzled face Meyer had seen a thousand times on television these past several years. Straight black hair. A slight frown on the face now. Wondering who these strange men were in their living room at close to seven in the morning.

"Where's Daddy?" she asked.

"Daddy's working," Shalah said, and lifted her daughter onto her lap. "Say hello to these nice men."

"Hello," the little girl said.

"This is Sabeen," Shalah said. "Sabeen is in the first grade, aren't you, Sabeen?"

"Uh-huh," Sabeen said.

"Hello, Sabeen," Meyer said.

"Hello," she said again.

"Sweetie, go read one of your books for a while, okay?" Shalah said. "I have to finish here."

"I have to go to school," Sabeen said.

"I know, darling. I'll just be a few minutes."

Sabeen gave the detectives a long look, and then went out of the room, closing the door behind her.

"Did a Jew kill my husband?" Shalah asked.

"We don't know that," Carella said.

"Then why did you ask if he knew any Jews?"

"Because the possibility exists that this might have been a hate crime," Meyer said.

"My husband was not a Palestinian," Shalah said. "Why would a Jew wish to kill him?"

"We don't know for a fact . . ."

"But you must at least *suspect* it was a Jew, isn't that so? Otherwise, why would you ask such a question? Bangladesh is on the Bay of Bengal, next door to India. It is nowhere near Israel. So why would a Jew . . . ?"

"Ma'am, a Star of David was painted on his windshield," Meyer said.

The room went silent.

"Then it *was* a Jew," she said, and clasped her hands in her lap.

She was silent for perhaps twenty seconds.

Then she said. "The rotten bastards."

"I shouldn't have told her," Meyer said.

"Be all over the papers, anyway," Carella said. "Probably make the front page of the afternoon tabloid."

It was ten minutes past seven, and they were on their way across the bridge again, to where Regal Taxi had its garage on Abingdon and Hale. The traffic was even heavier than it had been on the way out. The day was warming up a little, but not much. This had been the worst damn winter Carella could ever remember. He'd been cold since October. And every time it seemed to be warming up a little, it either started snowing or raining or sleeting or some damn thing to dampen the spirits and crush all hope. Worst damn shitty winter ever.

"What?" Meyer said.

"Nothing."

"You were frowning."

Carella merely nodded.

"When do you think she'll tell the kids?" Meyer asked.

"I think she made a mistake saying he was working. She's got to tell them sooner or later."

"Hard call to make."

"Well, she's not gonna send them to school today, is she?"

"I don't know."

"Be all over the papers," Carella said again.

"I don't know what I'd do in a similar situation."

"When my father got killed, I told my kids that same day," Carella said.

"They're older," Meyer said.

"Even so."

He was silent for a moment.

"They really loved him," he said.

Meyer figured he was talking about himself.

There are times in this city when it is impossible to catch a taxi. Stand on any street corner between three-fifteen and four o'clock and you can wave your hand at any passing blur of yellow, and—forget about it. That's the forty-five minutes when every cabbie is racing back to the garage to turn in his trip sheet and make arrangements for tomorrow's tour of duty. It was the same with cops. The so-called night shift started at four P.M. and ended at midnight. For the criminally inclined, the shift change was a good time for them to do their evil thing because that's when all was confusion.

Confusion was the order of the day at the Regal garage when Meyer and Carella got there at seven-thirty that morning. Cabs were rolling in, cabs were rolling out. Assistant managers were making arrangements for tomorrow's short-terms, and dispatchers were sending newly gassed taxis on their way through the big open rolling doors. This was the busiest time of the day. Even busier than the pre-theater hours. Nobody had time for two flatfoots investigating a homicide.

Carella and Meyer waited.

Their own shift would end in—what was it now?—ten minutes, and they were bone-weary and drained of all energy, but they waited patiently because a man had been killed and Carella had been First Man Up when he answered the phone. It was twelve minutes after eight before the manager, a man named Dennis Ryan, could talk to them. Tall, and red-headed, and fortyish, harried-looking even though all of his cabs were on their way now, he kept nodding impatiently as they told him what had happened to Khalid Aslam.

"So where's my cab?" he asked.

"Police garage on Courtney," Meyer told him.

"When do I get it back? That cab is money on the hoof."

"Yes, but a man was killed in it," Carella said.

"When I saw Kal didn't show up this morning . . ."

Kal, Carella thought. Yankee Doodle Dandy.

". . . I figured he stopped to say one of his bullshit prayers."

Both detectives looked at him.

"They're supposed to pray five times a day, you know, can you beat it? Five times! Sunrise, early afternoon, late afternoon, sunset, and then before they go to bed. Five friggin times! And two *optional* ones if they're *really* holy. Most of them recognize they have a job to do here, they don't go flopping all over the sidewalk five times a day. Some of them pull over to a mosque on their way back in, for the late afternoon prayer. Some of them just do the one before they come to work, and the sunset one if they're home in time, and then the one before they go to bed. I can tell you anything you need to know about these people, we got enough of them working here, believe me."

"What kind of a worker was Aslam?" Carella asked.

"I guess he made a living."

"Meaning?"

"Meaning, it costs eighty-two bucks a shift to lease the cab. Say the driver averages a hundred above that in fares and tips. Gasoline costs him, say, fifteen, sixteen bucks? So he ends up taking home seventy-five, eighty bucks for an eight-hour shift. That ain't bad, is it?"

"Comes to around twenty grand a year," Meyer said.

"Twenty, twenty-five. That ain't bad," Ryan said again.

"Did he get along with the other drivers?" Carella asked.

"Oh, sure. These friggin' Arabs are thick as thieves."

"How about your non-Arab drivers? Did he get along with them?"

"What non-Arab drivers? Why? You think one of my drivers done him?"

"Did he ever have any trouble with one of the other drivers?"

"I don't think so."

"Ever hear him arguing with one of them?"

"Who the hell knows? They babble in Bangla, Urdu, Sindi, Farsi, who the hell knows what else? They all sound the same to me. And they *always* sound like they're arguing. Even when they got smiles on their faces."

"Have you got any Jewish drivers?" Meyer asked.

"Ancient history," Ryan said, "I ain't *ever* seen a Jewish driver at Regal."

"How about anyone who might be sympathetic to the Jewish cause?"

"Which cause is that?" Ryan asked.

"Anyone who might have expressed pro-Israel sympathies?"

"Around here? You've got to be kidding."

"Did you ever hear Aslam say anything *against* Israel? Or the Jewish people?"

"No. Why? Did a Jew kill him?"

"What time did he go to work last night?"

"The boneyard shift goes out around eleven-thirty, quarter to twelve, comes in around seven, seven-thirty— well, you saw. I guess he must've gone out as usual. Why? What time was he killed?"

"Around two, two-thirty."

"Where?"

"Up on Ainsley and Twelfth."

"Way up there, huh?" Ryan said. "You think a nigger did it?"

"We don't know if who did it was white, purple, or black, was the word you meant, right?" Carella said, and looked Ryan dead in the eye.

And fuck you, too, Ryan thought, but said only, "Good luck catching him," making it sound like a curse.

Meyer and Carella went back to the squadroom to type up their interim report on the case.

It was almost a quarter to nine when they finally went home.

The day shift had already been there for half an hour.

Detectives Arthur Brown and Bert Kling made a good salt-and-pepper pair.

Big and heavyset and the color of his surname, Brown looked somewhat angry even when he wasn't. A scowl from him was usually enough to cause a perp to turn to Kling for sympathy and redemption. A few inches shorter than his partner—*everybody* was a few inches shorter than Brown—blond and hazel-eyed, Kling looked like a broad-shouldered farm boy who'd just come in off the fields after working since sunup. God Cop-Bad Cop had been invented for Kling and Brown.

It was Brown who took the call from Ballistics at 10:27 that Friday morning.

"You handling this cabbie kill?" the voice said.

Brown immediately recognized the caller as a brother.

"I've been briefed on it," he said.

"This is Carlyle, Ballistics. We worked that evidence bullet the ME's office sent over, you want to take this down for whoever's running the case?"

"Shoot," Brown said, and moved a pad into place.

"Nice clean bullet, no deformities, must've lodged in the brain matter, ME's report didn't say exactly where they'd recovered it. Not that it matters. First thing we did here, bro . . ."

He had recognized Brown's voice as well.

". . . was compare a rolled impression of the evidence bullet against our specimen cards. Once we got a first-sight match, we did a microscopic examination of the actual bullet against the best sample bullet in our file. Way we determine the make of an unknown firearm is by examining the grooves on the bullet and the right or left direction of twist—but you don't want to hear all that shit, do you?"

Brown had heard it only ten thousand times before.

"Make a long story short," Carlyle said, "what we got here is a bullet fired from a .38-caliber Colt revolver, which is why you didn't find an ejected shell in the taxi, the gun being a revolver and all. Incidentally, there are probably a hundred thousand unregistered, illegal .38-caliber Colts in this city, so the odds against you finding it are probably eighty to one. End of story."

"Thanks," Brown said. "I'll pass it on."

"You see today's paper?" Carlyle asked.

"No, not yet."

"Case made the front page. Makes it sound like the Israeli army invaded Majesta with tanks, one lousy Arab. Is this true about a Jewish star on the windshield?"

"That's what our guys found."

"Gonna be trouble, bro," Carlyle said.

He didn't know the half of it.

While Carella and Meyer slept like hibernating grizzlies, Kling and Brown read their typed report, noted that the dead driver's widow had told them the Aslams' place of worship was called Majid Hazrat-i-Shabazz, and went out at eleven that morning to visit the mosque.

If either of them had expected glistening white minarets, arches, and domes, they were sorely disappointed. There were more than a hundred mosques in this city, but only a handful of them had been originally designed as such. The remainder had been converted to places of worship from private homes, warehouses, storefront buildings, and lofts. There were, in fact, only three requirements for any building that now called itself a mosque: that males and females be separated during prayer; that there be no images of animate objects inside the building; and that the *quibla*—the orientation of prayer in the direction of the Kabba in Mecca—be established.

A light rain began falling as they got out of the unmarked police sedan and began walking toward a yellow brick building that had once been a small supermarket on the corner of Lowell and Franks. Metal shutters were now in place where earlier there'd been plate glass display windows. Grafitti decorated the yellow brick and the green shutters. An ornately hand-lettered sign hung above the entrance doors, white on a black field, announcing the name of the mosque: Majid Hazrat-i-Shabazz. Men in flowing white garments and embroidered prayer caps, other men in dark business suits and pillbox hats milled about on the sidewalk with young men in team jackets, their baseball caps turned backward. Friday was the start of the Muslim sabbath, and now the faithful were being called to prayer.

On one side of the building, the detectives could see women entering through a separate door.

"My mother knows this Muslim lady up in Diamondback," Brown said, "she goes to this mosque up there—lots of blacks are Muslims, you know . . ."

"I know," Kling said.

"And where she goes to pray, they got no space for this separation stuff. So the men and women all pray together in the same open hall. But the women sit *behind* the men. So this fat ole sister gets there late one Friday, and the hall is already filled with men, and they tell her there's no room for her. Man, she takes a fit! Starts yelling, 'This is America,

I'm as good a Muslim as any man here, so how come they's only room for *brothers* to pray?' Well, the imam—that's the man in charge, he's like the preacher—he quotes scripture and verse that says only men are *required* to come to Friday prayer, whereas women are not. So they have to let the men in first. It's as simple as that. So she quotes right back at him that in Islam, women are *spose* to be highly respected and revered, so how come he's dissing her this way? And she walked away from that mosque and never went back. From that time on, she prayed at home. That's a true story," Brown said.

"I believe it," Kling said.

The imam's address that Friday was about the dead cab driver. He spoke first in Arabic—which, of course, neither Kling nor Brown understood—and then he translated his words into English, perhaps for their benefit, perhaps in deference to the younger worshippers in the large drafty hall. The male worshippers knelt at the front of the hall. Behind a translucent, moveable screen, Brown and Kling could perceive a small number of veiled female worshippers.

The imam said he prayed that the strife in the Middle East was not now coming to this city that had known so much tragedy already. He said he prayed that an innocent and hard-working servant of Allah had not paid with his life for the acts of a faraway people bent only on destruction—

The detectives guessed he meant the Israelis.

—prayed that the signature star on the windshield of the murdered man's taxi was not a promise of further violence to come.

"It is foolish to grieve for our losses," he said, "since all is ordained by Allah. Only by working for the larger nation of Islam can we understand the true meaning of life."

Men's foreheads touched the cement floor.

Behind the screen, the women bowed their heads as well.

The imam's name was Muhammad Adham Akbar.

"What we're trying to find out," Brown said, "is whether or not Mr. Aslam had any enemies that you know of."

"Why do you even ask such a question?" Akbar said.

"He was a worshipper at your mosque," Kling said. "We thought you might know."

"Why would he have enemies here?"

"Men have enemies everywhere," Brown said.

"Not in a house of prayer. If you want to know who Khalid's enemy was, you need only look at his windshield."

"Well, we have to investigate every possibility," Kling said.

"The star on his windshield says it all," Akbar said, and shrugged. "A Jew killed him. That would seem obvious to anyone."

"Well, a Jew may have committed those murders," Kling agreed. "But . . ."

"May," the imam said, and nodded cynically.

"But until we catch him, we won't know for sure, will we?" Kling said.

Akbar looked at him.

Then he said, "The slain man had no enemies that I know of."

Just about when Carella and Meyer were each and separately waking up from eight hours of sleep, more or less, the city's swarm of taxis rolled onto the streets for the four-to-midnight shift. And as the detectives sat down to late afternoon meals which for each of them were really hearty breakfasts, many of the city's more privileged women were coming out into the streets to start looking for taxis to whisk them homeward. Here was a carefully coiffed woman who'd just enjoyed afternoon tea, chatting with another equally stylish woman as they strolled together out of a midtown hotel. And here was a woman who came out of a department store carrying a shopping bag in each hand, shifting one of the bags to the other hand, freeing it so she could hail a taxi. And here was a woman coming out of a Korean nail shop, wearing paper sandals to protect her freshly painted toenails. And another coming out of a deli, clutching a bag with baguettes showing, raising one hand to signal a cab. At a little before five, the streets were suddenly alive with the leisured women of this city, the most beautiful women in all the world, all of them ready to kill if another woman grabbed a taxi that had just been hailed.

This was a busy time for the city's cabbies. Not ten minutes later, the office buildings would begin spilling out men and women who'd been working since nine this morning, coming out onto the pavements now and sucking in great breaths of welcome spring air. The rain had stopped, and the sidewalk and pavements glistened, and there was the strange aroma of freshness on the air. This had been one hell of a winter.

The hands went up again, typists' hands, and file clerks' hands, and the hands of lawyers and editors and agents and producers and exporters and thieves, yes, even thieves took taxis—though obvious criminal types were avoided by these cabbies steering their vehicles recklessly toward the curb in a relentless pursuit of passengers. These men had paid eighty-two dollars to lease their taxis. These men had paid fifteen, twenty bucks to gas their buggies and get them on the road. They were already a hundred bucks in the hole before they put foot to pedal. Time was money. And there were hungry mouths to feed. For the most part, these men were Muslims, these men were gentle strangers in a strange land.

But someone had killed one of them last night.

And he was not yet finished.

Salim Nazir and his widowed mother left Afghanistan in 1994, when it became apparent that the Taliban were about to take over the entire country. His father had been one of the mujahideen killed fighting the Russian occupation; Salim's mother did not wish the wrath of "God's Students" to fall upon their heads if and when a new regime came to power.

Salim was now twenty-seven years old, his mother fifty-five. Both had been American citizens for three years now, but neither approved of what America had done to their native land, the evil Taliban notwithstanding. For that matter they did not appreciate what America had done to Iraq in its search for imaginary weapons of mass destruction. (Salim called them "weapons of mass deception.") In fact, Salim totally disapproved of the mess America had made in what once was his part of the world, but he rarely expressed these views out loud, except when he was among other Muslims who lived—as he and his mother did now—in a ghettolike section of Calm's Point.

Salim knew what it was like to be an outsider in George W. Bush's America, no matter how many speeches the president made about Islam being a peaceful religion. With all his heart, Salim knew this to be true, but he doubted very much that Mr. Bush believed what he was saying.

Just before sundown that Friday, Salim pulled his yellow taxi into the curb in front of a little shop on a busy street in Majesta. Here in Ikram Hassan's store, devout Muslims could purchase whatever food and drink was considered *halal*—lawful or permitted for consumption as described in the Holy Koran.

The Koran decreed, "Eat of that over which the name of Allah hath been mentioned, if ye are believers in His revelations." Among the acceptable foods were milk (from cows, sheep, camels, or goats), honey, fish, plants that were not intoxicant, fresh or naturally frozen vegetables, fresh or dried fruits, legumes (like peanuts, cashews, hazelnuts, and walnuts), and grains such as wheat, rice, barley, and oats.

Many animals, large and small, were considered *halal* as well, but they had to be slaughtered according to Islamic ritual. Ikram Hassan was about to slay a chicken just as his friend Salim came into the shop. He looked up when a small bell over his door sounded.

"Hey there, Salim," he said in English.

There were two major languages in Afghanistan, both of them imported from Iran, but Pushto was the official language the two men had learned as boys growing up in Kandahar, and this was the language they spoke now.

Salim fidgeted and fussed as his friend hunched over

the chicken; he did not want to be late for the sunset prayer. Using a very sharp knife, and making certain that he cut the main blood vessels without completely severing the throat, Ikram intoned *"Bismillah Allah-u-Albar* and completed the ritual slaughter.

Each of the men then washed his hands to the wrists, and cleansed the mouth and the nostrils with water, and washed the face and the right arm and left arm to the elbow, and washed to the ankle first the right foot and then the left, and at last wiped the top of the head with wet hands, the three middle fingers of each hand joined together.

Salim consulted his watch yet another time.

Both men donned little pillbox hats.

Ikram locked the front door to his store, and together they walked to the mosque four blocks away.

The sun had already set.

It was ten minutes to seven.

Among other worshippers, Salim and Ikram stood facing Mecca, their hands raised to their ears, and they uttered the words, *"Allahu Akbar"* which meant "Allah is the greatest of all." Then they placed the right hand just below the breast and recited in unison the prayer called *istiftah*.

"Surely I have turned myself, being upright holy to Him Who originated the heavens and the earth and I am not of the polytheists. Surely my prayer and my sacrifice and my life and my death are for Allah, the Lord of the worlds, no associate has He; and this I am commanded and I am one of those who submit. Glory to Thee, O Allah, and Thine is the praise, and blessed is Thy name, and exalted is Thy majesty, and there is none to be served besides Thee."

A'udhu bi-llahi minash-shaitani-r-rajim.
"I seek the refuge of Allah from the accursed devil."
Six hours later, Salim Nazir would be dead.

In this city, all the plays, concerts, and musicals let out around eleven, eleven-thirty, the cabarets around one, one-thirty. The night clubs wouldn't break till all hours of the night. It was Salim's habit during the brief early-morning lull to visit a Muslim friend who was a short-order cook at a deli on Culver Avenue, a mile and a half distant from all the midtown glitter. He went into the deli at one-thirty, enjoyed a cup of coffee and a chat with his friend, and left twenty minutes later. Crossing the street to where he'd parked his taxi, he got in behind the wheel, and was just about to start the engine when he realized someone was sitting in the dark in the back seat.

Startled, he was about to ask what the hell, when the man fired a bullet through the plastic divider and into his skull.

The two Midtown South detectives who responded to the call immediately knew this killing was related to the one that had taken place uptown the night before; a blue Star of David had been spray-painted on the windshield. Nonetheless, they called their lieutenant from the scene, and he informed them that this was a clear case of First Man Up, and advised them to wait right there while he contacted the Eight-Seven, which had caught the original squeal. The detectives were still at the scene when Carella and Meyer got there at twenty minutes to three.

Midtown South told Carella that both MCU and the ME had already been there and gone, the corpse and the vehicle carried off respectively to the morgue and the PD garage to be respectively dissected and impounded. They told the Eight-Seven dicks that they'd talked to the short-order cook in the deli across the street, who informed them that he was a friend of the dead man, and that he'd been in there for a cup of coffee shortly before he got killed. The vic's name was Salim Nazir, and the cab company he worked for was called City Transport. They assumed the case was now the Eight-Seven's and that Carella and Meyer would do all the paper shit and send them dupes. Carella assured them that they would.

"We told you about the blue star, right?" one of the Midtown dicks said.

"You told us," Meyer said.

"Here's the evidence bullet we recovered," he said, and handed Meyer a sealed manila envelope. "Chain of Custody tag on it, you sign next. Looks like you maybe caught an epidemic."

"Or maybe a copycat," Carella said.

"Either way, good luck," the other Midtown dick said.

Carella and Meyer crossed the street to the deli.

Like his good friend, Salim, the short-order cook was from Afghanistan, having arrived here in the city seven years ago. He offered at once to show the detectives his green card, which made each of them think he was probably an illegal with a counterfeit card, but they had bigger fish to fry and Ajmal Khan was possibly a man who could help them do just that.

Ajmal meant "good-looking" in his native tongue, a singularly contradictory description for the man who now told them he had heard a shot outside some five minutes after Salim finished his coffee. Dark eyes bulging with excitement, black mustache bristling, bulbous nose twitching like a rabbit's, Ajmal reported that he had rushed out of the shop the instant he heard the shot, and had seen a man across the street getting out of Salim's taxi on the driver's side, and leaning over the windshield with a can of some sort in his hand. Ajmal didn't know what he was doing at the time but he now understood the man was spray-painting a Jewish star on the windshield.

"Can you describe this man?" Carella asked.

"Is that what he was doing? Painting a Star of David on the windshield?"

"Apparently," Meyer said.

"That's bad," Ajmal said.

The detectives agreed with him. That was bad. They did not believe this was a copycat. This was someone specifically targeting Muslim cab drivers. But they went through the routine anyway, asking the questions they always asked whenever someone was murdered: Did he have any enemies that you know of, did he mention any specific death threats, did he say he was being followed or harassed, was he in debt to anyone, was he using drugs?

Ajmal told them that his good friend Salim was loved and respected by everyone. This was what friends and relatives always said about the vic. He was a kind and gentle person. He had a wonderful sense of humor. He was thoughtful and generous. He was devout. Ajmal could not imagine why anyone would have done this to a marvelous person like his good friend Salim Nazir.

"He was always laughing and friendly, a very warm and outgoing man. Especially with the ladies," Ajmal said.

"What do you mean?" Carella asked.

"He was quite a ladies' man, Salim. It is written that men may have as many as four wives, but they must be treated equally in every way. That is to say, emotionally, sexually, and materially. If Salim had been a wealthy man, I am certain he would have enjoyed the company of many wives."

"How many wives did he actually *have?*" Meyer asked.

"Well, none," Ajmal said. "He was single. He lived with his mother."

"Do you know where?"

"Oh yes. We were very good friends. I have been to his house many times."

"Can you give us his address?"

"His phone number, too," Ajmal said. "His mother's name is Gulalai. It means 'flower' in my country."

"You say he was quite a ladies' man, is that right?" Carella asked.

"Well, yes. The ladies liked him."

"More than one lady?" Carella said.

"Well, yes, more than one."

"Did he ever mention any jealousy among these various ladies?"

"I don't even know who they were. He was a discreet man."

"No reason any of these ladies might have wanted to shoot him?" Carella said.

"Not that I know of."

"But he *did* say he was seeing several women, is that it?"

"In conversation, yes."

"He said he was in *conversation* with several women?"

"No, he said to *me* in conversation that he was enjoying the company of several women, yes. As I said, he was quite a ladies' man."

"But he didn't mention the names of these women."

"No, he did not. Besides, it was a man I saw getting out of his taxi. A very tall man."

"Could it have been a very tall woman?"

"No, this was very definitely a man."

"Can you describe him?"

"Tall. Wide shoulders. Wearing a black raincoat and a black hat." Ajmal paused. "The kind rabbis wear," he said.

Which brought them right back to that Star of David on the windshield.

Two windshields.

This was not good at all.

This was a mixed lower-class neighborhood—white, black, Hispanic. These people had troubles of their own, they didn't much care about a couple of dead Arabs. Matter of fact, many of them had sons or husbands who'd fought in the Iraqi war. Lots of the people Carella and Meyer spoke to early that morning had an "Army of One," was what it was called nowadays, who'd gone to war right here from the hood. Some of these young men had never come back home except in a box.

You never saw nobody dying on television. All them reporters embedded with the troops, all you saw was armor racing across the desert. You never saw somebody taking a sniper bullet between the eyes, blood spattering. You never saw an artillery attack with arms and legs flying in the air.

You could see more people getting killed right here in the hood than you saw getting killed in the entire Iraqi war. It was an absolute miracle, all them embedded newspeople out there reporting, and not a single person getting killed for the cameras. Maybe none of them had a camera handy when somebody from the hood got killed. So who gave a damn around here about a few dead Arabs more or less?

One of the black women they interviewed explained that people were asleep, anyway, at two in the morning, wun't that so? So why go axin a dumb question like did you hear a shot that time of night? A Hispanic man they interviewed told them there were *always* shots in the barrio; nobody ever paid attention no more. A white woman told them she'd got up to go pee around that time, and thought she heard something but figured it was a backfire.

At 4:30 A.M., Meyer and Carella spoke to a black man who'd been blinded in Iraq. He was in pajamas and a bathrobe, and he was wearing dark glasses. A white cane stood angled against his chair. He could remember President Bush making a little speech to a handful of veterans like himself at the hospital where he was recovering, his eyes still bandaged. He could remember Bush saying something folksy like, "I'll bet those Iraqi soldiers weren't happy to meet *you* fellas!" He could remember thinking, I wun't so happy to meet *them,* either. I'm goan be blind the ress of my life, Mr. Pres'dunt, how you feel about *that?*

"I heerd a shot," he told the detectives.

Travon Nelson was his name. He worked as a dishwasher in a restaurant all the way downtown. They stopped serving at eleven, he was usually out by a little before one, took the number 17 bus uptown, got home here around two. He had just got off the bus, and was walking toward his building, his white cane tapping the sidewalk ahead of him . . .

He had once thought he'd like to become a Major League ballplayer.

. . . when he heard the sharp crack of a small-arms weapon, and then heard a car door slamming, and then a hissing sound, he didn't know what it was . . .

The spray paint, Meyer thought.

. . . and then a man yelling.

"Yelling at *you?*" Carella asked.

"No, sir. Must've been some girl."

"What makes you think that?"

"Cause whut he yelled was 'You *whore!*' An' then I think he must've hit her, cause she screamed an' kepp right on screamin an' screamin."

"Then what?" Meyer asked.

"He run off. She run off, too. I heerd her heels clickin away. High heels. When you blind . . ."

His voice caught.

They could not see his eyes behind the dark glasses.

". . . you compensate with yo' other senses. They was the sound of the man's shoes runnin off and then the click of the girl's high heels."

He was silent for a moment, remembering again what high heels on a sidewalk sounded like.

"Then evy'thin went still again," he said.

Years of living in war-torn Afghanistan had left their mark on Gulalai Nazir's wrinkled face and stooped posture; she looked more like a woman in her late sixties than the fifty-five-year-old mother of Salim. The detectives had called ahead first, and several grieving relatives were already in her apartment when they got there at six that Saturday morning. Gulalai—although now an American citizen—spoke very little English. Her nephew—a man who at the age of sixteen had fought with the mujahideen against the Russians—translated for the detectives.

Gulalai told them what they had already heard from the short-order cook.

Her son was loved and respected by everyone. He was a kind and gentle person. A loving son. He had a wonderful sense of humor. He was thoughtful and generous. He was devout. Gulalai could not imagine why anyone would have done this to him.

"Unless it was that Jew," she said.

The nephew translated.

"Which Jew?" Carella asked at once.

"The one who killed that other Muslim cab driver uptown," the nephew translated.

Gulalai wrung her hands and burst into uncontrollable sobbing. The other women began wailing with her.

The nephew took the detectives aside.

His name was Osman, he told them, which was Turkish in origin, but here in America everyone called him either Ozzie or Oz.

"Oz Kiraz," he said, and extended his hand. His grip was firm and strong. He was a big man, possibly thirty-two, thirty-three years old, with curly black hair and an open face with sincere brown eyes. Carella could visualize him killing Russian soldiers with his bare hands. He would not have enjoyed being one of them.

"Do you think you're going to get this guy?" he asked.

"We're trying," Carella said.

"Or is it going to be the same song and dance?"

"Which song and dance is that, sir?" Meyer said.

"Come on, this city is run by Jews. If a Jew killed my cousin, it'll be totally ignored."

"We're trying to make sure that doesn't happen," Carella said.

"I'll bet," Oz said.

"You'd win," Meyer said.

The call from Detective Carlyle in Ballistics came at a quarter to seven that Saturday morning.

"You the man I spoke to yesterday?" he asked.

"No, this is Carella."

"You workin' this Arab shit?"

"Yep."

"It's the same gun," Carlyle said. "This doesn't mean it was the same *guy,* it coulda been his cousin or his uncle or his brother pulled the trigger. But it was the same .38-caliber Colt that fired the bullet."

"That it?"

"Ain't that enough?"

"More than enough," Carella said. "Thanks, pal."

"Buy me a beer sometime," Carlyle said, and hung up.

At 8:15 that morning, just as Carella and Meyer were briefing Brown and Kling on what had happened the night before, an attractive young black woman in her mid twenties walked into the squadroom. She introduced herself as Wandalyn

Holmes, and told the detectives that she'd been heading home from baby-sitting her sister's daughter last night—walking to the corner to catch the number 17 bus downtown, in fact—when she saw this taxi sitting at the curb, and a man dressed all in black spraying paint on the windshield.

"When he saw I was looking at him, he pointed a finger at me . . ."

"Pointed . . . ?"

"Like this, yes," Wandalyn said, and showed them how the man had pointed his finger. "And he yelled 'You! Whore!' and I screamed and he came running after me."

"You whore?"

"No, two words. First 'You!' and *then* 'Whore!' "

"Did you know this man?"

"Never saw him in my life."

"But he pointed his finger at you and called you a whore."

"Yes. And when I ran, he came after me and caught me by the back of the coat, you know what I'm saying? The collar of my coat? And pulled me over, right off my feet."

"What time was this, Miss Holmes?" Carella asked.

"About two in the morning, a little after."

"What happened then?"

"He kicked me. While I was laying on the ground. He seemed mad as hell. I thought at first he was gonna rape me. I kept screaming, though, and he ran off."

"What'd you do then?" Brown asked.

"I got up and ran off, too. Over to my sister's place. I was scared he might come back."

"Did you get a good look at him?"

"Oh yes."

"Tell us what he looked like," Meyer said.

"Like I said, he was all in black. Black hat, black rain-coat, black everything."

"Was he himself black?" Kling asked.

"Oh no, he was a white man."

"Did you see his face?"

"I did."

"Describe him."

"Dark eyes. Angry. Very angry eyes."

"Beard? Mustache?"

"No."

"Notice any scars or tattoos?"

"No."

"Did he say anything to you?"

"Well, yes, I told you. He called me a whore."

"*After* that."

"No. Nothing. Just pulled me over backward, and started kicking me when I was down. I thought he was gonna rape me, I was scared to death." Wandalyn paused a moment. The detectives caught the hesitation.

"Yes?" Carella said. "Something else?"

"I'm sorry I didn't come here right away last night, but I was too scared," Wandalyn said. "He was very angry. *So* angry. I was scared he might come after me if I told the police anything."

"You're here now," Carella said. "And we thank you."

"He *won't* come after me, right?" Wandalyn asked.

"I'm sure he won't," Carella said. "It's not you he's angry with."

Wandalyn nodded. But still looked skeptical.

"You'll be okay, don't worry," Brown said, and led her to

the gate in the slatted wooden railing that divided the squadroom from the corridor outside.

At his desk, Carella began typing up their Detective Division report. He was still typing when Brown came over and said, "You know what time it is?"

Carella nodded and kept typing.

It was 9:33 A.M. when he finally printed up the report and carried it over to Brown's desk.

"Go home," Brown advised, scowling.

They had worked important homicides before, and these had also necessitated throwing the schedule out the window. What was new this time around—

Well, no, there was also a murder that had almost started a race riot, this must've been two, three years back, they hadn't got much sleep that time, either. This was similar, but different. This was two Muslim cabbies who'd been shot to death by someone, obviously a Jew, eager to take credit for both murders.

Meyer didn't know whether he dreamt it, or whether it was a brilliant idea he'd had before he fell asleep at nine that morning. Dream or brilliant idea, the first thing he did when the alarm clock rang at three that afternoon was find a fat felt-tipped pen and a sheet of paper and draw a big blue Star of David on it.

He kept staring at the star and wondering if the department's handwriting experts could tell them anything about the man or men who had spray-painted similar stars on the windshields of those two cabs.

He was almost eager to get to work.

* * *

Six hours of sleep wasn't bad for what both detectives considered a transitional period, similar to the decompression a deep-sea diver experienced while coming up to the surface in stages. Actually, they were moving back from the midnight shift to the night shift, a passage that normally took place over a period of days, but which given the exigency of the situation occurred in the very same day. Remarkably, both men felt refreshed and—in Meyer's case at least—raring to go.

"I had a great idea last night," he told Carella. "Or maybe it was just a dream. Take a look at this," he said, and showed Carella the Star of David he'd drawn.

"Okay," Carella said.

"I'm right-handed," Meyer said. "So what I did . . ."

"So am I," Carella said.

"What I did," Meyer said, "was start the first triangle here at the northernmost point of the star . . . there are six points, you know, and they mean something or other, I'm not really sure what. I am not your ideal Jew."

"I never would have guessed."

"But religious Jews know what the six points stand for."

"So what's your big idea?"

"Well, I was starting to tell you. I began the first triangle

at the very top, and drew one side down to this point here,"
he said, indicating the point on the bottom right . . .

". . . and then I drew a line across to the left . . ."

". . . and another line up to the northern point again,
completing the first triangle."

"Okay," Carella said, and picked up a pen and drew a
triangle in exactly the same way.

"Then I started the second triangle at the western
point—the one here on the left—and drew a line over to the
east here . . ."

". . . and then down on an angle to the south . . ."

". . . and back up again to . . . northwest, I guess it is . . . where I started."

Carella did the same thing.

"That's right," he said. "That's how you do it."

"Yes, but we're both right-handed."

"So?"

"I think a left-handed person might do it differently."

"Ah," Carella said, nodding.

"So I think we should call Documents and get them to look at both those cabs. See if the same guy painted those two stars, and find out if he was right-handed or left-handed."

"I think that's brilliant," Carella said.

"You don't."

"I do."

"I can tell you don't."

"I'll make the call myself," Carella said.

He called downtown, asked for the Documents Section, and spoke to a detective named Jackson who agreed that there would be a distinct difference between left- and right-handed handwriting, even if the writing instrument— so to speak—was a spray can. Carella told him they were investigating a double homicide . . .

"Those Muslim cabbies, huh?"

. . . and asked if Documents could send someone down to the police garage to examine the spray-painting on the windshields of the two impounded taxis. Jackson said it would have to wait till tomorrow morning, they were a little short-handed today.

"While I have you," Carella said, "can you switch me over to the lab?"

The lab technician he spoke to reported that the paint scrapings from the windshields of both cabs matched laboratory samples of a product called Redi-Spray, which was manufactured in Milwaukee, Wisconsin, distributed nationwide, and sold in virtually every hardware store and supermarket in this city. Carella thanked him and hung up.

He was telling Meyer what he'd just learned, when Rabbi A. Cohen walked into the squadroom.

"I think I may be able to help you with the recent cab driver murders," the rabbi said.

Carella offered him a chair alongside his desk.

"If I may," the rabbi said, "I would like to go back to the beginning."

Would you be a rabbi otherwise? Meyer thought.

"The beginning was last month," the rabbi said, "just before Passover. Today is the sixteenth day of the Omer, which is one week and nine days from the second day of Passover, so this would have been before Passover. Around the tenth of April, a Thursday I seem to recall it was."

As the rabbi remembers it . . .

This young man came to him seeking guidance and assistance. Was the rabbi familiar with a seventeen-year-old girl named Rebecca Schwartz, who was a member of the rabbi's own congregation? Well, yes, of course, Rabbi Cohen knew the girl well. He had, in fact, officiated at her *bat mitzvah* five years ago. Was there some problem?

The problem was that the young man was in love with young Rebecca, but he was not of the Jewish faith—which, by the way, had been evident to the rabbi at once, the boy's olive complexion, his dark brooding eyes. It seemed that Rebecca's parents had forbidden her from seeing the boy ever again, and this was why he was here in the synagogue today, to ask the rabbi if he could speak to Mr. Schwartz and convince him to change his mind.

Well.

The rabbi explained that this was an Orthodox congregation and that anyway there was a solemn prohibition in Jewish religious law against a Jew marrying anyone but another Jew. He went on to explain that this ban against intermarriage was especially pertinent to our times, when statistics indicated that an alarming incidence of intermarriage threatened the very future of American Jewry.

"In short," Rabbi Cohen said, "I told him I was terribly sorry, but I could never approach Samuel Schwartz with a view toward encouraging a relationship between his daughter and a boy of another faith. Do you know what he said to me?"

"What?" Carella asked.

" 'Thanks for nothing!' He made it sound like a threat."

Carella nodded. So did Meyer.

"And then the e-mails started," the rabbi said. "Three of them all together. Each with the same message. 'Death to all Jews.' And just at sundown last night . . ."

"When was this?" Meyer asked. "The e-mails?"

"Last week. All of them last week."

"What happened last night?" Carella asked.

"Someone threw a bottle of whiskey with a lighted wick through the open front door of the synagogue."

The two detectives nodded again.

"And you think this boy . . . the one who's in love with Rebecca . . . ?"

"Yes," the rabbi said.

"You think he might be the one responsible for the e-mails and the Molotov . . ."

"Yes. But not only that. I think he's the one who killed those cab drivers."

"I don't understand," Carella said. "Why would a Muslim want to kill *other* Mus . . . ?"

"But he's *not* Muslim. Did I say he was Muslim?"

"You said this was related to the . . ."

"Catholic. He's a Catholic."

The detectives looked at each other.

"Let me understand this," Carella said. "You think this kid . . . how old is he, anyway?"

"Eighteen, I would guess. Nineteen."

"You think he got angry because you wouldn't go to Rebecca's father on his behalf . . ."

"That's right."

"So he sent you three e-mails, and tried to fire-bomb your temple . . ."

"Exactly."

". . . and also killed two Muslim cab drivers?"

"Yes."

"Why? The Muslims, I mean."

"To get even."

"With?"

"With me. And with Samuel Schwartz. And Rebecca. With the entire Jewish population of this city."

"How would killing two . . . ?"

"The *magen David*," the rabbi said.

"The Star of David," Meyer explained.

"Painted on the windshields," the rabbi said. "To let people think a Jew was responsible. To enflame the Muslim community against Jews. To cause trouble between us. To cause more killing. That is why."

The detectives let this sink in.

"Did this kid happen to give you a name?" Meyer asked.

Anthony Inverni told the detectives he didn't wish to be called Tony.

"Makes me sound like a wop," he said. "My grandparents were born here, my parents were born here, my sister and I were both born here, we're Americans. You call me Tony, I'm automatically *Italian*. Well, the way I look at it, Italians are people who are born in Italy and live in Italy, not Americans who were born here and live here. And we're not *Italian*-Americans, either, by the way, because *Italian*-Americans are people who came here from Italy and *became* American citizens. So don't call me Tony, okay?"

He was nineteen years old, with curly black hair, and an olive complexion, and dark brown eyes. Sitting at sunset on the front steps of his building on Merchant Street, all the way downtown near Ramsey University, his arms hugging his knees, he could have been any Biblical Jew squatting outside a baked-mud dwelling in an ancient world. But Rabbi Cohen had spotted him for a *goy* first crack out of the box.

"Gee, who called you Tony?" Carella wanted to know.

"You were about to. I could feel it coming."

Calling a suspect by his first name was an old cop trick,

but actually Carella hadn't been about to use it on the Inverni kid here. In fact, he agreed with him about all these proliferating hyphenated Americans in a nation that broadcast the words "United We Stand" as if they were a newly minted advertising slogan. But his father's name had been Anthony. And his father had called himself Tony.

"What would you like us to call you?" he asked.

"Anthony. Anthony could be British. In fact, soon as I graduate, I'm gonna change my last name to Winters. Anthony Winters. I could be the prime minister of England, Anthony Winters. That's what Inverni means anyway, in Italian. Winters."

"Where do you go to school, Anthony?" Carella asked.

"Right here," he said, nodding toward the towers in the near distance. "Ramsey U."

"You studying to be a prime minister?" Meyer asked.

"A writer. Anthony Winters. How does that sound for a writer?"

"Very good," Meyer said, trying the name, "Anthony Winters, excellent. We'll look for your books."

"Meanwhile," Carella said, "tell us about your little run-in with Rabbi Cohen."

"What run-in?"

"He seems to think he pissed you off."

"Well, he did. I mean, why *wouldn't* he go to Becky's father and put in a good word for me? I'm a straight-A student, I'm on the dean's list, am I some kind of pariah? You know what that means, 'pariah'?"

Meyer figured this was a rhetorical question.

"I'm not even *Catholic*, no less pariah," Anthony said, gathering steam. "I gave up the church the minute I tipped to what they were selling. I mean, am I supposed to believe a *virgin* gave birth? To the son of *God,* no less? That goes back to the ancient Greeks, doesn't it? All their Gods messing in the affairs of humans? I mean, give me a break, man."

"Just how pissed off were you?" Carella asked.

"Enough," Anthony said. "But you should've seen *Becky!* When I told her what the rabbi said, she wanted to go right over there and kill him."

"Then you're still seeing her, is that it?"

"Of course I'm still seeing her! We're gonna get married, what do you think? You think her bigoted father's gonna stop us? You think Rabbi Cohen's gonna stop us? We're in *love!*"

Good for you, Meyer thought. And *mazeltov.* But did you kill those two cabbies, as the good *rov* seems to think?

"Are you on the Internet?" he asked.

"Sure."

"Do you send e-mails?"

"That's the main way Becky and I communicate. I can't phone her because her father hangs up the minute he hears my voice. Her mother's a little better, she at least lets me talk to her."

"Ever send an e-mail to Rabbi Cohen?"

"No. Why? An e-mail? Why would . . . ?"

"Three of them, in fact."

"No. What kind of e-mails?"

" 'Death to all Jews,' " Meyer quoted.

"Don't be ridiculous," Anthony said. "I love a Jewish *girl!* I'm gonna *marry* a Jewish girl!"

"Were you anywhere near Rabbi Cohen's synagogue last night?" Carella asked.

"No. Why?"

"You didn't throw a fire-bomb into that synagogue last night, did you?"

"No, I did not!"

"Sundown last night? You didn't . . . ?"

"Not at sundown and not at *any* time! I was with *Becky* at sundown. We were walking in the park outside school at sundown. We were trying to figure out our next *move*."

"You may love a Jewish girl," Meyer said, "but how do you feel about *Jews?*"

"I don't know what that means."

"It means how do you feel about all these *Jews* who are trying to keep you from marrying this Jewish *girl* you love?"

"I did not throw a fucking fire-bomb . . ."

"Did you kill two Muslim cabbies . . . ?"

"What!"

". . . and paint Jewish stars on their windshields?"

"Holy shit, is *that* what this is about?"

"Did you?"

"Who said I did?" Anthony wanted to know. "Did the rabbi say I did such a thing?"

"Did you?"

"No. Why would . . . ?"

"Because you were pissed off," Meyer said. "And you wanted to get even. So you killed two Muslims and made it look like a Jew did it. So Muslims would start throwing fire-bombs into . . ."

"I don't give a damn about Muslims or Jews *or* their fucking problems," Anthony said. "All I care about is Becky. All I care about is marrying Becky. The rest is all bullshit. I did not send any e-mails to that jackass rabbi. I did not throw a fire-bomb into his dumb temple, which by the way won't let women sit with men. I did not kill any Muslim cab drivers who go to stupid temples of their own, where *their* women aren't allowed to sit with men, either. That's a nice little plot you've cooked up there, and I'll use it one day, when I'm Anthony Winters the best-selling writer. But right now, I'm still just Tony Inverni, right? And that's the only thing that's keeping me from marrying the girl I love, and that is a shame, gentlemen, that is a fucking crying shame. So if you'll excuse me, I really don't give a damn about *your* little problem, because Becky and I have a major problem of our own."

He raised his right hand, touched it to his temple in a mock salute, and went back into his building.

At nine the next morning, Detective Wilbur Jackson of the Documents Section called to say they'd checked out the graffiti—he called the Jewish stars graffiti—on the windshields of those two evidence cabs and they were now able to report that the handwriting was identical in both instances and that the writer was right-handed. "Like ninety percent of the people in this city," he added.
That night, the third Muslim cabbie was killed.

"Let's hear it," Lieutenant Byrnes said.

He was not feeling too terribly sanguine this Monday morning. He did not like this at all. First off, he did not like murder epidemics. And next, he did not like murder epidemics that could lead to full-scale riots. White-haired and scowling, eyes an icy-cold blue, he glowered across his desk as though the eight detectives gathered in his corner office had themselves committed the murders.

Hal Willis and Eileen Burke had been riding the mid-night horse when the call came in about the third dead cabbie. At five-eight, Willis had barely cleared the min-imum height requirement in effect before women were gen-erously allowed to become police officers, at which time five-foot-two-eyes-of-blue became threatening when one was carrying a nine-millimeter Glock on her hip. That's exactly what Eileen was carrying this morning. Not on her hip, but in a tote bag slung over her shoulder. At five-nine, she topped Willis by an inch. Red-headed and green-eyed, she provided Irish-setter contrast to his dark, curly-haired, brown-eyed, cocker-spaniel look. Byrnes was glaring at both of them. Willis deferred to the lady.

"His name is Ali Al-Barak," Eileen said. "He's a Saudi. Married with three . . ."

"That's the most common Arabic name," Andy Parker said. He was slumped in one of the chairs near the win-dows. Unshaven and unkempt, he looked as if he'd just come off a plant as a homeless wino. Actually, he'd come straight to the squadroom from home, where he'd dressed hastily, annoyed because he wasn't supposed to come in until four, and now another fuckin Muslim had been aced.

"Al-Barak?" Brown asked.

"No, Ali," Parker said. "More than five million men in the Arab world are named Ali."

"How do you know that?" Kling asked.

"I know such things," Parker said.

"And what's it got to do with the goddamn price of fish?" Byrnes asked.

"In case you run into a lot of Alis," Parker explained, "you'll know it ain't a phenomenon, it's just a fact."

"Let me hear it," Byrnes said sourly, and nodded to Eileen.

"Three children," she said, picking up where she'd left off. "Lived in a Saudi neighborhood in Riverhead. No apparent connection to either of the two other vics. All three even worshipped at different mosques. Shot at the back of the head, same as the other two. Blue star on the windshield . . ."

"The other two were the same handwriting," Meyer said.

"Right-handed writer," Carella said.

"Anything from Ballistics yet?" Byrnes asked Eileen.

"Slug went to them, too soon to expect anything."

"Two to one, it'll be the same," Richard Genero said.

He was the newest detective on the squad and rarely ventured comments at these clambakes. Taller than Willis—hell, *everybody* was taller than Willis—he nonetheless looked like a relative, what with the same dark hair and eyes. Once, in fact, a perp had asked them if they were brothers. Willis, offended, had answered, "I'll give you brothers."

"Which'll mean the same guy killed all three," Byrnes said.

Genero felt rewarded. He smiled in acknowledgment.

"Or the same gun, anyway," Carella said.

"Widow been informed?"

"We went there directly from the scene," Willis said.

"What've we got on the paint?"

"Brand name sold everywhere," Meyer said.

"What's with this Inverni kid?"

"He's worth another visit."

"Why?"

"He has a thing about religion."

"What kind of thing?"

"He thinks it's all bullshit."

"Doesn't everyone?" Parker said.

"I don't," Genero said.

"That doesn't mean he's going around killing Muslims," Byrnes said. "But talk to him again. Find out where he was last night at . . . Hal? What time did the cabbie catch it?"

"Twenty past two."

"Be nice if Inverni's our man," Brown said.

"Yes, that would be very nice."

"In your dreams," Parker said.

"You got a better idea?"

Parker thought this over.

"You're such an expert on Arabian first names . . ."

"Arabic."

". . . I thought maybe you might have a better idea," Byrnes said.

"How about we put undercovers in the cabs?"

"Brilliant," Byrnes said. "You know any Muslim cops?"

"Come to think of it," Parker said, and shrugged again.

"Where'd this last one take place?"

"Booker and Lowell. In Riverhead," Eileen said. "Six blocks from the stadium."

"He's ranging all over the place."

"Got to be random," Brown said.

"Let's scour the hood," Kling suggested. "Must be somebody heard a shot at two in the morning."

"Two-twenty," Parker corrected.

"I'm going to triple-team this," Byrnes said. "Anybody not on vacation or out sick, I want him on this case. I'm surprised the commissioner himself hasn't called yet. Something like this . . ."

The phone on his desk rang.

"Let's get this son of a bitch," Byrnes said, and waved the detectives out of his office.

His phone was still ringing.

He rolled his eyes heavenward and picked up the receiver.

THIRD HATE KILLING
Muslim Murders Mount

All over the city, busy citizens picked up the afternoon tabloid, and read its headline, and then turned to the story on page three. Unless the police were withholding vital information, they still did not have a single clue. This made people nervous. They did not want these stupid killings to escalate into the sort of situation that was a daily occurrence in Israel. They did not want retaliation to follow retaliation. They did not want hate begetting more hate.

But they were about to get it.

The first of what the police hoped would be the last of the bombings took place that very afternoon, the fifth day of May.

Parker—who knew such things—could have told the other detectives on the squad that the fifth of May was a date of vast importance in Mexican and Chicano communities, of which there were not a few in this sprawling city. *Cinco de Mayo,* as it was called in Spanish, celebrated the victory of the Mexican Army over the French in 1862. Hardly anyone today—except Parker maybe—knew that *La Battala de Puebla* had been fought and won by Mestizo and

Zapotec Indians. Nowadays, many of the Spanish-speaking people in this city thought the date commemorated Mexican independence, which Parker could have told you was September 16, 1810, and not May 5, 1862. Some people suspected Parker was an idiot savant, but this was only half true. He merely read a lot.

On that splendid, sunny, fifth day of May, as the city's Chicano population prepared for an evening of folklorico dancing and mariachi music and margaritas, and as the weary detectives of the Eight-Seven spread out into the three sections of the city that had so far been stricken with what even the staid morning newspaper labeled "The Muslim Murders," a man carrying a narrow Gucci dispatch case walked into a movie theater that was playing a foreign film about a Japanese prostitute who aspires to become an internationally famous violinist, took a seat in the center of the theater's twelfth row, watched the commercials for furniture stores and local restaurants and antique shops, and then watched the coming attractions, and finally, at 1:37 P.M.—just as the feature film was about to start—got up to go to the men's room.

He left the Gucci dispatch case under the seat.

There was enough explosive material in that sleek leather case to blow up at least seven rows of seats in the orchestra. There was also a ticking clock set to trigger a spark at 3:48 P.M., just about when the Japanese prostitute would be accepted at Juilliard.

Spring break had ended not too long ago, and most of the students at Ramsey U still sported tans they'd picked up in Mexico or Florida. There was an air of bustling activity

on the downtown campus as Meyer and Carella made their
way through crowded corridors to the Registrar's Office,
where they hoped to acquire a program for Anthony
Inverni. This turned out to be not as simple as they'd
hoped. Each and separately they had to show first their
shields and next their ID cards, and still had to invoke the
sacred words "Homicide investigation," before the yellow-
haired lady with a bun would reveal the whereabouts of
Anthony Inverni on this so-far eventless Cinco de Mayo.

The time was 1:45 P.M.

They found Inverni already seated in the front row of a
class his program listed as "Shakespearean Morality." He
was chatting with a girl wearing a blue scarf around her
head and covering her forehead. The detectives assumed
she was Muslim, though this was probably profiling. They
asked Inverni if he would mind stepping outside for a
moment, and he said to the girl, "Excuse me, Halima,"
which more or less confirmed their surmise, but which did
little to reinforce the profile of a hate criminal.

"So what's up?" he asked.

"Where were you at two this morning?" Meyer asked,
going straight for the jugular.

"That, huh?"

"That," Carella said.

"It's all over the papers," Inverni said. "But you're still
barking up the wrong tree."

"So where were you?"

"With someone."

"Who?"

"Someone."

"The someone wouldn't be Rebecca Schwartz, would it? Because as an alibi . . ."

"Are you kidding? You think old Sam would let her out of his sight at two in the morning?"

"Then who's this 'someone' we're talking about?"

"I'd rather not get her involved."

"Oh? Really? We've got three dead cabbies here. You'd better start worrying about *them* and not about getting *someone* involved. Who is she? Who's your alibi?"

Anthony turned to look over his shoulder, into the classroom. For a moment, the detectives thought he was going to name the girl with the blue scarf. Hanima, was it? Halifa? He turned back to them again. Lowering his voice, he said, "Judy Manzetti."

"Was with you at two this morning?"

"Yes."

His voice still a whisper. His eyes darting.

"Where?"

"My place."

"Doing what?"

"Well . . . you know."

"Spell it out."

"We were in bed together."

"Give us her address and phone number," Carella said.

"Hey, come on. I told you I didn't want to get her involved."

"She's already involved," Carella said. His notebook was in his hand.

Inverni gave him her address and phone number.

"Is that it?" he asked. "'Cause class is about to start."

"I thought you planned to marry Becky," Meyer said.

"Of *course* I'm marrying Becky!" Inverni said. "But meanwhile . . ."—and here he smiled conspiratorially—". . . I'm fucking Judy."

No, Meyer thought. It's Becky who's getting fucked.

The time was two P.M.

As if to confirm Parker's fact-finding acumen, the two witnesses who'd heard the shot last night were both named Ali. They'd been coming home from a party at the time, and each of them had been a little drunk. They explained at once that this was not a habit of theirs. They fully understood that the imbibing of alcoholic beverages was strictly forbidden in the Koran.

"Haram," the first Ali said, shaking his head. "Most definitely *haram.*"

"Oh yes, unacceptable," the second Ali agreed, shaking his head as well. "Forbidden. Prohibited. In the Koran, it is written, 'They ask thee concerning wine and gambling. In them is great sin, and some profit, for men; but the sin is greater than the profit.'"

"But our friend was celebrating his birthday," the first Ali said, and smiled apologetically.

"It was a party," the second Ali explained.

"Where?" Eileen asked.

The two Alis looked at each other.

At last, they admitted that the party had taken place at a club named Buffers, which Eileen and Willis both knew was a topless joint, but the Alis claimed that no one in their party had gone back to the club's so-called private room but had instead merely enjoyed the young ladies dancing around their poles.

Eileen wondered *whose* poles?

The young ladies' poles?

Or the poles of Ali and Company?

She guessed she maybe had a dirty mind.

At any rate, the two Alis were staggering out of Buffers at two o'clock in the morning when they spotted a yellow cab parked at the curb up the block. They were planning on taking the subway home, but one never argued with divine providence so they decided on the spot to take a taxi instead. As they tottered and swayed toward the idling cab—the first Ali raising his hand to hail it, the second Ali breaking into a trot toward it and almost tripping—they heard a single shot from inside the cab. They both stopped dead still in the middle of the pavement.

"A man jumped out," the first Ali said now, his eyes wide with the excitement of recall.

"What'd he look like?" Eileen asked.

"A tall man," the second Ali said. "Dressed all in black."

"Black suit, black coat, black hat."

"Was he bearded or clean-shaven?"

"No beard. No."

"You're sure it was a man?"

"Oh yes, positive," the second Ali said.

"What'd he do after he got out of the cab?"

"Went to the windshield."

"Sprayed the windshield."

"You saw him spraying the windshield?"

"Yes."

"Oh yes."

"Then what?"

"He ran away."

"Up the street."

"Toward the subway."

"There's an entrance there."

"For the subway."

Which could have taken him anywhere in the city, Eileen thought.

"Thanks," Willis said.

It was 2:15 P.M.

Parker and Genero were the two detectives who spoke once again to Ozzie Kiraz, the cousin of the second dead cabbie.

Kiraz was just leaving for work when they got there at a quarter past three that afternoon. He introduced them to his wife, a diminutive woman who seemed half his size, and who immediately went into the kitchen of their tiny apartment to prepare tea for the men. Fine-featured, dark-haired and dark-eyed, Badria Kiraz was a woman in her late twenties, Parker guessed. Exotic features aside, she looked very American to him, sporting lipstick and eye shadow, displaying a nice ass in beige tailored slacks, and good tits in a white cotton blouse.

Kiraz explained that he and his wife both worked night shifts at different places in different parts of the city. He worked at a pharmacy in Majesta, where he was manager of the store. Badria worked as a cashier in a supermarket in Calm's Point. They both started work at four, and got off at midnight. Kiraz told them that in Afghanistan he'd once hoped to become a schoolteacher. That was before he started fighting the Russians. Now, here in America, he was the manager of a drugstore.

"Land of the free, right?" he said, and grinned.

Genero didn't know if he was being a wise guy or not.

"So tell us a little more about your cousin," he said.

"What would you like to know?"

"One of the men interviewed by our colleagues . . ."

Genero liked using the word "colleagues." Made him sound like a university professor. He consulted his notebook, which made him feel even more professorial.

"Man named Ajmal, is that how you pronounce it?"

"Yes," Kiraz said.

"Ajmal Khan, a short-order cook at a deli named Max's in Mid-town South. Do you know him?"

"No, I don't."

"Friend of your cousin's," Parker said.

He was eyeing Kiraz's wife, who was carrying a tray in from the kitchen. She set it down on the low table in front of the sofa, smiled, and said, "We drink it sweet, but I didn't add sugar. It's there if you want it. Cream and lemon, too. Oz," she said, "do you know what time it is?"

"I'm watching it, Badria, don't worry. Maybe you should leave."

"Would that be all right?" she asked the detectives.

"Yes, sure," Genero said, and both detectives rose politely. Kiraz kissed his wife on the cheek. She smiled again and left the room. They heard the front door to the apartment closing. The men sat again. Through the open windows, they could hear the loud-speakered cry of the muezzin calling the faithful to prayer.

"The third prayer of the day," Kiraz explained. "The *Salat al-'Asr*," and added almost regretfully, "I never pray anymore. It's too difficult here in America. If you want to be American, you follow American ways, am I right? You do what Americans do."

"Oh sure," Parker agreed, even though he'd never had any problem following American ways or doing what Americans do.

"Anyway," Genero said, squeezing a little lemon into one of the tea glasses, and then picking it up, "this guy at the deli told our colleagues your cousin was dating quite a few girls . . ."

"That's news to me," Kiraz said.

"Well, that's what we wanted to talk to you about," Parker said. "We thought you might be able to help us with their names."

"The names of these girls," Genero said.

"Because this guy in the deli didn't know who they might be," Parker said.

"I don't know, either," Kiraz said, and looked at his watch.

Parker looked at his watch, too.

It was twenty minutes past three.

"Ever *talk* to you about any of these girls?" Genero asked.

"Never. We were not that close, you know. He was single, I'm married. We have our own friends, Badria and I. This is America. There are different customs, different ways. When you live here, you do what Americans do, right?"

He grinned again.

Again, Genero didn't know if he was getting smart with them.

"You wouldn't know if any of these girls were Jewish, would you?" Parker asked.

"Because of the blue star, you mean?"

"Well . . . yes."

"I would sincerely doubt that my cousin was dating any Jewish girls."

"Because sometimes . . ."

"Oh sure," Kiraz said. "Sometimes things aren't as simple as they appear. You're thinking this wasn't a simple hate crime. You're thinking this wasn't a mere matter of a Jew killing a Muslim simply because he *was* a Muslim. You're looking for complications. Was Salim involved with a Jewish girl? Did the Jewish girl's father or brother become enraged by the very *thought* of such a relationship? Was Salim killed as a warning to any other Muslim with interfaith aspirations? Is that why the Jewish star was painted on the windshield? Stay away! Keep off!"

"Well, we weren't thinking *exactly* that," Parker said, "but, yes, that's a possibility."

"But you're forgetting the *other* two Muslims, aren't you?" Kiraz said, and smiled in what Genero felt was a superior manner, fuckin guy thought he was Chief of Detectives here.

"No, we're not forgetting them," Parker said. "We're just trying to consider all the possibilities."

"A mistake," Kiraz said. "I sometimes talk to this doctor who comes into the pharmacy. He tells me, 'Oz, if it has stripes like a zebra, don't look for a horse.' Because people come in asking me what I've got for this or that ailment, you know? Who knows why?" he said, and shrugged, but he seemed pleased by his position of importance in the workplace. "I'm only the manager of the store, I'm not a pharmacist, but they ask me," he said, and shrugged again. "What's good for a headache, or a cough, or the sniffles, or this or that? They ask me all the time. And I remember what my friend the doctor told me," he said, and smiled, seemingly pleased by this, too, the fact that his friend was a doctor. "If it has the symptoms of a common cold, don't go looking for SARS. Period." He opened his hands to them, palms up, explaining the utter simplicity of it all. "Stop looking for zebras," he said, and smiled again. "Just find the fucking Jew who shot my cousin in the head, hmm?"

The time was 3:27 P.M.

In the movies these days, it was not unusual for a working girl to become a princess overnight, like the chambermaid who not only gets the hero onscreen but in real life as well, talk about Cinderella stories! In other movies of this stripe, you saw common working class girls who aspired to become college students. Or soccer players. It was a popular theme nowadays. America was the land of opportunity. So was Japan, apparently, although Ruriko—the prostitute in the film all these people were waiting on line to see— was a "working girl" in the truest sense, and she didn't even want to become a princess, just a concert violinist. She was about to become just that in about three minutes.

The two girls standing on line outside the theater box office also happened to be true working girls, which was why they were here to catch the four o'clock screening of the Japanese film. They had each separately seen *Pretty Woman*, another Working Girl Becomes Princess film, and did not for a moment believe that Julia Roberts had ever blown anybody for fifty bucks, but maybe it would be different with this Japanese actress, whatever her name was. Maybe this time, they'd believe that these One in a Million fairy tales could really happen to girls who actually did this sort of thing for a living.

The two girls, Heidi and Roseanne, looked and dressed just like any secretary who'd got out of work early today . . .

It was now 3:46 P.M.

. . . and even sounded somewhat like girls with junior college educations. As the line inched closer to the box office, they began talking about what Heidi was going to do to celebrate her birthday tonight. Heidi was nineteen years old today. She'd been hooking for two years now. The closest she'd got to becoming a princess was when one of her old-fart regulars asked her to come to London with him on a weekend trip. He rescinded the offer when he learned she was expecting her period, worse luck.

"You doing anything special tonight?" Roseanne asked.

"Jimmy's taking me out to dinner," Heidi said.

Jimmy was a cop she dated. He knew what profession she was in.

"That's nice."

"Yeah."

In about fifteen seconds, it would be 3:48 P.M.

"I still can't get over it," Roseanne said.

"What's that, hon?"

"The *coincidence!*" Roseanne said, amazed. "Does your birthday *always* fall on Cinco de Mayo?"

A couple sitting in the seats just behind the one under which the Gucci dispatch case had been left were seriously necking when the bomb exploded.

The boy had his hand under the girl's skirt, and she had her hand inside his unzipped fly, their fitful manual activity covered by the raincoat he had thrown over both their laps. Neither of them really gave a damn about whether or not Ruriko passed muster with the judges at Juilliard, or went back instead to a life of hopeless despair in the slums of Yokohama. All that mattered to them was achieving mutual orgasm here in the flickering darkness of the theater while the soulful strains of Aram Khacaturian's *Spartacus* flowed from Ruriko's violin under the expert coaxing of her talented fingers.

When the bomb exploded, they both thought for the tiniest tick of an instant that they'd died and gone to heaven.

Fortunately for the Eight-Seven, the movie-theater bombing occurred in the Two-One downtown. Since there was no immediate connection between this new outburst of violence and the Muslim Murders, nobody from the Two-One called uptown in an attempt to unload the case there. Instead, because this was an obvious act of terrorism, they called the Joint Terrorist Task Force at One Federal Square further downtown, and dumped the entire matter into their laps. This did not, however, stop the talking heads on television from linking the movie bombing to the murders of the three cabbies.

The liberal TV commentators noisily insisted that the total mess we'd made in Iraq was directly responsible for this new wave of violence here in the United States. The conservative commentators wagged their heads in tolerant understanding of their colleagues' supreme ignorance, and then sagely suggested that if the police in this city would only learn how to handle the problems manifest in a gloriously diverse population, there wouldn't be any civic violence at all.

It took no more than an hour and a half before all of the

cable channels were demanding immediate arrests in what was now perceived as a single case. On the six-thirty network news broadcasts, the movie-theater bombing was the headline story, and without fail the bombing was linked to the cab-driver killings, the blue Star of David on the windshields televised over and over again as the unifying leitmotif.

Ali Al-Barak, the third Muslim victim, had worked for a company that called itself simply Cabco. Its garage was located in the shadow of the Calm's Point Bridge, not too distant from the market under the massive stone supporting pillars on the Isola side of the bridge. The market was closed and shuttered when Meyer and Carella drove past it at a quarter to seven that evening. They had trouble finding Cabco's garage and drove around the block several times, getting entangled in bridge traffic. At one point, Carella suggested that they hit the hammer, but Meyer felt use of the siren might be excessive.

They finally located the garage tucked between two massive apartment buildings. It could have been the underground garage for either of them, but a discreet sign identified it as Cabco. They drove down the ramp, found the dispatcher's office, identified themselves, and explained why they were there.

"Yeah," the dispatcher said, and nodded. His name was Hazhir Demirkol. He explained that like Al-Barak, he too was a Muslim, though not a Saudi. "I'm a Kurd," he told them. "I came to this country ten years ago."

"What can you tell us about Al-Barak?" Meyer asked.

"I knew someone would kill him sooner or later," Demirkol said. "The way he was shooting up his mouth all the time."

Shooting *off,* Carella thought, but didn't correct him.

"In what way?" he asked.

"He kept complaining that Israel was responsible for all the trouble in the Arab world. If there was no Israel, there would have been no Iraqi war. There would be no terrorism. There would be no 9/11. Well, he's a Saudi, you know. His countrymen were the ones who *bombed* the World Trade Center! But he was being foolish. It doesn't matter how you feel about Jews. I feel the same way. But in this city, I have learned to keep my thoughts to myself."

"Why's that?" Meyer asked.

Demirkol turned to him, looked him over. One eyebrow arched. Sudden recognition crossed his face. This man was a Jew. This detective was a Jew.

"It doesn't matter why," he said. "Look what happened to Ali. *That* is why."

"You think a Jew killed him, is that it?"

"No, an angel from Paradise painted that blue star on his windshield."

"Who might've heard him when he was airing all these complaints?" Carella asked.

"Who knows? Ali talked freely, *too* freely, you ask me. This is a democracy, no? Like the one America brought to Iraq, no?" Demirkol asked sarcastically. "He talked everywhere. He talked here in the garage with his friends, he talked to his passengers, I'm sure he talked at the mosque, too, when he went to prayer. Freedom of speech, correct? Even if it gets you killed."

"You think he expressed his views to the wrong person, is that it?" Meyer asked. "The wrong *Jew.*"

"The *same* Jew who killed the other drivers," Demirkol

said, and nodded emphatically, looking Meyer dead in the eye, challenging him.

"This mosque you mentioned," Carella said. "Would you know . . . ?"

"Majid At-Abu," Demirkol said at once. "Close by here," he said, and gestured vaguely uptown.

Now *this* was a mosque.

This was what one conjured when the very word was uttered. This was straight out of *Arabian Nights,* minarets and domes, blue tile and gold leaf. This was the real McCoy.

Opulent and imposing, Majid At-Abu was not as "close by" as Demirkol had suggested, it was in fact a good mile and a half uptown. When the detectives got there at a little past eight that night, the faithful were already gathered inside for the sunset prayer. The sky beyond the mosque's single glittering dome was streaked with the last red-purple streaks of a dying sun. The minaret from which the muezzin called worshippers to prayer stood tall and stately to the right of the arched entrance doors. Meyer and Carella stood on the sidewalk outside, listening to the prayers intoned within, waiting for an opportune time to enter.

Across the street, some Arabic-looking boys in T-shirts and jeans were cracking themselves up. Meyer wondered what they were saying. Carella wondered why they weren't inside praying.

"Ivan Sikimiavuçlyor!" one of the kids shouted, and the others all burst out laughing.

"How about Alexandr Siksallandr?" one of the other kids suggested, and again they all laughed.

"Or Madame Döllemer," another boy said.

More laughter. Carella was surprised they didn't all fall to the sidewalk clutching their bellies. It took both of the detectives a moment to realize that these were *names* the boys were bandying about. They had no idea that in Turkish "Ivan Sikimiavuçlyor" meant "Ivan Holding My Cock," or that "Alexandr Siksallandr" meant "Alexander Who Swings a Cock," or that poor "Madame Döllemer" was just a lady "Sucking Sperm." Like the dirty names Meyer and Carella had attached to fictitious book titles when they themselves were kids . . .

The Open Robe by Seymour Hare.

The Russian Revenge by Ivana Kutchakokoff.

The Chinese Curse by Wan Hong Lo.

Hawaiian Paradise by A'wana Leia Oo'aa.

. . . these Arab teenagers growing up here in America were now making puns on their parents' native tongue.

"Fenasi Kerim!" one of the boys shouted finally and triumphantly, and whereas neither of the detectives knew that this invented name meant "I Fuck You Bad," the boys' ensuing exuberant laughter caused them to laugh as well.

The sunset prayer had ended.

They took off their shoes and placed them outside in the foyer—alongside the loafers and sandals and jogging shoes and boots and laced brogans parked there like autos in a used-car lot—and went inside to find the imam.

"I never heard Ali Al-Barak utter a single threatening word about the Jewish people, or the Jewish state, or any Jew in particular," Mohammad Talal Awad said.

They were standing in the vast open hall of the mosque

proper, a white space the size of a ballroom, with arched windows and tiled floors and an overhead clerestory through which the detectives could see the beginnings of a starry night. The imam was wearing white baggy trousers and a flowing white tunic and a little while pillbox hat. He had a long black beard, a narrow nose and eyes almost black, and he directed his every word to Meyer.

"Nor is there anything in the Koran that directs Muslims to kill anyone," he said. "Not Jews, not anyone. There is nothing there. Search the Koran. You will find not a word about murdering in the name of Allah."

"We understand Al-Barak made remarks some people might have found inflammatory," Carella said.

"Political observations. They had nothing to do with Islam. He was young, he was brash, perhaps he was foolish to express his opinions so openly. But this is America, and one may speak freely, isn't that so? Isn't that what democracy is all about?"

Here we go again, Meyer thought.

"But if you think Ali's murder had anything to do with the bombing downtown . . ."

Oh? Carella thought.

". . . you are mistaken. Ali was a pious young man who lived with another man his own age, recently arrived from Saudi Arabia. In their land, they were both students. Here, one drove a taxi and the other bags groceries in a super- market. If you think Ali's friend, in revenge for his murder, bombed that theater downtown . . ."

Oh? Carella thought again.

". . . you are very sadly mistaken."

"We're not investigating that bombing," Meyer said.

"We're investigating Ali's murder. And the murder of two other Muslim cab drivers. If you can think of anyone who might possibly . . ."

"I know no Jews," the imam said.

You know one now, Meyer thought.

"This friend he lived with," Carella said. "What's his name, and where can we find him?"

The music coming from behind the door to the third-floor apartment was very definitely rap. The singers were very definitely black, and the lyrics were in English. But the words weren't telling young kids to do dope or knock women around or even up. As they listened at the wood, the lyrics the detectives heard spoke of intentions alone not being sufficient to bring reward . . .

When help is needed, prayer to Allah is the answer . . .

Allah alone can assist in . . .

Meyer knocked on the door.

"Yes?" a voice yelled.

"Police," Carella said.

The music continued to blare.

"Hello?" Carella said. "Mind if we ask you some questions?"

No answer.

"Hello?" he said again.

He looked at Meyer.

Meyer shrugged. Over the blare of the music, he yelled, "Hello in there!"

Still no answer.

"This is the police!" he yelled. "Would you mind coming to the door, please?"

The door opened a crack, held by a night chain.

They saw part of a narrow face. Part of a mustache. Part of a mouth. A single brown eye.

"Mr. Rajab?"

"Yes?"

Wariness in the voice and in the single eye they could see.

"Mind if we come in? Few questions we'd like to ask you."

"What about?"

"You a friend of Ali Al-Barak?"

"Yes?"

"Do you know he was murdered last . . . ?"

The door slammed shut.

They heard the sudden click of a bolt turning.

Carella backed off across the hall. His gun was already in his right hand, his knee coming up for a jackknife kick. The sole of his shoe collided with the door, just below the lock. The lock held.

"The yard!" he yelled, and Meyer flew off down the stairs.

Carella kicked at the lock again. This time, it sprang. He followed the splintered door into the room. The black rap group was still singing praise to Allah. The window across the room was open, a curtain fluttering in the mild evening breeze. He ran across the room, followed his gun hand out the window and onto a fire escape. He could hear footsteps clattering down the iron rungs to the second floor.

"Stop!" he yelled. "Police!"

Nobody stopped.

He came out onto the fire escape, took a quick look below, and started down.

From below, he heard Meyer racketing into the back-yard. They had Rajab sandwiched.

"Hold it right there!" Meyer yelled.

Carella came down to the first-floor fire escape, out of breath, and handcuffed Rajab's hands behind his back.

They listened in total amazement as Ishak Rajab told them all about how he had plotted instant revenge for the murder of his friend and roommate, Ali Al-Barak. They listened as he told them how he had constructed the suitcase bomb . . .

He called the Gucci dispatch case a suitcase.

. . . and then had carefully chosen a movie theater showing so-called art films because he knew Jews pre-tended to culture, and there would most likely be many Jews in the audience. Jews had to be taught that Arabs could not wantonly be killed without reprisal.

"Ali was killed by a Jew," Rajab said. "And so it was fit-ting and just that Jews be killed in return."

Meyer called the JTTF at Fed Square and told them they'd accidentally lucked into catching the guy who did their movie-theater bombing.

Ungrateful humps didn't even say thanks.

It was almost ten o'clock when he and Carella left the squad-room for home. As they passed the swing room down-stairs, they looked in through the open door to where a uni-formed cop was half-dozing on one of the couches, watching television. One of cable's most vociferous talking heads was demanding to know when a terrorist was *not* a terrorist.

"Here's the story," he said, and glared out of the screen. "A green-card Saudi-Arabian named Ishak Rajab was arrested and charged with the wanton slaying of sixteen movie patrons and the wounding of twelve others. Our own police and the Joint Terrorist Task Force are to be highly commended for their swift actions in this case. It is now to be hoped that a trial and conviction will be equally swift.

"However . . .

"Rajab's attorneys are already indicating they'll be entering a plea of insanity. Their reasoning seems to be that a man who *deliberately* leaves a bomb in a public place is not a terrorist—have you got that? *Not* a terrorist! Then what is he, huh, guys? Well, according to his attorneys, he was merely a man blinded by rage and seeking retaliation. The rationale for Rajab's behavior would seem to be his close friendship with Ali Al-Barak, the third victim in the wave of taxi-driver slayings that have swept the city since last Friday: Rajab was Al-Barak's roommate.

"Well, neither I nor any right-minded citizen would condone the senseless murder of Muslim cab drivers. That goes without saying. But to invoke a surely inappropriate Biblical—*Biblical,* mind you—'eye for an eye' defense by labeling premeditated mass murder 'insanity' is in itself insanity. A terrorist is a terrorist, and this was an act of terrorism, pure and simple. Anything less than the death penalty would be gross injustice in the case of Ishak Rajab. That's my opinion, now let's hear yours. You can e-mail me at . . ."

The detectives walked out of the building and into the night.

In four hours, another Muslim cabbie would be killed.

The police knew at once that this wasn't their man.

To begin with, none of the other victims had been robbed. This one was.

All of the other victims had been shot only once, at the base of the skull.

This one was shot three times through the open driver-side window of his cab, two of the bullets entering his face at the left temple and just below the cheek, the third passing through his neck and lodging in the opposite door panel.

Shell casings were found on the street outside the cab, indicating that the murder weapon had been an automatic, and not the revolver that had been used in the previous three murders. Ballistics confirmed this. The bullets and casings were consistent with samples fired from a Colt .45 automatic.

Moreover, two witnesses had seen a man leaning into the cab window moments before they heard shots, and he was definitely not a tall white man dressed entirely in black.

There were only two similarities in all four murders. The drivers were all Muslims, and a blue star had been spray-painted onto each of their windshields.

But the Star of David had six points, and this new one had only five, and it was turned on end like the inverted pentagram used by devil-worshippers.

They hoped to hell yet *another* religion wasn't intruding its beliefs into this case.

But they knew for sure this wasn't their man.

This was a copycat.

CABBIE SHOT AND KILLED
FOURTH MUSLIM MURDER

So read the headline in the Metro Section of the city's staid morning newspaper. The story under it was largely put together from details supplied in a Police Department press release. The flak that had gone out from the Public Relations Office on the previous three murders had significantly withheld any information about the killer himself or his MO. None of the reporters—print, radio, or television—had been informed that the killer had been dressed in black from head to toe, or that he'd fired just a single shot into his separate victims' heads. They were hoping the killer himself—if ever they caught him—would reveal this information, thereby incriminating himself.

But this time around, because the police knew this was a copycat, the PR release was a bit more generous, stating that the cabbie had been shot three times, that he'd been robbed of his night's receipts, and that his assailant, as described by two eyewitnesses, was a black man in his early twenties, about five feet seven inches tall, weighing some hundred and sixty pounds and wearing blue jeans, white sneakers, a brown leather jacket, and a black ski cap pulled low on his forehead.

The man who'd murdered the previous three cabbies must have laughed himself silly.

Especially when another bombing took place that Tuesday afternoon.

The city's Joint Terrorist Task Force was an odd mix of elite city detectives, FBI Special Agents, Homeland Security people, and a handful of CIA spooks. Special Agent in Charge Brian Hooper and a team of four other Task Force officers arrived at The Merrie Coffee Bean at three that afternoon, not half an hour after a suicide bomber had killed himself and a dozen patrons sitting at tables on the sidewalk outside. Seven wounded people had already been carried by ambulance to the closest hospital, Abingdon Memorial, on the river at Condon Street.

The coffee shop was a shambles.

Wrought iron tables and chairs had been twisted into surreal and smoldering bits of modern sculpture. Glass shards lay all over the sidewalk and inside the shop gutted and flooded by the Fire Department.

A dazed and dazzled waitress, wide-eyed and smoke-smudged but remarkably unharmed otherwise, told Hooper that she was at the cappuccino machine picking up an order when she heard someone yelling outside. She thought at first it was one of the customers, sometimes they got into arguments over choice tables. She turned from the counter to look outside, and saw this slight man running toward the door of the shop, yelling at the top of his lungs . . .

"What was he yelling, miss, do you remember?" Hooper asked.

Hooper was polite and soft-spoken, wearing a blue suit, a white shirt, a blue tie, and polished black shoes. Two detectives from the Five-Oh had also responded. Casually, dressed in sport jackets, slacks, and shirts open at the throat, they looked like bums in contrast. They stood by trying to look interested and significant while Hooper conducted the questioning.

"Something about Jews," the waitress said. "He had a foreign accent, you know, so it was hard to understand him to begin with. And this was like a rant, so that made it even more difficult. Besides, it all happened so fast. He was running from the open sidewalk down this, like, *space* we have between the tables? Like an *aisle* that leads to the front of the shop? And he was yelling Jews-this, Jews-that, and waving his arms in the air like some kind of nut? Then all at once there was this terrific explosion, it almost knocked *me* off my feet, and I was all the way inside the shop, near the cap machine. And I saw . . . there was like sunshine outside, you know? Like shining through the windows? And all of a sudden I saw all body parts flying in the air in the sunshine. Like in silhouette. All these people getting blown apart. It was, like, awesome."

Hooper and his men went picking through the rubble.

The two detectives from the Five-Oh were thinking this was very bad shit here.

If I've already realized what I hoped to accomplish; why press my luck, as they say? The thing has escalated beyond my wildest expectations. So leave it well enough alone, he told himself.

But that idiot last night has surely complicated matters. The police aren't fools, they'll recognize at once that last night's murder couldn't possibly be linked to the other three. So perhaps another one *was* in order, after all. To nail it to the wall. Four would round it off, wouldn't it?

To the Navajo Indians—well, Native Americans, as they say—the number four was sacred. Four different times of day, four sacred mountains, four sacred plants, four different directions. East was symbolic of Positive Thinking. South was for Planning. West for Life itself. North for Hope and Strength. They believed all this, the Navajo people. Religions were so peculiar. The things people believed. The things he himself had once believed, long ago, so very long ago.

Of course the number four wasn't *truly* sacred, that was just something the Navajos believed. The way Christians believed that the number 666 was the mark of the beast, who was the Antichrist and who—well, of course, what else?—had to be Jewish, right? There were even people who believed that the Internet acronym "www" for "World Wide Web" really transliterated into the Hebrew letter *"vav"* repeated three times, *vav, vav, vav,* the numerical equivalent of 666, the mark of the beast. *Let him that hath understanding count the number of the beast: for it is the number of a man; and his number is six hundred threescore and six,* Revelations 13. Oh yes, I've read the Bible, thank you, *and* the Koran, *and* the teachings of Buddha, and they're all total bullshit, as they say. But there are people who believe in a matrix, too, and not all of them are in padded rooms wearing straitjackets.

So, yes, I think there should be another one tonight, a tip of the hat, as they say, to the Navajo's sacred number four, and that will be the end of it. The last one. The same signature mark of the beast, the six-pointed star of the Antichrist. Then let them go searching the synagogues for me. Let them try to find the murdering Jew. After tonight, I will be finished!

Tonight, he thought.

Yes.

Abbas Miandad was a Muslim cab driver, and no fool.

Four Muslim cabbies had already been killed since Friday night, and he didn't want to be number five. He did not own a pistol—carrying a pistol would be exceedingly stupid in a city already so enflamed against people of the

Islamic faith—nor did he own a dagger or a sword, but his wife's kitchen was well stocked with utensils and before he set out on his midnight shift he took a huge bread knife from the rack . . .

"Where are you going with that?" his wife asked.

She was watching television.

They were reporting that there'd been a suicide bombing that afternoon. They were saying the bomber had not been identified as yet.

"Never mind," he told her, and wrapped a dishtowel around the knife and packed it in a small tote bag that had BARNES & NOBLE lettered on it.

He had unwrapped the knife the moment he drove out of the garage. At three that Wednesday morning, it was still in the pouch on the driver's side of the cab. He had locked the cab when he stopped for a coffee break. Now, he walked up the street to where he'd parked the cab near the corner, and saw a man dressed all in black, bending to look into the back seat. He walked to him swiftly.

"Help you, sir?" he asked.

The man straightened up.

"I thought you might be napping in there," he said, and smiled.

"No, sir," he said. "Did you need a taxi?"

"Is this your cab?"

"It is."

"Can you take me to Majesta?" he said.

"Where are you going, sir?"

"The Boulevard and a Hundred Twelfth."

"Raleigh Boulevard?"

"Yes."

Abbas knew the neighborhood. It was residential and safe, even at this hour. He would not drive anyone to neighborhoods that he knew to be dangerous. He would not pick up black men, even if they were accompanied by women. Nowadays, he would not pick up anyone who looked Jewish. If you asked him how he knew whether a person was Jewish or not, he would tell you he just knew. This man dressed all in black did not look Jewish.

"Let me open it," he said, and took his keys from the right-hand pocket of his trousers. He turned the key in the door lock and was opening the door when, from the corner of his eye, he caught a glint of metal. Without turning, he reached for the bread knife tucked into the door's pouch.

He was too late.

The man in black fired two shots directly into his face, killing him at once.

Then he ran off into the night.

"Changed his MO," Byrnes said. "The others were shot from the back seat, single bullet to the base of the skull . . ."

"Not the one Tuesday night," Parker said.

"Tuesday was a copycat," Genero said.

"Maybe this one was, too," Willis suggested.

"Not if Ballistics comes back with a match," Meyer said.

The detectives fell silent.

They were each and separately hoping this newest murder would not trigger another suicide bombing some-place. The Task Force downtown still hadn't been able to get a positive ID from the smoldering remains of the Merrie Coffee Bean bomber.

"Anybody see anything?" Byrnes asked.

"Patrons in the diner heard shots, but didn't see the shooter."

"Didn't see him painting that blue star again?"

"I think they were afraid to go outside," Carella said. "Nobody wants to get shot, Pete."

"Gee, no kidding?" Byrnes said sourly.

"Also, the cab was parked all the way up the street, near the corner, some six cars back from the diner, on the same side of the street. The killer had to be standing on the passenger side . . ."

"Where he could see the driver's hack license . . ." Eileen said.

"Arab name on it," Kling said.

"Bingo, he had his victim."

"Point is," Carella said, "standing where he was, the people in the diner couldn't have seen him."

"Or just didn't *want* to see him."

"Well, sure."

"Cause they *could've* seen him while he was painting the star," Parker said.

"That's right," Byrnes said. "He had to've come around to the windshield."

"They could've at least seen his back."

"Tell us whether he was short, tall, what he was wearing . . ."

"But they didn't."

"Talk to them again."

"We talked them deaf, dumb, and blind," Meyer said.

"Talk to them *again*," Byrnes said. "And talk to anybody who was in those coffee shops, diners, delis, whatever, at the scenes of the other murders. These cabbies stop for coffee breaks, two, three in the morning, they go back to their cabs and get shot. That's no coincidence. Our man knows their habits. And he's a night-crawler. What's with the Inverni kid? Did his alibi stand up?"

"Yeah, he was in bed with her," Carella said.

"In bed with who?" Parker asked, interested.

"Judy Manzetti. It checked out."

"Okay, so talk to everybody *else* again," Byrnes said. "See who might've been lurking about, hanging around, casing these various sites *before* the murders were committed."

"We *did* talk to everybody again," Genero said.

"Talk to them *again* again!"

"They all say the same thing," Meyer said. "It was a Jew who killed those drivers, all we have to do is look for a god-damn Jew."

"You're too fucking sensitive," Parker said.

"I'm telling you what we're getting. Anybody we talk to thinks it's an open-and-shut case. All we have to do is round up every Jew in the city . . ."

"Take forever," Parker said.

"What does that mean?"

"It means there are millions of Jews in this city."

"And what does *that* mean?"

"It means you're too fucking sensitive."

"Knock it off," Byrnes said.

"Anyway, Meyer's right," Genero said. "That's what we got, too. You know that, Andy."

"What do I know?" Parker said, glaring at Meyer.

"They keep telling us all we have to do is find the Jew who shot those guys in the head."

"Who told you that?" Carella said at once.

Genero looked startled.

"Who told you they got shot in the head?"

"Well . . . they *all* did."

"No," Parker said. "It was just the cousin, whatever the fuck his name was."

"What cousin?"

"The second vic. His cousin."

"Salim Nazir? *His* cousin?"

"Yeah, Ozzie something."

"Osman," Carella said. "Osman Kiraz."

"That's the one."

"And he said these cabbies were shot in the *head?*"

"Said his cousin was."

"Told us to stop looking for zebras."

"What the hell is that supposed to mean?" Byrnes asked.

"Told us to just find the Jew who shot his cousin in the head."

"The *fucking* Jew," Parker said.

Meyer looked at him.

"Were his exact words," Parker said, and shrugged.

"How did he know?" Carella asked.

"Go get him," Byrnes said.

Ozzie Kariz was asleep when they knocked on his door at nine-fifteen that Wednesday morning. Bleary-eyed and unshaven, he came to the door in pajamas over which he had thrown a shaggy blue robe, and explained that he worked at the pharmacy until midnight each night and did not get home until one, one-thirty, so he normally slept late each morning.

"May we come in?" Carella asked.

"Yes, sure," Kariz said, "but we'll have to be quiet, please. My wife is still asleep."

They went into a small kitchen and sat at a wooden table painted green.

"So what's up?" Kariz asked.

"Few more questions we'd like to ask you."

"Again?" Kariz said. "I told those other two . . . what were their names?"

"Genero and Parker."

"I told them I didn't know any of my cousin's girlfriends. Or even their names."

"This doesn't have anything to do with his girlfriends," Carella said.

"Oh? Something new then? Is there some new development?"

"Yes. Another cab driver was killed last night."

"Oh?"

"You didn't know that."

"No."

"It's already on television."

"I've been asleep."

"Of course."

"Was he a Muslim?"

"Yes."

"And was there another . . . ?"

"Yes, another Jewish star on the windshield."

"This is bad," Kiraz said. "These killings, the bombings . . ."

"Mr. Kiraz," Meyer said, "can you tell us where you were at three o'clock this morning?"

"Is that when it happened?"

"Yes, that's exactly when it happened."

"Where?"

"You tell us," Carella said.

Kiraz looked at them.

"What is this?" he asked.

"How'd you know your cousin was shot in the head?" Meyer asked.

"Was he?"

"That's what you told Genero and Parker. You told them a Jew shot your cousin in the head. How did you . . . ?"

"And did a Jew also shoot this man last night?" Kiraz asked. "In the head?"

"Twice in the face," Carella said.

"I asked you a question," Meyer said. "How'd you know . . . ?"

"I saw his body."

"You saw your cousin's . . ."

"I went with my aunt to pick up Salim's corpse at the morgue. After the people there were finished with him."

"When was this?" Meyer asked.

"The day after he was killed."

"That would've been . . ."

"Whenever. I accompanied my aunt to the morgue, and an ambulance took us to the mosque where they bathed the body according to Islamic law . . . they have rules, you know. Religious Muslims. They have many rules."

"I take it you're not religious."

"I'm American now," Kiraz said. "I don't believe in the old ways anymore."

"Then what were you doing in a mosque, washing your cousin's . . . ?"

"My aunt asked me to come. You saw her. You saw how distraught she was. I went as a family duty."

"I thought you didn't believe in the old ways anymore," Carella said.

"I don't believe in any of the *religious* bullshit," Kiraz said. "I went with her to help her. She's an old woman. She's alone now that her only son was killed. I went to help her."

"So you washed the body . . ."

"No, the *imam* washed the body."

"But you were there when he washed the body."

"I was there. He washed it three times. That's because it's written that when the daughter of Muhammad died, he instructed his followers to wash her three times, or more than that if necessary. Five times, seven, whatever. But always an *odd* number of times. Never an *even* number. That's what I mean about all the religious *bullshit*. Like having to wrap the body in *three* white sheets. That's because when Muhammad died, he himself was wrapped in three white sheets. From Yemen. That's what's written. So God forbid you should wrap a Muslim corpse in *four* sheets! Oh no! It has to be three. But you have to use *four* ropes to tie the sheets, not *three,* it has to be four. And the ropes each have to be seven feet long. Not three, or four, but *seven!* Do you see what I mean? All mumbo-jumbo bullshit."

"So you're saying you saw your cousin's body . . ."

"Yes."

". . . while he was being washed."

"Yes."

"And that's how you knew he was shot in the head."

"Yes. I saw the bullet wound at the base of his skull.

Anyway, where *else* would he have been shot? If his murderer was sitting behind him in the taxi . . ."

"How do you know that?"

"What?"

"How do you know his murderer was inside the taxi?"

"Well, if Salim was shot at the back of the head, his murderer *had* to be sitting . . ."

"Oz?"

She was standing in the doorway to the kitchen, a
diminutive woman with large brown eyes, her long ebony
hair trailing down the back of the yellow silk robe she wore
over a long white nightgown.

"Badria, good morning," Kiraz said. "My wife, gentlemen.
I'm sorry, I've forgotten your names."

"Detective Carella."

"Detective Meyer."

"How do you do?" Badria said. "Have you offered them
coffee?" she asked her husband.

"I'm sorry, no."

"Gentlemen? Some coffee?"

"None for me, thanks," Carella said.

Meyer shook his head.

"Oz? Would you like some coffee?"

"Please," he said. There was a faint amused smile on his
face now, "As an illustration," he said, "witness my wife."

The detectives didn't know what he was talking about.

"The wearing of silk is expressly forbidden in Islamic law,"
he said. " 'Do not wear silk, for one who wears it in the world
will not wear it in the Hereafter.' That's what's written.
You're not allowed to wear yellow clothing, either, because
'these are the clothes usually worn by nonbelievers,' quote

unquote. But here's my beautiful wife wearing a yellow silk robe, oh shame unto her," Kiraz said, and suddenly began laughing.

Badria did not laugh with him.

Her back to the detectives, she stood before a four-burner stove, preparing her husband's coffee in a small brass pot with a tin lining.

" 'A man was wearing clothes dyed in saffron,' " Kiraz said, apparently quoting again, his laughter trailing, his face becoming serious again. " 'And finding that Muhammad disapproved of them, he promised to wash them. But the Prophet said, *Burn* them!' " That's written, too. So tell me, Badria. Should we burn your pretty yellow silk robe? What do you think, Badria?"

Badria said nothing.

The aroma of strong Turkish coffee filled the small kitchen.

"You haven't answered our very first question," Meyer said.

"And what was that? I'm afraid I've forgotten it."

"Where were you at three o'clock this morning?"

"I was here," Kiraz said. "Asleep. In bed with my beautiful wife. Isn't that so, Badria?"

Standing at the stove in her yellow silk robe, Badria said nothing.

"Badria? Tell the gentlemen where I was at three o'clock this morning."

She did not turn from the stove.

Her back still to them, her voice very low, Badria Kiraz said, "I don't know where you were, Oz."

The aroma of the coffee was overpowering now.

"But you weren't here in bed with me," she said.

*   *   *

Nellie Brand left the District Attorney's Office at eleven that Wednesday morning and was uptown at the Eight-Seven by a little before noon. She had cancelled an important lunch date, and even before the detectives filled her in, she warned them that this better be real meat here.

Osman Kiraz had already been read his rights and had insisted on an attorney before he answered any questions. Nellie wasn't familiar with the man he chose. Gulbuddin Amin was wearing a dark-brown business suit, with a tie and vest. Nellie was wearing a suit, too. Hers was a Versace, and it was a deep shade of green that complimented her blue eyes and sand-colored hair. Amin had a tidy little mustache and he wore eyeglasses. His English was impeccable, with a faint Middle-Eastern accent. Nellie guessed he might originally have come from Afghanistan, as had his client. She guessed he was somewhere in his mid fifties. She herself was thirty-two.

The police clerk's fingers were poised over the stenotab machine. Nellie was about to begin the questioning when Amin said, "I hope this was not a frivolous arrest, Mrs. Brand."

"No, counselor . . ."

". . . because that would be a serious mistake in a city already fraught with Jewish-Arab tensions."

"I would not use the word frivolous to describe this arrest," Nellie said.

"In any case, I've already advised my client to remain silent."

"Then we have nothing more to do here," Nellie said, briskly dusting the palm of one hand against the other.

"Easy come, easy go. Take him away, boys, he's all yours."

"Why are you afraid of her?" Kiraz asked his lawyer.

Amin responded in what Nellie assumed was Arabic.

"Let's stick to English, shall we?" she said. "What'd you just say, counselor?"

"My comment was privileged."

"Not while your man's under oath, it isn't."

Amin sighed heavily.

"I told him I'm afraid of no woman."

"Bravo!" Nellie said, applauding, and then looked Kiraz dead in the eye. "How about you?" she asked. "Are *you* afraid of me?"

"Of course not!"

"So would you like to answer some questions?"

"I have nothing to hide."

"Yes or no? It's your call. I haven't got all day here."

"I would like to answer her questions," Kiraz told his lawyer.

Amin said something else in Arabic.

"Let us in on it," Nellie said.

"I told him it's his own funeral," Amin said.

Q: Mr. Kiraz, would you like to tell us where you were at three this morning?

A: I was at home in bed with my wife.

Q: You wife seems to think otherwise.

A: My wife is mistaken.

Q: Well, she'll be subpoenaed before the grand jury, you know, and she'll have to tell them under oath whether you were in bed with her or somewhere else.

A: I was home. She was in bed with me.

Q: You yourself are under oath right this minute, you realize that, don't you?

A: I realize it.

Q: You swore on the Koran, did you not? You placed your left hand on the Koran and raised your right hand . . .

A: I know what I did.

Q: Or does that mean anything to you?

Q: Mr. Kiraz?

Q: Mr. Kiraz, does that mean anything to you? Placing your hand on the Islamic holy book . . .

A: I heard you.

Q: May I have your answer, please?

A: My word is my bond. It doesn't matter whether I swore on the Koran or not.

Q: Well, good, I'm happy to hear that. So tell me, Mr. Kiraz, where were you on these *other* dates at around two in the morning? Friday, May second . . . Saturday, May third . . . and Monday, May fifth. All at around two in the morning, where were you, Mr. Kiraz?

A: Home asleep. I work late. I get home around one, one-fifteen. I go directly to bed.

Q: Do you know what those dates signify?

A: I have no idea.

Q: You don't read the papers, is that it?

A: I read the papers. But those dates . . .

Q: Or watch television? You don't watch television?

A: I work from four to midnight. I rarely watch television.

Q: Then you don't know about these Muslim cab drivers who were shot and killed, is that it?

A: I know about them. Is that what those dates are? Is that

when they were killed?

Q: How about Saturday, May third? Does that date hold any particular significance for you?

A: Not any more than the other dates.

Q: Do you know who was killed on that date?

A: No.

Q: Your cousin. Salil Nazir.

A: Yes.

Q: Yes what?

A: Yes. Now I recall that was the date.

Q: Because the detectives spoke to you that morning, isn't that so? In your aunt's apartment? Gulalai Nazir, right? Your aunt? You spoke to the detectives at six that morning, didn't you?

A: I don't remember the exact time, but yes, I spoke to them.

Q: And told them a Jew had killed your cousin, isn't that so?

A: Yes. Because of the blue star.

Q: Oh, is that why?

A: Yes.

Q: And you spoke to Detective Genero and Parker, did you not, after a third Muslim cab driver was killed? This would have been on Monday, May fifth, at around three in the afternoon, when you spoke to them. And at that time you said, correct me if I'm wrong, you said, "Just find the fucking Jew who shot my cousin in the head," is that correct?

A: Yes, I said that. And I've already explained how I knew he was shot in the head. I was there when the imam washed him. I saw the bullet wound . . .

Q: Did you know any of these other cab drivers?

A: No.

Q: Khalid Aslam . . .

A: No.

Q: Ali Al-Barak?

A: No.

Q: Or the one who was killed last night. Abbas Miandad, did you know any of these drivers?

A: I told you no.

Q: So the only one you knew was your cousin, Salim Nazir.

A: Of course I knew my cousin.

Q: And you also knew he was shot in the head.

A: Yes. I told you . . .

Q: Like all the other drivers.

A: I don't know how the other drivers were killed. I didn't see the other drivers.

Q: But you saw your cousin while he was being washed, is that correct?

A: That is correct.

Q: Would you remember the name of the imam who washed him?

A: No, I'm sorry.

Q: Would it have been Ahmed Nur Kabir?

A: It could have. I had never seen him before.

Q: If I told you his name was Ahmed Nur Kabir, and that the name of the mosque where your cousin's body was prepared for burial is Masjid Al-Barbrak, would you accept that?

A: If you say that's where . . .

Q: Yes, I say so.

A: Then, of course, I would accept it.

Q: Would it surprise you to learn that the detectives here—Detectives Carella and Meyer—spoke to the imam at Masjid Al-Barbrak?

A: I would have no way of knowing whether or not they . . .

Q: Will you accept my word that they spoke to him?

A: I would accept it.

Q: They spoke to him and he told them he was alone when he washed your cousin's body, alone when he wrapped the body in its shrouds. There was no one in the room with him. He was alone, Mr. Kiraz.

A: I don't accept that. I was with him.

Q: He says you were waiting outside with your aunt. He says he was alone with the corpse.

A: He's mistaken.

Q: If he was, in fact, alone with your cousin's body . . . ?

A: I told you he's mistaken.

Q: You think he's lying?

A: I don't know what . . .

Q: You think a holy man would lie?

A: *Holy* man! *Please!*

Q: If he was alone with the body, how do you explain seeing a bullet wound at the back of your cousin's head?

Q: Mr. Kiraz?

Q: Mr. Kiraz, how did you know your cousin was shot in the head? None of the newspaper or television reports . . .

Q: Mr. Kiraz? Would you answer my question, please?

Q: Mr. Kiraz?

A: Any man would have done the same thing.

Q: What would any man . . . ?

A: She is not one of his *whores*! She is my *wife*!

I knew, of course, that Salim was seeing a lot of women. That's okay, he was young, he was good-looking, the Koran says a man can take as many as four wives, so long as he can support them emotionally and financially. Salim wasn't even married, so there's nothing wrong with dating a lot of girls, four, five, a dozen, who cares? This is America, Salim was American, we're all Americans, right? You watch television, the bachelor has to choose from *fifteen* girls, isn't that so? This is America. So there was nothing wrong with Salim dating all these girls.

But not my wife.

Not Badria.

I don't know when it started with her. I don't know when it started between them. I know one night I called the supermarket where she works. This was around ten o'clock one night, I was at the pharmacy. I manage a pharmacy, you know. People ask me all sorts of questions about what they should do for various ailments. I'm not a pharmacist, but they ask me questions. I know a lot of doctors. Also, I read a lot. I have time during the day, I don't start work till four in the afternoon. So I read a lot. I wanted to be a teacher, you know.

They told me she had gone home early.

I said, Gone home? Why?

I was alarmed.

Was Badria sick?

The person I spoke to said my wife had a headache. So she went home.

I didn't know what to think.

I immediately called the house. There was no answer. Now I became really worried. Was she seriously ill? Why wasn't she answering the phone? Had she fainted? So I went home, too. I'm the manager, I can go home if I like. This is America. A manager can go home if he likes. I told my assistant I thought my wife might be sick.

I was just approaching my building when I saw them. This was now close to eleven o'clock that night. It was dark, I didn't recognize them at first. I thought it was just a young couple. Another young couple. Only that. Coming up the street together. Arm in arm. Heads close. She turned to kiss him. Lifted her head to his. Offered him her lips. It was Badria. My wife. Kissing Salim. My cousin.

Well, they knew each other, of course. They had met at parties, they had met at family gatherings, this was my *cousin!* "Beware of getting into houses and meeting women," the Prophet said. "But what about the husband's brother?" someone asked, and the Prophet replied, "The husband's brother is like death." He often talked in riddles, the Prophet, it's all such bullshit. The Prophet believed that the influence of an evil eye is *fact.* Fact, mind you. The evil eye. The Prophet believed that he himself had once been put under a spell by a Jew and his daughters. The Prophet believed that the fever associated with plague was due to the intense heat of Hell. The Prophet once said, "Filling the belly of a person with pus is better than stuffing his brain with poetry." Can you believe that? I *read* poetry! I read a lot. The Prophet believed that if you had a bad dream, you should spit three times on your left side. That's what Jews do when they want to take the curse off something, you know, they spit on their fingers, ptui, ptui, ptui. I've seen elderly Jews doing that on the street. It's the same thing, am I right? It's all bullshit, all of it. Jesus turning water into wine, Jesus raising the dead! I mean, come on! Raising the *dead.* Moses parting the Red Sea? I'd love to see that one!

It all goes back to the time of the dinosaurs, when men

huddled in caves in fear of thunder and lightning. It all goes back to Godfearing men arguing violently about which son of Abraham was the true descendant of the one true God, and whether or not Jesus was, in fact, the Messiah. As if a one *true* God, if there *is* a God at all, doesn't know who the hell he himself is! All of them killing each other! Well, it's no different today, is it? It's all about killing each other in the name of God, isn't it?

In the White House, we've got a born-again Christian who doesn't even realize he's fighting a holy war. An angry dry-drunk, as they say, full of hate, thirsting for white wine, and killing Arabs wherever he can find them. And in the sand out there, on their baggy-pantsed knees, we've got a zillion Muslim fanatics, full of hate, bowing to Mecca and vowing to drive the infidel from the Holy Land. Killing each other. All of them killing each other in the name of a one true God.

In my homeland, in my village, the tribal elders would have appointed a council to rape my wife as punishment for her transgression. And then the villagers would have stoned her to death.

But this is America.

I'm an American.

I knew I had to kill Salim, yes, that is what an American male would do, protect his wife, protect the sanctity of his home, kill the intruder. But I also knew I had to get away with it, as they say. I had to kill the violator and still be free to enjoy the pleasures of my wife, my position, I'm the manager of a pharmacy!

I bought the spray paint, two cans, at a hardware store near the pharmacy. I thought that was a good idea, the Star of David. Such symbolism! The six points of the star symbolizing God's rule over the universe in all six directions, north, south, east, west, up and down. Such bullshit! I didn't kill Salim until the second night, to make it seem as if he wasn't the true target, this was merely hate, these were hate crimes. I should have left it at three. Three would have been convincing enough, weren't you convinced after three? Especially with the bombings that followed? Weren't you convinced? But I had to go for four. Insurance. The Navajos think four is a sacred number, you know. Again, it has to do with religion, with the four directions. They're all related, these religions. Jews, Christians, Muslims, they're all related. And they're all the same bullshit.

Salim shouldn't have gone after my wife.

He had enough whores already.

My wife is not a whore.

I did the right thing.

I did the American thing.

They came out through the back door of the station house—a Catholic who hadn't been to church since he was twelve, and a Jew who put up a tree each and every Christmas—and walked to where they'd parked their cars early this morning. It was a lovely bright afternoon. They both turned their faces up to the sun and lingered a moment. They seemed almost reluctant to go home. It was often that way after they cracked a tough one. They wanted to savor it a bit.

"I've got a question," Meyer said.

"Mm?"

"Do you think I'm too sensitive?"

"No. You're not sensitive at all."

"You mean that?"

"I mean it."

"You'll make me cry."

"I just changed my mind."

Meyer burst out laughing.

"I'll tell you one thing," he said. "I'm sure glad this didn't turn out to be what it looked like at first. I'm glad it wasn't hate."

"Maybe it was," Carella said.

They got into their separate cars and drove toward the open gate in the cyclone fence, one car behind the other. Carella honked "Shave-and-a-hair-cut," and Meyer honked back "Two-bits!" As Carella made his turn, he waved so long. Meyer tooted the horn again.

Both men were smiling.

Diamond Dog

Dick Lochte

Dick Lochte, a *Los Angeles Times* columnist and reviewer as well as writer, has published *Laughing Dog, Sleeping Dog,* a short story collection *Lucky Dog and Other Tales of Murder,* and co-authored (with attorney Christopher Darden) several legal thrillers, including *Lawless, The Last Defense,* and *LA Justice.* The Independent Booksellers Association named Lochte's *Sleeping Dog* one of the 100 Favorite Mysteries of the Century. He was also the recipient of the 1985 Nero Wolfe Award and a nominee for the Shamus Award.

The animal shelter described in the opening section of "Diamond Dog" actually exists, which is more than I can say about the mythical town in which I have placed it. A number of years ago, when I became a first-time house owner, I took one look at my new large backyard and decided it was time I had a dog. Marriage and fatherhood were still in the offing. I wanted

a loyal companion, a bodyguard, and, I suppose, the slightly
stabilizing responsibility of having another mouth to feed.

That brought me to a rather remarkable animal shelter
where, as in the story, an array of well-bred homeless dogs
vied for attention. Beau, the giant black Bouvier who plays
a key part in the following fiction, was there. But I didn't
pick him. I signed up for a smaller dog, an eerie-looking toy
collie that seemed more manageable.

Animals were held at the facility for fourteen days,
allowing their owners time to find and reclaim them. During
that period, those wishing to adopt a pet would place their
names on a wait list, timed and dated. On the morning of
their fifteenth day, unclaimed animals became available for
adoption. Interested parties had to be there at eight-thirty
A.M. when the shelter opened. If you were on time and your
name was first on the list, the dog was yours. I was there
that morning, bright and early. My name was first on the list
for the toy collie. Second on the list was a six-year-old girl.
When her father explained to her that I would be getting the
little collie, she started to cry.

"What else have you got?" I asked the attendant. She
took me back to a cage that was almost filled by a huge
black dog I'd seen during my first tour.

"He's house-trained. He's obedient. And he's beautiful,"
she said, opening the cage door. The creature lumbered out.

"That's not a dog," I said. "I don't know what it is. A bear,
maybe, or a Wookie, but it's not a dog."

"Bouviers are wonderful watchdogs," she said, ignoring
my outburst. "Police departments use them in Europe.
They're intelligent and loyal. And, unless someone adopts
him today, we're going to have to put him to sleep."

"You're not serious," I said.

But she was. Large dogs took up too much space and ate too much food, she explained. That's why they were hard to place and why the shelter was unable to provide unlimited care for them. Beau's time was up.

So, due to a couple of circumstances, or possibly con jobs, I wound up with a magnificent, handsome, utterly lovable animal with the body of a bear, the heart of a lion, and the appetite of a Great White shark. He has been such a large part of my life, it's high time he was introduced to Serendipity and Leo.

—DICK LOCHTE

1. Serendipity's Tale

The Bay City Animal Shelter is a one-story, U-shaped, pale orange brick building at the end of a drab little cul-de-sac named, appropriately, Wistful Street. With the Pacific Ocean only two blocks to the west, its four-pawed inmates, discarded, forgotten, or lost, can at least breathe some of the cleanest air in the Greater Los Angeles area. And, Lord knows, the city employees who staff the shelter are caring and knowledgeable and die-hard animal lovers to a woman or man. Still, what else but wistful could the clear little orphaned canines and felines be, knowing that they have only two weeks to attract new owners before facing the big sleep?

This particular shelter houses some of the very finest canines one could hope to own and love. Samoyeds. Weimaraners. Beautiful collies, though I understand they tend to be snippy. I imagine the reason for this abundance of well-bred animals is that Bay City has become a stopping off place for the upwardly mobiles of Southern California. The downwardly mobiles, too, I suppose. Its highways and byways are filled with families leaving the area for loftier haunts like Brentwood or Pacific Palisades or Bay Heights, where my grandmother, the actress Edith Van Dine, and I live. Or they're moving on to less pricey locations like the Hollywood flats or the Valley or the tawdrier sections of Venice.

According to Officer Rina Rose, who handles the records at the shelter, these near-transients often forget their animals or simply leave them behind. How callous! Today's urban jungles are no places for helpless domestic animals. Those that manage to survive turn up at the shelter.

I discovered the house of the lost canines more than three years ago, when I still harbored the adolescent twelve-year-old notion that I would be spending my future in the field of animal husbandry (wifery?). This was before I discovered criminology to be my true vocation. Since then, I have sung the praises of the shelter and been responsible for several happy pairings.

That day in the middle of Spring Break, however, I was on my own errand, skating four miles down Bay Drive from the Heights to Wistful Street. The early morning traffic was surprisingly dense, and I arrived a few minutes late. Lieutenant Rudy Cugat of the Bay City Police Department, trim and dapper as always in a pastel lime suit, was in front of the shelter. He tapped his slightly vulgar gold wristwatch.

"In the wealthy land of the prompt, the tardy cannot raise a dime," he said, as I skated up to him. "Someone was here, demanding possession of the animal. I know the man—a miserable, mean-spirited cur. Claimed to be the dog's owner. But he had no proof. Still, I suspect Officer

Rose would have awarded him the canine, if I had not been here to plead your case."

"Is the man still here?"

"He left. With blood in his eye." The lieutenant seemed to be savoring the memory.

"I wouldn't want to take anyone's dog," I said.

"Believe me, chica, the man is a lying *bas*—a teller of untruths. And he is a lousy writer."

Ah. A writer. That explained the lieutenant's hostility. I well understood writers' temperaments. The great private detective, Mr. Leo Bloodworth, and I had collaborated on two moderately successful books based on our adventures among the criminal element, *Sleeping Dog* and *Laughing Dog*. Not to be outdone, Lieutenant Cugat had written a novel, *Bay City Heat,* a rather fanciful tale about a superhuman police detective obviously modeled on himself. The softcover original had not earned back its obscenely large advance, and the foolhardy publisher had canceled his contract. But an orphaned writer was a writer still.

"Who is this teller of untruths?" I asked.

"Diamond Jack Barker," Lieutenant Cugat said with distaste.

"Oh." I knew the name, of course. How could one not? In a world seemingly filled with obnoxiously aggressive and obsessive self-promoting authors, Diamond Jack Barker was a nonpareil. So excessive were his stunts that the fact that his dark, well-researched true crime stories were rather elegantly written seemed almost beside the point. His last, "*The Rapist,* had been based on events that had occurred in Los Angeles in the late 1980s—the search for, capture, and conviction of a serial rapist. Because the guilty party, who took his own life shortly after the sentencing, had been the son of a former governor of California, the story had been safely buried. Until Diamond Jack Barker unearthed it. That was his forte: digging up things that people hoped would remain hidden. "Still, if the dog is his . . ." I said.

"I have had dealings with Diamond Jack," the lieutenant said. "If it was his dog, he'd have brought the ownership papers, several copies of his latest tome, and a camera crew from *Entertainment Tonight*."

"Then what's he want with the animal?" I asked.

"I don't know and I don't care. The man is scum. Let's get this done, please, chica. The city is festering with criminals in need of my attention."

The lovely Bouvier des Flanders, a large black sheepdog, was waiting for us. He'd just been given a nice bath. He smelled of strawberry soap, and the dark curly hair on his huge frame had the shine of health. "He's a big boy, that's for sure," the lieutenant said as the animal was led from his temporary cage by the cheery Officer Rose. Though short and slight, she seemed to be having no trouble maneuvering the dog.

"Here he is, all seventy-eight pounds of him," she said. "I'm real happy you picked him, Serendipity. We don't always find homes for dogs as large as Bozzetto. They're a little more high-maintenance than the little Benjis."

The lieutenant raised an eyebrow and said to me. "You certain Leo is fine with this?"

I smiled and changed the subject. "Officer Rose, where did the name 'Bozzetto' come from?"

"On his collar," she said. "No address. No phone number. Just 'Bozzetto.' We checked the area directories to see if maybe it was a family name. Not around here, it isn't."

"Are we stuck with it?"

"He responds to it. If you decide to change it, you might want to pick something close. Bozo. Boz."

"Beau?" I asked. The big dog turned my way.

"Looks like that'll do," Officer Rose said.

The paperwork took only a few minutes. Officer Rose was explaining the importance of neutering when Diamond Jack Barker burst into the shelter. I had seen him on various TV talk shows, but he was much scarier in person. His thick black hair was poking out in all directions. His eyes, usually covered by aviator sunglasses, were naked and slightly bulging as they took in the dog, then the lieutenant.

"Okay, Cugat," he said. "A thousand bucks? That buy my dog back?"

"Is he really yours?" I asked.

The true crime writer stared at me as if I'd suddenly beamed down from the USS *Enterprise*. "Yes, he's really mine," he said, mocking me.

"What's his name?"

"Bozzetto, if it's any of your goddamn business." He turned to the lieutenant. "A grand do it, amigo?"

"It's not my dog, Diamond Jack." The lieutenant seemed genuinely amused.

"Damn right, it's not," Mr. Barker said, misunderstanding. "Now you're talking sense." He snapped his fingers, evidently expecting me to hand over the leash.

Instead, I asked, "What do you feed him?"

"Huh? Dog food. What else?"

"What kind of dog food?"

"I don't know. Chow."

"Wet or dry?"

He scowled at me. "I don't have time for this crap, kid. Gimme my dog."

"I don't think it is your dog," I said. "Every owner knows exactly what brand and type of food their animal eats. Who's your vet?"

Mr. Barker's face was crimson. Suddenly, he grabbed the leash, tearing it from my hand.

Just as suddenly, he was on the ground, with the lieutenant's elegantly shod left foot pressed against his chest. "Naughty move, Jack," he said. "Where are all the photographers when you need them?"

"Let me up," the writer yelled.

"I'm going to remove my foot, now, Jack. And you're going to bid us adios."

Mr. Barker got up. He dusted himself off, glaring daggers at the lieutenant. "You blindsided me, Cugat," he said. "Nobody beats Diamond Jack when he's on guard."

"Bye-bye, Jack," the lieutenant said.

"Have your fun. You're going to pay heavily for it."

He slammed the door behind him.

"Wow," Officer Rose said. "Something is definitely eating on that dude. If he was a dog, I'd treat him for worms."

"His bark is worse than his bite," the lieutenant said. "I think."

There was no sign of Mr. Barker outside the shelter. Lieutenant Cugat's thoughts turned to Beau. "Chica, when I agreed to help you convey the animal to Leo's home in my brand-new Lexus, I did not envision quite so large a passenger. I assume he's car-trained?"

"He must be, don't you think?" I said.

*   *   *

Beau, née Bozzetto, behaved himself admirably during the half-hour drive to Mr. Bloodworth's coach house on the far edge of Hollywood. He alternated from sticking his huge handsome head out of the window to feel the breeze, to slumping on the rear seat with his chin on my thigh.

When we arrived, the lieutenant surveyed the street and said, "I don't like leaving you here, chica. This is a high-crime neighborhood."

"I'll be fine," I said. "I've got this big boy for protection. I'm going to take advantage of Mr. Bloodworth's absence to do some tidying up and let Beau get used to his new home. I've ordered a little cake."

"Long as I've known Leo," the lieutenant said, "he's been like the Lone Ranger. Even when he was married. You sure he's gonna like this surprise birthday present?"

I nodded. "He told me he wanted a dog. He said, and I quote: 'You know, Sarah,' and I love it when he uses that diminution of my name, 'you know, Sarah, when a guy gets to be my age, he starts thinking of a pipe and slippers and a dog to bring the morning paper.'"

"You asked him if he wanted a dog and that's what he said?"

"Actually, his comment was in response to my observation that he was a bit overweight and needed an exercise program."

For some reason this seemed to amuse the lieutenant. "What's so funny?" I asked.

"Life," he said.

He watched me retrieve the front door key from under the plaster statue of Curly Stooge that Mr. Bloodworth used to decorate his overgrown garden. "Alas, chica, I must go. You can get home okay?"

"Gran isn't expecting me until dinner. If Mr. B. comes here right after work, he'll drive me home. If not, I'll take a cab. But I do hope I'm still here where he arrives. I want to see his face when he gets his first look at Beau."

"I wish I could see that myself," the lieutenant said.

2. Leo's Tale

Birthdays! Who the hell needs 'em?

I celebrated my latest at The Horse's Neck, a sports bar I save for those special occasions—income tax day, Christmas Eve, the anniversary of my getting booted out of the LAPD, and my birthday. Morning found me on the couch in my living room, dressed in my suit and tie. And shoes. If I'd been living on the East Coast and it'd been winter, I'd still be wearing a hat and topcoat and muffler.

It was not quite dawn. Chilly. I was in that awful in-between state—still a little drunk but hurting from the hangover. And there was a big black dog pissing on my living room throw rug.

At the sound of my groan, the dog finished up his business and trotted over to give me an eyeball-to-eyeball inspection. He was a goddamn giant, with hunks of pink and white stuck to his black beard. He opened his mouth, showing me a set of choppers that looked like a beat trap with gums and giving me a whiff of something vaguely liverish. I probably didn't smell so sweet myself at the moment, but I wasn't thinking about that. I was too busy trying to figure out how I could be having a nightmare with my eyes open.

The animal wasn't really threatening. I think he was trying to be friendly. He unfurled a tongue the size of a triple kielbasa, and before he could slap it against my cheek stubble, I rolled upright and shoved off the sofa.

My stomach flipped over and I realized that, with all the fun I'd been having listening to the depressed Russian bartender at the Neck describe the suicide rate in the Ukraine, I'd forgotten to take my Achiphex. Which meant I was not only drunk and hungover, I was having an attack of acid reflux. Staggering around the bemused dog on my way to the bathroom, I noticed there was a red ribbon hooked to its collar. Later for that. Later, too, for the remains of something that was probably a birthday cake on the freshly gouged and icing-smeared dining room table.

When I finally was able to begin gargling away some of the residue of another misspent night, I spied, reflected in the mirror above the washbasin, the big dog standing in the bathroom doorway looking at me with what I took to be disdain.

"Yeah, well, at least I don't have birthday cake all over my chin," I told him.

I wasn't the least bit curious about what he was doing in my house. The ribbon gave it away. I'm a detective.

I was hanging the urine-soaked throw rug on the back fence, preparing to spray it down with the hose, when the phone rang. Sighing, I walked past the dog into the house. The dog followed. I picked up the kitchen extension and said, "Hi, kid."

"How'd you know it was me?"

"Lucky guess. Look, about the dog . . ."

"His name is Beau. But that's not why I'm calling."

"Maybe not, but—"

"It's on the news. Lieutenant Cugat is in custody," she said. "They think he murdered Diamond Jack Barker."

"Well," I said, "it's high time somebody did."

They were holding Cugie without bail at the Beverly Hills lockup before shipping him downtown to Bauchet Street. He wasn't looking so hot. The guy prided himself on his appearance, but he didn't seem to care that he needed a shave, and his suit looked worse than mine.

"You up on this?" he asked me.

"Sarah told me about the scene at the animal house and Jamie just gave me the rundown on why they picked you up." The homicide detective in charge of the investigation, Jamie Hernandez, was an old pal of Cugie's and mine. He'd explained that Barker had called a press conference yesterday afternoon in which he charged Cugie with unprovoked assault and battery. It was a nuisance claim, but a nasty one that would tie up my buddy in legal and official police red tape for a while. Then, last night at approximately nine o'clock, Cugie showed up at Barker's condo on Charleville Street in Bev Hills. According to the doorman on duty, he looked drunk, an observation he made to Barker. Regardless, the writer told him to send Cugie back. The doorman did not see my buddy leave. Barker's corpse was discovered at nine in the morning with a letter opener stuck in its neck.

"Jack and I had our talk and I left through his garden out back," Cugie told me.

"Why not go out the front?"

"That was his idea. He said he'd sleep better if I snuck out the back."

"Sleep better why?"

Cugat shrugged. "Who the hell knows? Probably didn't want his neighbors to see a drunk greaser leaving his place. Hound, you know I didn't kill the *cabron,* right?"

"I know you sure wouldn't have used a letter opener with your Police Special on your hip. What the hell were you doing there, anyway?"

"I had a couple Cuba Libras and decided to explain to the man the serious mistake he made with those charges. See, two can play that game. We cut this deal a few years ago."

"What kind of deal?"

"I helped him write his 'masterwork,' *The Rapist.*"

"Yeah?"

"I dug out all those hidden records of the case. He thanked me in his introduction. Didn't you read the book?"

"I get enough true crime every time I leave the house," I told him. "I don't go paying for it in bookstores. Especially not to make a weasel like Diamond Jack Barker a millionaire. How much did he pay you?"

"Twenty-five large," Cugie said.

"Not bad."

"For all I did?" he said with indignation. "He promised I would be the coauthor. My name was supposed to be on the cover, not on the acknowledgment page. It's in the deal memo, all signed and sealed."

"You shoulda sued him."

"I threatened. That's how I got the twenty-five grand. I let it go at that, but then the *pendejo* accused me of assaulting him. I went to his place to wave that deal memo under his litigious nose. He messes with my rep, I'll mess with his."

"And?"

"He agreed to withdraw his complaint. He sure wasn't happy about it, though."

"You guys do a little shouting?" I asked. "Something the neighbors might mention in court?"

Cugie gave me a sheepish look. "Maybe. I, ah, even made

a move to slug the son of a bitch. But he pulled a gun on
me. A little K3."

"He was carrying?"

"Had it on his desk." Cugie frowned. "I guess that
doorman's warning about me made him nervous."

"Going there wasn't such a great idea, amigo."

"Really? I was wondering about that."

"He didn't happen to mention what he wanted with the
big dog?" I asked.

"No. He offered me another thousand bucks to get it for
him, though."

"We could have split the loot," I said. "The dog's more
trouble than my last wife."

"Forget about the dog, huh, Leo. Find out who killed the
lowlife son of a bitch and get me out of this mess."

"Your brothers in blue should be helping. . . ."

"They've got their man, and that's that. I been a cop long
enough to know how it works. All the effort from here on
will be to build the case against me. Jamie's a pal, but he
has to walk the line. You don't."

I stood up and signaled for the guard that I was through.
"Jamie's feeling guilty enough he's promised to open a few
doors," I said. "I'll see what I can do."

Serendipity was at my place, cleaning up the dog's assorted
messes. When I'd finished filling her in on Cugie, we went
into the backyard, where the King Kong of dogs was
chasing butterflies. "Beau's definitely special," she said.

"I guess he is," I said. "He's not housebroken. He'll eat
your shoes if you don't keep 'em on your feet. And, in an
indirect way, he's responsible for Cugie being in the slams.
Definitely special."

"You don't like him," she said, her face falling.

"I didn't say that. He just takes some getting used to." I looked at the big monster obeying nature on the crab grass. "You think I can just leave him out here during the day?" I asked.

"He's fenced in," she said. "He should be fine. Just make sure he has water and food."

"I wouldn't want him to get out and bite anybody." I was thinking primarily of the Vietnamese gangstas squatting in an empty house two lots over.

"He's a beautiful animal, Mr. B. But if you don't like him . . ."

"Stop saying that. I like him. I like him. I just don't . . . no, I like him."

She smiled. I couldn't remember exactly when her smiles had started meaning so much to me.

"How do you plan on helping poor Lieutenant Cugat?"

"Detective Hernandez has agreed to let me take a look at the crime scene."

"When?"

"Around five. He's tied up till then."

"Five. That works for me," she said.

The Prince Charles on Charleville Street was a three-story building with a fishbowl front and a revolving team of uniformed doormen who kept tabs on anyone who entered or exited. The elderly evening doorman paused in his contemplation of the ugly metal sculpture in the center of the lobby to tell us he'd just come on duty and wasn't sure if Hernandez was in the house. He was tall, a little bit more than my six-two, with white sideburns showing under his officer's cap and a matching white moustache and beard combo. In his dark blue uniform with gold piping and epaulets, there was something naggingly familiar about him. That was par for the course in Southern California, where the guy selling you auto parts probably had his own cowboy series in the Sixties.

The doorman, who I suppose could have been an ex-cowboy star, too, dialed Barker's number. After listening for a while, he said, "I'll give it a few more rings, in case Detective Hernandez is on the patio."

"It's okay," I told him. "He said he might be running late. We'll take a stroll while we wait."

Serendipity and I went on a tour of the outside of The Prince Charles. "It's always a good idea to get the lay of the land," I told her. "Unless Cugie turned psycho in the last twenty-four hours, somebody paid a call on Barker after he left without the doorman or anybody else seeing him. The question is, how."

The building occupied a corner of the block. To its left was a small enclosed garage for the condo dwellers. It required an electronic key to enter. As far as I could tell from the sidewalk, the garage was a separate structure from the main building. The only connection was a leaf-green canvas awning that began at an exit door near the garage entrance and fed into the matching awning in front of The Prince Charles.

Halfway along the right side of the building, the one exposed to the sidewalk and the street, there was a bolted fire door that someone could have used to exit. But there was no knob or handle, so no one could have entered through it without the help of a party inside the building. At the rear, a ten-foot wall topped with spikes separated the building from an alley wide enough for automobile access. The wall was broken by four metal doors behind which, I assumed, were the patios of the garden apartments. Barker had died in the one on the northwest corner.

"It's not likely anyone hopped over that wall," Sarah said as we stood near Barker's back door. She kicked the door with her flat-toed shoe. It responded with a deep solid gong and didn't budge. "Pretty formidable."

There was a wad of paper flattened on the asphalt by the day's traffic. I cracked my knees to give it a closer gander and then rose with a grunt. "Okay. Let's go see if Hernandez made it."

The elderly doorman was under fire when we got there. A woman his own age was on him like a rabid dog. "Your apology means nothing to me, Anthony," she said, her wrinkled face crimson, her deep blue eyes flashing. "I don't trust the streets at night, which is why I'm living in a building that has a doorman. I don't want my daughter and granddaughter to have to leave here when it's dark without someone watching their progress to their car."

"I really am sorry, Miz Palmer." The doorman looked like he was about to bend in two. Hearing the name "Palmer," I realized the old lady was Hildy Palmer, who'd won an Academy Award for a movie she made with Brando back in the Fifties. God, she'd been beautiful then. Now she was just another over-pampered ill-tempered old lady.

"Sorry doesn't cut it, you son of a bitch," she said. "I'm paying for security and I expect to get it."

She pivoted on her Joan and Davids and strode toward the thick glass inner door, seething. She stayed there, a foot from the door, facing forward, waiting for the doorman to unlock it. When he did, with the key attached to his belt, she marched angrily into the building.

"There goes the Christmas present, huh, Anthony?" I said.

"I was just away from my post for a minute," he said. He looked sheepish. "A fella my age, nature calls. Miz Palmer can be rather demanding. And the name is Tony, sir. Tony Prima. I never much cared for Anthony."

"Okay, Tony. Detective Hernandez show up yet?"

"Yes, sir," he held the inner door open. "He said to just send you back. Suite One-D."

"Your 'nature call'?" Serendipity asked, "Was that last night?"

"Every night, ma'am," he said with a faint smile. "Even when I don't drink coffee."

"Did you mention it to Detective Hernandez?" she asked.

"Not to him, but to the officer who questioned me."

Detective Jamie Hernandez, small, wiry, and dark, met us at the door to suite 1-D. He seemed a little nervous and wasn't at all pleased that I'd brought Sarah. Watching her move past us to enter the study where Diamond Jack met his fate, Jamie said, "It's a crime scene, Hound. Not the Universal City Tour."

"She's a natural at this detective business, Jamie. Comes up with good stuff. She just found out that the doorman was away from his post last night."

"That's in the report," Jamie said, a little defensively. "Ten minutes to take a leak, at approximately ten-fifteen. The thing is, you still need a key to get through the inner door."

I followed him into the murder room. It was the sort of den you'd expect a bestselling writer to have. Books lined one wall. TV set and other electronic garbage along the other. There was a soft oxblood-colored leather couch, several stuffed chairs, and an antique desk of dark wood with gold accents. It and one of those chairs for people with back problems were facing away from French doors leading to the patio.

A dark-brown carpet covered the floor. It looked like it might have been nice and plush yesterday. Now it was splotched with powders and chemicals from the lab. White marking tape had been laid down, outlining the position of the absent corpse, head about two feet from the bookshelf. For some reason, there was a second outline, a rectangle approximately eight inches by ten inches beside the body.

"Here's the deal," Hernandez said, keeping an eye on Sarah as she poked around the room. "Accordin' to the door guys, there was on'y four people to visit Barker yesterday. Cugat was the last in. At," he consulted a sheet of paper, "nine-oh-five in the pee-em. Barker was alive when Cugie went in; the door guy talked to him. Medical examiner says death occurred sometime between then and eleven."

Sarah had been looking at a paperback edition of *The Rapist* that had been resting on Barker's desk beside a laptop computer. She replaced it and asked, "Anything missing, that you know of, detective?"

Hernandez hesitated as if he were wondering if he should bother to answer her question. Finally, he said, "Doesn't seem to be. But we haven't given the people who worked for him the chance to make sure."

She pointed to several reddish-brown drops marring the glass desktop. "Was there a lot of blood?"

"You see it," Jamie said. "The real damage was internal. He died fast, the medical examiner says. Weapon was a silver letter opener usually on the desk, next to the wooden in-out baskets."

"Did you find a gun, a little K3?"

"Yeah. In his desk drawer. The guy had handguns all over the place. Purchased and registered a couple weeks ago. They sure did him a lot of good."

"What's with the second outline on the carpet?" I asked.

"That's where the book was," Hernandez said. "The one that made him famous. *The Rapist.*"

"Is the size of the outline accurate?" Sarah asked.

"They know what they're doing," Jamie said, a defensive edge to his voice.

"So how do you figure it went down?" I asked.

"Following the blood trail, it looks like he got stuck over there," Jamie said, pointing at the desk. He indicated the splotchy rug. "More blood drops form a line over to the book-case. We figure he grabbed the book just before he passed."

"Then the book is pretty important," Sarah said.

"A dying man stumbles across the room for it. Yeah, 'important' fits," Jamie said.

"It was a hardcover?"

"Uh-huh. If you notice the shelf, all the books are hard-covers. On that top shelf are the ones he wrote, several copies of each. The others look like research. L.A. history. Organized crime. Books on poisoners, stranglers. Like that."

Sarah went to the shelf and took down one of the other copies of *The Rapist.*

"First printing," she said. "Doesn't look like it's been opened before."

"Any idea what Barker had in mind when he grabbed the book?" I asked.

Jamie looked glum. "Cugat's name is in it. It's part of the evidence against him."

"They're through dusting and everything, aren't they?" Sarah asked.

"Yeah, but don't go . . ."

Too late. She'd nipped open the black leather appointment book on Barker's desk. "This says that two people were supposed to meet with Mr. Barker yesterday," she said. "At three-thirty, someone named Tina. At six, Doctor L. *The Rapist* is dedicated to Tina."

"Who's she?" I asked Jamie.

"The stiff's sister," Hernandez answered. "Tina Barker. Late twenties. Unmarried. Not much family resemblance, lucky for her. Kinda hot, if you like neurotics. She was his editorial assistant. Bottom of the suspect list. They seemed to get along. No apparent motive. Doctor L. is Doctor Louisa Lemay, a shrink Barker wanted to help him with his next book. Claims she barely knew the guy. Says she left him at six-thirty and that jibes with the doorman's memory."

"Anybody else here yesterday?" I asked, walking to the French doors that led to the patio.

"Young guy named Stephen Page. He's not on the calendar because he worked for Barker. A gofer. Did the computer stuff, answered the phone, ran errands. Like that. It was he who found the body this morning."

"He have a key?" Sarah asked.

"No. The sister says nobody did except Barker."

"The gofer mentioned in *The Rapist,* too?" I asked.

"Not in the front, which is about as far as I got."

"But his name *is* Page," Sarah said.

"Yeah." Jamie almost smiled. "That's good. But he's not our guy. He's a wimpy college punk. All shook up, like Elvis. Worked here mornings only. Part of an intern program at his school. Three other people saw Barker alive after Page went home yesterday. And as the old guy at the door is gonna testify, Cugat was the last he opened up for."

"Maybe another occupant let in the killer while the doorman was relieving himself," Sarah said. "Or maybe a neighbor did the actual killing."

Jamie looked at me and rolled his eyes. "First thing we did was talk to the other people in the building, the ones who were home last night. This is a high-end condo, Hound. One-bedrooms start at half a mil. Before the murder, this suite might have been worth as much as one point five mil. Notoriety plays hell with this kinda real estate. These folks would think twice before murdering their next-door neighbor."

"Even people who care about property values wind up committing crimes of passion," Sarah said. I wondered if she was trying to needle him.

"Where's the passion here, kid?"

"The killer used a weapon at hand, the dead man's own letter opener. That doesn't seem to suggest premeditation."

"Unless the killer had been here before and knew about the letter opener," Jamie said.

I was siding with him on that one. I pointed to the French doors. "Barker keep those locked or open?"

"Closed and locked," Jamie said, "except for the half-hour he spent sunning himself everyday."

"Any prints on 'em?"

He sighed. "Our pal's. Otherwise clean."

"If Cugie had just killed Barker, you'd have thought he'd have been more careful," I said. I opened the doors to the evening smog and a well-cared-for patio and garden. There was a chaise longue covered by a beach towel decorated with a drawing of the cover of *The Rapist.* Beside the chaise was a wrought iron table with a spotless ashtray, sunglasses, and a day-glo bottle of tanning lotion.

Beyond the brick patio, near the rear wall, camellia bushes were in full bloom, their white and pink blossoms looking moist and healthy. On the brick walkway, just past the French doors, I spotted a wad of paper and bent over to look at it.

"That's like the one in the alley," Sarah said.

Before I could stop him, Jamie picked up the wad and unfolded it. "Just a hunk of white paper," he said.

"Could loosen up the case against Cugie," I said.

"How do you figure?"

"Fold it up like it was and see if it fits in the door slot opposite the latch bolt."

Hernandez obeyed. The wad fit neatly into the recess in the striker plate along the frame. When he swung the door shut, the paper stopped the latch bolt from connecting.

"There's another wad in the alley near the patio door," I said. "Any of Barker's previous visitors could have fixed it for a homicidal return without the doorman being any the wiser. So much for Cugie being the last person to see the dead man."

Hernandez nodded. "Not bad," he said. "Except that opens things up too much. Who's to say the doors weren't fixed two days ago? Or four?"

"That doesn't seem likely," Sarah said. "If Mr. Barker or anybody used the doors, they'd know right away that they didn't click shut. He sunned himself every day and the bushes look moist enough to have been watered very recently."

"The go-for, Page, says that Barker liked 'em wet down first thing every morning," Jamie said, nodding. "So I guess we're back to the people who were here yesterday. Cugat included, of course, only now he's got company."

As we reentered the apartment, Jamie looked at his watch. "Hell, I'm on golden time," he said. "I'm gonna invite the possibles down to Parker Center tomorrow to chew the fat a little more."

"Any way you can fix it for us to listen in?" I asked.

"You, maybe." He shifted his glance to Sarah and shrugged. "What the hell. You, too, I guess. Gimme a call in the ay-em, Hound, and I'll tell you when exactly."

Leaving The Prince Charles, Serendipity seemed distracted, but snapped out of her funk long enough to return the doorman's wave as we drove away. "Isn't one of your favorite singers named Tony Prima?" she asked.

"Louie," I told her. "Louie Prima."

"Oh," she said.

While she slipped back into her thoughts, I dug out a cassette and popped it into the player. Backed by the incomparable Sam Butera and the Witnesses, Prima and Keely Smith swung their way through "Just A Gigolo," "That Old Black Magic," and "Embraceable You" and were well into a stirring rendition of "Jump Jive An' Wail," when we arrived at the apartment Sarah shared with her grandma.

She didn't seem at all moved by the music. She thanked me for the lift, reminded me to pick up some flea powder for the dog, and said she would be ready and waiting the next morning by nine o'clock.

"I know you, kid," I said as she was getting out of the car. "Something's on your mind?"

"I just want to do a little cruising along the Information Highway, Mr. B. To check out an idea."

I waited until she'd entered her building, then burned rubber away from there. There was an idea I wanted to check out, too.

3. Serendipity's Tale

It was the Beau-Barker connection that was so puzzling.

As soon as Gran wandered off to bed—she retires early on the nights before the taping of her soap—I gathered the dinner dishes and placed them in the washer. Then I settled down in front of the PC for a workout with my favorite Internet search engine, Copernic.

That kept me up later than usual, which, I suppose, is why I had trouble waking up the next morning. Then Mr. Bloodworth called, doing the job better than any alarm clock. Detective Hernandez had scheduled a ten o'clock meeting with the suspects at Parker Center. Could I be ready in twenty minutes? Could I not?

The big sleuth was strangely quiet on the drive downtown. Quiet but grinning like the Cheshire Cat. Odd.

We shared the elevator to the fourth floor with a pixieish, shaggy-haired blonde in black leather who turned out to be Tina Barker, the dead man's sister. Detective Hernandez and his partner, Detective Marcella Schott, a black woman, walked us to an interrogation room down a hall past the robbery-homicide bullpen.

I had seen the room once before. Then it had had just three chairs and a table. There were eight chairs that morning. No sooner had we occupied five of them, than another detective walked Lieutenant Cugat in and handed him over to Detective Schott, who purposely placed her chair between him and the door. The poor man didn't look like he could make a break for it, even if he were so inclined. He was depressed and pasty and unkempt. He moved as if his body had sprung a leak and all energy and confidence had drained away.

"Any hopeful news, Hound?" he asked Mr. Bloodworth.

"Hang in there, partner," Mr. B. replied. He was still grinning. Definitely up to something.

Detective Hernandez ducked out of the room and came back a few minutes later with the corpse's former part-time assistant, Stephen Page. The boy was as nervous as we'd been told. He was also making little gulping noises and, from time to time, clutching his stomach.

The final suspect, Dr. Louisa Lemay, was last to arrive, but even she made it before ten. She was a tall, full-bodied woman with a generous mouth and shoulder-length, slightly curled brown hair. I've often wondered what it would be like to be a brunette. They invariably seem more intelligent and serious than blondes, and Dr. Lemay was no exception. She wore a sedate skirt and jacket combination and no-nonsense glasses with tortoise-shell frames that drew attention to her lovely green eyes.

She stared intently at Detective Hernandez while he informed them that, since his initial chats with each of them had been one-on-ones, he thought he'd make it a group discussion today. "But before I begin," he said, extending his hand in Mr. B.'s direction, "I've agreed to let Mister Leo Bloodworth ask a few questions."

This was a surprise. I wondered what Mr. B. could possibly have told the detective to convince him to make such a break from police protocol. I hoped it didn't mean Mr.

Bloodworth had leaped to the wrong conclusion about the book on Mr. Barker's floor and sold his assumption to Detective Hernandez. But as soon as he turned to Dr. Lemay, my heart sank.

"Doctor, you were working with Mr. Barker on his next book, right?"

"As I informed an officer yesterday, I met with him two days ago to discuss the possibility of my working with him," she said, speaking in a precise manner, with just a hint of a Southern accent. "Mr. Barker showed me a good-sized green box filled with clippings, notes, and audio tapes that he said pertained to an unresolved crime, a very famous—I suppose I should say infamous—one. Some of the material—he held up one of the tapes—contained information that he felt would provide evidence of a psychological nature. He needed an analyst's evaluation. It was an intriguing idea and I agreed to assist him."

"Which infamous unresolved crime are we talking about?"

"He . . . wouldn't tell me. He said that he feared it might prejudice my analysis. I assured him of my professionalism, but he remained adamant."

"Jack could be a real bug on secrecy," Tina Barker said.

"The police didn't find any green box," Mr. Bloodworth said. "Maybe that's because—"

"Did anyone else see the box?" I asked. I wasn't supposed to participate in any way, but I felt I had to do what I could to stop Mr. B. from making a serious mistake.

"S-s-sure. I've s-s-seen it," Stephen Page said. "It's b-b-been on his desk for the last couple of weeks."

"When my brother gets down to the nits and grits of a project, he puts the blinders on," Tina Barker added. "Lately, he's been in and out of that box constantly."

Mr. Bloodworth looked perplexed.

"Does anyone know which unsolved crime Mr. Barker was researching?" I asked, risking Detective Hernandez's ire.

"All my brother would say about it was that this incredible murder story had been laid on his doorstep. He was at the stage when he wouldn't dare even give a clue about the subject matter. There are so few really good stories that haven't been done to death and so many true crime writers out there sniffing around."

"We're getting off track here," Mr. Bloodworth said. "Let's take a look at what really went down the day of the murder."

Don't do this, I begged silently. Please don't.

"We know for a fact that it was one of you who decided Diamond Jack Barker needed killing," he said.

They gawked at him, registering an array of emotions— from incredulity (Dr. Lemay) to fear (Stephen Page). "Leaving motive aside for the moment, the main problem was accessibility," Mr. B. went on recklessly. "How do you dodge the doorman to get in to do the job? Well, you have to find another way."

Filled with confidence and, I'm sorry to report, displaying no small degree of smugness, he explained his theory about the killer sticking paper wads in the rear doors to keep them unlocked for re-entry.

"But, Hound," Lieutenant Cugat said, "Barker was still kicking when I left through the back. And I could swear I heard those door locks click behind me."

Then Stephen Page let even more wind out of Mr. B's

sails. "Uh, those p-p-paper wads, they were mine," he said. "Mr. B-B-Barker liked me to water the p-p-plants in the morning and take out the trash. The study doors tend to swing open if they're not l-l-locked, and he wanted 'em shut, especially when the air conditioner was on. B-B-But he didn't want to keep getting up to unlock them for me. The alley door is self-locking and if I wasn't careful, I'd wind up having to walk around to the front of the b-b-building. So I just p-p-plugged the locks. I unp-p-p-plugged 'em, soon as I was finished with the p-p-plants."

The two police detectives exchanged glances and Detective Hernandez said, "Ah, Leo, maybe we should—"

But Mr. Bloodworth was not to be denied. "Okay, let's sideline the accessibility problem for the moment and move on to the clue to the killer that Barker left with his last strength. The medical examiner tells us that he must've died quickly. The killer had to have been there in the den to see him struggle to get to the shelf and grab his book. If the killer had thought the book to be in any way incriminating, it would have wound up back on the shelf, right?"

Tina Barker and Stephen Page nodded.

"So we can assume the killer was not someone connected to the book. That immediately eliminates Lieutenant Cugat and Tina Barker, both of whom were mentioned in the dedication and acknowledgment." It was good to see the light of hope return to the lieutenant's eyes, even temporarily. "It also eliminates Stephen Page," Mr. Bloodworth continued, "since his name has an obvious connection to any book."

"But, Hound," Lieutenant Cugat said, "if the book doesn't point to the murderer, why did Barker bother to grab it?"

"It points to the murderer, all right," Mr. Bloodworth said. "It points to Dr. Lemay, who was probably going to be the subject of Barker's next expose. Well, doctor, what nasty secret of yours did Barker uncover?"

The doctor's jaw dropped and she stared at Mr. B. in abject amazement.

"I still don't get what the book says about Dr. Lemay," Lieutenant Cugat said.

"Neither did Dr. Lemay," Mr. Bloodworth said with insufferable pride. "When she saw *The Rapist* lying on the floor beside the man she'd just murdered, she didn't realize what its title would spell if the two words ran together."

"Therapist," Lieutenant Cugat said, catching Mr. B.'s grin.

Dr. Lemay wasn't grinning. She'd risen to her feet, anger robbing her face of its natural beauty. "This is absurd," she said, heading for the door.

Detective Schott stood to intercept her, but she clearly wasn't certain she should.

Dr. Lemay said to her in a quiet fury, "If you are not out of my way in ten seconds, I shall notify my lawyer to sue you, your associate, the LAPD, the county of Los Angeles, and especially that fat buffoon who has just defamed me by accusing me of murder on the strength of a book title. By God, I'd love to hear what a jury would say about that evidence."

Detective Schott looked to her partner for guidance and got it in the form of a quick nod. She stepped aside, allowing the furious therapist to storm away.

Those remaining seemed thoroughly perplexed.

Mr. Bloodworth, to his credit, saw some humor in the situation. "Gee, that worked well," he said.

Detective Schott escorted Lieutenant Cugat back to the Bauchet Street lockup. Detective Hernandez told Tina Barker and Stephen Page that he was sorry he'd called them in for nothing and thanked them for their cooperation. He left to walk them to the elevator, then stuck his head back in to tell us to stay where we were. He did not look happy.

Alone with Mr. B. in the interrogation room, I said, "You were right about the book being a clue."

"No kidding," he said. "The doc killed him."

"No. You were wrong about that."

"What are you talking about? 'The Rapist.' 'Therapist.' It's gotta be."

"Think back to Mr. Barker's den," I said. "What was on his desk?"

"The usual junk. A lamp. A laptop. Phone." Then he said, "Oh, yeah," evidently remembering the paperback edition of *The Rapist.*

"He was stabbed near the desk," I said. "If it was the book's title that was so important, he could have just picked up the paperback. He didn't have to go across the room. He wanted the hardcover edition."

"Okay. What does that tell us?"

"The murderer," I said. "I mean, there's some other stuff you have to know, too, but that and what Tina Barker said just a while ago should tell you who it is."

"Never mind the games," he said. "Let's hear it."

"Well, to begin, it's not just one murder, it's more."

"How many more?"

"Thirty maybe."

I wasn't trying to shock him, but I evidently did. He

seemed to pale. "I know you catch stuff I overlook," he said. "But thirty murders."

"There's no way you could know about that part of it," I said. "Unless, like me, you were curious about why Mr. Barker was so interested in Beau. I did tell you that his given name was 'Bozzetto,' did I not?"

"Uh-huh."

"Well, I had two questions. Who was Beau's previous owner? And why was the beautiful dog set free? To find out the first answer, I fed 'Bozzetto' into my search engine and came up with an Italian cartoon animator and a French snowboard champion. I doubted Beau's owner had either of them in mind when naming the animal. 'Bozzetto' also turns out to be an art term, referring to a model that a sculptor might use in constructing a large work. This seemed a more likely possibility.

"As for question two, all the talk of murder made me think that Beau's owner might have experienced something bad around the time he wound up on his own. I checked the Web site www.socalcrimenews.com, which lists all major crimes in this area by date, and discovered that a sculptress had been brutally murdered in her home on the Venice canal on the same day that the Bay City police spotted Beau dodging traffic and brought him to the shelter.

"Bouviers are notoriously protective of their owners. My guess is Beau chased the murderer's vehicle and wound up lost."

"This is all interesting stuff, kid. But what ties it to Barker?"

"The murdered sculptress was named Jenny Sargon. She was sixty-eight. I'd never heard of her before, but maybe you did?"

"I don't think so. But I'm not really into sculpture."

"Not even the Seaside Sculptor?" I asked.

"Yeeeaaahhhh," Mr. Bloodworth said, drawing the word out thoughtfully. "That was about thirty years ago, but it's not something you forget. Stanley . . . no, Sidney Furst. He was world famous. Became a multimillionaire forging realistic-looking bronze statues of people and animals. The Brentwood and Holmby Hills crowd coughed up the big bucks to have a Furst for their front lawn. A couple on a bench. A postman carrying a letter up the walk."

"Then came the San Fernando Earthquake in 1971," I said. "Seven point six. One of the Furst statues cracked. . . ."

"And there was a corpse inside. Furst was exposed as a nut case who'd been bronzing human beings in his foundry. They went after Furst, but he was in the wind. Thirty of 'em, huh? As I recall, they were homeless, most of 'em."

"Except for Harry Ambrose," I said, the Internet being my source.

"Right. 'Hurlin' Harry,' " he said. "Heisman Trophy–winner. Superstar. Pride of the Raiders. Got stoned one night with his pals and wound up a lawn jockey in Pasadena. People went nuts after they peeled the bronze off Harry. It was one thing to kill homeless people, even in those numbers, but it was a different deal with Harry. He was well-loved, and his killer was still out there some-where. Pressure was applied. Heads rolled on the force. But they never found Sidney Furst."

"He left a fiancée behind," I said. "She claimed to know nothing of his crimes or his whereabouts. After a while, they left her alone. Like Mr. Furst, she was an artist and a sculptor. Her name was Jenny Sargon."

Mr. Bloodworth brightened. "I get it. She was helping Barker write a book about Furst. And Furst killed 'em both."

"Looks like," I said. "That's probably what Mr. Barker was trying to tell us when he grabbed the hardcover edition of his book. The 'first' edition. Or maybe he was trying to get a true-crime book about Furst from the shelf below and made a mistake."

"In either case, Furst is the guy. And I bet you know where he is, right?" he asked.

"No, I don't," I told him. Then I smiled. "But I know where he will be at five o'clock."

4. Leo's Tale

We pulled up to The Prince Charles apartments a little after five. Jamie and Detective Schott were in their unmarked police car behind us. I could see old Tony Prima, at his post in full uniform. The big dog could see him, too, I guess. He started throwing himself against the door of my sedan. I wasn't sure the door would hold.

"Looks like you were right, kid. The monster recognizes Prima."

"Beau," she said. She was seated on the backseat beside the dog, holding his thick leather leash. "The dog's name is Beau and he's not the monster. Prima is."

"Point well taken," I said. I was proud of her, proud of the way she'd knocked Jamie off his high horse. When he'd returned from bowing and scraping to Barker's sister and the go-for, he just wanted to vent. That's why he'd kept us, to have somebody to shout at. He wasn't interested in anything we had to say. I was ready to blow but Sarah stayed cool as a cumquat. Ignoring his insults, she told him her theory linking the Jenny Sargon murder to the Barker killing.

His eyes started to light up when she dropped Furst into the mix. The idea of catching the infamous Seaside Sculptor was so appealing, he started acting like a lap dog while she piled on the circumstantial evidence. The "first" edition. The name "Prima," Italian for "first." The doorman's absence from his post around the time of the murder. The murder of Jenny Sargon taking place in the early morning, an odd time unless the killer was just getting off a night shift. And there was the comment from Tina Barker that her brother had said his next book idea had been dropped on his doorstep.

Hernandez had been so impressed, he'd even gone along with the kid's plan to use the dog. "It's what Mr. Barker was going to do," she said. "If Beau recognizes Mr. Prima, that tells us something. If Mr. Prima recognizes Beau, and makes a run for it, that'll tell us even more."

The animal in question definitely recognized Prima. And he wasn't glad to see him, "You gonna be able to hold back Beau?" I asked Sarah. "We just want Prima scared, not eaten."

"I think so," she said.

Actually, the point was moot. As soon as Prima spied us heading for the front door with the growling animal, he made a beeline into the building. His keys would open all locks, but as the kid and I had learned, there were only five other exits. Sarah stayed at the car with the dog. Detective Schott took the side fire door, gun in hand. Jamie and I ran to the alley, scanning the four garden exits.

Prima pushed through the rear door next to Barker's. Age didn't do him any favors in the quick-getaway department. Jamie had him on the ground and in cuffs in jig time.

As they carted him off, I heard him ask Jamie if there was a good fine arts program at Pelican Bay Prison.

Sarah and I were waiting when they turned Cugie loose an hour or so later.

On the drive to his house, he took the passenger seat and Sarah shared the back with Beau. He listened quietly while we gave him a rundown on the events of the evening. Then he took a minute or so to digest it all. "Jack was an idiot," he said finally. "He should have gone to the police as soon as he began to suspect that his doorman was Sidney Furst."

"Mr. Furst had been working at The Prince Charles for nearly seven years without bothering a soul that we know of," Sarah said. "I guess Mr. Barker figured he wasn't a threat."

"But Jenny Sargon's murder must have wised him up. It meant Furst knew he was planning an exposé. He had to be next on the guy's People To Kill list. Hell, Furst even had a key to his apartment."

It was a point both Hernandez and I had raised earlier. Sarah gave Cugie the same answer she gave us. "I can't say for sure what was in Mr. Barker's mind. But we know he was adamant about keeping his story ideas a secret. He must have felt that going to the police would open up the possibility of his being scooped. Instead, he went out and bought a small arsenal. He must have thought that was all he needed. He was convinced he was the top dog. Furst may have been able to subdue Jenny Sargon, but no seventy-year-old man, not even one as seriously homicidal as Mr. Furst, could get the better of Diamond Jack Barker."

Cugat nodded, "He was a conceited bastard, all right. He

once told me that's why he was 'Diamond' Jack, because no one was any tougher or sharper or more valuable. What a fool. Diamond? He wasn't even a zircon."

He turned in his seat to face the rear. "But speaking of diamonds, Ms. Dahlquist," he said, "as far as this nearly railroaded hombre is concerned, your friendship is rarer than the brightest jewel. Thanks for saving me."

"That's very sweet, Lieutenant," she said, "but Beau is the one who flushed out Mr. Furst and sent him scurrying. He's a handsome, brave, intelligent animal. And he'll make a wonderful companion, don't you think so, Mr. B.?"

I flashed on my throw rug, drying on the line, my smelly backyard, the three-pound bag of kibble sitting in the middle of the kitchen, the upcoming trip to the vet for shots, the exterminators I had to call to get rid of the fleas, the prospect of accepting responsibility for another living creature. "A wonderful companion," I agreed.

Anything to see that smile.

~~~~~~~~~~~~~~

Arizona Heat

Clark Howard

~~~~~~~~~~~~~~

Clark Howard's fifth Ellery Queen Readers Award merely indi-
cates that his more than thirty years of writing and more than
200 short stories have not gone unappreciated. He's also been
honored with an Edgar Award for Best Short Story, and his work
has also been adapted for film and television, including Alfred
Hitchcock Presents. Howard has seen his work published in
AHMM, EQMM, a number of anthologies including the just
released of *The Widow of Slane.* Some of his stories have been
collected in *Crowded Lives and Other Stories of Desperation.*

Tim Murray had covered the Paley murder case since the
morning after it happened, first as a reporter for the *Bisbee
Eagle,* later for the *Douglas Enterprise.* He was trying to
work his way up to the *Phoenix Sun,* but so far his resume
had been ignored. Now the Paley case was winding down.
Horace Paley's killer, Stuart Percy, after eight years on

Arizona's death row, was facing imminent execution; Percy's former lover, Jane Paley, the murdered man's wife, was beginning her ninth year of a life sentence at the women's prison. Murray thought that if he could break a last-minute story on the case, the Phoenix editors might take note of it and see something in his ability that had not surfaced in his resume. Make that resumes, plural.

So Murray put on a pair of swim trunks, took his clipboard with the yellow legal pad attached, a couple of ball-point pens, and a thermos of Gatorade, and went out to the pool at the little apartment complex where he lived, and began to write . . .

ARIZONA HEAT
by Tim Murray

She was a young woman with a bitter past.

He was a man looking for one more chance.

When they happened to meet . . . in the Arizona heat . . . something raw happened.

In the low desert of southeast Arizona, the company mining town of Lavender lay on the landscape like a series of tiny Monopoly houses around a great open pit mine that fed precious copper to teams of rugged, sun-browned, sweaty men who pulled the malleable, ductile metal out of the earth. The place was twenty-one miles from nowhere.

To Lavender there came a man and a woman who met and for a time could not stay away from each other. They loved freely, fiercely, wantonly,

like wild creatures. Then, after a time, they parted and went their separate ways.

The woman had once been married and had two children. She wanted a better life for them and for herself. So she married an older man, a mining superintendent, who gave her all of that—and had a big company life-insurance policy besides.

For a while, the woman's life was good. Then her lover showed up—down on his luck, as usual. He wanted his woman back—and he also wanted the money from her husband's life-insurance policy.

One night, as the woman's husband returned home from a late shift, two bullets were fired out of the darkness, and the man fell dead.

The police said the lover did it. The lover said the wife did it. The courts said they both did it.

Now the lover waits for the gas chamber, while the woman serves a life sentence in a sweltering desert prison.

There was never any doubt about the lover's guilt. But the evidence against her came from him.

Only he, by admitting that he lied, can save her before the gas chamber takes him to its long sleep.

And time is running out. . . .

The woman serving a life sentence in the Arizona women's prison had been known as Jane Fuller when she was fourteen years old and had walked into a high-school counselor's office in Lincoln, Nebraska, and said, "I need help.

My twenty-four-year-old brother has been raping me since I was twelve. Him and his wife leave me every night to take care of their three kids while they go out drinking. Lately they've been bringing men home to have sex with me. My mom's dead and my dad's a drunk. I'm about ready to kill myself—"

That visit to the counselor's office was all it took. The teenager was taken into the protective custody of county authorities that very day and never had to return to her brother's home. Instead, after an investigation, county authorities made arrangements for Jane to go live with her sister, Betty, who was twenty-two and had run away from a life similar to Jane's several years earlier. Betty was married to a man named Kevin Lund, had two toddlers, and lived in a little company mining town in Arizona.

When Jane learned that Betty and her husband had agreed to take her in, she silently thought: *Thank God.* She knew that her sister's husband was a decent, churchgoing man, and that Betty had a good life—the kind of life Jane herself wanted someday: husband, children, home, respectability.

Before long, Jane Fuller was on a Greyhound bus traveling across country to a place in Arizona called Lavender.

The first time reporter Tim Murray interviewed Jane, after she had become the wife of Horace Paley, was when she was awaiting trial for his murder. Jane was twenty-four, two years younger than Murray himself. They spoke in the visiting room of the Geronimo County jail. The accused woman spoke of what life had been like for her when she first arrived at her new home in Lavender.

"I was like a square peg pounded into a round hole," she said. "Understand, I had been functioning almost as an adult for a couple of years by the time I got here. I mean, my older brother had been raping me since I was twelve. I had an ulcer by the time I was thirteen. I'd been taking care of his kids every night like a grown woman. I was sexually involved with grown men, a lot of them married—a couple of them fathers of kids I was in ninth grade with. I mean, I wasn't prepared to be an average teenager, you know?"

At that first interview, Tim Murray found Jane to be friendly, personable, attractive: She had curly, darkish-red hair over eyes the color of macadamia nuts, and a figure that was not blatantly voluptuous but nevertheless shapely enough to turn male heads for a second look. Tim, four years out of journalism school and going nowhere in his career, found himself uneasily drawn to her, not all that much physically but more so because of her candor, her easygoing openness with him. He had to keep reminding himself that there was a possibility that she either murdered or conspired with Stuart Percy to murder her own husband.

"Anyway," Jane continued, "needless to say, things didn't work out quite the way I'd've liked. My sister Betty and her husband were Jehovah's Witnesses. There were only three places I was allowed to be: school, church, and home. Talk about culture shock . . ."

Jane had remained in the Lund home for two years, until she was old enough to quit school and go to work. Then she left and found a full-time job in a Tastee-Freez in the hamlet of Bisbee, two miles away. She boarded with a local family. It was not exactly a giant step forward in her life, but at least she was on her own, at least she had some *freedom*. Jane still wanted what her sister Betty had: a home and family of her own. But she wanted it to be a life somewhere in-between the sordid existence she had left back in Nebraska and the restrictive, often stifling world she had found with Jehovah's Witnesses.

Shortly after Jane's eighteenth birthday, a girl named Sissy Dornan, whom Jane had known in Lavender High before she quit school, came into the Tastee-Freez with her husband and new baby. Sissy had also left school, and married a young copper miner, had a baby, and was living in one of the company houses in Lavender. Sissy invited Jane to Sunday dinner and Jane accepted. It was there that she was introduced to Andy Tyler, a miner friend of the Dornans.

Andy was a big, strapping guy; he was, Jane thought, somebody a girl could lean on, depend on. He was close to thirty, but Jane didn't care. The important things were that he seemed good-natured, didn't smoke, drank nothing stronger than beer, and loved kids. Sometimes at the Dornan home, he would spend entire evenings after supper playing with Sissy's toddler on the floor.

Andy lived in a trailer near the mine pit.

Before long, Jane was living there, too.

"I'm two months late," Jane told Andy a few weeks before Christmas, when they had been living together for six months. "I guess I'm pregnant."

"Thought you was taking care of yourself," Andy said.

Jane shrugged. "I must have messed up."

"Want to get rid of it?" Andy asked.

Another shrug. "Not really." She looked away. "I haven't

ever had anything of my own that was worth anything before. And, you know, I like kids. You do too." When she looked back at him, her eyes were teary. "I think it'd be nice to have a little baby."

Andy stared solemnly at her for a moment. Then he shrugged too. "Guess we ought to get married, then."

Nothing could have made Jane happier. At last her dream was going to start coming true.

They married on Christmas Eve and Andy got them into a little company house near the pit mine. Jane was sick almost every day of her pregnancy, but she didn't care; while the baby was growing inside her, she felt it was the purest, most precious time of her young life, and she believed that she was truly blessed. Andy was a wonderfully attentive husband. Every night Jane gave thanks in prayer for the life she had found.

That summer, a baby girl arrived after six hours of labor, all coached by Andy, who had gone to classes with Jane. It was one week before Jane's nineteenth birthday. They named the child Emily.

Jane breast-fed her infant. She and baby Emily were inseparable. Andy got less attention and was a little jealous. But his complaints seemed good-natured. Jane made it up to him by being special to him in bed. Nine months later, she was pregnant again.

The second pregnancy was much easier. "That was because Emily and I went through it together," Jane told Tim Murray in another interview. "I felt like it was Emily's baby, too, not just Andy's and mine."

The delivery was harder this time around, however; the

doctor had to induce labor and it lasted nine hours, Andy again coaching her through every contraction. It was a baby boy this time, whom they named Edward. Jane had a tubal ligation; she was twenty years old, and felt she now had her dream family.

"I really enjoyed the early years of my marriage," Jane told Tim Murray. "I nursed both children for Edward's first nine months, then I weaned Emily and nursed only my son for two more years." She smiled shyly at the young reporter, whom she found quite handsome. "Andy bitched a lot because I was selfish with my, uh—ample breasts. But when you're nursing, you know, your nipples are sore a lot. And at night, in bed, I was too tired for sex a lot of the time."

Tim glanced at the accused woman's breasts several times. They were still ample. He felt a little embarrassed at Jane's candor.

"Andy began coming home late after work," she said. "He got in the habit of stopping off with some of the other miners at the Lavender Bar. And he started drinking Jack Daniels with his beer . . ."

It was when Andy began acting strange the following year that Jane discovered he had also taken up the habit of smoking marijuana. She complained about it, though not as vehemently, she realized later, as she should have. Her main concern was not what those new habits might be doing to Andy, only that he keep both his drinking and smoking out of the house, away from the children—which was fine with Andy. His young wife had made the not uncommon mistake of centering her life around their two children. Her husband slowly drifted away.

Jane did not realize the seriousness of the matter until a year later, when she found cocaine hidden in the house. Then she realized that Andy had become a full-blown addict. More and more alienated from his wife, he refused her offers of help, scoffed at suggestions of therapy, and shunned all her attempts to make up for the inattentiveness she now realized had created the problem.

Andy became unreachable. He came home only to sleep a few hours between midnight and dawn, and virtually ignored the children. The money he gave Jane to run the house began to get tight. When she could, Jane took care of other children in her home to make ends meet; when she had to, she borrowed money from her sister.

Christmas that year was the event that ended the marriage. Toys for the children and a few family gifts had been put on lay-away in a Bisbee department store, and money was being saved for them. However, when it came time to pick them up, a few days before Christmas, the money was gone. Andy had blown it on a holiday dope binge. For Jane, depriving her kids of Santa Claus was the ultimate offense. Shortly after the first of the new year, she took the children and left.

Jane moved back in with her sister's family. Over the next few months, Andy begged her to come back. He entered a program to kick his cocaine habit, and swore to her that he would stay clean when he did. But Jane rejected his pleading.

"I don't trust him anymore," she told Betty. "He's weak. I don't think he'll ever be a good provider again. Drinking and drugs will always be out there, tempting him. I can't take the chance that he'll choose them over Emily and Edward. My kids are everything to me."

Jane determined to find someone else to be a daddy to her kids. She started looking for her dream all over again.

Horace Paley was a forty-one-year-old man, never married, who worked as a shift superintendent at the pit mine. Jane had met him years earlier through her brother-in-law, Betty's husband, and known him casually when she first arrived to live with her sister. Unknown to Jane, Horace Paley had always been attracted to her, but kept his distance because at the time she was still a minor. But when Horace learned that Jane had left Andy Tyler and filed for divorce, he began, as Jane said in a later interview, "paying attention to me.

"We'd run into each other here and there, on the street or in a store, and just stand and talk, you know, like people do in a little community. Eventually he started calling me on the phone at Betty's, where I'd moved with my kids to get away from Andy. It was obvious that he liked me a lot. When I finally got Betty and Kevin to let me invite him around, my kids took to him right away. I mean, they were *crazy* about him. He'd pay attention to them, always brought them little gifts of some kind, played with them. That was very important, because my kids were everything to me."

While her divorce was pending, Jane and Horace began seeing each other regularly. It became clear to Jane that Horace was seriously courting her. They went to dinner, to dances at the company recreation building, to movies, and, eventually, to bed in Horace's little company house.

Sex with Horace, Jane found, was not much different than sex with Andy had been. Jane enjoyed pleasing him, but like all the sex she had ever known, beginning with her brother Jack, she derived no personal satisfaction from it, no intense passion, no orgasms. With Horace, it was just a way to get a new, better daddy for Emily and Edward. When her divorce was final, she planned to reestablish her modest little dream life with a new husband.

But, like a lot of Jane's plans, it was not to be that easy.

While she was waiting for her divorce to be finalized, Jane put Emily and Edward in a day-care facility and found a job as a nursing assistant in the Vista Valley Convalescent Center for the elderly in Bisbee, two miles away.

"It was my first real job," she boasted to Tim Murray. "I didn't count slinging ice cream at Tastee-Freez; that wasn't a *job,* it was just work. But as soon as I started at Vista Valley, I somehow felt naturally suited for the work. I seemed to have a genuine knack for taking care of old folks. I loved it, I really did, and I loved them. I even started thinking seriously about studying to be a real nurse after Horace and I got settled."

Shortly after starting at Vista Valley, a handsome, polished man, about ten years her senior, wearing a white physician's coat, introduced himself as Dr. Stuart Percy. He was charming, very friendly, and after a while began instructing her in more efficient ways to take care of her patients. Jane was immediately attracted to him, almost with a physical urgency. His smooth self-confidence, easy smile, even the way he smelled when she stood close to him, aroused feelings in her that she had never before experienced. Several times, she caught him looking at her while she was working, and sensed that there was also something stirring in him.

It was summer, Arizona heat seeping into every crack and corner despite air conditioning; a time when an extra blouse or shirt button might be opened, when a line of perspiration would settle on a person's upper lip, when bodies felt the need for some kind of *release*—from clothing, restraints, inhibitions. Jane and Stuart were being moved by that Arizona heat—and they both knew it. They were drawn to each other by a demanding passion that neither was able to resist.

The first time they made love was, for Jane, like a scene from an erotic movie. The heat that day had been dispelled for an hour by one of the typical violent summer thunderstorms that sometimes assaulted the desert. A driving rain was pelting the convalescent home when Stuart walked up, took Jane's hand, and led her into an unoccupied room.

"We should be calming the patients," she said, drawing back.

"You and I need calming more than the patients do," he told her, and braced the closed door with a chair.

In seconds, he had her white uniform and his own clothes off, and they were doing things to each other as naturally and easily as if they had been doing them for years. Looking back, Jane would say, "It was the most perfect lovemaking I can imagine two people ever having. It was like being naked in Heaven and making love on a cloud. I *must* have had a dozen orgasms, almost nonstop, like a line of speeding cars on a highway. I'll probably be thinking about that the moment I die."

I wonder if Stuart Percy will, too, Tim Murray asked himself, thinking of the man waiting to die in the gas chamber.

Nearly every day after that first time, Jane and Stuart wallowed in each other's lust, when and where they could, both of them professing the greatest love they had ever felt.

"I want to take you and run away from here," Stuart said to her one day in the third week of their intimacy.

"Run away from what?" It was her first uneasy moment with him.

"Look, I have a wife, Jane. Her name is Corinne. And I have a little boy named Carlton." Seeing the surprised expression on her face, he said, "Why are you looking at me like that? You're married too, and you have a little boy and a little girl."

"Sure, but I'm getting a divorce," Jane reasoned.

"I will, too. Let's go away together; let's make a new life."

"What about my kids?" That was Jane's gauntlet. She loved this man fiercely, but she was not about to trade her children for him.

"We'll take them with us," Stuart replied at once, passing the ultimate test.

"What about your son?" Jane asked guiltily.

"I can make some kind of arrangement about Carlton after we get settled." He took her in his arms. "Where do you want to go? I've lived in Nevada, Oregon, Texas, Florida, even up in Maine for a while—"

"I've never been anywhere except Nebraska, besides here," she said, feeling less than worldly.

"Did you like Nebraska?"

"I liked the place—I didn't like my life—"

"Your life is going to be different now. Let's start with Nebraska. If we don't like it, we can move on."

A fully realized woman, really in love for the first time, Jane agreed to run away with Stuart Percy. She was elated at the prospect. She would have her kids, a husband she was wild about, and the beginning of a new life. Thoughts of Horace Paley were simply put out of her mind. Once again, she seemed to have a future that was bright.

As usual in Jane's life, the brightness soon dimmed.

On the long drive toward Nebraska, somewhere in Colorado, Jane casually asked, "Where did you go to school to become a doctor?"

Stuart looked at her incredulously.

"I'm not a doctor, Jane. I thought you knew. I was just trying to impress you when I said that. I was a nursing assistant, just like you."

Jane was stunned; further, she was deeply embarrassed because Stuart seemed to think it was her own fault for not knowing. She became chagrined when he spoke again.

"Do you really love me, Jane, or do you just love the thought of being a doctor's wife?"

Made vulnerable by this shocking turn of events, Jane swore that she truly loved him. She swore that it did not matter what he was.

Her surprises, however, were just beginning. The next blow came the following day.

"How about we detour east to Kansas?" he said. "There's somebody I'd like you to meet."

"Oh? Who?" She thought at first it might be his parents. No such luck.

"Well, I didn't tell you before because I was afraid of upsetting you. Corinne isn't my first wife. I was married before, to a woman named Esther. We have three kids. Stuart, Jr., is nine, and Irene is seven. My five-year-old's name is Edward, same as your boy. Isn't that funny?"

Yeah, it's a scream, Jane thought. *God, what next?*

* * *

In Salina, Kansas, Jane and Stuart stayed for two weeks with Esther and the three children. They lived in a tacky little house and subsisted on state welfare. Stuart's children were crazy about Jane's two little ones, and Esther seemed to be a kind and understanding person. All of which made the visit at least tolerable for Jane.

When Stuart was not around, Esther told Jane of the nomadic life she had led with Stuart, moving from San Francisco, where they met and married, to Wisconsin, then Florida, Maine, Kansas.

"Like we were gypsies. Finally the kids and I stopped. We'd had enough. He just kept on going. I lost him."

At night, after relentless sex with Stuart, during which Jane did not care about anything except the orgasms he brought to her, she would lie in the darkness and wonder how the other women, Corinne and Esther, felt; thinking how awful it would be, after finding Stuart, to lose him. The thought, Jane later told Tim Murray, gave her chills and made her cling fearfully to his naked, sleeping body.

She vowed never to lose him, whatever it took.

Before they left, Jane thanked Esther for her hospitality. "I really didn't know what to expect before I got here," she confessed. "I had no idea Stuart had a first wife and children this old."

"Oh, I'm not his first wife," Esther said with a sly smile. "He was married to a woman named Charlotte before me. He's got a boy of fourteen by her. I think they live somewhere in Oregon." She gripped Jane's arm. "Please don't tell Stuart I told you. Not until you're a few hundred miles away, anyhow."

Jane decided not to mention it at all. "I mean, what the hell," she said later, "what was one more wife and another kid coming out of the woodwork?"

If he left all those women behind—Charlotte, Esther, Corinne, and who knew who else—Jane reasoned that there must have been something lacking in the relationship. She chose to think that the something was love: powerful love, *real* love—the kind she and Stuart had together.

She was determined to make a life with this true love of hers, whatever it took, whatever baggage of his she had to accept and overlook. The modest dream she had pictured for herself throughout the years was still obtainable—and it would be better than ever, because she would be sharing it with Stuart.

"I just had to chase my dream a little longer," she recalled deciding. "But I was determined to do it."

When they finally got to Lincoln, Nebraska, and found a place to live, Jane put her children in a day-care facility again, and she and Stuart both got jobs at Albermar Adult Care Home, as nursing assistants.

Within a month, because of her efficiency and dedication, Jane was promoted and put in charge of her own section of rooms and patients—and Stuart was working for her. It was a situation that bothered Stuart.

The two of them got along very well in their off hours, acting much like newlyweds freshly in love. But during working hours, tension started to build between them, particularly when Jane instructed Stuart to do something, or when she felt it necessary to criticize his sloppy work.

"I taught you how, boss lady, remember?" he would say sarcastically. And Jane would back off and do the work right herself.

"After three months," Jane recalled, "of being together morning, noon, and night, hardly ever being out of each other's sight—eating, sleeping, living, and working together—Stuart developed kind of an edge. At home he would brood and complain about my two noisy children and the lack of money to go out in the evening. At work I noticed that he was becoming verbally abusive and sometimes physically aggressive with some of our patients. I tried to handle it without offending him. One day I kidded him by saying, 'If I didn't love you, honey, I think I'd fire you.'"

"Go ahead, do it," Stuart challenged. It was clear from his tone that he meant it. Jane tried to laugh it off, but he wouldn't let her. "If you don't have the nerve to fire me, then I quit!"

Tossing his smock onto her desk, he walked out.

When Jane got home after work, Stuart was packed and ready to leave. "I'm going to try California again," he said. "Want to come?"

"Stuart, please don't do this," Jane pleaded. "We've started a new life here—"

"I'm tired of the new life, and I'm going to California," he repeated emphatically. "You want to come or not?"

"What happens when you get tired of California?" she asked. "Do we hit the road to Florida or Maine or wherever, like you did with Esther? Or do you leave me behind like you did Corinne in Arizona? And like you probably did Charlotte in Oregon?"

It was the first time she'd ever mentioned that she knew about Charlotte.

Stuart stared coldly at her for a moment, as if she had committed an unpardonable sin. Then he picked up his suitcase and left.

Three days later, Jane called Horace Paley and he sent three plane tickets for her and the children to fly back to Arizona. Horace met them at the airport in Phoenix. Back in the company mining town of Lavender, Jane and her children moved into Horace's little house at the edge of the pit mine.

The following month, Jane picked up her final divorce papers ending her marriage to Andy Tyler. That weekend, she and Horace drove up to Laughlin, Nevada, and were married.

Once again, Jane began her dream life: husband, kids, little house, respectability.

It lasted all of three months.

The soft knock at the back door came one night an hour after Jane had put the children to bed. When she opened the door, she almost fainted. It was Stuart.

"How's married life?" he asked casually.

"What—what are you doing here?" It was impossible to conceal her shock. "I thought you were in California."

"I couldn't stay away from you," he replied, touching her cheek with his fingertips. "Can I come in?"

"No—you'd better not. Horace—my husband—will be home any minute—"

"No, he won't, Jane. He's working the late shift at the mine. He won't be home for three hours."

Stuart slowly eased past her into the kitchen, letting his body drag along hers as he moved. . . .

Thinking back on the moment, Jane recalled to Tim Murray that Stuart's presence, his touch, had turned her on. "I couldn't help it," she admitted. "Stuart had that effect on me. The look in his eyes, the sound of his voice, the way he dragged himself against me like that. I couldn't resist him; I'd never been able to resist him. He knew it. I barely had time to turn off the kitchen light before he had me on the floor. . . ."

He had left her there on the kitchen floor an hour later. Then he called her the next day, a little while after Horace left for work.

"Stuart, please leave me alone," she begged.

"I want to come over in a little while. After it gets dark."

"Stuart, no, you can't! I'm married now! If Horace found out about last night—"

"He *will* find out," Stuart said evenly, "unless you let me come over tonight."

"You wouldn't tell him, Stuart, you wouldn't do that to me—"

"I love you, Jane. I'd do anything to have you. And you want me, too. You know you do."

"Stuart, don't do this to me, *please!* Let me make a life for myself and my kids—"

"Tonight, Jane. Leave the back door unlocked."

He hung up.

So it started all over again. Jane maintained in her interviews with Tim Murray that there was nothing she could do about it; she was terrified that Horace would find out.

At the same time, she did not deny experiencing the same body-shuddering multiple orgasms that Stuart had always given her. Before he got to her house, when he was on the phone, she invariably pleaded with him to stay away, and when their sweating, grinding sex was over, she implored him not to come back. But during the act itself, she hoped it would never end. She claimed in retrospect that the situation was driving her toward a nervous breakdown.

When Stuart started talking about Horace's company life insurance, Jane did not take him seriously. She knew quite well by then that *Doctor* Stuart Percy talked a very good game, but he never followed through. Stuart was a dreamer, a wisher, a planner; he had never been a *doer.* Even when he outlined a plan to kill Horace one night, Jane dismissed it.

"In my wildest imagination, I never thought Stuart could—or would—commit murder," she later swore to Tim Murray. "It would have been like believing he could stop telling lies, stop using women the way he did. Basically, Stuart was a coward. Even after all this time, with him on Death Row, it's still hard for me to believe it happened."

But happen it did.

One night, Horace Paley returned home after working the three-to-eleven shift at the Lavender Mine and was fatally shot two times outside his carport. He died within an hour.

One week later, Stuart Percy was arrested at the Cochise Motel in Phoenix, where he was working as a relief desk clerk. Someone who recognized him had seen him running from the scene after the shooting. When he was found in Phoenix, he still had the murder weapon in his car. He was taken back to Geronimo County and charged with first-degree murder.

Stuart's story was that Jane had fired the fatal shots.

"I was there," he admitted at his trial four months later. "Jane and I had been making love and lost track of the time. Before we knew it, Horace was driving up. Jane got angry at us being interrupted. She'd been trying for weeks to get me to kill Horace for his insurance money. When she heard him come home, she said she'd had enough of him and was going to get rid of him herself, once and for all. She ran outside and shot him twice. I took the gun away from her and got the hell out of there. I figured she could say some burglar had done it or something—"

When Jane testified at the trial, she admitted that she and Stuart had been having an affair, but stated that on the night of the killing she was inside the house with her children, all of them asleep, and that she had never at any time asked Stuart to kill her husband or been part of any plan for him to do it.

There had been no fingerprints on the gun; Stuart had wiped it clean. Then he had carelessly left it in his car, believing that no one would suspect him.

The jury found Stuart Percy guilty of murder in the first degree. He was sentenced to death in the gas chamber.

Stuart Percy's story about Jane trying to get him to murder her husband did not go away after his conviction. He had told his wife, Corinne, to whom he was still married, as well as several other people in the area, that Jane wanted him to kill Horace Paley for her. And Jane had admitted at the trial that in addition to having an affair with Percy, she had also given him two hundred dollars out of her household money when he told her that his car was about to be repossessed. Investigators learned that shortly after Jane gave him the money, he used it to buy the murder weapon at a pawnshop in Tucson.

Circumstantial evidence began to pile up. Even though Stuart's story of Jane herself doing the shooting was disbelieved, a conspiracy theory, in light of her adulterous behavior, became strong enough for her to be indicted.

Jane was arrested, pled not guilty, and eventually faced a jury trial. Like Stuart, she was found guilty. The circumstantial evidence, as well as her history with Stuart and her own admission of the recent affair, and her giving Stuart the money he used to buy the gun, convinced the jury that she had, in fact, conspired with Stuart Percy to kill Horace and collect his life insurance. Like Stuart, Jane could have received the death penalty—but in her case, as a mother of two little children, mercy was shown. She was sentenced to life in prison, and required to serve a mandatory fifty years of that term.

"All I ever wanted," Jane told Tim Murray in an interview after her conviction, "was a decent husband, a nice little house to raise my kids in, and respectability. I thought I'd found it with Andy, but he turned into a junkie. I know that was partly my fault; hell, maybe it was *all* my fault for making my kids more important than my husband.

"But the biggest mistake I made was taking the job at Vista Valley, because that's where I met Stuart. As far as the men in my life are concerned, Stuart was the best and the worst thing that ever happened to me. I still have very intense feelings for him even now. Half the time those feelings are hatred, but the other half they're love. He was the only man I ever loved completely—body, mind, heart, soul, spirit. I love him for making me a whole woman, for keeping me from going through life without ever being physically fulfilled. But I hate him with all my heart for killing Horace, because Horace was such a good and kind man. And I hate him most of all because he cost me my kids. My little Emily and my little Edward. I'll never be a mother to them again. That's the worst part of everything that's happened to me . . ."

Tim Murray spent an hour with Jane on the morning she was taken to prison. By now they had become familiar and comfortable with each other. They were, oddly, almost like old friends. "How are the kids doing?" Tim asked.

"Good. Thank God for my sister Betty and her husband for taking them in. They've moved back to Nebraska; the scandal in Lavender was too much for them. Kevin's got a good job servicing farm equipment." She shrugged. "I guess my kids will grow up to be Jehovah's Witnesses, but what the hell. It's a lot better than the way I grew up." Sighing, Jane changed the subject. "What about you, Tim? What are you going to do now that you don't have me to write about anymore?"

"I don't know," he said, grunting softly. "I made it from the *Bisbee Eagle* to the *Douglas Enterprise.* Maybe that's as far as I'll ever get. Small-town reporter on a small-town newspaper."

"No," Jane said, shaking her head, "you'll make it to the big time one of these days, wait and see. And you'll meet a nice young lady, get married, have kids, a home, respectability . . ." Her voice faded off to silence. That was *her* life she was wishing for him.

Now Tim was the one to shake his head. "No, I'll probably stay a bachelor until I'm old and gray."

"Someone will come along," she promised.

For just a moment, a split instant, their eyes locked and something passed between them; something that had been barely buoyant in each of their minds for a long time now, but which each of them had dismissed out of hand as being frivolous. It was a brief thought of what might have been. . . .

"Can I write to you, Tim?" she asked when it came time for her to go.

"If you want to."

Tilting her head slightly, Jane said, "You've never asked me if I really did plan with Stuart to kill Horace, have you?"

"No, I've never asked you that."

"Do you want to ask me now?"

"No."

A little while later, Tim stood outside the Geronimo County jail as Jane was escorted—handcuffed, belly-chained, and ankle-shackled—to a transport van to be taken to prison.

Tim Murray job-jumped for a few years, but always laterally, never upwardly. He worked for the *Benson Banner,* the *Nogales Press,* even spent some time up north on the *Flagstaff Sentinel.*

Jane wrote him, at first every week, then twice a month, finally monthly or less frequently. She really had little to correspond about. Her days were maddeningly uniform, like reading the same book over and over again. The women's prison sat on the scorching Sonora Desert just north of the Mexican border. She worked in the sweltering, steaming prison laundry. The only happy aspect of her life was that when Emily and Edward were old enough, Jane's sister Betty encouraged them to begin writing to their mother. She loved getting childish letters from them.

But even that happiness carried heartbreak with it.

At the men's prison near Florence, Stuart Percy sat on Death Row, watching time go by as one appeal of his sentence after another was turned down. Slowly but with a methodic, maddening sureness, the state and federal appellate appeals process moved him closer and closer to the gas chamber.

Stuart was a surly, irksome inmate, disliked by other prisoners as well as staff. He grew more and more unpleasant as each year one or two or three men on the Row went to their deaths, and for him time moved inexorably on.

In the women's prison, Jane's cellmate was an older woman named Belle, doing life for killing her boyfriend and a woman with whom he had been cheating on her.

Jane talked constantly to Belle about finding some way to convince Stuart Percy to recant his story that she had been part of a plan to murder her husband.

"If only he would admit that he had lied at his own trial, they would have to give me a new trial, or commute my sentence, or *something*. Wouldn't they, Belle?"

"Seems likely," the older woman said. "But you never know, kid," she qualified her statement. Belle was in her twenty-third year in prison. She was nothing if not jaded.

"If I could only get in touch with him." Jane would pace the cell or the yard or the rec room, wringing her hands. "If

I could only talk to him. He loved me, Belle, I know he did. Maybe he would listen to reason and help me."

"I wouldn't count on it, honey."

"He might do it for my kids. He liked my kids." Pausing a beat, she added quietly, "Some of the time, anyway."

But there was no way for Jane to contact Stuart. "It's impossible," her prison counselor told her. "There's absolutely no way for you to do it. It's strictly against Department of Corrections policy for an inmate in any prison facility to correspond or otherwise communicate with anyone on Death Row. Look, why don't you have your lawyer talk to his lawyer?"

"I don't have a lawyer anymore. My appeals have run out and the state won't appoint any other lawyers to represent me. And I don't have any money to pay for a lawyer myself."

"Well, I'm sorry, Jane, but there's nothing I can do for you."

In desperation, Jane wrote to Tim Murray and asked if he would come visit her. Tim was now the editor of the *Dos Cabezos Weekly* in the little town of Willcox. He was still a bachelor, still dreaming of a job with a big-time newspaper in a big-time town. He and Jane had not seen each other for eight years, and their exchange of letters had, over time, become infrequent.

At first sight of her in the visiting room, Tim was shocked. Only thirty-two, Jane looked ten years older. The expression on his face told Jane exactly what he was thinking.

"Yeah, I know," she said. "It happens to all of us in here. Too much starchy food. Not enough exercise. Too many cigarettes. No sex—or at least none to speak of." She forced a half smile. "But you look good, Tim. An editor now, huh?"

"Yeah. Of a *weekly.* Twelve pages of ads, local gossip, and front-page stories about Indians getting in fights at the Friday night American Legion baseball games. I go home every night, drink gin, and wish I had all that journalism school tuition back."

Studying Jane, Tim could not help wondering how much better she would have looked if she and he had met under different circumstances . . .

"Why did you ask me to come see you, Jane?"

"Can you get in to visit Stuart on the Row?"

"Probably. But why would I want to?"

"To read a letter to him. From me." Before Tim could respond in any way, Jane leaned forward urgently. "Look, the only chance I have of ever getting out of here is if Stuart retracts his testimony and I get a commutation, or maybe a retrial based on new evidence—"

"Jane, Jane," he cut in. "Do you seriously think there's even a remote possibility that Stuart would do that? He's been protesting his innocence for eight years. Do you think he's going to admit to the world now that he's guilty?"

"He might, Tim. He *might.* The closer he gets to the gas chamber, the more he might consider doing the right thing for a change—"

"You're kidding yourself, Jane."

"It's a *chance,* Tim—"

"Why do this to yourself? Why build your hopes up when all it's going to get you is a big letdown?"

Sitting back in her chair, Jane fixed him with a flat, unblinking stare. "I've been in this hellhole for eight years, Tim. I have to serve forty-two more to even be considered for parole. *Forty-two* more years, Tim. I'll be seventy-four years old. My kids will be middle-aged. I'll probably be a grandmother. If there's even a one-in-a-*million* chance, don't you think it's worth me taking it?"

Tim contemplated her position. And the woman herself. The once-pretty, darkish red hair was no longer curly, but combed straight back now with, no style to it; the brightness of her macadamia eyes had faded to dullness; her complexion had coarsened; her shapely figure was tending toward thickness. It hurt his heart to see her that way. But the last thing in the world he wanted to do was enhance any remote hope she had of being released from prison. That would only cause anguish for her—and for him.

Yet in the end he found himself incapable of refusing to help her. He could not look into her pleading eyes and say no.

"What would you say to Stuart in the letter?"

Jane brightened at once. "I'm not sure. I mean, I know what I'm going to say but I don't know how I'm going to say it. I need to think about it."

"Well, don't think too long," Tim said. "The U.S. Supreme Court declined to review Stuart's case this morning. I heard it on the radio driving down here. That was the last of his appeals. The state will set an execution date now. He's probably got less than thirty days left."

Jane turned somber. "You'll help me, then, Tim."

"Yes. Any way I can."

When he left the women's prison that day, he felt as if he had just driven a nail into Jane's heart.

The letter to Stuart came in an envelope addressed to Tim Murray. It read:

Dear Stuart,

I am writing to beg you to help me. If you ever truly cared for me, please—please—try to find it in your heart to tell the truth about what happened. There is nothing I can do to help you, Stuart, but if there was, I think you know I would do it. You are the only man I ever truly loved; please don't let me rot in prison because of it. . . .

The letter went on to explain how Jane felt that if Stuart would retract his trial testimony and issue a statement that she did not conspire with him to kill her husband, it would mean at least a retrial for her, perhaps even a commutation of her sentence.

Tim went to the prison that housed Death Row and used his newspaper credentials to ask for an interview. Prison policy was to allow media representatives access to condemned inmates if the prisoner consented to it.

The Death Row visiting room was divided down the middle by a counter with an eighty-gauge steel wire grille that extended from the countertop to the ceiling. The condemned inmate sat on one side of the counter and grille, the visitor on the other. Stuart Percy was brought in on his side dressed in a white jumpsuit, wrists handcuffed to a belly chain. Pale, haggard-looking, head shaved because of the heat, he stared at Tim through the tight-gauged grille.

"You the same guy that wrote all those stories about Jane eight years ago?" he asked.

"I'm the one," Tim said.

"How come you never wrote any stories about me?"

"Because nobody cared about you. A lot of people were sympathetic to Jane."

"So what do you want to talk to me now for?"

"Jane asked me to come. She wrote you a letter. She asked me to read it to you."

"Is it a love letter?" Stuart asked smugly, almost with a leer.

Tim shrugged. "Partly, I guess. You decide."

Taking the letter from his pocket, Tim unfolded it and slowly, quietly, read Jane's pleading words. Stuart's expression did not change. After watching Tim put the letter away, he merely stood and smiled.

"Thanks for dropping in. Tell Jane I said hello."

"You won't even consider helping her?"

"Look," the condemned man responded with an edge, "right now I'm not interested in helping anybody but myself. I've got one more shot at beating the gas chamber. That shot is a petition to the governor for clemency to commute my death sentence to life in prison. The appeals lawyer appointed to my case by the state tells me I've got a pretty good chance. There's a big anti-death-penalty movement all over the country right now—"

"You're dreaming, Percy," Tim cut in flatly. "This is an election year. The governor's not going to grant clemency to a cold-blooded killer like you."

"What makes you so sure I *am* a cold-blooded killer?" Stuart asked bluntly. "No fingerprints on the gun, remember? All my lawyer has to do is convince the governor that there's a fifty-fifty chance that *Jane* pulled the trigger, not me. So why shouldn't he be fair and give us both the same sentence?"

Tim stared at the condemned man. Mixed scenarios and wild thoughts bombarded his mind. Was it possible that—?

No, that was unthinkable.

Turning his back on Stuart Percy, Tim walked out of the visitors' room. Outside in the parking lot, he sat in his car with both hands gripping the steering wheel, staring at the haze of Arizona heat that the blazing afternoon sun drew up from the flat Pinal desert. He would not believe that Jane was a murderer; he *could* not believe it. Nor did he believe that she was in any way involved in a conspiracy to kill Horace Paley. For one thing, he reasoned with himself, she loved her kids too much to become involved in anything that might remotely cause her to lose them. And for another thing—

Well, he just didn't believe it, that was all.

As he drove away toward the highway, he swore to himself that somehow, some *way,* he was going to get Jane out of prison.

During ten years of bouncing around from one small Arizona newspaper to another, Tim Murray had built up a network of friends and acquaintances at various levels of state and local government. One person with whom he had periodic amiable encounters, and whom he had watched move up the ladder of responsible jobs at the state house, was a young man his own age named Danny Lopez, who was currently serving as press secretary to the governor. Tim invited Lopez to lunch in Phoenix.

"I've got an idea for you, my friend," he told Lopez. "It's something your boss might like, and if he does you can take full credit for it."

"And what do you get, Timmy?" the press secretary asked.

"An eight-hour lead on breaking the story."

"Last time I heard, pal, you were working for a *weekly*."

"I won't break the story in my paper. I'll break it on one of the wire services. And I'll get a byline that'll go out all over the country."

"Still shooting for the big time, huh? Okay, what's the story?"

"This is an election year for your boss. There's a strong anti-capital-punishment movement in the state that could cost him some critical votes. Are you familiar with the Stuart Percy case?"

"Yeah. We just got an application for clemency on him. The trial judge has already set an execution date. I hope this idea of yours doesn't involve commuting this guy. Because if it does—"

"Wait, Danny, don't get negative on me before I finish. You know about Jane Paley, who was convicted in the same case?"

"Yeah. Her appeals have run out."

"Right. But she thinks she can convince Stuart Percy to recant his testimony against her if she can speak with him face-to-face. Think about the press coverage your boss would get if he allowed an unprecedented visit between the two of them to allow Jane Paley to plead her case. Jane has two kids. The public would eat this up, Danny. The anti-death-penalty crowd, too; giving a condemned killer a chance to make some kind of retribution for what he's done by helping to release an innocent convicted woman from prison—"

"I don't know," Lopez said, shaking his head. "It's going to look like a ploy to get his own sentence commuted."

"Not to the anti-death-penalty crowd. To them it's going to show the world that even a condemned killer has some humanity in him. And if Percy does recant his testimony and get a mother of two released, it may make him some kind of hero and your boss might even consider it politically advisable to commute *him.* But whether he goes that far or not, Danny, it's a win-win situation for him." Tim paused a beat, then added, "It's the kind of story that could help get a governor into the U.S. Senate in a few years."

Danny Lopez pursed his lips in thought and began drumming his fingers spiritedly on the table.

Bingo, Tim thought.

One week later, after two more meetings with Danny Lopez to clarify a few incidental matters, Tim Murray was back in the Death Row visiting room facing Stuart Percy.

"I've got a deal for you, Percy. It might—and I'm emphasizing *might*—just save your life."

He told the condemned man about the meeting that could be arranged between him and Jane Paley, the publicity it would no doubt generate, and the sympathy it could conjure up for him if he aided Jane in securing either a new trial or a commutation of her sentence.

Percy shook his head irritably. "I already told you: I've got my own executive-clemency petition pending before the governor."

"Not anymore, you haven't," Tim told him evenly. "Your petition will be denied at the governor's weekly press conference today."

"How the hell do you know that?"

"Doesn't matter how I know it. Point is, you've got a date

with the gas chamber in two weeks. Your only hope is a last-minute reprieve by the governor—*after* you meet with Jane, and you retract your testimony about her."

Percy angrily got to his feet. "I don't know what kind of scam you're trying to pull on me, Murray, but it's not going to work!" His eyes narrowed. "You've got something going with Jane, haven't you? You're hot for her, aren't you? You want her out for yourself! Well, you can go to hell, Mr. Reporter! I'm not falling for it!"

Tim rose to leave. "It's up to you. Enjoy your last few days."

Just then, a corrections officer entered the room on the inmate's side. "Percy," he called, "the governor denied your clemency petition. It just came over the noon news." The officer then left.

Tim was standing at the exit door, waiting.

Stuart Percy sat back down and buried his face in his hands. After several moments, he looked over at Tim.

"Okay. What do I have to do?"

Bingo, Tim thought again.

The story, written by Tim at poolside that afternoon, went out on one of the wire services the next day. Broadcast news picked it up at once.

"In a copyrighted story by reporter Timothy Murray, National News Service has reported that Arizona governor Neal Harris has approved an unprecedented meeting between a condemned man facing the gas chamber in less than two weeks and his former lover, both of whom were convicted of the murder eight years ago of the woman's husband. . . ."

Courthouse News anchor Gracie Nance interrupted regularly scheduled programming with a half-hour special report. "Arizona governor Neal Harris today gave permission for an extraordinary face-to-face meeting between condemned killer Stuart Percy and his former lover, Jane Paley, widow of the man Percy was sentenced to death for killing, ostensibly to collect the victim's life insurance. Paley, a mother of two who is serving a life sentence in prison for her part in the same crime, has long maintained that her ex-lover Percy could prove her innocence. Now, with Percy very close to his execution date, with no further appeals left, she will have the opportunity to personally plead with him to do so. . . ."

On the day of their meeting, Jane was brought handcuffed and shackled to the men's prison by an escort of Arizona State Rangers. The warden and a team of corrections officers took her to the Death Row visitors' room, which had been reserved for the occasion. Stuart was brought in on the inmate side. The two could be observed but not heard by prison staff. They were left completely alone. No media or cameras were allowed inside the prison during the meeting.

Jane and Stuart spent a minute just staring at each other through the wire grille. It had been nearly ten years since each had last seen the other. Jane's eyes teared up and she briefly bit her lower lip at the memory of the love she had once felt for the man facing her. Stuart, on the other hand, was reserved and early on displayed the attitude that it was Jane's fault that he was where he was. The preliminary dialogue between them was strained. Jane tried desperately to convince Stuart to support her innocence. She begged and pleaded. But Stuart could not get past the fact that he was going to die, while Jane would go on living.

"You know what happened that night as well as I do, Jane," he accused. "You didn't want to spend the rest of your life with a man twice your age, a man who could never, *ever*, make you feel the way I made you feel. You said yourself a hundred times that you'd never even had an orgasm with any other man! This isn't *fair*, Jane—you go free and I have to die!"

Stuart dismissed out of hand Jane's assertion that there was nothing she could do about his situation, only something that he could do about hers.

"Not true." He shook his head vehemently. "You could tell them that *you* pulled the trigger that night, Jane. Then I could be commuted and we could both go on living."

The thirty minutes that they had been allowed together went by before either of them realized it, and guards came to take Jane away. "Stuart, please!" she screamed as she was hustled toward the door, "Please—for my kids, Stuart—please—!"

Then it was over.

Outside, she was hurried through a phalanx of media people, all seeming to ask variations of the same question: "Jane, do you think Stuart will help you?"

She could only shake her head helplessly. "I don't know—I don't know—"

Back in her cell at the women's prison, Belle asked, "What do you think, honey?"

Jane, wasted from her frantic, emotional pleading, lit a cigarette and shook her head despondently.

"I think you and Tim have been right all along. Stuart is going to be a world-class, low-life bastard all the way to the gas chamber."

*   *   *

Tim Murray, however, was not of the same mind. He continued to carry out his plan. Two days after Jane's visit, Tim himself went to see Percy again.

"I had breakfast with my friend, the governor's press secretary, this morning, Stuart. He told me, strictly off the record, that the governor is going to seriously consider a last-minute reprieve for you—depending on how you respond to Jane's pleas, and what the public opinion polls show."

"Why the hell should I believe that?" Stuart asked with a sneer.

Tim shrugged. "Why *not* believe it? What do I have to gain by lying to you?"

"I know why you're doing this, Murray. You're doing it to help *her.*"

"I'm doing it to help myself," Tim asserted. "I'm doing it for the *story.* This is going to make me a big-time reporter. Look, Stuart, here's how it works. You tip me in advance when you're going to hold a press conference to declare Jane's innocence. You let me break the story first on a wire service. The governor's press secretary has agreed to do the same when the governor grants you a last-minute reprieve; I break that story first, too. After that, I can write my own ticket. It's a no-lose situation, Stuart. Everybody wins. I get my big-time job. Jane goes free. And you beat the gas chamber."

"How do I know the governor will come through?"

"He'll come through," Tim assured him. "Look, right now it's a national news story. After you clear Jane, it'll be an *international* news story. The governor will be in the limelight around the world. He'll *have* to commute you for the act of mercy you showed to that world. If he doesn't, he'll be dead politically." Tim suddenly snapped his fingers. "I just thought of something. I want you to give me an exclusive interview the night you're supposed to be executed. It'll make a great human-interest piece. You'll be contrite, remorseful. You'll be resigned to going to your death, but at the same time at peace with yourself knowing you helped free an innocent woman so that she could return to her kids." Tim smiled. "I'll make a martyr out of you, Stuart. After you're commuted to life, bleeding-heart liberals all over the country, all over the *world*, will be lining up to make you their poster boy, their hero. You'll get so much mail from prison groupies, they'll have to give you an extra cell to use as an office."

Stuart Percy's eyes began to reflect interest. He wet his lips several times as he contemplated the prospects of being a famous person, even if it was behind bars. Maybe he could persuade Jane to visit him, maybe even to marry him in a televised prison ceremony, and maybe they could have conjugal visits. She hadn't looked all that desirable when they met the previous week—it was obvious that prison had taken its toll on her—but after she got out, he knew she'd fix herself up again, get that red hair curled, get her body back in shape—

"I need to think about this," Stuart said. Tim shook his head.

"You haven't got time to think about it, Stuart. I have to get word back to the governor's press secretary. Things have to be put in motion. I need to arrange an interview with Jane for right after you hold your press conference, so she can tell the world what a great person you are, and how grateful she is, maybe even how much she still loves you—*and* she has to begin pleading with the governor to commute your sentence like he commuted hers—"

Stuart loved that part of the plan. "Okay!" he said abruptly. "All right! I'll do it!"

The condemned man's eyes shone with an excitement Tim had never seen before. Saliva formed in the corners of his mouth. He looked like a cannibal who had just been thrown somebody's liver. Tim rose to leave.

"You're a smart man, Stuart. I'll get the ball rolling on the outside. You start working on what you'll say at your press conference. Get word to me as soon as you decide when you want to hold it."

Stuart Percy held his press conference on the third day before he was scheduled to go to the gas chamber.

In a quiet, controlled, seemingly sincere voice, he admitted that he had lied at his trial about Jane's complicity in the murder of Horace Paley—and he at last admitted his own guilt.

"I did it because I loved Jane so much," he said contritely. "I'm very ashamed of it now. I know I have to be punished for my terrible crime, and I am ready to take that punishment. I hope Jane can find it in her heart to forgive me, and I hope that Governor Neal Harris will find it in his heart to set her free so she can be reunited with her two wonderful children." At that point, Stuart blinked his eyes several times as if trying to hold back tears. "That's all I have to say," he concluded, his voice weakening. "Thank you all for listening to me."

The media representatives rushed out to file their stories.

Only to find that National News Wire Service had already released a copyrighted exclusive report, bylined by Timothy Murray, an hour earlier.

* * *

Two days later, some eighteen hours before Stuart Percy was scheduled to die, Tim Murray scored another copyrighted exclusive on the news wires just minutes after Governor Neal Harris signed commutation papers releasing Jane from prison. She was not pardoned; that would have left the state vulnerable to a civil lawsuit. Instead, her conviction was allowed to stand, but her sentence was reduced to time served. It was an agreement worked out secretly between Tim Murray and Danny Lopez.

Tim was waiting for Jane when she walked out of prison. He drove her to Phoenix, to a beauty salon where he had arranged for her to have a private makeover, from shampoo to pedicure. He had also purchased for her a stylish, expensive pantsuit, blouse, shoes, and everything she needed to wear, following size and color instructions she had given him before her release. And he bought her a one-way first-class airline ticket to Lincoln, Nebraska, where her children were being raised by her sister and brother-in-law, the Lunds.

"What do you think you'll do with your life now?" Tim asked her at the boarding gate for her flight. Jane shrugged, pushing her sunglasses up into her again curly reddish hair. Macadamia eyes bright now, fashionably attired, fresh from a facial, with new makeup and eyeliner, she no longer looked ten years older than she was.

"I guess I'll just start trying to find my dream again," she told him. "A decent husband, good daddy for my kids, nice house somewhere, respectability." Tilting her head coquettishly, she took him by the coat and pulled him close to her. "Any chance you'd like to apply for the job?"

"Can't," he told her. "I'm going to Paris. Bureau chief for National News Wire Service. Big-time job."

Jane put her arms around his neck and stood on tiptoe to kiss him full on the lips. It was delicious right down to his heels, as he had always imagined it would be.

"You're sure I can't change your mind?"

"I'm sure."

As he watched her walk into the jetway, hips swaying just enough to turn several heads, he thought: *Good thing she didn't kiss me a second time.*

Then he remembered that he never had asked her whether she had been involved in the killing or not.

At ten that night, Tim was let into the Death Row visiting room where Stuart Percy was waiting on the other side of the grille to grant an exclusive interview. He smiled widely as Tim walked up.

"Jane get off all right?" he asked.

"Yes."

"How'd she look?"

"Like a movie star."

"Damn!" Stuart exclaimed. "I can't wait to start writing to her. I'm going to have her send me some pictures of herself, you know what I mean? Private pictures, just for me."

"Stuart," Tim said quietly, "I'm afraid I've got some bad news for you. The governor's not giving you a reprieve."

For a second, Percy's expression froze, then he grinned. "Hey, don't kid about that."

"I'm not kidding."

Now the condemned man's expression froze and remained that way. "But—you said—you said he'd *have* to—"

"Well, things change, Stuart. Newspaper editorials and public opinion polls show that most of the citizens of Arizona think you should be executed."

"But—but, wait a second now—that wasn't the deal. Look, I did my part in this! They can't do this to me!"

"I'm afraid they can, Stuart. And they have. You're going to be executed tonight."

Angry blood now filled Stuart Percy's face. Closing his cuffed hands into fists, he began to pound on the wire grille.

"No! No! This isn't right! This isn't *fair!* You—cannot—let—them—execute—me!"

"I have to, Stuart. My exclusive story of your execution is already written. I'm a reporter. . . . You can't expect me to change my story."

Stuart Percy was still pounding on the grille and screaming when Tim Murray left the visiting room.